Las Bugambilias

A bilingual queer novel

Lalo León

Edited by: Amy Snyder

ISBN: 979-8-9913824-0-3

To those who can't speak...

EXPLICIT CONTENT

This novel depicts scenes of physical, emotional and psychological abuse as well as language describing sexual assault, self-mutilation, and domestic violence. Reader discretion is advised.

1

The Saturday morning sun peeked over the jagged silhouette of the mountains to the east as light raced across the desert floor, illuminating the dusty air with a turbid yellow glow. The glass and metal towers of downtown shimmered in the early light, scattering sunbursts across the wide expanses of sparse suburbia. Perfectly straight streets extended in infinitely long but shallow canyons of asphalt, lined with clean and empty sidewalks. Brute square-mile blocks of tangled side streets housed the vast repetition of stucco boxes painted every possible shade of dirt. This was the regimented antithesis to the chaotic gardens of L.A., where sunny California dreams go to die in the solar-bleached sands of the interior desert. Here in Phoenix, every man has their own patch of dirt, but the measure of any man was not only the size of his castle but also how quickly he could turn that dirt into a lush, green fantasy. It took quite a bit to make the sand bloom; in fact, it would take the work of many a dark-skinned man to reverse blight back into Eden. Manny happened to be one of those men, now covered by a straw hat, a long-sleeved shirt, and faded Wrangler jeans to protect him from the rays of the blazing sun.

It was six a.m., and Manny and his crew were already hard at work on the north side of town where the rhythmic tick-tick-tick of golf course sprinklers mixed with the whir of leaf blowers and trimmers. He was trying to get a few of his regular jobs done before he had to head back down to South Phoenix. If it wasn't the heat that was making him sweat that morning, it would have been the bottled frustration at having to stop work in the middle of the day to take his stepson to his appointment once again. Two years at the same old grind and still he couldn't see the change that he had hoped for.

All he really wanted was for it to be over, for private embarrassment to stop and then evaporate into the Arizona air. But even with the drone of gasoline motors around him, he could never drown out the burning doubt of whether he should have even married Magdalena at all and taken on the burden of her son. She never knew, or at least he didn't think she knew. But this truth never set him free, like Pastor Roberts would say in his Sunday sermons. It made him wonder whether Pastor Roberts and the other men of the church ever looked at him more derisively because of it. It was the only thing stopping him from standing still in the long bobbing shade of a palm tree to think, "Why is this my problem?"

Meanwhile in South Phoenix, Michael was still lying in bed with his eyes wide open and unconsciously gripping the sheets as if he was about to be dragged down the hall. It had come back to him in the twilight hours that morning, almost like a ghost. A haunting image that whispered things that he wished were never true, things that came from an unconscious darkness. A dream that felt like a love longing to held but that easily killed like a deadly poison if he ever were to touch it. He couldn't stand going to the appointments, but as Pastor Roberts told him time and time again, Jesus can purify only what we let him see. And after years of sermons, Michael wholeheartedly believed that the purity of a man's soul was above all else the most valuable thing he could possess. He felt bad that he didn't go to work with Manny that morning, but yesterday had been the fifth night in a row that he couldn't sleep. It didn't help that Manny's voice echoed in his sleep-drunk head, "Asi las viejas se quedan dormidas como tu!"[1] Michael's eyelids twitched in little side spasms as he tried to focus on a single crumb of popcorn plaster directly above him on the ceiling, and even though his body felt heavy, sinking into the old mattress, he fought to stay awake so the dream wouldn't return.

Over the past year and a half, the appointments had started to focus mostly on this one dream, and every little practice and exercise prescribed to him was meant to bury the evil. Ironically, this work served only to make it more real and palpable the few times he did drift off to sleep. The dream itself was never frightening; the only thing Michael truly feared was that its truth would leak into his waking hours and that its meaning was a bad omen of things to come.

Even though it was just past six in the morning, Michael knew that before long, Manny would be home to pick him up, pounding on his bedroom door to tell him to hurry up, and Michael would have to face these demons again. He got up and walked into the bathroom and cupped water in his hands and splashed his face a few times to rinse out the grainy crusts from his eyes. He stared intently

---

[1] "You're just like all the old ladies that stay asleep!"

into the mirror as the water trickled down his face and into the sink. His dark brown eyes were bloodshot with tangled threads of red vessels pulling at his irises. His reflection stared back at him unflinchingly, like a stranger on the other side of the glass. It was a stranger with golden brown skin and short jet-black hair who wanted nothing more than to be free from the prison of Michael's psyche and was hopeful that one day he would live out his secret, far beyond the confines of the mirror.

Michael couldn't look at him for very long, this loathsome and unwanted presence who was a source of embarrassment and shame. A beastly and savage part of him that ran on the passionate and instinctual nature of his humanity contrary to the teachings of The Jesus of Pastor Roberts. A nature that was loud, colorful, and Latin but also a nature of desire and sensual taboo. A true sin of the flesh that must be kept away from the eyes of everyday people lest it bring judgment upon him. Michael started to tear up at the thought of anyone knowing that stranger in the mirror, and that his blackest sin would be discovered. He eventually splashed more water on his face to rinse out his eyes and turned them from the mirror as he walked away.

Michael walked into the kitchen and the wafting smell of bitter coffee and corn tortillas that was filling the small house. The radio in the corner was softly playing Juan Gabriel under the hissing of water flowing through the old copper pipes.

"Ay no aguanto este pinché calorón!"[2] blurted out Magdalena as she walked in from the front door, flapping her long skirt. "Pobrecita mi bugambilia, no se como

---

[2] "I can't stand the damn heat!"

aguanta tanto calor!"[3]

"Mornin', Mom!"

"Buenos dias, mijito. Sírvete una taza de café, lo acabo de hacer!"[4] she shouted to him as she turned to flapping her blouse.

"Did Manny hide the hose again?"

"Si, el cabrón la escondió."[5]

"What for this time?"

"No mas porque mi matita le rompió su camisa otra vez con las espinas!"[6]

"Hmmmm."

"Le dije que mi matita es mas corajuda que el!"[7]

"Why donchu just let 'em cut it?"

"No, hijo … porque es mia. Quiero que mi bugambilia sea como yo."[8]

"It's just a plant, Mom."

"Si, pero es lo unico que Manuel me deja hacer en la casa."[9]

Michael peered out the front door to see the arching boughs of the bougainvillea bobbing in the hot morning breeze. Her massive trunks undulated in voluptuous curves around the wooden post holding up the front porch. A deep green umbrella shot outward, speckled with paper flowers of fuchsia petals that fluttered like

---

[3] "My poor bougainvillea, I don't know how it can stand so much heat!"

[4] "Good morning, son. Serve yourself some coffee, I just made it!"

[5] "Yeah, that asshole hid it from me."

[6] "Just because my little plant ripped his shirt with the thorns!"

[7] "I told him that my little plant has a temper!"

[8] "No, son … because it's mine. I want my bougainvillea like me."

[9] "Yeah, but it's the only thing Manny lets me do in this house."

batting eyelashes. She stood tall as a guardian to Manny's house, shedding her confetti of papers flowers when Magdalena and Michael passed by, and every so often snagging Manny's shirt.

"Mijo! Quieres huevos rancheros?"[10] she asked as she headed back into the kitchen to start cracking eggs.

"Yeah … I'll have some."

Michael went straight for the coffeemaker and poured himself a mug of black coffee. He sat down at the small dining room table in the kitchen, hoping that the caffeine might brighten up his eyes before his mother had a chance to notice. The steam from the frying pan rose up while daggers of light through the mini blinds stabbed through onto the table. The house was filled with the smell of onions, green chile, and tomato, bringing him back to his childhood.

"Dormistes?"[11] she asked him.

"Yeah, a bit."

"Y por que estabas llorando anoche?"[12] She began to shovel the eggs onto plates. He felt as if a stone had just hit the pit of his stomach and was trying to pull him to the floor.

"I wasn't crying … it's just my allergies," he mumbled.

"Ay mijito crees que todavía tengo la 'P' en la frente?"[13] she said calmly.

For Michael, it just added to the awkwardness at the table, as he felt naked. His mind quickly ran through

---

[10] "Son, do you want ranch style eggs?"
[11] "Did you sleep?"
[12] "Then why were you crying last night?"
[13] "Oh son, you think I still have the "P" on my forehead" (a euphemism meaning "Do I look like an idiot to you?").

the possible ways he could separate himself from this moment, but luckily Magdalena found a way out for him.

"Cuando es tu cita?"[14] she asked as she reached for a warm corn tortilla.

"At lunchtime, I guess? Manny's comin' to pick me up," he said while pinching eggs with a piece of tortilla. "Guess he wasn't that mad at me for not goin' to work," he added.

"Pero todavia se encabronó?"[15] she asked.

"Yeah, he was pretty mad at me for not gettin' up in time."
Magdalena sat resolute in the game she was playing with her son.

"Hmmm … oye … Y que chingados hacen alla?"[16] she asked inquisitively.

"Pastor Roberts just talks about Bible stuff," Michael muttered, feeling nauseatingly warm all over again. "He thinks I should go to a Christian school after I graduate."

"Que, que!?"[17]

"He thinks goin' to ASU is gonna be hard for me or somethin' like that," he said, looking at her and shrugging his shoulders. In the midst of this conversation, Michael remembered one of the first catechisms he was ever taught in these Saturday appointments: "Only God needs to know your secrets."

"Está insinuando que porque eres Mexicano, no

---

[14] "What time is your appointment?"
[15] "And still he got mad?"
[16] "Hmmm, hey, what the fuck do you guys do over there?"
[17] "Wait, what!?"

puedes ir a la universidad, o que?"[18]

"No! Not that! He just thinks that it's not a good place for Christians to go."

"Adio … yo se lo que ese cabrón quería decír," she said. "Te apuesto que el te quiere ver trabajando asi como Manuel!"[19]

"It's not like that!" Michael whined.

"Que no te vayan a convencer de no ir," she said rather forcefully before sipping her coffee. Then she raised one eyebrow in a show of ire. "Tu no vas andar cortando ramitas, todo asoleado! N'hombre! Asi ven los Gringos a los Mexicanos, sierviendo nada mas para limpiar los pinches patios."[20]

"Gawd, Mom, you're makin' it more than what it is!"

"No, no, no es cierto hijo," she exclaimed. "Hay que darse valor si queres salir adelante."[21]

Michael was aware of the impassioned resentment his mother had toward White people since marrying Manny and subsequently the church as well. It was common to walk into a Sunday morning service and be subtly ignored by familiar people. Not rudely or with malintent, but just glossed over as if a ghost. Magdalena

---

[18] "Is he insinuating that because you're Mexican, you can't go a university?"

[19] "Bullshit … I know what what that asshole was trying to say. I bet you he wants to see you working like Manuel!"

[20] "He better not try to convince you that you shouldn't go. Even though I'm grateful for the work that Manuel has, you're not going to be out there cutting bushes out in the sun! No way! That's the way Gringos see Mexicans, only good for cleaning the fucking yards."

[21] "No, no, no, son, it's true. You gotta have your own self-worth if you want to get ahead."

didn't find this horrifically offensive, as she figured she was off the hook from having to make innocuous small talk. What she was bothered when random women came up to her assuming that the only way she could serve society was to stand for an open repository of kitschy stereotypes and expectations. It took a year of being married and hearing such commentary to teach her fuel her how to survive being Brown in "Gringolandia." She had a stealthy tactic of letting White people live in the fantasy that they were better than Mexicans, all the while living in a way in which she never garnered sympathy but firmly held hostage the indispensable respect and necessary utility that she knew they needed. They were hungry for authenticity, in the same way that people hired Manny to clean their yards. She knew they needed him so they could have the luxury of beauty without getting a sunburn. This she distilled down to one simple message: "Donde hay hambre hay necesidad."[22]

The two of them sat in silence as she watched her beloved bougainvillea boughs bobbing in the hot breeze. Her purplish pink petals provided the only color at the dreary home. In that she wondered if her necessity to Manny held her hostage the same way she held other people hostage. Her quiet and dull sadness filled the room and pushed out the tension she had built between her son, and she too wanted to find some escape from the truth that she could not run from. Looking over to the clock on the stove, she saw the morning was passing and Manny would be home soon to pick up Michael.

"Andale, ve y bañate![23]" she said to her son as she

---

[22] "Where there is hunger, there is necessity."
[23] "Go on, go take a shower."

stood, picking up the empty breakfast plates from the table.

She sat them in the sink as Michael, eager to escape, pushed his chair out and then headed to the bathroom. Before he shut the door, he could hear the sliding static of the radio as she changed stations.

… shshshshshshsh … You're listening to K-P-R-Y broadcasting the Word of God to all of Arizona …"

******

The lukewarm shower had done little to wash away the wrenching anxiety in Michael's stomach as he sat waiting in the small living room for Manny to pick him up. His scuffed-up workboots, and Wrangler jeans felt heavy against his skin, which was already starting to sweat in the moist air from the evaporative cooler. Among the drabber parts of the house, Manny's living room exuded an excruciating sense of basicness that rivaled even the most ascetic of monasteries. Decorations never lasted long in the house, as Manny deemed most of them to be in some way an offensive indulgence and thus they had to be removed. The primer-white nature of the walls made even the presence of a human being feel intrusive within this drab inner sanctum. However, a few pictures in thin brass frames did manage to stay and offer crumbs of color, but even then, there was always the threat of their being thrown away during one of those awful nights.

The few things that Manny did allow in the living room were purely for utility. An old couch and love seat with mismatched upholstery were pushed up against the wall, and where a TV would normally be, a large, heavy leather-bound Bible sat on a thoroughly scratched-up table. Manny's clients assumed he couldn't afford much, so in the name of noble Christian charity, people regularly gave him their hand-me-downs. However, a TV was one of the few things he never accepted, or anything else through which the devil may enter. When Michael started high school, Manny had relented and allowed a radio so that he family could at least hear the hymns and Bible studies broadcast on the off nights from church. Manny had a suspicion, though, that while he was away, Magdalena would turn the radio to "Worldly" stations. The clinging evil from her past was filled with Catholic idol worship, Mexican debauchery, and womanizing mariachi music. In most circumstances he wouldn't have it, but he knew that it was often a losing battle and as long as she kept the evil of this world away from him, he could on occasion extend Christian grace to her.

Michael picked up the faint engine noise of Manny's truck rounding the corner on Central Avenue. He drove a 1982 Ford pickup with a faded forest green paint job except where gouges and dents gave way to the parasitic earth-colored rust growing on it. The truck was only 10 years old, but Manny had a tendency to be rough with all of his things. After he pulled up into the driveway, a creak and slam of the truck door coupled with the thick-heeled clack of Manny's worn-out boots on the dusty walkway put Michael at attention.

Michael saw Manny's silhouette cast an austere shadow into the room from the front doorway as the bougainvillea branches seemed to reach out and spitefully snag Manny's shirt from behind. The sharp smell of fresh-cut grass and half-burnt gasoline exhaust quickly filled the doorway. Manny emitted the aroma of a hardworking man. Michael tried his best to exude the same working-man persona, all the while thinking, "This is the man I'm supposed to try to be like?" Manny did little to hide his irritation at coming home in the middle of the day or that he was short a worker that morning as he looked Michael up and down. It had been an ongoing competition of Latin Male dominance just waiting to see which of the two could "out-man" the other.

"Whatcha waitin' for?" Manny said sternly. "Anda! Let's go or we're gonna be late."

As Michael was biting the corner of his lip, he sighed and stood up, trying to preserve his dignity in front of the man whom he had come to loathe. He stepped up to Manny and, face-to-face, gave him one last look up and down in return before walking past him and to the passenger side of Manny's truck.

"Magda! I'm leavin'!" Manny shouted into what seemed like empty house, and his cry fell into resentful chasm of silence. Normally it would put Manny in a bad mood if Magdalena didn't acknowledge that the man of the house had come in, but he already had enough to deal with, and the day wasn't getting any longer.

The two headed down Central Avenue toward the stoplight at Broadway in Manny's old truck. The city rolled by through the dirt-speckled glass as Michael stared out aimlessly. South Phoenix was a different world from the green lawns and tree-lined streets of the desert utopias on the north side of town. Here the streets were lined with abandoned buildings punctuated by industrial yards storing sun-bleached car parts. A few scraggly Palo Verde and mesquite trees stood in stark contrast to the lonely unkempt palm trees and dried-up shrubs that the city put in years ago as part of their beautification of the neighborhood.

They drove passed the boxing gym that Michael had been going to for about 2 years now, which had become a secret sanctuary for him. It was in an old storefront building of white plaster and hazy glass, with a hand-painted sign that read "Round One Boxing" in large, bold black type. Similar hand-painted signs seemed to march down the street as they drove by, advertising everything from "Llanteros" to "Mofles" to "Cataliticos," in what became the ubiquitous hallmark of Mexican hustle and free market entrepreneurialism. Farther down Central, on the corner of Broadway, stood the small brick church that had come to dominate Michael's and Magdalena's lives over the years. The unassuming building stood out ironically from the rest of the neighborhood in its mundane plainness, except for the tall white steeple perched on the asphalt shingle roof. The beige bricks were punched out only a few times by thin hazy windows, caked with dust, and one set of double doors, well set in the shadow of a small vestibule beyond the sidewalk.

The truck bounced and bobbed when they turned into the parking lot with all the well-worn wheel ruts and potholes that cratered the neglected pavement. Manny parked in the first row of parking spaces so they could see the front doors through the noon day sun that was already beaming through the windshield. Cracks and stars in the glass amplified the light further into tiny explosions of sun daggers, making Michael squint. The heat was quickly rising inside the cab, with the windows only slightly cracked open. Sweat began to bead on Michael's forehead and lower back, but he tried to not show his discomfort in front of Manny, even though the thought of the appointment loomed over him.

They could hear the low rumble of old pickup trucks flocking into the church parking lot behind them. One by one the cabs popped open, and a flood of dark-skinned men scurried out, putting on their wide-brimmed hats and pulling tools and leaf blowers out from the truck beds. Soon, light tan clouds of dust billowed from the old sidewalks like a monsoon storm, and the mass overwhelmed even the pure white steeple.

Parked far from the flock of pickup trucks was a freshly waxed maroon Cadillac owned by an older stout man. He was balding and trying to beat the inevitable with a freshly shaved head. The few stray stubbly hairs on the sides did little to hide his pink scalp, which was still trying to heal from the latest sunburn. He stepped out of the car in his polo shirt, dull from too may washes, and cleanly pressed khaki pants, sharp creases running down the legs. Safely tucked under his arm was a leather-bound Bible with shimmering gold-leafed edges.

Pastor Roberts hailed from the buckle of the Bible belt and had relocated to Phoenix as part of a self-proclaimed mission to save the souls of men. It wasn't long after arriving that he became entrenched in returning to what he called "Good Ol'-Time Religion." As so often happens, he took a contingency from a larger church for himself and in the name of Jesus. A few weeks later, a young and unmarried Manny had wandered into the church looking to undo the damage that years of whiskey drinking had done. Within a year he was fully baptized with the promises of salvation and peace with his creator God, and it was only a matter of time before Pastor Roberts took a particular liking to his fledgling acolyte, since he was his first convert. It was that abiding trust that prompted him to bring Michael for "pastoral counseling" when he discovered his stepson's secret. In exchange for counseling, Manny would clean the meager grounds of the church for free. An act of protestantized penance that

Manny still could not shake from his own Catholic past.

Pastor Roberts waved to them both as he walked to the front doors, and Michael immediately bolted out of the sweltering truck.

"Howdy there, Michael, how's the Lord treatin' ya today?" the pastor shouted.

"I'm doin' all right, you?", Michael shouted back as he walked closer.

"Oh, just trying to beat this heat! But praise God, it sure does makes a sermon on hell that much easier, am I right?" he said with a kindly smile, putting his hand on Michael's shoulder.

Away from the immediate presence of Manny, Michael could feel his working-man persona start to fade while a sense of apprehensive piety began to grow. In front of Magdalena, he had to be the son who would make something of himself, and in front of Manny he had to show his worth as a man. But on Saturdays with Pastor Roberts, he knew that he didn't have to put on a face. He had been well trained that only God needed to know his secrets, and Pastor Roberts was the closest he could get to God on earth. While the disappointment and fear of the recurring dream rattled in his brain, he still had an intrinsic faith that he would find absolution and deliverance from his affliction. With good reason he believed, since he had been absolved week after week, but he still wanted something permanent, to be forgiven by God in a way that he could say with definitive proof, "God saved me from my sin, and I never had to see my sin again." He saw people on Sunday morning experience that same miracle, and he waited to have his.

Manny's crew had started to pull clippers and sheets of burlap from their truck beds to clean as Manny slowly got out from his truck, watching as client and patient climbed up the few steps to the locked double doors of the church. Leaning up against the truck, he adjusted his hat to keep his face in the shadow, watching to make sure Michael went inside. As Pastor Roberts fumbled through the myriad of keys to open the padlock on the chain through the door handles, Michael looked up above the entrance where the words to a Bible verse had been handpainted in elegant cursive script. "Come all ye who are heavy laden and burdened and I will give you rest." As Pastor Roberts opened the padlock, Michael thought, "I hope this time I get my 'rest.'"

2

Pastor Roberts shut the doors behind them, letting the echo clamor through the still darkness. A few beams of faint daylight were spilling in through a row of dirty windows on the side, illuminating bits of floating dust like tiny stars twinkling in the night sky. Even though it had been years since Michael had stepped foot into the church of Mexico, he had not been able to abandon the reverence he felt whenever he walked into any sacred space, no matter whether it was clad in gold leaf or crumbling drywall. On Sundays his imagination would often drift to Bible passages such as the creation story, and from there he would picture God inhabiting the little church when the lights were turned off and the people were absent. A cosmic God that would brood over the swirling light and dust, forming planets and stars in a microcosm of the universe. If anything, it made him feel hopeful that in these brief peaceful moments of silence he would be able to have a highly-sought-after communion with God, regardless of how much of a failing Christian he was, but by the simple virtue of his own humanity.

"Let me turn on the lights for us," Pastor Roberts said as he patted Michael on the shoulder, startling him out of his serenity.

With a flip of a few switches, the room was flooded with the dull white-bluish glow from fluorescent bulbs, immediately drowning out the miniature galaxies and stars of his personal universe and bringing him back to the hard reality of this terrestrial Christian living.

The old church had the same amount of inert personality on the inside as it did on the outside, with a laissez-faire materialistic detachment to things bordering on extreme. The floors were covered with a tired royal-blue commercial carpet, fraying in some places and patched with strips of curling gray duct tape in others. The pews had seen better days, pockmarked from key chains that nicked and pitted the orange-colored varnish to reveal the natural blond wood underneath. The ceiling was girded with dark wooden beams angling upward toward the modest pitch. A popcorn plaster ceiling stretched between them like stunted stalactites. Although no one could see it from the street, the roof had been badly damaged by a monsoon some years back, and brown stains that looked like dried rose petals bloomed above him in a dirty watercolor.

The stage was up front and only a few steps high, covered in the same worn-out royal-blue carpet as the rest of the church. Pastor Roberts called this "The Altar," the place where men meet God to reconcile their fallen state and find absolution, or even redemption. To mark that intersection between the divine and the profane was a simple but austere pulpit. From the congregation's side, the cross-shaped pulpit looked imposing, thick, and authoritative; however, the back toward the pastor was purposefully hollow so that it reflected the thunderous pounding during a sermon. Many a Sunday sermon boomed out the words "This house will pass away, but the Word of God remains" from this spot.

Farther back in the church, in a wall behind the pulpit, was a small opening where a humble mural of Jesus's baptism in the river Jordan blended into an in the otherwise unremarkable tub of the baptistry. As the story was told to Manny and eventually to Michael, once Pastor Roberts had liberated the congregation from the grips of the corrupt and modernizing church, a loyal follower came to Pastor Roberts offering his talents. He called it "reaching the unchurched through art." The result was what Michael called the "Pastel Jesus" standing in the tranquil blue waters of an Edenic Judean Wilderness, which then dreamily cascaded down into the baptistry in a waterfall of blue glitter.

Pastor Roberts had no qualms about introducing the once-forbidden practice of making graven images of God, as he had always struggled with knowing the God he prayed to, but he'd never been able to picture Jesus's face on his own. Because few Christlike models were available at the time, the mysterious artist who had left the church shortly after finishing his magnus opus used the closest thing he could find to represent the God of Love, Grace, and Redemption, and that was Pastor Roberts himself. Although the rough texture of the plastered drywall erased any possibility of an accurate likenesses to the mortal man, the downcast blue eyes and the sharp Caucasian shape of his nose still managed to overcome the crudely drawn locks of dirty blond hair. As a young boy, Michael had known the likeness of Jesus to be the one he saw on prayer candles of "El Sagrado Corazón": European in likeness but still an identifiable Catholic root. Similarly, pictures of the

La Virgen de Guadalupe, which were drastically different from other Catholic images he saw as a child, still managed to have the same color of mestizo skin as Michael, and he felt some sort of faint connection either by tradition or likeness to them. But this Jesus was different. It was the Jesus of this particular church, of this particular faith, and of this single man who led them. It was this likeness that Michael had to please, that mattered to Michael, and that Michael was taught to believe would provide atonement for all of his sins. It was the Pastel Jesus of Pastor Robert to whom he asked daily in desperation to heal his sick mind.

Suddenly, the squeal of air-conditioning units spooling up echoed in the air ducts overhead. "Now hopefully we can git some col' air in here!" Pastor Roberts shouted back at Michael, who was still standing in the entrance watching his imagination evaporate, taking with it his Cosmic God. Pastor Roberts waddled around to bring two chairs from the back closet and set them down in front of the altar and the pulpit.

"All right, son, ya ready to git started?" he called out.

Michael began to make his way down the aisle, quietly mumbling to himself, "You gotta go through this if you wanna change, you gotta go through this if you wanna change."

Every step forward felt more and more like the day when he came forward to accept Jesus as his personal savior. He imagined a solemn but quietly joyous ceremony that everyone in the church would eventually have to go through. Answering what the church referred to as "The Altar Call" from Pastor Roberts at the pulpit, coaxing him to come down amidst the soft singing of an old hymn. He could see all the people around him vividly, like ghosts from his memory filling the empty church. Even with the droning buzz of fluorescent lights above him, he could hear their song in his head as the soft voices began to sing.

> *Just as I am, without one plea, but that thy blood was shed for me, and that thou bidd'est me come to thee, O Lamb of God, I come, I come.*

After Michael finally got to the front, he turned back around to see that the singing ghosts had evaporated like the Cosmic God and he was once again alone with Pastor Roberts. Standing again in the place where God and men were supposed to meet, as he did the week before, and the week before that, and so on.

"I'm just lookin' for my list, Michael. I know I left it in here somewhere," said Pastor Roberts while thumbing through chunks of pages in his Bible.

Michael clenched his hands in his pockets and could feel the nervous sweat making his work clothes heavy.

"Ah, here it is!" he exclaimed as he pulled out a folded-up sheet of yellow legal pad paper. Before sitting down, Michael looked at the Pastel Jesus, quietly praying in his heart,

> *Let this be the last time I gotta go through this*
.

"Alrighty, son, how ya been this week? Everythin' workin' a'ight like we talked about?"

Michael avoided eye contact with him.

"Son, look at me. I asked you how you are doin'?"

"I'm … I'm doin' OK, I guess."

"You sure don't look OK. What's on your mind?"

"I'm … I'm just dealin' with some things, you know …"

Pastor Robert's cheery and lighthearted disposition hit a hard stop when he heard those words.

"No, I don't know. What kinda things we talkin' 'bout here, son. You slippin' into sin again?"

Michael took a second while he scanned the space above his head for some sort of dignified and justifiable answer but found only the yellowish-brown water stains on the ceiling.

"Speak up, son. God already knows if you've sinned. Ain't no use hidin' it, and if you don't confess it, well, then God can't forgive you."

"I know, it's just …"

"Spit it out, son!"

"It's the dream."

"Hmmm," Pastor Roberts ruefully snorted

"It came back again … last night," Michael said softly.

"The one 'bout the boy? The one in the desert?"

Michael looked down at the floor and nodded, trying to block out the frustrated inhalation of Pastor Roberts. He was tired of it too, since the all the exercises and catechisms that he was told to practice never seemed to work consistently. The healing would last only for a day or two. Not to mention there was the constant worry of when the dream would slither from the darkness and strike like a rattlesnake. Michael believed its sinfulness would kill his communion with the Pastel Jesus. It was like reaching the edge of a faraway land, knowing that the answer to everything somewhere beyond the horizon and the implausibility of traversing the churning ocean with no seaworthy vessel kept him stranded on the shores of his own understanding. It left him wishing that God, in some bit of mercy, would bring a whale to swallow him up and take him across, or never bring him back up at all.

For all he could do, Pastor Roberts just sat staunchly in the chair, massaging away the coming headache from his temple.

"I, uhm … I just kept askin' … God why this is happenin' … to me, you know! I try … and I try … to do everything right … and nothin' works." He sputtered while weeping and burying his tear-soaked face in already-clammy hands. "What's wrong with me?" he asked. "WHY CAN'T I CHANGE, GOD DAAAMNIT!!!" he screamed out toward the ceiling, only to collapse into a heaving mess in the chair. His voice was muffled by the locked doors and the leaf blowers outside.

"Son, ya know betta than to use God's name in vain like that, 'specially in the church."

"I'm sorry," Michael said while wiping the tears and snot with the sleeve of his shirt.

After a few moments in the near-quiet church, Pastor Roberts took to his Bible and jotted down another line of blue scribbles on the growing list he kept on the yellow paper. "Boy, these lil' outbursts of yours just keep gettin' worse and worse."

"I'm sorry, it's just …"

"Oh, don't start with that, son! You know that there ain't nothin' that God can't handle."

"I know that, it's just …"

"It's just what, son? Too much to ask of you?"

"All the stuff I try don't work!"

"Son, if God can create the heavens and the earth, then he can sure as all get-out change you. You believe God can do that?"

"Yeah …"

"Then if God can do that, there's only one thing standin' in the way of God doin' his work, and what do you think that is?"

"It's … it's me."

"That's right, it's you!"

"I'm tryin' not to."

"Well, if that's the case, then there's only one other thing left."

"What?"

"God really isn't in you, boy."

"No! I swear he is!"

"You do believe Jesus is your savior?"

"I do … ever since I was a lil' kid."

"Well then, son, you best start actin' like it."

"Yes, sir …" Michael said sheepishly.

"Ya gotta trust God, lean into them promises he's givin' you. Ya gotta have faith that God'll heal you. Ya gotta trust that the blood o' Jesus Christ'll save you from all that sin that's tryin' to lead you away. Am I right?!"

"Yes, sir …"

"What does First Corinthians 10:13 say?"

"Huh?"

"You heard me. Recite that verse I told you to memorize."

Michael strained to open his mouth and peel his dry, sticky tongue from its roof, obstinate to recite on command.

"There hath no temptation take you but such as is common to man but God is faithful, who will not suffer you to be tempted above that ye are able but will with the temptation also make a way to escape that ye may be able to bear it."

"There you go, son, you got faith in Jesus?

"Yeah …"

"Well then, all these times that you've sinned, he's always made a way for you to get out of it. Only one standing in the way, son, and that's you."

Michael was flushed with heat despite the cool air from the air-conditioning. He could feel the drops of sweat condense and run down his spine in nervous rivulets. The fires of hell and their divine judgment were licking at his feet, taunting him and reminding him of the consequences of his failures. He resigned himself that the best he could do was once again cast himself on the mercy of God.

"I guess I'm just gonna have to try harder next time," said Michael.

"Gotta do a lot more than just try harder, son. God's forgiveness is a gift and you can't be takin' advantage like that!"

"I don't wanna do that. I wanna be good, and I wanna be over this!"

"But you're still havin' them ungodly feelins. We gotta do something 'bout that!"

"I know, but what? I've been readin' my Bible, I've been doin' all those exercises you taught me, I've been avoiding guys my age …"

"It's comin' down to your faith in Jesus, son. Where you're fallin' short is your faith that you've got a way to beat this sin. If Jesus can beat sin, so can you! Am I right?"

Michael could do nothing more than dejectedly stare at all the random patterns of blue specks in the carpet by his feet. He couldn't hide himself from Pastor Roberts's indictment. As long as he indulged in his sinfulness, the dream would always come back. Haunting him like a thorn in the flesh, week after week, month after month, and year after year. There was more that was needed of him to get better, to seek God out more fervently lest he fall into the sin again and again.

"How bad you want it, son? Hmmm? You wanna end up in hell like every other sinner who rejects God?"

"No, I wanna be with Jesus. I wanna be with my family!" wept Michael.

"That's what I wanna hear!"

Michael tried wiping the snot from his nose as the little nugget of positive affirmation that Pastor Roberts welled up within him and made him start crying again.

"And stop cryin'! What I tell you 'bout cryin', son?" added Pastor Roberts. "Godly men don't cry, they pray!"

"Yeah ... they do," Michael squeaked out, trying to hold back the tears.

For Michael, the type of hope that Pastor Roberts gave was a complex hope. On one hand, there was the chance that divinity could grant special clemency from the shackles of damnation. But on the other, a world of imaginative violence came with obtaining such hope. Violence that he had come to know more and more when the mundane exercises and catechisms lost their power to do anything. Redemption had become a blood sport in which this little piece of his psyche would be murdered again and again in the name of salvation. A crusade of sorts toward the holy land of his soul, where the offending root of undesirable residents must be driven out.

The first time Pastor Roberts told him to imagine and twist his dream around, it was novel and spectacular, a quenching rush of relief from the omnipresent sensation of sin. But with every passing week the twisting became increasingly dramatic, increasingly visceral. If there was a reason for Michael's hesitancy to accept the escape that the Pastel Jesus offered him, it was the cost of inviting death into his young mind. With time the solution of violently twisting his dream seemed to be more and more reasonable even though deep down, he still resisted its seductive simplicity.

"You ready to git started?"

"I am."

"All right, son, we're gonna do this just like before."

"OK."

"I'll open us in prayer, then just let God speak to you. You got that, son?"

"Yeah, I got it."

Michael gave a willing nod as he waited.

"Let's bow our heads," Pastor Roberts said as he took a deep breath and raised his right hand in the air.

Following suit, Michael closed his eyes as he let the stillness engulf him and the empty church. He could still hear the leaf blowers outside, which blended with the soft buzz of the lights to create the church's meditative background noise. The only nonharmonic sound was Pastor Roberts's nasally breathing, turbulent inhaling and exhaling, which cut through the white noise with faint whistles. There they sat, sequestered from others, except for Pastel Jesus. Pastor Roberts was knocking at the door of Michael's inner life, and Michael with much apprehension was opening the door to let him in again to the secret place.

"Our heavenly Father above, creator of life. We humbly come before knowin' that your truth never fails us. We know that your faithfulness is beyond our comprehension, and that you never allow more temptation in our lives than what we can handle. We know that these temptations and ungodly desires that Michael has been experiencin' are what you've allowed in his life, because you know that this is what he can resist. Open his eyes to see that if he were to just put his faith in you, he can overcome them. Please hear my prayer for him and open his heart to accept your truth. The truth that this kinda life is not in your plan of salvation for him. Let him see that there's a life for him to live in fellowship with you, free from these corrupt and sinful feelins. We know that it's not in your will that he would fall into the abomination of unnatural lust, so I ask that you guide him to your light. I ask that you provide him with your strength, that as we dive deep into this dream that the enemy keeps on showin' him, you reveal your mercy and grace to him."

Pastor Roberts paused to allow his prayer to soak deep into Michael's brain. Even though the prospect of venturing into his own imaginative soul was frightening, Michael felt a mixed exhilaration much like a first kiss. He could feel the knotting nerves in his stomach, and the shivers and shakes would soon be on their way. As a preventative practice, Michael had learned to clench his teeth at the beginning of every prayer so he could stop their chattering whenever he felt cool, anxious-ridden blood course through his body. Pastor Roberts continued his prayer.

"Lord, we ask that you open Michael's mind to these thoughts to receive the wisdom and knowledge of your son, Jesus Christ."

Pastor Roberts paused once more to allow the remnants of his voice to faintly echo in silent space, and all the while Michael felt the flush run over his body as his eyelids twitched.

"All right, son, I'd like you to just go back your mind to the dream. Just let God guide your mind to his truth, son. Remember there ain't no secrets in here, God's gonna show you what he wants you to confess."

Michael sat motionless in his chair, his eyes closed and slightly burning from the salty tears. He took a deep breath as his mind drifted back into the meditative fog of the dream. It was like slowly drowning in the waters of his memory, and his head effortlessly slipped into the liquid of his imagination as the fluorescent glow of reality shrank into a single speck of light before vanishing completely. The vision was obscured at first, as the dark red shadows of eyelids faded away, then slowly the brightness of the dream began to open up around him. His eyes fluttered as he felt a burst come up from his neck, like ten thousand blossoms of color blooming from his spine, the airy tones of his secret place surrounding him in a sensual bouquet of exotic flowers.

Tell me what you see, son.
I'm … I'm standin' in this huge valley.
There are mountains all around me.
And they're blue and. Purple.
It's a desert 'cept it doesn't feel like sand.
It feels like dried-up salt.
It's white and crusty and warm on my toes.

Mmm-hmm … what else.

The sun is bright and
its settin' in front of me…
and the sky…the sky is like a
pretty color of blue.
Like I'm inside a big glass marble.

Keep on goin', son

I can see the sky,
it's changing colors like,
from orange, to pink, to purple.
But there's one big shadow
that's comin' toward me.
It's a wired-shaped shadow,

curvy like a fat snake.

What's it doin'?

When I try to walk toward it,
it moves away from me,
back to where it came from.
I keep trying to walk toward it
and it just moves away more.
I start runnin' just to keep up
but I can never catch up to it.
It's like it knows that I'm chasin' after it.

Anythin' else?

Yeah, the air feels warm on my face,
and I can hear the salt crunchin' when I run.

Keep going.

I keep runnin' and runnin' till
I can finally catch up to the shadow.

And whaddya see?

I see a huge dead tree in front of me.
The branches are all twisted and salty and white.
It kinda looks like a dried-up octopus
comin' outta the ground.

Anythin' else you see there?

Michael hesitated as his mind's eye drifted off to
the side of the tree, because sitting next to trunk of the tree
was the cause of so much grief.

Son?!

Yeah?

Is it that guy again?

Yeah … it's him ...

Michael immediately felt butterflies in his belly whenever he got to this part of the dream. A sensual warmth coursed through his body as an intense magnetism drew him. He never knew how to explain it, only that he felt the same thing whenever he saw a pretty girl. It scared him to think that in gazing on something he wanted so bad, he might get caught up in the lust again. But before he could pull his subconscious self from the desert, Pastor Robert intervened.

>   Whaddya feel when you see this guy?

I … uhm … I …
I'm tryin' to not feel anythin'.
I'm trying to fight against that sin.

>   Son, if you want God to save you
>   from this, you best be honest.

I'm tellin' you the truth.

>   Then why you are you blushin'? Hmmm?

>   I'm gonna ask you again, son.
>   What are you feelin' when you
>   see this boy?

>   You like him?

Whaddya like 'bout him?

While it pained Michael to admit it again, he knew Pastor Roberts would not stop until he answered. He couldn't hide anything from God, and if God was using Pastor Roberts to provide the escape from this sin, then he had to tell him every private and immoral thought. He imagined himself coming close to the young man who was now leaning up against the tree, coyishly smiling at Michael. The setting sun struck him with a halo, glowing around him in a golden aura. Even the short distance that separated them seemed to drip with desire, especially here in the privacy of his inner world under the azure blue sky.

Well, he's … uhm …
he's kinda tall … like me.

OK, that's a start, what else?

And he's …
got black hair like me.
It's short and faded on the sides.

Keep on goin'.

It's kinda weird …
it feels like I know him.
I've never seen him before,
but it feels like …

Feels like what, son?

I don't know …
like I should know him.

Is that so?

Well, that's new.
Anything else you wanna tell me?

What do you feel when you see him?

Uhm … well he's muscular.

He's a well-built guy.

He's lean and …
and he's Brown like me …

What do you feel, son?

I … I swear he looks like someone I know …

Whoa whoa whoa,
hold your horses there, son.
I'm askin' you how ya feel and you

keep tellin' me things I already know.

I'm sorry.

Now we've been through this,
you're gonna have to
come clean on how ya feel,
otherwise God can't help you …

Yes, sir …

Go 'head, son, say it to the Lord
what you like about this boy.

The anxious shivers started in Michael's belly,
traveling up his gullet to quiver in his jaw. Eventually his
whole body vibrated with pubescent shame as the
awakening of this, his second sexuality, became apparent.
His fingertips and toes felt ice cold with clammy eager
sweat. With the all-consuming numbness to the world
beyond the salt desert of his dream, he was flesh hungry.
Ready to reach across the imaginary space between him
and his fantasy.

I, uhm … like his lips …
I like how he's got just a
lil' bit of stubble for his goatee.

You wanna kiss him?

Son, did you hear me?

I asked you if you …

… Yeah … I do.

I wanna kiss him …

And if you could, would you?
Remember, there ain't no
secrets with God.

Yeah, I would.

Would you wanna kiss him
like boys and girls kiss?

Yeah.

You want him to kiss you?

Yeah.

You want him to kiss you
like a boy kisses a girl?

I guess so … I don't know.

You guess so?

I mean ... yeah I want to kiss him.

Sounds to me like you'r
wantin' to act like the woman.
Don't you think?

I mean, I guess so …

Would you rather kiss him
like he was the girl?

Well, yeah …

Why?

'Cause then it wouldn't be as bad.

But you know either way
it's wrong, don't you?

Michael could feel the draw of sensual energy radiating through his body all the while he was fighting against the pull of his pastor's dogma ringing in his ears. The indescribable mash-up of sensations from exhilaration and guilt to fear and arousal had become embattled conflicts so profound that he couldn't tell which side he was on anymore, or which side was winning. He felt like he was on the edge of committing a grave sin by wishing to touch his fantasy and wanting it to be real this time. Not to mention that he selfishly hoped that just beyond the threshold of what was permissible was a place where it didn't matter whether it was right or wrong. A place where the pressures of what Pastel Jesus wanted evaporated into sublime reconciliation, and where even the mere mention of these feelings as the vilest sinful act didn't bring them austere judgment.

Are ya havin' feelins toward this boy?

More than the last time?

Michael felt his whole body tense up while his stomach nauseatingly churned in his belly. He couldn't lie anymore, not to Pastor Robert and not before God. Another week had gone by and the sexual desires for this young man had not abated. In fact, they had grown stronger.

I … I do have those feelins.

> Hmmm, do you like them
> feelins for men?

I just want 'em to go away!

> That's not what I asked, son.
> Do you like havin' them
> feelins toward other men?

I can't do this anymore …

> Now, don't you start backin' out of this, son!
> Be a man of God and confront your sin!

I'm sorry … I can't be that!

Michael began sobbing as he doubled over in his chair, sucking in gasps of air. He didn't know that he could feel any more shame then he already did, but somehow saying it out loud again and again reminded him of his own inadequacies to vanquish the demons within this awakening. Remorse was just as unwelcome an emotion as the damn butterflies in his stomach that seemed to taunt him incessantly.

> Why you feelin' sorry?

'Cause every week it's the same thing!
It's the same thing,

and it ends up the same way!

Get it through your head, son!
That's why God brought you here!
So that he can heal you!

Then how come it
hasn't happened yet?!

It ain't me that's lackin' faith, son!

I just can't find a way to get
this guy outta my head!
It's not like he doesn't want to leave,
it's like he can't!

Don't start believin'
the lies of the Devil.
You can and you will!

I just don't know what to do anymore!
I've tried so hard to not think this way,
and every week I keep
comin' back like a failure.
A failure to you! A failure to God!

I like him, all right?!

Is that what you wanna hear?!

I want him, OK?!
I just dunno how to stop wantin' him!

Michael felt the stinging pain on his legs after screaming and beating his fists into his thighs. The trails of salty tears were down his neck and to his chest as he quivered uncontrollably with every exhalation. His breath stuttered and spasmed as he whimpered in front of Pastor Roberts. He opened his swollen brown eyes to escape the dreamy desert he was in and see whether maybe, by some miracle, the Pastel Jesus had made himself manifest in the flesh before him. And that for once he would turn his gaze away from heaven and to the bewildered pilgrim before him, absolving his mortal sin like Mary Magdalene and admonishing him to go and sin no more. Instead, Pastor Roberts sat in front of him, wide-legged and with a furrowed brow. He, unlike his young acolyte, managed to maintain his pious meditative state, keeping his eyes closed as if waiting for God to move through him and impart some immediate revelation.

"Son, I'm receivin' a word a knowledge from the Lord." Pastor Roberts reached his hand upward. "First Corinthians, chapter 3, verse 15 says, 'If any man's work shall be burned, he shall suffer loss: but he himself shall be saved; yet so as by fire.'"

Michael wiped more snot and tears onto his sleeves as he tried to catch his breath from his outburst.

"Praise Jesus, thank you, Lord," Pastor Roberts whispered as he slowly opened his eyes.

"What's gonna happen now?" Michael asked.

"It means that we're gonna do another exercise."

The past two years had generated a thick compendium of catechisms, exercises, and rituals that had become a sort of spiritual prescription from his pastor and sometimes soul doctor. The godly and biblically rooted psychological practice was meant to root out offending sexual immorality. The exercises had ranged from the practical and mundane, such as "bouncing his eyes," constantly moving his focus around a room and fixating on different inanimate objects every five seconds. Michael did this when he saw an attractive man who could cause him to sin. However, other exercises were more draconian in nature, such as willfully isolating himself from friends or situations that might trigger same sexual desires.

Every week, Michael assured his pastor that he had completed all tasks that were assigned to him with exacting precision, and despite the discomfort—or in some cases, emotion pain—he still felt that at the very least the side effects of such "soul medicines" had their benefit in the end. But exercises that involved the dream carried with them the most severe side effects, and with each passing week the practices themselves became increasingly strange and violent. Michael eventually called it "dream twisting." When he began this treatment, he naively thought that imagining such things was self-contained in the realm of the subconscious. But as much as he worried about the queer truth of the dream leaking into reality for others to see, he also worried that the violence brewing in the salt desert could forcefully explode into his life.

"I want you to close your eyes and go back to the part of your dream where you finally meet this boy. Can you do that for me?"

"I don't know ..."

"Son, the Lord is callin' out to you, so you best listen to him."

"But what if it doesn't work this time?"

"Son, God can use your failures for your own good. You just gotta have faith in him."

"I don't know if I can do any more."

"Son, you ain't got a whole lotta options. You wanna spend eternity in hell 'cause of this?"

"No, but …"

"Well then, you deal with this now. It's up to you, son."

"OK," he said hesitantly.

Michael closed his eyes as he felt the vivid rush of his imagination flood over him, and he drifted back to the dead tree in the soft afternoon light of the salt desert. Standing next to the sinuous tree trunk, he saw the young man just as he had left him. Butterflies fluttered in his belly again as he admired the flexing musculature of his fantasy in the warm light of the setting sun. He tried to soak up his untarnished image in these last few seconds before Pastor Roberts boomed from the outside world into the subconscious dream.

You got that image in your mind, son?

Yeah.

Good. Now listen carefully, son.
Do you confess that you've lusted in your
heart toward this man and others like him?!

Yes.

And son, do you again renounce that
ungodly lust and lay it at the feet of Jesus?!

Yes.

And do ya repent of these evil abominations
and return back to the light of God?!

Yes.

Then you purge that vile
boy from your mind
with the holy fire of God that
purifies all things!

What do you want me to do?

You heard me, son!
Just like the Bible said,
… any man's work shall suffer loss.
but he himself shall be saved …

Michael looked at the boy standing against the tree as his kind and familiar smile seemed to call out to him to return the same kindness. It pained Michael to see this idealized handsome man innocently unaware of the judgment that had just been pronounced upon him, but Michael feared that his redemption would once again elude him if he didn't comply with another bizarre and violent request.

The month before, he was told to meditate on a verse in the book of Galatians that said,

> *… and they that are Christ's have crucified*
> *the flesh with the affections and lusts.*

After which his "dream twisting" involved him imagining himself digging a hole and burying the boy alive. The month before that, he was told to memorize another passage in the Gospel of Matthew, which said,

> *… and whoso shall offend one of these*
> *little ones which believes in me,*
> *it were better for him that a millstone*
> *were hanged around his neck,*
> *and that he were drowned in the depths of the sea.*

That episode of "dream twisting" involved him imaging a great flood coming in over the salt desert and holding the boy's head underwater to make sure that this

sin of lust would stay buried in the oceanic depths of his
psyche.

You … just want me to picture him on fire?
That's right, son. Every believer is
eventually gonna have to sacrifice
somethin' of himself to the Lord.
You wantin' me to kill him?

Son, sin is sin.
And if you don't kill sin,
sin will end up killin' you.
You sure 'bout this?

Sure as the Lord is good.
Just start off slowly, son
and describe to me how you do it.
It's for your own good.

Michael took a deep breath as he stood in the salt
desert with his fantasy in front of him. His body began to
shake again at the thought of psychological arson, let alone
immolating another human being. The sun still hovered
above the deep blue mountains, but the warmth he once
felt in his fingers and toes was fading quickly as he readied
himself to do the work of purifying his mind and soul.

Go on, son.

I … I can see a can of gasoline next to me.

All right, keep goin'.

And he's standing in front of me.

I pick up the gas can and pour out the gas on the ground.

It looks like a dirty river that moves toward him.

It makes a little puddle at his feet.

                                      What's he doin'?

He knows somethin' is wrong.
But he doesn't do anythin'.

He's just standin' there … waitin'.

There's a noise all around.
Like desert bugs buzzin' in the summer.
They're getting louder, and louder.

It's almost like they are screamin'.

                                    You wanna keep goin'?

I've gotta.

                                      All right …

I found a box of matches in my pocket.

I light one …
I can feel it warm on fingers.

The bugs are screamin' louder now …
it's hurtin' my ears.

                                               You can do this, son.

I drop the match in the gas.

                                                       Hallelujah.

The fire is bright …

The bugs are screamin' really loud.

He's burnin' up.

It's so bright …
I can barely see him.

                                             What's he doin'?

Nothin', he's just standin' there …
takin' it.

He ain't fightin' it.

He's quiet while his legs
turn black like charcoal.

                                      Are the bugs still screamin'?

Yes.

Is he still on fire?

Yes.

Now, repeat after me, son.
Sin, you've got no place in my life.

Sin, you've got no place in my life.

I put my lusts on the altar of sacrifice.

I put my lusts on the altar of sacrifice.

Jesus, come down and cleanse my mind.

Jesus, come down and cleanse my mind.

Praise God for deliverin' me from my sin.

Praise God for deliverin' me from my sin.

And savin' me from bein' a fag.

And savin' me from …

Savin' me from …

Go ahead and say it, son.

And savin' me from bein' a …
from bein' …
from bein' a faggot …

   Thank you, Jesus. Thank you for savin' this boy.
  Smoke was rising from the body and billowing out
against the velvet blue sky as the column of fire grew
upward and black soot stained the pure white salt.
Whatever life had been there in the fantasy, it was
dispersed to the wind and carried the ashes like gray snow
onto Michael and the twisted old tree.
  Pastor Roberts opened his eyes to peek at Michael
weeping in the chair, no longer trying to wipe his face. Just

numb and exhausted as he soaked in the devastation behind his eyelids. Michael was resigned to stop fighting against the commands or catechisms and to mourn the loss of someone whom he believed to be so integrally connected to him but whom he had never really met.

What's happenin' now?

He's … he's gone now …

He's all burned up.

Thank you, Jesus.

The fire had begun to die down as the sun dipped farther below the horizon of the salt desert. Slowly the glowing embers cooled to reveal the charred remains of Michael's fantasy, his sacrifice for redemption. A blackened humanoid form was void of any resemblance to the boy who had stood in the salt. Like the remains of Lot's wife, all that was left was an inert asexual statue of human ash. Here was the seared reality of what was to come if Michael could not change—it wouldn't be the willful flames of one's imagination but the unrelenting fires of hell that could render him into an eternal facsimile of the boy in front of him. The slow decrescendo of a thousand desert cicadas droning in his head quieted enough to leave a sharp ringing in his ears, signaling that the worst was over.

Anythin' else God is revealin' to you?

Michael turned to look around in the dwindling sunlight as the indigo night shadows started marching toward him. From behind him came the gentle touch of fingers on his shoulders, caressing him. He turned around to see a fine young woman standing innocently and coyishly behind him. Her wavy black hair cascading down in swirling locks to her voluptuous breasts. Her curves were smooth like a fine tequila while her eyes burned like the desert sun. Her smile spoke of a passionate, strong woman who was just as good a fighter as she was a lover. Michael watched the second apparition make her way to the tree opposite to where her male counterpart was. As much he wanted to touch the body of his now-scorched fantasy, he felt this deeply rooted need to woo her with the melodies of the Mexican songs his mother listened to. She was the one to calm his soul after these exercises, a welcome respite.

Son! Did ya hear me?
I asked you if you're seein'
anything else.

Uhm … naw, that's it. There's nothin' else.

He had never let on to Pastor Roberts that she was always there waiting for him after the purges, when the "dream twisting" was over. Michael assumed just as much that her presence was proof that all the catechisms and exercises were working. That when his mind was rid of the attraction to men, then his attraction to women would surface. It was strange for him, though, that she was so intrinsically linked to the boy. Bonded to each other by the ties of humanity, like Adam and Eve. He was, however, afraid to even mention her existence to Pastor Roberts. He didn't want to even think about the possibility that it might be just as much of a sin to have a woman in his mind as it was to have a man. He could not go through another round of this and have two columns of human ash burned into his mind.

> Now, son, you feelin' any kinda
> sinful attractions right now?
> Anything I should know 'bout?

Pastor Roberts got up from his chair and stood next to Michael, sliding his hand onto his shoulder. Michael's eyes were still tightly shut, and his lips began to quiver nervously when he felt the heavy and pudgy hand rubbing his back. The sensation of another man made his skin tense and feel contaminated after just being purified. Out of fear that this might be a way for his same-sex attractions to come surging in again, Michael began to squirm subtly from side to side trying to escape while his mind was still focused on the morenita in the desert.

> Anythin' else ya see in your dream?

Michael looked around at the white salt desert reflecting the dim sunlight that was slowly dipping behind the horizon. He turned to face the twisted and dried-up tree in front of him, bathed in the warm glow of the coming twilight, while she walked behind the tree and gazed at the pillar of charcoal next to her. Michael followed her, his eyes tracing the undulating curves of the tree limbs, starting from the small splintering ends of the branches. As his eyes moved down, he noticed a small drop of liquid forming on one of the branches, swelling up spontaneously from the surface of the soft wood. He looked at the other bare branches and began to see other drops beading the naked tree bark like blossom buds in early spring. Each dark drop grew steadily until it was too heavy to cling to the tree and fell like a little seed onto the crusty salt below. In the diminishing light, the tiny splashes were difficult to distinguish.

Michael got close to one of the drops on the tree trunk as it began to trickle down through every imperfection in the bark. To Michael, the drops looked almost like black tears, and when he stepped forward and touched one, he felt that the liquid was warm and thick. He pulled his hand closer to his face and saw the color red glistening in the last bit of light. It was blood. He looked back to see his handprint stamped in crimson on the trunk as more blood trickled down the tree. Then he looked around to see the growing splatter pattern on the crust of salt around him, as if he were in a horror movie. Outside this vision, in the real world, Michael's body began to shiver ever so lightly.

The tree … it's … bleeding.

Pastor Roberts, finally sensing that Michael had reached his limit for the day, knelt down beside him and began to pray.

"Father, we thank you for what you
have shown Michael today,
and for how you have extended
your grace and mercy to him.

Above all else, we thank you for
lovin' him with all of his blemishes.
I know that your will for him is
that he would leave the same-sex attraction
behind and that he would walk
in the knowledge of you.
We ask that you bless him and continue to
guide him though this challengin' time in his life.
In your name we pray, Amen."

3

"How you feelin', son?"

Michael tried to peel open his eyelids. The salty tears had crusted them together. The ashes of his fantasy were now locked deep in the inner folds of his brain, like smeared graffiti on a neighborhood wall. All he could really feel was the after-pain, a lingering and lasting throbbing that didn't come from his body or skin but from some unknown invisible layer of himself.

"Did you fall asleep on me, son?"

"Hey, son! I'm talkin' to you!"

He could feel the firm jiggling on his shoulder that tried to wake him from his trance. When he did manage to open his eyes, the blurry fluorescent lights still made everything look as if he had been swallowed up by the salt desert. A misty whiteness that was disorienting and consuming. One by one, the sensations of the real world started to come back to him: the hard wooden chair, the stiff fabric of his work jeans on his legs, and the soft touch of Pastor Roberts's hand on his back. Even though it was usual for him to be touched after these exercises, the almost dead weight of Pastor Roberts's hand made him feel cold and eerily strange, as if he were alien and uninvited. Besides the strangeness, it was still enticing to feel the touch of another human being. But it scared him to think that each stroke of a man's hand could awaken the ashes of his fantasy to haunt him. He did his best to wriggle away from the pastor as the lights came into focus.

"Looks like that one took a lot outta you," said a winded Pastor Roberts.

"Yeah … it um … it was … a lot."

"Well, gotta do what we can to get that gay outta you!"

"Yeah, gotta try everythin' …"

"How you feelin', son?"

"I'm, I'm … OK, I guess."

"Them gay thoughts botherin' you?"

Michael sat for a minute, waiting to see if he could resurrect the ashes of the boy into memory or fantasy. Just as a test. Anything from his kind smile to his soft brown eyes, something that could make Michael remember what he looked like. But every bit of the boy that Michael tried to remember quickly became engulfed in gasoline-fueled flames, eventually smoldering again in the dim smoky glow of twilight. His tan skin had instantly become charred and then like embers. The desire for men had been tamed once again, and the threat of the dream faded away like the last sultry streams of white smoke. Even the weird dead feeling he got from Pastor Roberts touching him seemed to be numbed. Still, there was a part of him that wanted to resist hijacking his own subconsciousness.

"No … I don't feel anythin' …"

"Feelin' nothin' is a good thing, son … it's a really good thing!" said Pastor Roberts as he sat back down in his chair.

"But I feel somethin' else …"

"You do?"

"Yeah …"

"Well, what is it, son?"

"I feel … like … sad … like really sad …"

"You feel sad for what?"

"Just that … it makes me sad to think about hurtin' someone for me to feel better. Even if they ain't real. It makes me sad that I've gotta do this. How bad am I that I've gotta hurt other people to be good?"

"Lord, help me! Look, son, does God hate sin?!"

"Well, yeah …"

"And that boy, does he make you want to fall into sin?

"Y-yeah …"

"Well, that boy is sin! Plain 'n simple, son!"

"So, God hates him?"

"Don't you, son? He's been the one makin' your life miserable, ain't he? Makin' you lust after men all the time. I'll tell you what … if anythin' gets in the way of me and Jesus, I'm gonna hate it. I'm gonna hate it just like God hates it. Am I right?"

"Yeah …"

"Well then … love the things God loves, and hate the things God hates. It's as simple as that."

For Michael, this was the great schism, the chasm that he found difficult to cross, where the restraints of hatred were obliterated and the ability to harbor such justifiable hatred was now sanctified. He read in the Bible how he was to love his neighbor. He had been hearing these admonishments long before Manny and the church on the corner were even in his life. But for now, love had to take a back seat—or at its best, sit in the passenger front seat. It was strange to Michael that the two spectral ends of humanity were bent and folded over on themselves to be one and the same and yet were distinct and polarized at the same time.

"Pastor?"

"Yes, son?"

"Can I ask you somethin'?"

"Sure, son, go ahead."

"Does God hate me 'cause I'm like this?"

"No, son, God just hates the sin that in you. That's all."

"Then why does all this happen to me?"

"Why does 'what' happen to you, son?"

"Feelin' like this … Why is it happenin' to me?"

"You mean feelin' pain, or feelin' like you need to act out your sin?"

"Having these feelins toward guys."

"You think that it's God's fault?"

"No … I just … I dunno … It just feels like … like I just can't change …"

"Oh come on, son! You know the answer to that. Donchya remember?"

Pastor Roberts reached down and pulled out the yellow paper that was folded up in his Bible. He opened it and handed it over to Michael.

"Why donchya read the first couple of lines out loud, son? It'll do you good to remember how you got here."

Michael the paper and started to read the blue ink statement in his own cursive handwriting.

Reasons:

June 24, 1995

My dad never played football with me.
I didn't grow up with my dad telling me I was a
man.
I didn't like playing outside with other boys in
school.
Without other boys, I never knew how much of a
man I was.
My dad didn't teach me what sin is.
Without God's truth, I'd believe any lie as truth.
My mom and dad were Catholic.
I didn't know real Christianity till I came here.
My dad died before I hit puberty.
I had no role model, so my mom took over and
taught me to think like a woman.
I started having these feelins when I was 12.
I started looking for my dad's love in other men.
I kept it a secret from everyone.
I knew it was wrong.

As his eyes swept across the familiar page, he could vividly remember the day he wrote this with Pastor Roberts's help. He was sixteen when he came for his first appointment. Embarrassed and scared, he could think of only his one true fear: that he could lose Magdalena. It was bad enough to lose one parent to the grave, but it was incomprehensible to lose his mother on account of him—if not by her own abandonment or Manny's banishment, then surely by the great expanse of hell that would divide them in the next life. He just could not allow circumstance to

take not only his father but her as well. It was bad enough
that it was Manny, the man he had come to despise since
childhood, who happened to stumbled onto his secret. But
in a strange and begrudging mercy, Manny never said
anything to anyone; he just quietly and secretively brought
him to the church to be fixed. In Manny's mind, it was
easier to make Michael change than to suffer the awkward
embarrassment of having to explain why his stepson was a
queer. In a sense they were holding each other hostage,
bound by the burden of silent closeted shame.

During Michael's first appointment, the initial
round of questions from Pastor Roberts came at him like a
rapid-fire Stasi-like interrogation, small exploratory cuts
into his person to see exactly when and where this sin had
entered him. Michael was questioned about the type of
men he liked, or what exactly he liked about a particular
man. Pastor Roberts even went as far as to pull out a health
and fitness magazine with photographs of bare-chested
men and ask if any of the sweaty guys aroused him. But
once his father's profound absence was discovered, the
pastor zeroed in on a diagnosis and Michael began to zero
in on every nuanced mishap of his childhood. Michael was
asked to write down all his seemingly benign responses,
like daily affirmations. There were reminders of how the
lie of his being born this way was just that, a lie. Like
reading the tea leaves at the bottom of a cup, the jumbled
unrelated facts of his past were arranged into a single
coherent thought, a diagnostic premonition of his sickness.
Every damaging incident of his masculinity was paired
with a truth, a response that was carefully crafted by Pastor
Roberts, ensuring that the path of his deviation into
perdition could be easily recalled at times like this.

"You remember now, son?"

Michael silently and remorsefully nodded while holding the yellow sheet of paper.

"It's a lotta daddy issues that made you this way, son! I can't say how many times I seen boys like you grow up without a daddy and end up livin' in that lie thinkin' they're gay and wastin' their whole lives in that filth."

Since that summer in 1995 it had become painfully easy for Michael to place the blame on the dead. Cold, lifeless lips could not cry out and defend themselves from the immense conspiracy being spun by the living. It was just as easy to believe that if death had not taken his father so soon, then the pain of loss wouldn't have been so deep that it left him looking for his daddy in the arms of another man. Michael often wondered if maybe his father had played tackle football instead of soccer just once in his life, it may have saved him from this tragic lack of maleness. Despite what he thought was a normal Mexican childhood, the train of reasoning made him believe more and more often that perhaps his Mexican upbringing had somehow hindered him from growing up to be the ideal straight All-American young man.

"I've got faith that God'll deliver you from this, son, just you see."

Michael turned to the empty church that was bathed in that drab light, wanting to find the God hidden in front of him. What he really wanted to do was scream out with absolute certainty that he did in fact like the boy, that he liked him just as much he liked the girl in his dream. He wanted to get up in Pastor Roberts's face and yell that he wanted to feel something for the boy. He wanted to know what it was like to hold the boy's hand or kiss the girl. He wanted to feel his heart flutter after hearing "I love you" from either one. He could hear his own voice in that scenario, shouting to Pastor Roberts, "I can't change it! I don't wanna have to be fixin' everyone mistakes they made on me, all right?!"

"You doin' OK, son?" interrupted Pastor Roberts.

"Uhm, yeah … It's … you know …"

"You have faith that Jesus can save you from this?"

"Yeah … yeah, I do."

"Do you, son?"

By this time the sound of leaf blowers had died down, and the church was filled with the low howling sound of damp air moving through the air ducts as the two of them sat quietly in front of the Pastel Jesus.

"Why donchya go ahead and stand up, son."

"I'm OK, really … I believe … I believe Jesus can save me. Honest!"

"I know, I heard ya. But I think you need to hear it, son."

"But really, I'm good."

"It's for your own good. Come on, now! Git up!"

Michael hesitantly stood, as he was taught to do in instances like this, when he needed reassurance of his faith. Standing tall with his feet apart, he clasped his hands behind his back and puffed up his chest as much as he could as he thought,

Stand like a man, nice and tall.

"All right, son. Go on … let's hear it."

Michael took in a deep breath as he tried to squeeze his shoulder blades together.

"I am a man, made in God's image,

I'll serve God like the Man he wants me to be,
I'll love my wife like Jesus loves the church,
I'll do things like other men do,
I'll think like a man, and not like a woman,
I'll defend and fight for the people God's put in
my life,
I'll fight against anything that tells me I'm not a
man,
I won't look at a man the way I'm supposed to
look at a woman,
I'll see other men as role models instead,
I'll be the Man of God that he wants me to be,
I am a man."

"A-men! Praise God!"

Michael exhaled and deflated his masculine shoulders and let his body collapse back into himself. He always felt like a sideshow clown miming a cartoonish version of a man whenever he had to perform this particular exercise. He wasn't even sure that it was the "right version" of a man to be, but it seemed to be the one who Pastor Roberts like him to be.

"Uh-uh … keep it up, son. You gotta keep it up. Always be tryin' to show the world what kinda man you are. Now stand up straight!"

"Sorry!"

Since the dream twisting began, Michael had learned a trick to help him be outwardly manly. He forced himself to think about the boy being destroyed over and over, using the hatred for his fantasy to fuel his determination. He couldn't see the boy's eyes or body, but he could see the end result. It made him feel numb, soothing like cold water trickling down his spine. His whole body seemed to shiver with the internal coldness and his teeth started to chatter. Despite the shivering, the numbness allowed him to clear his mind, letting him recall all the men he knew in church, his repertoire of "Straight Role Models," examples that Pastor Roberts encouraged him to study and to imitate how they stood, acted, and carried themselves. He always remembered that all these men were White, with no expression of any sexuality, and stalwart like good Christians. He randomly picked out a few of these examples, focusing intensely on how they presented their inert maleness to the world in hopes that by pure mental osmosis, his pores would exude the same sexless character.

"You've been practicin' in front of the mirror like I told you, son?"

"Yes, sir. Every night before I go to bed."

"How 'bout the other stuff …"

"Other stuff?"

"Yeah, your handshake."

"What about it?"

"Let's see it!" Pastor Roberts stood up in front of Michael, his faded shirt dampened with sweat and clinging to his soft convex body. He stuck out his clammy hand toward Michael. "Howdy there, son, I'm Pastor Roberts. It sure is nice to meet you!" he said in his typical Sunday welcoming voice, smiling.

In a fraction of a second, Michael ran through his handshake sequence, infusing this week's dream twisting image until his body felt cold and numb again.

Burn
Hand out
Flames
Grab the palm

Searing
Grip it tight
Ashes
Not like a woman
Death
Good shake
Numb
Look 'em in the eye

"Nice to meet you, I'm Michael Mendoza."

"You like football, son?"

"Football? You betcha!"

"Did you happen to catch the game last week?"

"Yeah ... I did ... I uhm ... uhm ..."

"Oh come on, son! You gotta be able to answer a simple question like that!"

"I'm sorry!"

"I know you Mexicans like to watch soccer, but ain't no one gonna understand that. This is 'merica, son!"

"OK, OK ... Lemme try again!"

"Focus son, focus!"

Pastor Roberts took a moment to reset for his role-play. "So, did you see the game last week, son?"

Burn – Flames – Searing – Ashes – Death – Numb

"Nah, my team wasn't playin' last week," responded Michael with shivering determination.

"Hmmm ... so, who's your team?"

"... The Cardinals."

Pastor Roberts examined his young acolyte up and down, confirming that he had passed the test, this time.

"Not bad. I guess that's one way of dodgin' a question."

"Thanks."

"But I don't want you to be gettin' in the habit. You better be watchin' football, son."

"But it ain't football season right now …"

"Don't be mouthin' off to me, son. You know what I mean!"

"OK … I'm sorry, I'm sorry … I'll … I'll do it."

"Just do what other men do! You got that?"

Pastor Roberts frustratingly plopped himself back down in his chair while pulling out his white handkerchief to dab the beading sweat from his forehead.

"Is there anythin' else you want me to do this week?"

"As a matter of fact there is, son! I'd like you to study 'nother Bible verse."

"More verses?"

"Oh absolutely! In fact, it looks like they've been helpin'."

"OK, well … which one?"

"Lemme see," exhaled Pastor Roberts as he picked up his Bible and started leafing through the shimmering golden pages. "Here we go, son. Matthew, chapter 5, verse 30."

Pastor Roberts handed over the black Bible, giving a penetrating stare deep into Michael's tired brown eyes.

"Why don't you read it out loud, son."

Michael took the Bible in his hands and tried to focus on the red letters of the text.

"And if thy right hand offend thee, cut it off, and cast it from thee: for it is profitable for thee that one of thy members should perish, and not that thy whole body should be cast into hell."

"Amen!"

"Well, that's cool and all, but what's it mean for me?"

"God can't make it any plainer for you, son! If there's somethin' that's causin' you to sin, then you gotta cut it outta your life."

"Anythin'?"

"Anythin' and everythin'! You wanna get better, don't you?"

"Well, yeah."

"Then just 'member this verse whenever you feel them urges comin' on … just repeat that verse over and over again … pray through it if you have to."

Michael looked back down at the red text on the tissue-thin pages while a familiar and more nagging question bubbled in his brain.

"Will all this really help me?"

"Will this help you?!? Son, I've been a pastor for longer than you've been alive, and I've seen boys and young men in the same place as you are. Just strugglin' with the same kinda demons and come out this. And you're gonna ask me if this is really gonna help?!" Pastor Roberts huffed before he continued. "You know, it just breaks my heart to see the devil lie to so many boys. Pullin' them away from God's truth. The devil's real, son. And he ain't gonna stop, unless we say no."

"It's just that I've been fightin' all of this for two years. Is it ever gonna stop?"

"One day, son … one day it'll stop."

"Just wish it was now."

"I know, son. But you just gotta look forward to the day when all this is behind you. And by then you'll be married, to a woman. And everything'll be OK."

"Will I ever be loved?"

"Son!? What kinda question is that?"

"I dunno … It's just …"

"Son, Jesus loves you. He loves you so much that he came and died on the cross so you can go to heaven. Ain' that enough for you?"

"Well, I know that, but I don't feel it sometimes, you know?"

"Son, love ain't a feelin'. You just know it right here in your heart. Just like you know that Jesus loves you too much to let you stay this way. He'll give you chance after chance to get things right …"

"He will?"

"Absolutely he will, that's what love is. No matter how many times you stumble, God's always there to pick you up and set you back on your feet. It ain't the kind them gays think it is. Hoppin' from one bed to another. That ain't love, that's fornicatin'. This right here, this is love. Getting' all that sin outta you. That's God's great love"

Michael glanced over at the Pastel Jesus, still standing in the water, seemingly distant from the conversation with his soft blue eyes steadfastly gazing toward heaven. Michael wanted Jesus's face to inflate into true carnal humanity and look down at this young devotee and say for himself that he loved him. He wanted to hear it just once, personally from his pastel God, instead of hearing it secondhand. He wanted to feel that deep sense of love, a love that lived and was real to his soul. A love that made him feel ten feet tall because someone in this world thought he was worth it. He could just as easily say he loved Jesus too; that's what he had been taught to do since he was a kid. But the girl of his dream and the ashes of his nightmare represented a new kind of a love. A human love. A love that seemed to easily transcend the erotic laws of attraction and yet awaken them to arrive at the same place of worthiness. A love more than sex. A love that he couldn't describe but would recognize.

"It's gettin' kinda late, son. I think Manny's about near done outside."

"Yeah, it's gettin' time for me to go."

"By the way, how're things with your stepdaddy?"

"Do we really gotta talk 'bout that?"

"Son, I told you. There are no places to hide durin' these appointments."

"They're fine."

"Just fine?"

"Yeah, they're fine."

"You gettin' short with me again, son?"

Michael could feel his heart racing. It was a strange reaction that would make the memories of the salt desert and the dream twisting fade into seething, impotent rage. For the first time today, his brain could let the image of the flames and ashes go without the cold numbness he had learned. Just hearing Manny's name changed Michael into someone who didn't feel the paralyzing coldness. Rather, he felt red indignation, like an angry furnace that burned more fervently than any Arizona sun. Ironically these were the times that Michael knew he felt like man, thought like a man, and wanted to act out like a man. The kind of Latin man who didn't see American Christian pacifism as a virtue but rather called for stern and brute aggression as a very real necessity.

"No it's just that … things are fine, OK?"

"Still can't get over all that stuff, can you?"

"… Well, no, I can't!"

"C'mon, son. We've been through this before. You're only hurtin' yourself …"

"You know, Pastor … I'll do all the exercises you tell me to do, I'll memorize the whole Bible if I have to, and I'll pray on my knees till it hurts, but I just can't let him have that. Not like that, and not without really sayin' he's sorry!"

"Maybe all them bad dreams is tryin' to tell you to let go of it."

"I just can't … It hurts me so bad, but it feels like no one cares that he hurts me. It hurts, it really hurts. It hurts me that he does this to my mom and …"

"Bible says we should forgive, son."

"Yeah, I know it does! But there's a huge difference between doing what I aught to do and doin' what I wanna do."

"Son, I know he's got problems, but it's not like you ain't got yours. Besides, God don't like to see families apart. It's just not right!"

"But there's all the …"

"Son, listen, listen, listen. Maybe that boy keeps comin' back in your dreams 'cause you're not wantin' to accept Manny. Did you ever think about that? Hmmm? I betcha if you start openin' up to him, a lot of them urges of wantin' to be with another man will go away. I know he ain't your daddy, but God's givin' you a shot at havin' one even if it ain't your real daddy."

"I wish it was someone else …"

"Son, you can't fight against God's will. If he's sent Manny into your life, it's for a good reason."

"You know, I come in here and I git up and say those words over and over again hopin' I'll be straight one day. Every week I hear myself sayin' that I should git up and fight … and I wanna. I wanna fight! But everything I've heard on Sundays says that I shouldn't. That I've gotta be a good boy, when all I wanna do it hit back! I wanna punch him!"

"Son, I'm only gonna tell you once, so you best listen good. The second you lay a hand on your stepdaddy, you'll be committin' a sin as big fornicatin' with another man."

"But I wanna hit him … I wanna fight back!"

"Son, if you wanna be a man of God, then you fight back with prayin'! Askin' God how to forgive him …"

"Forgive him? I can't stand it whenever he's around. It hurts me that I see everythin' he does and then to think that this is who God's sent to help me …"

"Well, son, sometimes you gotta hurt before God saves you."

"Yeah, but …"

"Look, don't it hurt when you do all them exercises in your head? Or were you lyin' to me about all that earlier?"

"Yeah, but …"

"And you feel better after, don't you?"

"A little bit, yeah."

"Then God's gotta purpose when you hurt like that."

"Yeah? What is it?" Michael pressed his lips tight as puffs of angry air snorted from his flaring nostrils.

"Look here, son, I know I'm hard on you. But it's 'cause I know what God wants in your life. He don't want you to be like all them faggots and fornicators out there. He wants somethin' more for you. And if that means he don't want you to be growin' up without a daddy, then so be it."

"I don't want a dad."

"And look where that's gotten you, son."

"Can't it be someone else?"

"Like who? You've got a lotta men here in church to choose from …"

"What about my coach?"

"You know I don't like you hangin' around him, son."

"Why?"

"'Cause he ain't a good Christian influence on you. He looks like one of them … oh, what do y'all call 'em … a gangbanger … what do you call 'em in Spanish?"

"A cholo?"

"Yeah, that's right, a cholo!"

"Well, he ain't."

"I just wonder if he ain't gonna get you into more trouble."

"But ain't he showin' me how to be a man?"

"Yeah, the wrong kinda man. You wanna be a good Christian man who fights with the truth of God in your heart, not some hoodlum who turns to violence. God don't want that for you either."

Michael turned again toward the mural of Jesus standing in his heavenly aura, forever waiting to be baptized in the soft-blue water outlined with crusted, shiny glitter. Still hopelessly waiting for Jesus to make himself real and say to him, "No, my son, that's not what I want for you. I want you to be happy." But there were no words, no miracle. Just the stinging treatment and the sickening feeling that this cure would be the one thing he hated most in the world. Who knew that all those years ago, when he stood in the baptistry under the same crusty fake water, his baptism would wash away something and still leave filth behind. His Spanish, his culture, and even his choice of whom he wanted in his life trickled off him into the serene waters of Protestantism. But it never washed away his sin, it just made it clearer for others to see.

"I guess I can try again with Manny …"

"Amen, son, Amen! You'll see I'm right. Just you wait!"

Pastor Roberts took out his handkerchief again to wipe the sweat off his head while Michael leaned forward in his chair. He was stuck with no other options. He had no leverage to say that he wanted something other than being stuck between being queer and his nemisis. But what else could he do? The dreams were torture enough, and it seemed less painful to accept the lie in full godliness and call Manny "Dad" than suffer another sleepless night worrying that he would be banished to hell.

"Well, is there anythin' else you wanna talk about before you go, son?" asked Pastor Roberts as he started to fold up the yellow sheet of paper into his Bible.

"I don't think so."

"Alrighty, son, I just want you to know that no matter how hard all this gets, I still love you. I may get upset and start hootin' and hollarin' about things, but that's only 'cause I love you. You hear me?"

"Yeah, I do."

"God loves you too much to let you be this way, so just let him do what he's gonna do to make it better. Don't fight it, just be open to all the pain and hurtin'," Pastor Roberts said as Michael was trying to block out any burgeoning temptations.

Love was customary for Pastor Roberts, and this particular love was for Michael's own good. Despite every objection or mistake he had committed during the week, Michael found it oddly comforting that he felt something from Pastor Roberts at the end of each appointment. He assumed that, at best, this was somewhat genuine love. The more Pastor Roberts hated the queerness in Michael, the more he tried to see that he was cured. It was as if he actually cared whether Michael went to hell. It wasn't until today that Michael realized what he had seen all this time was the fluidity of hate in love, and love in hate. Maybe if he just tried hard enough, his love for God would drive him to hate the ashes of the boy, and perhaps in his hatred for Manny he would find the love that would save his soul. Even in the middle of this labyrinth of Bible verses, catechisms, exercises, creeds, and handshakes, this could be at least one bit of assured truth for him to work from. Still, it didn't seem right to Michael from the outside looking in, but maybe that had been the hinderance all this time. Maybe that's why the dream came back over and over again. Maybe it was time to surrender from the bounds of love and hate. He had nothing else to lose.

"I think we're done here, son. Why don't you help me git these chairs back up here?"

Michael jumped to his feet, taking the immediate opportunity to distance himself from the cold, dead touch of Pastor Roberts. He could try to hatelove/lovehate later at home, but for now he just didn't want to have to feel anything. They both plopped their chairs back into place behind the choir risers, as Pastor Roberts headed toward the switch and began shutting off the lights inside the church. Michael stayed on the stage staring at the mural in the baptistry one last time, the blue eyes of Pastel Jesus piously gazing at the parting white clouds. One by one the droning fluorescent bulbs fell silent as the dull light vanished into the darkness. Michael turned to the back of the church to once again see the small daggers of natural light coming through the narrow windows, illuminating the swirls of nebulous dust in the microuniverse of this dark space. Cosmic God was allowed back in now that Pastel Jesus was done trying to save the boy. There was no need for Cosmic God to witness the violence of this week's dream twisting. No need for him to see the institution of hatelove/lovehate like a new communion rite.

"All right, son, it's gettin' hot. Let's git up on outta here."

As they opened the doors to the bright daylight, Manny was waiting in a settling cloud of dust as his crews loading up tools and equipment into their trailers.

"Howdy there, Manny. You 'n your boys all finished up out here?" Pastor Roberts asked.

"Yup, all done!"

"Well, I figure I'd just walk your boy out."

Manny looked at his stepson as he squinted in the bright sun. Michael was trying to hold back the reactionary angry that he was so accustomed to, but he quickly found his opportunity to practice his new skill.

Hatelove/lovehate
Hatelove/lovehate
Hatelove/lovehate

Manny looked back at Pastor Roberts and asked, "How'd he do?"

Pastor Roberts looked at Michael and, with a big smile, said, "Well, I think he did just fine. Time will tell, brotha Manny, time will tell."

Glancing once more at Michael, Manny nodded in agreement. He turned and gestured to Michael to go on ahead and get into the truck. Michael tried his best not to show contempt for Manny and forced a smile as he head back to the truck. As he walked away, he could hear Pastor

Roberts's voice continue to ramble on with Manny.

"Manny, I wanted to ask if you had thought 'bout the position on the deacons board."

"Yeah, I did."

"Well, me and the other deacons were talkin' …"

The conversation drifted away as Michael walked closer to the truck. He pulled the door open and immediately felt the blast of hellish hot air that had built up inside. He climbed in and left the door open. Manny and Pastor Robert were still talking at the front of the church in the blistering sunlight, and the pastor's pale skin became redder and beaded with fat drops of sweat that reflected off his bald head like press-on rhinestones. He watched as Pastor Roberts gave Manny a conciliatory smile, shook hands, and walked away. Manny swiftly walked back to the truck and stood at the open door, where Michael was waiting.

"You gonna work today or what?!" he sternly asked his stepson.

Michael gave a resigned nod to his stepfather.

"Y no quiero pedo! Entendiestes?"[24]

"I won't … Dad."

"Dad?!"

As Manny started the engine, he reached under the seat and pulled out some old leather work gloves. He tossed them next to Michael as they left the church, heading to the north part of town.

"I don't know what you're tryin' to do … pero nunca tendre un maricón como hijo."[25]

Burn – Flames – Searing – Ashes – Death – Numb

---

[24] "I don't want any trouble. You understand me?"
[25] "I'd never have a son that's a faggot."

4

The silence between Michael and Manny might as
well have been as wide as the Grand Canyon. Both were
seething under the sweltering sun, working in lockstep,
trading stabs of wordless glances. Their throats were dry
and itchy as the metallic flavor of dirt and gasoline vapor
settled in their lungs. But neither of them wanted to say out
loud how tired they were, neither wanted to chicken out.
With parched tongues they still managed to carry on with
all the other men of Manny's crew that afternoon. Shouts
between the dark-skinned men echoed in the green tree-
lined street between the revving of leaf blowers and
trimmers.

"Ya casi, Juanito?"

"No mames, güey!"

Soon the lawns were neatly mowed and every
untamed bush was shaped like a life-size gumdrop.
Stepfather and stepson slid into opposite sides of Manny's
beat-up truck, never looking at each other until they pulled
up to the next job at the next house or the next street.

Over the few years that he had been working with
Manny, Michael had learned to mimic the other men in

Manny's crew. Not so much for the purpose of achieving his long-awaited straight epiphany as for the necessity of getting work done. Hoisting burlap sacks of branches and leaves onto his back and tossing them into trailers, sweating heavily until his shirt was crusted white with salt. And just like them, he learned not to complain about the heat or the cuts and scrapes from dead branches. Experience taught him about the ridicule and backlash that would happen if he did: torrents of quick jabs and name-calling, names such as "joto,"[26] "maricón,"[27] and "faldillón,"[28] against which Michael knew that he couldn't defend himself, honestly at least. Beyond the name-calling, Michael had always perceived these men as a different type than the men at church. Men who said little about themselves when they worked. Men who had little time for life's pleasures, like watching football to make them "straight" or staying late on Sunday night for Bible study. Even though all their hard work was burned into their rich brown skin, Michael had a deep-rooted sense that he would never see those men as the type that he needed to be. They were not the White men of status and suits on Sundays. And from that, it was easy for Michael to surmise that everything Pastor Roberts wanted him to be could be distilled into a simple idea: His manliness was a hobby to practice and perfect.

It was already three o'clock in the afternoon, and the sun was at its hottest when it started to wane in the azure sky. Even though the towering trees at this last house provided a lot of shade, Michael was starting to feel the

---

[26] Fag

[27] Faggot.

[28] Someone who holds tightly to the apron string.

heat getting to him. He felt dizzy as he tried to push through the final loads of palm fronds that needed to be dumped into the trailers. His tongue was sticky, and his skin was hot under his long-sleeved shirt. When he got into the truck, he was lightheaded and discretely nodding off in front of Manny.

Stay up, don't act like a joto! he said to himself, hoping Manny wouldn't say anything. But he was so shaky from the heat exhaustion that it finally prompted Manny to speak.

"Anda! Drink this!"

Manny tossed over a bottle of lukewarm sports drink. Michael couldn't stand the sickening feeling of blacking out, so he took the bottle and gulped it down without stopping. He would deal with his obliged gratitude later.

"Ya, ya, ya, hombre ... you're gonna get sick."

Michael finished the bottle and then gasped in air as he started to perk up a bit.

"Andale, keep tryin' to show off like you're the tough guy! See what's gonna happen!"

"I wasn't showin' off, Manny."

"You better not. I don't have time to take you to the hospital."

"I'll live!"

"Roll down your window, tambien. Gotta get some air in here!"

Michael did as he was told. At least he had started to sweat again, and even the hot street air coming into the truck as they drove north started to feel cool on his sweaty face.

"Where we goin' now?"

"Gotta go to George's house."

"George? From church?"

"Yeah."

"I thought we cleaned his house last week."

"Yeah, we did …"

Michael sat back in the damp musty seat, cradling the empty bottle in his hand. He had run through his typical repertoire of simple things to say and was coming up short on ways to reciprocate the olive branch of a warm bottle of sports drink. However, Manny was festering with impatience when it came to his stepson. It took only a few more stoplights before Manny finally broke down to ask him.

"Is Pastor helpin' you with your problem?"

"What problem?"

"Ay hombre, no seas tan burro![29] You know what I'm talkin' 'bout!"

"It's not a problem, and yeah, he's helping me."

"You sure?!"

"Why, you don't believe me?"

"I wanna, but I just don't trust you."

"Yeah … right, you don't trust me …"

"You're not lyin' to me?!"

"God, why do you have be on my ass all the time?!"

"Ey! Don't use that language with me! Have some respect!"

"What do you care? I'll be gone when summer's over!"

"Hey! Just because you're not gonna be in my house don't mean that I don't want to have to deal with your tonterias. You gotta lotta evil in you, you know

---

[29] "C'mon, man, don't act so stubborn!"

that?!"

"And what are you gonna do 'bout it, huh?"

"I'm takin' you to the pastor, ain't I?"

"Then leave me alone!"

"You think I'm just gonna leave this alone? Who knows what else you're hidin'!"

"What, you're gonna go through my backpack again?!"

"Hey, hey, hey! I had my reasons, OK?"

"Yeah? And what were they?"

"I wanted to see if you were sellin' mota!"

"I told you I wasn't!"

"No, but you had other things in there!"

"… So?!"

"I told you I don't want no cochinadas[30] in my house! My home is for God, not jotos!"

"What do you want? Huh?! I've been goin' to see Pastor like I promised!"

"Has it gone away?"

"It's goin' away, OK! God, what do you care?!"

"Hey, I just wanna know if all that's gone! I think I deserve that. I could've thrown you out of that house so fast that day …"

"Yeah? And why didn't you?"

"'Cause we're supposed to be a family! A good Christian family."

"Some family we turned out to be."

"Hey, you don't know how bad I've wanted a family, all right? I didn't have this growin' up. When you get older, you'll see what I mean."

"See what?"

---

[30] Dirtiness.

"That you'll want things just like everyone else."

"When I'm as old as you, I don't wanna be anythin' like you."

"Hmpf … You think you know everythin', don't you. You think you've got it all figured out …"

"No, I just know who you are. I've seen you fight with my mom. I know what the fights are 'bout."

"You think it's wrong to be like that, don't you."

Michael said nothing and resumed watching the buildings and sidewalks flow by as if they were sailing down a flat asphalt river.

"Look around you, boy. You see all these nice houses? These pretty buildings? It's all Gringos here. This is theirs, and you wanna know somethin'? They don't care 'bout you. They only care 'bout one thing. And you either have it or you don't. And if you want it so bad, you'll do anythin' to get it."

It was a tragic reality, and one that Manny had learned early on, even as a boy. Being Brown brought with it certain expectations and liabilities from Gringos. Speaking English only made it easier to mingle with people who had 'made it' in life, those who had successfully attained the American Dream. But if either one of them was ever caught letting a little bit of their accent slip out, they might as well be a few days out from having walked across the border. Therefore, they had to resort to the tried-and-true method of just being a ghost of a Mexican. Getting aimlessly lost in Americana had become such an endemic problem for Manny, and even for Michael, that every time either one of them talked to Magdalena, she frustratingly refused to answer in English. But for Manny, the more he let his Brownness evaporate, the more he wanted to dive deep into the baptistry of White culture and be washed of the culpabilities of being a Mexican. Manny had a ravenous and insatiable craving to be like a White man. And the allure of all these White lives that he worked for, and their White American Dreams that he kept clean and trim, was just as intoxicating as Michael's hidden fantasies of men.

After a few turns off the main roads and onto narrow side streets, they found themselves in one of the more well-to-do neighborhoods of the city. Here was where the sweat of Manny and his crew really made the desert bloom and flourish like the idyllic Eden of the American West. The old ranch-style homes that at one time were considered to be in the boonies of Phoenix were now nestled in the ever-expanding suburban sprawl of concrete and stucco. Each house sat on a large stretch of verdant green and perfectly mowed lawn. Rows of lush bougainvilleas were formed into colonnades of bloated green pillars with speckled dots of fuchsia throughout the neighborhood. There was not a patch of desert dirt to be found, or even a weed reaching out of the ground like the arms of some long-dead spirit.

When Manny finally pulled over, Michael immediately recognized the house at the end of the street as George and Rebecca's stately home. The lawn was still bright green and trim, just as Manny had left it last week. Michael could always pick out George's house by the way George liked to keep his bougainvilleas. The other houses had them as stubby columns or rounded gumdrops, but his home had a pair of elegant and full bushes at the entrance, like Magdalena's, each one standing near the front door like a stately guardian angel. It was Manny's job to keep every wild and thorny branch tamed, since George was not a fan of the constant pink confetti that littered his front patio. Keeping the bushes from turning into their natural unbridled form was a must.

Manny called to his crew as they threw bundles of burlap into his truck.

"Ya casi muchachos?!"[31] he yelled.

"Si, patron!"[32] answered one of the newest workers.

"Que te falta?"[33]

"Pues …"[34]

"Pues que? Que paso?"[35] he asked all of them.

"Pues, es que ese pinche Gringo alla …"[36]

"Cual Gringo?"[37]

"… el de la ultima casa, pues."[38]

"Que te dijo?"[39]

"Pues, no mas … andaba chingue, chingue, chingue, patron!"[40]

"Que, que?!"[41]

"Si, nos regañó que porque estabamos ensuciando su bandera,"[42] he said as he pointed to George and Rebecca's house.

"Y porque no lo le hecistes caso? Huh? No te estoy pagando para buscar pedo con mis clientes, no'hombre!"

---

[31] "Almost done, boys?!"
[32] "Yes, boss! "
[33] "What's left? "
[34] "Well …"
[35] "Well what? What goin' on? "
[36] "Well, it's that damn Gringo over there …"
[37] "Which Gringo?"
[38] "… the one in the last house, over there."
[39] "What did he tell you?"
[40] "Well, you know … he's there fuckin' bustin' my balls, boss!"
[41] "Wait, what?!"
[42] "Yeah, he yelled at us because we were dirtying his flag."

Manny shouted at his worker. "Hay que respetar a quien nos paga! Me entiendes?!"[43]

"Si … si patron, perdón,"[44] mumbled the contrite man.

"Anda! Ya no quiero oir nada de eso!"[45] shouted Manny as he glared straight through the worker. The others slowly backed away from what would be an even more severe retribution for standing up the guy.

"You know, sometimes I think these guys are more hardheaded than you," he said to Michael with a slightly frustrated chuckle as he creaked his door open and slithered out.

As they both made their way toward George's house, the towering trees around them seemed to extend their branches even farther overhead, closing the street into a natural cathedral of rough-hewn bark and leaves. A chorus slowly animated with the symphonic song of buzzing cicadas in the warm orange light of the late-afternoon sun that pierced the dust clouds. Michael could just close his eyes and be instantly transported to the salt desert of his dream as it spread out before him on the backs of his eyelids. The insects began a crescendo in the green leafy vaults above him, and he swore that he could see the erratic dancing of firelight and the twisted shadow of the old dead tree slithering like a serpent.

Burn - Flames - Searing - Ashes - Death - Numb

---

[43] "And why didn't you listen to him? Huh? I'm not payin' you to be lookin' for fights with my clients. We better respect those that are payin' us, you got that?!"

[44] "Yes … yes, boss, I'm sorry."

[45] "Get back to work! I don't hear any more of this!"

Don't think about it ...
be a man ...
be strong ...
fight it ...
just let him burn, just let him burn.

The front door to the house opened and out walked a skinny White man in khaki shorts and a navy-blue polo shirt carrying a large American flag wrapped around a short chrome flagpole.

"How's it goin', George?"

"Oh, not too bad, Manny. Just puttin' the ol' Stars and Stripes back out. Didn't want it gettin' all dusty when your boys were out here."

"Well, they aughtta know better ..."

George chuckled as he unfurled the flag and slid it into the holder. The soft breeze had suddenly stopped, and the flag hung limp but solemn.

"It's just hard to get through to some people. But whatcha gonna do, right?" George laughed.

Michael stood back, still trying to choke down the thoughts of the burning boy as if vomit were coming up. He had the sense that the ability to conquer these thoughts while out in public would help him in the long run to battle the surprise of these evil fantasies rearing up out of nowhere. He was silently but desperately trying to numb himself, as he learned today, feeling nothing so that nothing could bother him.

"Hey, Michael. I don't ever see you here. Are you working with your stepdad now?"

Stand up straight.

"No, I'm just helpin' out while on summer break," responded Michael.

Act like a man.

"Well, good for you! You're gettin' to be about done with high school, though, aren't ya?"

"Yeah, I'll be graduating soon."

"Well, Amen to that! What are you gonna do afterward? You plan on workin' with Manny, or are you gonna go to a trade school or somethin'?"

Be a man and show him that you
can be more than Manny.

"I'm actually going to ASU, gonna major in pre-law …"

George's eyes widen with a bit of surprise, even as Michael felt the sting of disappointment at the self-perception of his faltering masculinity.

"Pre-law, huh? Wow! That's, uhm … that's a tough major. You ready for all that studyin'?"

"Yeah, I am."

He respects you.

George turned to Manny, grimacing. "Looks like you're gonna have to pick up a few more yards to clean up, am I right?" He let out a loud belly laugh.

Manny laughed along with him before Michael interjected again.

Be your own man.

"I'm actually going on a full-ride scholarship."

Both men stopped laughing, and an awkward silence gripped them as the droning hymn of the cicadas continued, seemingly louder with every attempt by Michael to exert maleness into the world. George looked at Michael with a bit of wonderment and appreciative fascination, while Manny's pride quietly screamed blasphemies at Michael behind the glares of his brown eyes.

"At least till the fall he be workin' with me. See if we can't man him up," said Manny under stiff lips.

He caught you! Told you, you look like fag!

"Boy, I'll tell you what, you best be prepared for goin' away to school. Don't let them professors teach you any of that liberal nonsense, ya hear?"

"What kinda nonsense?" asked Michael.

"Oh, you know, all that wordly garbage they're teachin' in those universities these days. How it's OK to kill babies and that it's OK to be gay, you know … lies like that. It's why I ended up going to a Christian university. Gotta keep on the straight and narrow, you know what I mean?"

"Yeah, straight and narrow …"

He knows you're a joto. Gotta try and hide it!

"Actually, George, it's kinda what I wanna to talk to you 'bout," Manny chimed in.

"You wantin' to be liberal, Manny?" George asked jokingly.

"Oh no! Nothin' like that, but Pastor Roberts been

talkin' to me about being on the deacon board …"

"Oh yeah, he mentioned somethin' 'bout that at the last meetin'."

"How straight and narrow are we talkin'?"

"Well, brother Manny, it's hard to say, you know …"

"Look, I know it's all 'bout how the board feels, but I just wanna know what they're gonna be lookin' for."

"Well, I guess the biggest thing that I can think of is that they're gonna look at how you carry your home. Bible says that a deacon can't have any addictions, can't be greedy, gotta be blameless before the Lord, married and never divorced, and able to manage his home. You know, all the wife and kids kinda stuff."

"Manage his home?"

"Sure, you know … just gotta make sure Michael here ain't sacrificing cats to the devil or that your wife ain't havin' a night on the town without you." George smirked as he playfully winked at Michael.

"I don't think there's any cats missin' on our street …"

"Oh, I'm just kiddin' ya, Manny! All the board wants is to make sure that your heart and your home are in the right place. That God is first and foremost, that's all."

"Well, we do … no issues there."

"Amen, brother! Like the Bible says, 'God searches a man's heart for righteousness.'"

"Does that mean you're gonna look at everythin'?"

"Well, mostly everythin'. But it ain't gonna be nothin' too deep. We ain't the government. We're not gonna be looking at your taxes or anythin' like that. It's not like you got anythin' to hide, right?"

George laughed as he slapped Manny's back,

almost knocking him over.

"In all honesty, Manny, if you've been called to be a deacon, it's 'cause Pastor Roberts sees that God's callin' you."

"You think so?" asked Manny.

"Sure! Most of us on the board can say that we ain't perfect, but if it wasn't for the grace of God ..."

"Right ..."

Just then a coyish and shapely figure appeared in the doorway.

"Here you go, honey, thought you'd might like some iced tea."

George's wife, Rebecca was the kind of woman to be saccharine sweet to the point of nausea even in the most dull situations. She was never ill-willed, but at times her overt optimism tended to make her the target of gossip and ridicule, and most of the other women at church developed a sadistic penchant for polite backstabbing just for the sake of bringing her helium-filled personality back to earth. She still tried her best to embody the Baptist female modesty even outside of church. She was wearing a navy-blue ankle-length skirt and a blue-and-white floral pattern blouse with sleeves to her elbows and a collar up to her neck. She was the perfect companion to a husband who served for years on the deacon board.

"Why, thank you, sweetheart," George said to her as he took the glass of tea. "Look who stopped by, hon'."

"Well, good afternoon, boys." She smiled as George wrapped his arm around her waist, making sure to keep her tightly at his side.

"Afternoon, Rebecca," said Manny as Michael sheepishly stood off to the side and waved.

"So, Manny, I hear you're bein' considered for the

board."

"Becky!" snapped George.

"Oh, I'm so sorry for being such a gossip, honey!" she said as she sweetly smiled at her husband. "Just lookin' forward to havin' another lady to go have coffee with when you boys are at church all day."

"It's a'ight," Manny chimed in.

"So, have you told your wife yet?"

"Not yet, need to talk to her 'bout it."

"Well, you let her know. I'm sure we'll have a great ol' time gettin' to know each other."

"She might like that."

"Oh, I hope so. I just wish I knew lil' more Spanish so we could talk. Most I can do is ask for extra salsa on my burrito." She laughed.

Her sunny disposition and bubbly answers made Manny smile for the first time that day, and all the embittered and hardened anger that he carried melted away. For that brief second, he could forget his wife's obstinance to conformity, his stepson's shameful secret, and the heavy scent of half-burned gasoline fumes and fresh-cut grass on his clothes. If all he ever wanted was the life of a White man, then to have a wife like Rebecca by his side would be the icing on the cake. A sign telling him that he had arrived.

"Well … uhm, guess we better be goin' now, let you guys enjoy your Saturday," Manny said.

"All right, Manny!" bellowed George.

"See you at church tomorrow?"

"Sure thing!"

"All right, boys!" said Rebecca.

"Oh, before I forget, here is your pay for this week," said George as he pulled a folded check from his pocket.

"Thanks, George, but it's a'ight …"

"Hey, you and your boys do a pretty good job of keepin' the yard lookin' presentable."

"This week is on me, really!"

"What?! No! Take it, Manny."

"I'm serious, it's OK."

"Manny, take it. You got a kid that's going to college soon. Let me be a blessin' to you, brother, please!"

"I, uhm …"

"C'mon, take it, Manny."

Manny reluctantly reached out as George slid the folded-up check into his fingers, and the smile he had earlier was instantly dashed against the rocks of reality.

"See you boys tomorrow!" called out Rebecca one last time.

"Yeah, see ya …" Manny sulked as he walked away.

Both Manny and Michael waved goodbye to the couple before heading back to Manny's truck. Once they were out of earshot of George and Rebecca, Michael bluntly asked, "That money really going to help me go to school?"

Manny's envy caused his blood to flash boil, and he pulled Michael by the sleeve and sternly whispered in his ear, "Your lil' problem better not cost me a place on the board! Me entiendes?!"

"If you don't tell them mine, I won't tell them yours. How 'bout that?"

As they walked back to the truck, the last of the burlap bundles were being picked up by Manny's crew. The end of the workday had finally come for them, and while pickup truck doors slammed shut and windows rolled down, the tun-ta-ta-tun-ta-ta of mariachi and banda music trickled out and faintly echoed down the cathedral of trees. By now the cicadas had finished their song for the day, and a lonely yellow rusted pickup truck with two of the newest workers pulled up next to Manny's truck.

"Oye, no se les vaya a olvidar, muchachos,"[46] shouted Manny

"Si, patron!" the two men said in unison before they drove off down the tree-lined street.

"Nos vemos!" said Manny as he tersely waved them off.

Manny, resigned once again to face the unchangeable truth of his place in the world, turned the key and started driving down the nave within trees and leaves. Michael sat quietly looking out the window, watching the clean, lush front yards whiz by him. Each man was trying to come to grips with who he was and not really knowing how to change into the man that they wanted to be.

They made their way home just as the sun was dipping below the peaks of the western mountains to radiate faint streaks of shadows across the dusty rose dome of the sky. As they turned the corner, Magdalena's large and unrestrained bougainvillea greeted them in the dying daylight, waving her thorny branches in the hot breeze while her pink velvety flowers fluttered gently in the wind. In the twilight she was animated and full of life, as if she had been waiting all day just to see them return, even if she tended to spite Manny. She stood alone among the starkness of the neighborhood, where there was no cathedral of nature to house her like a shrine, only the stark reality of South Phoenix that gave her the honest desert

---

[46] "Hey, boys, don't forget about tomorrow."

landscape.

As they were parking the truck, Michael bolted out and walked straight into the house under the bobbing boughs of fuchsia flowers, greeted immediately with the smell of beans boiling on the stove. Their nutty scent paired with the rich aroma of the manteca they were cooking in made an already hungry Michael wide-eyed and ready to devour. The slight smoking of the comal added its own pungent fragrance to the char of fresh flour tortillas cooking and puffing up. The sound of the kitchen radio playing boleros that Magdalena used to listen to with her father wove the smell of the food into a tapestry of memories that transported Michael back to childhood. An overwhelming feeling of security and fondness took over, as if all the problems that he had dealt with that day could be left at the feet of Magdalena's bougainvillea until the next morning.

"Ya llegaron?"[47] shouted his mother from the kitchen.

"Yeah, we're home!" Michael shouted back as he tried to pull off his dusty shoes at the front door.

His mother walked out of the kitchen with a dish towel to dry her hands as she went to meet her men. Manny was still in his truck making sure his work tools were locked up for the night. She saw Michael trying to pull off his remaining shoe, struggling to get the laces undone as he hopped on one leg trying to keep his balance.

"Ay mijito, te ayudo?"[48] she asked as she walked toward him.

---

[47] "You home now?"
[48] "Oh, son, you want me to help you?"

Be a man. Don't let a woman do that for you!

Tersely he looked up and stopped her.

"I'm fine! Really! I got it!" he said defensively.

Like a mongoose staring down a cobra, she gazed deep into the inner recesses of his skull to make him know that he should not have done that. She cocked her head, watching him fight the knots until they were free.

"Ya!?" she asked sarcastically.

"Yeah," Michael huffed as pulled his foot free and almost lost his balance.

"Andale ve bañate! Apestas a puro sol y cuerpo!"[49]

"That bad?!"

"O si! Como hombre que ha trabajado todo el dia!"[50] she said bluntly as she winced and tried to lean away.

Someone said you're a man, it just wasn't from a man.

It wasn't until right then, in the last hours of the day, that he realized that Pastor Roberts said nothing to him about having to face his queer side. Nothing from Manny about sweating all day like him and the rest of his crew. And even George couldn't say anything about him being able to go to school on his own. The hopes of the day had extinguished with the sunset and not one man in his life had given him what he wanted from them. The coveted salve to make the queer scales fall off his eyes to see the truth of his heterosexual self. Only the words of his mother could give him that, and from what he was told in

---

[49] "Hurry up and go bathe! You smell like body odor!"
[50] "Oh yeah! Like a man that's been workin' all day!"

his earlier catechisms, it was not only not enough but just as damaging.

"Andale hijo, ve bañate! Ahorita te sirvo,"[51] she urged him.

As he skulked into the dark and shadowy hallway toward the bathroom, Manny made his way into the house. Magdalena turned and marched back into the kitchen, and then the music died suddenly. All that was left was the rattling lid of the stock pot from the boiling beans and a music-less house for Manny to come home to.

In the bathroom, the clinical fluorescent light flickered and buzzed as Michael took off his clothes. He turned on the water, feeling that it was scalding hot from sitting in the attic pipes all day. As he leaned up against the wall waiting for the water to run cold, he looked at himself in the mirror. His brown eyes traced up and down his nude 18-year-old body, analyzing every curve and shadow that was cast on him. A body that had begun showing the final changes from the little boy he once was to the young man he was turning out to be.

Joto!

He ran his fingers along the top of his chest, feeling his bones push outward against his flesh, making graceful divots around his neck. He continued to trace the shape of his skin curiously as it stretched over his physique while the dim light caught a few beads of sweat, making him glow in tones of burnished copper. His skin felt strange, as if he were wearing someone else's shirt. The troubling part was that he couldn't take off, no matter how

---

[51] "Hurry up, son, and bathe. I'll serve you dinner later."

many times he tried to.

You still ain't a man!

He could remember a time before this foreign skin, when he would look at himself in the mirror with disappointment and see nothing but a skinny kid staring back at him. However, two years of sparing at the boxing gym with Coach Padilla had done him some good. His chest had become broad and started to show definition, a bulk wrapped tightly against his frame. His shoulders were rounded and undulated like muscular waves with his toned biceps and forearms. In the past few weeks, his hands had started to darken to a deep rich brown just like the men in Manny's crew. As he leaned up against the sink, he flexed his lean arms, letting his eyes follow the taught fibers of his forearm muscles twisting around the bone in subtle strands of light and shadow.

You even stand like a faggot.

His short dark hair was like rich black coffee, littered with dust and pieces of dry leaves from the day's work. Coincidentally, Michael's stubble had started to come in about six months ago, which left his chin and upper lip peppered with the same coarse black hair as the bottom of his sideburns and the slopes of his jawline.

You've gotta be straighter;
no one's gonna believe you.

Naked and in front of the mirror like this was one of only a few times that he ever saw himself for who he was. Without the clothes of a landscaper. Without the typical button-up shirt that he wore on Sundays. Here, locked away from prying eyes, he could see himself honestly and truthfully. Peering into his dark pupils, he could see his own fantasies that he secretly kept from those around him. These were pleasures that he truly felt guilty for having, trapped in the world of the salt desert, all the nuances of both men and women swirled together in the tiny globes staring back at him.

Burn - Flames - Searing - Ashes - Death - Numb

The growing tha-thump of his heartbeat pulsated into a pounding rhythm in his head. Like a reflex, the innocent fantasy was once again consumed by the flames, as he was trained. Hurling pain and loss to the extremities of his body. Pain that vibrated in the muscular arms that he was leaning on before the cold numbness trickled down his spine and made his foreign skin feel ice cold. Determined, he tried to think of the girl in his dream, but even then, the blurred lines, desire, and gender jumbled him into a vortex of anxiety that kept pulling him deeper and deeper. Searching for a way to stop it, he began whispering at a volume only he could hear.

"I am a man, made in God's image,
I'll serve God like the Man he wants me to be,
I'll love my wife like Jesus loves the church,
I'll do things like other men do,
I'll think like a man and not like a woman,
I'll defend and fight for the people God's put in.
my life,
I'll fight against anything that tells me I'm not a
man,

I won't look at a man the way I'm supposed to
look at a woman,
I'll see other men as role models instead,
I'll be the Man of God that he wants me to be,
I am a man."

The tinny sound of water hitting the bathtub was drowned out as he intensely stared at himself with growing dissatisfaction.

"Gotta man up, Michael, gotta man up," he whispered to himself while extending his right hand, practicing shaking hands with an imaginary man just as he had done with Pastor Roberts. Determined on getting this right, he stuck his hand out again and again and again, picturing any of the men from church standing in front of him, trying desperately to win their approval, and each time finding some sort of feminine fault.

"No! That was too limp!" He tried again.

"Not like that! No one's gonna kiss my hand." He attempted again.

"Grip harder!" he said to himself, tightly gripping the hand of the imaginary person in front of him.

The more he practiced, the less he imagined any one man whom he was trying to impress and the more he found himself shaking hands with his own reflection. The more he tried to practice, the more the young man in the mirror seemed to taunt him and ridicule him. He could see plainly that his reflection was just as much male as he was, but even with the evidence staring back at him, he could not shake the thought that his eyes and body were traitors in conspiracy.

No, you ain't straight!

Stop it!
Act like a man!

You faggot!

Stop shakin' my hand like a woman!

Stop it! Why can't you just be normal?!

Michael's frustration had boiled over to where he got up into the face of his own reflection to growl "Stop it!" over and over again. His nostrils flared and his breath steamed up the mirror. He didn't want to feel the cold numbness, but he did want to feel the searing anger that had been brewing inside. Short of punching the glass, he felt reason creep back into his brain once his breath fogged up the mirror to blur his reflection. He stood back to recognize himself again as the cloudy glass faded and the intense rage melted away into the linoleum tile.

"I can't do this … I can't do this," he repeated, embarrassed that he was having to wrestle with his own psyche.

To avoid having to look in the mirror, he pulled the plastic shower curtain back and stepped into the lukewarm water. He hoped that it would wash away all the feelings of regret, failure, and disappointment. Instead, his legs turned to jelly and his stomach felt sour as he contemplated the insurmountable consequences of giving up. A rush of anxiety shuttered through his bones as muscles twitched in spasmodic chaos. He feared the retribution of God, Pastel Jesus, and Pastor Roberts for not even making it a day without his internal filth tainting the pure and gracious deliverance he'd received that morning.

"If I can't do this … then what?"

His legs got weaker as the question sank deep into his conscience, so much so that he sat down in the tub, curled up into a ball, and hugged his legs close to his naked body. The warm water continued to fall on him, trickling in rivulets around his neck and down his back. His tanned flesh became speckled with stray drops as he hoped that this crude baptism could cleanse his mind once and for all. He tried to think of any scripture that he could pray through to absolve him of the immense guilt that he was feeling. Only one verse came to mind, and that was from Pastor Roberts that morning,

"If thy right hand offend thee,
cut it off, and cast it from thee."

The words reverberated between his ears as he stared through the sliver of space between his calves and as the cascading water flowed past his feet toward the swirling drain. He thought for a moment about the implications of such a verse, caught between the mystique and frustration he felt for the treacherous part of his body that ultimately led him to lust for men, time and time again. He was most frustrated that his mind was the birthplace of the two fantasies of the salt desert, these forbidden fruits of a pubescent Eden. He could not find a way to dissect one from the other. It was as if their very existence was dependent upon the survival of the other.

Do I cut it off?

The plausibility of such an action seemed to suck the air out of the room as he sat there with his head buried between his legs. His eyes pictured torrents of water running past him, with diluted swirls of bright red streaming down the drain. A plague of imagined pain coursed up from his belly as the horrid sound of silent screaming in his head resonated louder and louder. His heart began to race at the reality of having to make such a drastic choice to save his own soul; even more frightening was the insane possibility that he was trying to give logical reason for his action should he find himself in the emergency room. The internal dyne of his thoughts blended in an ever-growing crescendo of noise that rivaled the earlier chorus of a thousand cicadas. To break away from this vision, he began slapping his face hard enough to sting.

"Snap out of it … snap out of it … snap out of it … snap out it," he whispered hoarsely through the water running down his face. The raw pain felt oddly soothing; at least it was a real feeling, on his skin and not in his mind.

"Men fight through the pain … they fight through it … no cryin'!"

And as quickly as the anxiety came on, the water around him returned to being crystal clear, void of any crimson stains.

As best he could, he shoved the images of blood and handshakes and the burned-up fantasy deep down into some familiar dark place in his heart—a place that had already been packed full of the rotting images and thoughts he crammed in there from the last time this happened. With the cacophonous buzz pressing on his eardrums, he pushed himself to his wobbly feet and tried to push through the muck of his inner life to find the path back to reality. He grabbed the bar of soap and began lathering up his body and rinsing away the dirt and sweat from the day. He tried to think of something innocuous to occupy his mind, something like cars or how was he going to celebrate his graduation in a few weeks. The buzz began to subside, and his breath slowed as he leaned forward, planting his hand on the wall under the shower head. The water spraying on his back rinsed away the white foamy lather, with the last rivulets running down his golden-brown skin, thinning quickly to single drops of water clinging to him.

"I'm done. Can't try anymore tonight …" he thought as he shut off the water and grabbed an old towel. To him, the day was lost like so many others in a long line of days marked by his inability to do what he often felt was an achievable goal. Pastor Roberts seemed to have sufficient faith that it was possible to be straight, so why couldn't he just do it? Why couldn't he resist the temptation of men?

He gathered his dirty clothes from the floor and checked that the towel was secure around his waist as he opened the door. When he walked out, he thought once again, "Try, just one more time." He wadded up his dirty clothes as best he could and carried it bundled together in one hand as he tried to strut confidently from the bathroom to his room. Although no one was watching, he knew it was practice for the next day, when he would have to perform in front an audience of everyday people and show his "masculinity."

*****

It was later that night when Michael poked his head out of his bedroom to look around and noticed that the hallway was completely dark. He could be sure that he was alone now, safe from any intrusion. He quietly knelt down next to his bed, looking back at his bedroom door one more time to make sure that it was closed and locked. He lifted up the sheets on the side and then pulled up the mattress, just enough for him to stick his hand between the mattress and box spring. He fished around in one of his secret hiding places until he grabbed what he was looking for and pulled out a composition notebook that had the words "Hopefully, tomorrow …" written in ballpoint pen on the cover. He looked around again, making sure that even his overactive imagination hadn't got the best of him and that Manny wasn't secretly hanging over him. He sat back down on his bed and began flipping through the pages one by one.

Every day for the past two years was chronicled in this book, every reflection and catechism from Pastor Roberts's Saturday morning lessons etched with blue pen. The text was intentionally written in an almost indecipherable cursive so no one else could read it if the book were found. But even among the swirly blue hieroglyphics, he could clearly make out all the daily pleas he wanted answered.

> *God, please help me!*
> *How do I make this stop?*
> *I just want to be good!*

He fought back against contributing one more cry

out to Pastel Jesus this time. But even though he was standing and pushing back against the floodgates of horrific images from his psyche, he couldn't give himself the luxury of tears. Tears that might as well have marked him as less than a man, but given the state he was in, it mattered little compared with his other transgressions. He wanted to write another entry, of how the boy burned in front of him today, or about the sight of blood in the shower water. But even now he couldn't bring himself to do it. There was nothing these pages didn't already know. There had to be some way of trying to become a man, some way that he had overlooked that could fix him. Would he have to become more than the men around him? How much more could Pastel Jesus ask of him?

Frustrated, he picked up the notebook and shoved it back in between the mattress and box spring, then lay down in his bed staring up at the popcorn ceiling again. As he closed his tired eyes, his imagination drifted back to the salt desert in his dream. There the charred remains of the fantasy stood as black as night in contrast to the warm glow of the white salt grains on ground. The faceless humanoid of solid ash, the boy he had murdered that morning, served as a permanent reminder of his willingness to sacrifice innocence in exchange for his purity.

In his thoughts he tried to conjure up the young woman whom he had kept secret from Pastor Roberts. He decided to let his mind wander as he had done that morning, but this time he let her lead him to where she wanted to go. As he immersed himself back into the dream, he found her there already waiting for him. She had a warmth about her as if she had been waiting for him until they were alone. She turned to the pillar of ash and reached out her hand and ran her delicate fingers across the blackened head of her fellow fantasy as if trying to smear the blackness across the salt. The ash crumbled into a fine delicate powder, and in a miraculous wonder, the warm face of his male fantasy emerged from the charred remains into living flesh, trapped in the makings of Michael's death prison.

When Michael saw him, his heart sank, since it seemed that this stubborn lust, this sexual attraction that should not be, had beaten him again. She could also feel his fear, and it seemed to make the desert feel eerily cold. He could not bring himself to set fire to the ashes that remained, and he could no longer try to make himself feel numb; he could only feel awestruck at the resilience of these two, that these two intrinsic pieces of him, primordial in humanness and consciences, stood in direct defiance of everything that Pastor Roberts said and did. Then, as quickly as she had wiped the ashes from the boy's face, she turned to Michael and softly kissed him on the cheek. Michael felt warm blood rush up his body, both sensual and innocent. It was the same pure and unadulterated exhilaration of euphoria and peace that he always felt when he wanted to touch the boy. He stood back, seeing both of them in front of him, as the anxiety of trying to please Pastel Jesus, trying to change for the Church, or trying to act "manly" enough melted and slipped below the grains of salt on the ground. He was alone with the objects of his desire, and tonight he was able to sleep soundly.

5

Bee-beepbee-beepbee-beep …

Michael rolled over in a tangled mess looking more like an overgrown newborn. He was still drowsy when he slammed his hand on the alarm clock and broke the crust around his eyes to see the digital numbers staring back at him. It was seven on Sunday morning, and the new day's sun had already started to peek around the struggling AC unit in his window and through the old sheer curtains. He rolled onto his back to see the popcorn ceiling above him statically shimmering in the bright peach daylight, like a thousand fake stars in a sky of dingy white. Yet he could see something more in the dull sky above him, something lurking past the plaster stars. The haunting images of his fantasy, his dream, animated itself in the random shapes and shadows. Phantoms played out again and again, the destruction that he was taught to perform and the rebirth that his mind called out for.

"Today's gotta be different …"

It would be time for church in a few hours, and he could bet on the fact that Manny would be standing in the living room, tapping his watch, scolding him and Magdalena to get in the truck on time. Such was Manny's dedication that one time all three of them were sick with the flu, but Manny, being the ever-faithful follower, still managed to drag them all to church and stay for the whole service. Not even the most virulent contagion would keep Manny from missing one Sunday sermon.

Michael yawned and stretched with unrelenting tiredness, until he heard a frustrated rattling of the doorknob jiggling violently.

"Crap!" he whispered as he jumped to his feet, rushing to unlock the door. Manny was on the other side, already pounding on the door with his fist.

Thud, thud, thud.

"Michael! Abréme la puerta carajo!"[52] he demanded as he tried to get in. Michael switched over the latch and opened the door to find Manny standing with a closed fist ready to pound on the door.

"Que te he dicho, ehh?![53] I don't like locked doors. Me entendieste?!"

"Sorry, I forgot that this isn't my house."

"Sabes que?! … Ahora no! It's Sunday!"

"And … ?"

"And I'm not gonna get into it with you."

"Finally a break …"

---

[52] "Open the door damnit!"

[53] "What have I told you, huh?"

Manny's lip tightened as he glared at Michael. Manny took a deep breath to calm himself before he finally said, "A listate, church is at nine!"

"Whatever you say," said Michael.

Manny looked around Michael's room with an uneasy suspicion, as if he could sense the secrets allowed to squat in his house. It had been a long time since Michael shared Manny's idealization for a better life. They both knew where Magdalena stood on trying to get just a little bit of that Gringo Life, but there was hope early on that in this family he was stitching together, he could give Michael what he knew. He had a dream that one day he could bestow upon him those hard-learned "Man Lessons" and instill in him the sense that even though he was not his son by blood, at the very least he could see the dream he wanted for himself carried on by the boy. But on that day two years ago, when he looked through Michael's backpack and saw that the threat to his dream had nestled in his home, Manny's trust in his family died. Michael could remember a time when Manny did have some amount of love in him, but any love that has been hurt eventually rots into bitterness and conspiracy. In Manny's eyes, Michael's effeminate sexuality conspired against him in the most abhorrent and embarrassing way possible.

"Get dressed!" Manny said sternly as he turned and made his way down the dark hallway.

Michael closed the door, breathing a sigh of relief while he looked back at his bed to make sure the sheets were not tucked under the mattress. His book of secret confessions was safe, but even in the chaotic folds and curves of his dangling bedsheets, the fantasies had managed to squeeze out from under the mattress and slip across the fabric, re-creating their epic drama on the white sheets.

He wanted to get sucked into it. He wanted to watch their grand seduction again and again. Perhaps destiny, or perhaps revelation, but something profound was being said to him, more profound than the hour-long services on Sunday, all of it spoken in splendid wordlessness. A language of the soul, in primal and almost savage meanings, and he wanted to know it. He just could not translate what they were telling him.

"Michael, hurry up and get in the shower!" shouted Manny from down the hall.

"I'm goin' to!" Michael shouted back.

He looked over to see that the alarm clock read 7:18 a.m. Rushing to avoid another chastisement, Michael went over and pulled the bedsheets tight so the fantasies would be lost in the flatness while he got ready.

Michael went about setting out his usual church clothes before showering. Slacks and a solid cornflower-blue button-up dress shirt. He hated blue, but it was a manly color, so he tolerated wearing it every chance he could. When he was much younger, he was required to wear obnoxiously colored hand-me-down ties to church. He would eventually end up loosening the uncomfortable noose after Pastor Robert was about five minutes into his sermon. Remembering how Manny would get silently angry at him for things like that brought a welcome and rare smile.

He pulled open his sock drawer and started digging around for a pair to match his shirt and pants. While he was feeling around toward the back of the drawer, he felt an odd lumpy object that hadn't been there before. It wasn't unusual for him to find things hidden in his room, nor was it the first time. Magdalena had gotten into the habit of hiding things in his room that she felt Manny had become aware of. Objects and tokens of her and Michael's life before Manny. Objects that were a threat to the life he was making with them now. Even though Manny often threatened to raid the house to search and destroy these things, he rarely succeeded in finding anything to throw in the trash or smash in the backyard. Among some of the more notable hidden treasures, Michael had found pictures of his dad, hidden in a manilla envelope carefully tucked under his T-shirts. Another time he found a Mother's Day card made out of construction paper from when he was in elementary school, tucked safely and inconspicuously in his school notebooks like a mundane bookmark. These normal bits and pieces of one's life helped him remember in fragments, what life was like before Manny, before Pastel Jesus and the church, and especially before the dream. A life written only in Spanish and blessed by the sign of the cross.

"What's she hidin' this time?" Michael wondered as he pulled at a small lumpy velvet bag.

He slid his finger inside and dug around to fish out what felt like a wadded-up ball of beads and metal chain. He hooked an open loop of the chain on his finger and pulled out a silver and glass bead rosary. The tiny facets refracted the warm sunlight into sparkling specks of color while the silver crucifix on the end tried to glow through black tarnish. He held it up, watching the beads untwist and gracefully cascade in the light, and he immediately thought of his grandmother using this very same rosary. Michael had a vivid image of her sitting in her house on a quiet afternoon with the drizzling mountain rain in Cananea softly tapping on the tin roof while she prayed. A formidable woman with a dignified elegance, she sat with her legs crossed, rocking in her rocking chair while her lips softly whispered,

> "Padre nuestro,
>   santificado sea
>   tu nombre …"

Wine-colored fingernails gingerly gripped each faceted bead with personal conviction and reverence and slowly inched their way around the rosary with every Ave Maria. As a boy he would hide behind the open door, watching with curiosity as she prayed in the stillness of her home.

"Ves esa silla?" she would ask him as she pointed to her chair. "Alli es mi iglesia."[54]

Her words made God seem like a definable abstraction, a paradox of infinite divinity and mortal humanity, where faith was not complicated but a simple and profound act of personal belief that had no room for others to say what or how to believe.

"Michael, hurry up!" Manny shouted from the living room.

"Ya no andes chingandolo, Manuel! Por Dios!"[55] Magdalena shouted from the kitchen.

He knew what he must do with all the treasures Magdalena had entrusted to him. Michael opened the door just a bit and leaned out, peeking through the sliver to the hallway to make sure that Manny wasn't there watching or spying on him. Seeing that all was clear, he closed the door and locked it before he knelt beside his bed. He reached

---

[54] "You see that chair? That's my church."
[55] "Jesus Christ, Manuel! Leave him alone."

under the bed frame and into the open underside of the box spring. There he had made a little cradle of old shoestrings that he tied in a chaotic web among the metal springs. Sitting in the cradle like the freshly caught prey of a spider was an old shoebox laminated with layers of packing tape to hold the fraying cardboard together.

He pulled out the little treasure box and opened it to see where he stashed all the things his mother had intended to hide from Manny. Among the rescued treasures were wedding pictures and folded-up coloring book pages on which he had scribbled as a kid "Te quiero Mama" in blue crayon. Here in his makeshift safety deposit box would be where he carefully laid the rosary next to a leather scapular that he had found in his sock drawer the week before.

When he reached down to grab the velvet pouch and put it the box as well, it felt as if something heavy was still inside. He shook the little bag upside down and a silver medal threaded with a thin silver chain fell out onto his open hand. It was round, with the engraved picture of a man in a toga holding a staff and a lick of flame above his head. Around the edge were the words "San Judas—Patrón de Causas Perdidas—Ruega por Nosotros."[56] Running his fingers across the worn silver, he felt the faint remnants of initials engraved on the back. Looking closely at the other side in the bright light, he could make out two faint letters: J.L. for Julio Lopez, his grandfather. Michael could remember J.L. clearly, dressed in his button-up shirt and Tejano hat, riding on his horse through the mountainous grasslands and ocotillos. His rough chaps were worn down by the thorns and spines as he herded heads of cattle to

---

[56] Saint Jude—Patron of Lost Causes—pray for us.

greener pastures. Just holding the warm silver medal in his hand, Michael could smell the sweaty leather of a saddle and saddle blanket when J.L. brought the horse in to feed, mixed with the pungent and dusty aroma of alfalfa in the trough. Michael remembered that even as a child he would get into his jeans and get help from his grandfather to put his leg over the saddle and feet into the stirrups. Then his grandfather led the horse by the bridle so Michael would be accustomed to the beast and its every movement. It was memories like this that made Michael wonder why this wasn't enough to cure him. Was the vaquero life that he was born into not enough to save him from these fantasies? Or could this memory even save him now? Was the palpable real memory of a long-dead father figure better than the daily reluctance of a surrogate?

When Michael saw that the rosary was long enough that he could hide it under his shirt, he slipped it over his head and put it around his neck. The warm crucifix rested against his bare chest as he stood up in front of the mirror. Then he slipped on a white T-shirt to make sure the rosary would be hidden from Manny's and Pastor Roberts's eyes. He looked back at his alarm clock and saw that time was quickly passing by. He closed up the shoebox and hid it back in its cradle in the box spring before unlocking the door. With no sight of Manny, he headed to the bathroom.

******

Manny stood in the living room fully dressed in his Sunday best, pacing while he waited for Michael and Magdalena. The stubborn wrinkles on his pants and jacket still showed even after he spent most of the morning trying to steam them out. The silvery loose threads on his cuffs seemed more frayed this week than in the past and became more noticeable against the sun-darkened skin of his hands. He had always wanted to buy himself at least one other suit, but matching the dapperness of his male counterparts at church was far out of his reach.

"Ya! We're gonna be late!" he yelled at them.

Michael stumbled out of the hallway still buttoning up the cuffs on his sleeves while trying to tuck his blue shirt into his slacks.

"You're worse than a woman! You know that?!" Manny sneered.

Michael rolled his eyes as he brushed by Manny on his way out.

"Ya Magda!" he yelled again.

"Como chingas!" she retorted as she stepped out from her bedroom.

She wore her standard issue long flowing skirt, which came down to her calf as required by the church, but instead of her usual high-collar top, she wore a fitted white short-sleeve blouse that hugged her curves and elegantly accentuated her body. Around her shoulders she'd draped herself with an exquisitely embroidered shawl that her mother gave her, a black fanciful and airy lace interwoven with bright flowers of maroon, azure blue, and golden yellow threads. The needlework colors brilliantly contrasted the smooth earth-colored tones of her skin underneath. Her jet-black hair was pulled straight back and wound tightly into a simple but sophisticated bun, and her tiny and delicate gold stud earrings glistened like the midmorning sun.

"You can't go to church dressed like that!"

"Y porque no?"[57]

"It's disrespectful. There are men there. Godly men!"

"Y que?"[58]

"Go change!"

"No, a mi me gusta como me veo."[59]

"Magda, I'm not goin' into church with you lookin' like that!"

"Ó si? Mejor me quedo en la casa. Puedes irte solo para que los jítones vean que ejemplo de diacòno eres. … A ver dime, que quieres?"[60]

"Get in the truck!" Manny quietly snorted as she gracefully walked out under the boughs of her bougainvillea.

When they got to church, Manny drove his truck to the very last parking space in the farthest row possible. Big fancy cars filed into the lot, but the three of them sat in the truck with the engine off watching every couple get out of their cars and head inside. The men wore sharply pressed suits and matching ties, leading their wives into the church on their arms in a weekly pageantry of old southern charm and etiquette. Women strolled in with their modest long skirts that never hiked up past the calf and that perfectly complemented their loose high-neck blouses to hide their womanly figures. Each woman was capped with white or golden blond cotton candy hairdos, delicately shaped in

---

[57] "And why not?"

[58] "So what?"

[59] "No, I like the way I look."

[60] "Oh really? Well, I can go change but we'll be late, or would you rather me stay home? You can go by yourself so those hotshots see that you're a grand example of a deacon, without a wife. …Tell me what would you like?"

undulating waves contained in a sphere. Hairsprayed halos shone brightly in the blistering Phoenix sun, no doubt a self-imposed endowment of Protestant sainthood for the loyalty to their respective husbands.

Manny sat pensively in the truck watching the parade of happy couples.

"Why can't you be like them," Manny said to Magdalena.

"Y porque me voy a rebajarme al mismo nivel de esas viejas? Ni me llegen a los talones,"[61] she retorted as she cocked her head, all the while looking Manny in the eye.

"Vamonos, Mijito, a ver que chiles pelan aqui."[62]

Michael knew all too well the unflappable tone of his mother's voice in situations like this. She could be calculating and spiteful, and oftentimes her aim was to wound Manny in the one place that hurt him the most. It wasn't lost on Michael that this was the type of behavior that Pastor Roberts had talked to him about. A man was supposed to be a man, be the leader of the house.

Michael opened the door, and he and his mother slid out of the truck and began walking toward the church. They left Manny sitting in the truck, stunned and disappointed yet again with Magdalena's defiant insolence. It was a while before he finally opened his door and got out, pulling up the waist of his wrinkled pants and fixing himself in his old creased suit.

Manny worked his face into a contrived yet constipated smile as the three of them walked through the

---

[61] "And why should I have to lower myself to their level? None of them can even compare with me."

[62] "Come on, son, let's see what they have to offer here."

double doors. The church was filled with the saccharine conversations as clusters of people, some standing in the rows of wooden pews and some seated but twisting back around, shared the latest gossip.

"… Well, did ya hear 'bout Frank and Darla?"

"Oh my Lord, it's such a cryin' shame …"

"I just can't believe they're callin' it quits after so many years together!"

"Oh honey, I know! They didn't seem to be goin' through any problems, but she just up and left."

"Can you believe she was tired of havin' to depend on Frank for everythin'. Said she was goin' back to school!"

"Oh that poor Darla! She don't need school, Jesus is

what she needs."

"I just wonder if
she was even
saved at all!"

"If she really was, she
wouldn't be needin' to
find anythin' out in there
the world."

After they passed that group of older women, they walked by a group of men in their freshly pressed Sunday suits.

"Oh I'm just appalled by it …"

"This administration is really takin' us
down a road headed straight to hell."

"And then this whole 'Don't ask, Don't tell' nonsense ..."

"Now, don't you get me started on that!"

"My daddy didn't serve in Korea for a bunch of queers to ruin the army!"

"Amen, brother Paul, my Stars and Stripes
are defended by real God-fearin' men."

"I'm afraid that one of these days, the Good Lord is gonna get tired of the way this country is turnin' its back on him."

"Oh yes, brother, all 'em gays and
abortionists are to blame for it. Just you
see, God'll judge 'em."

The conversation was casual enough, but even the
seemingly innocuous words drifted through the mess of
noise and splashed into Michael's ears, rippling a thought
of conspiracy into his head.

Did they see somethin'?
Was I walkin' like a fag?
God, what did I do?
I need to stop this
It's that boy's fault.

Burn - Flames - Searing - Ashes - Death - Numb

Flashes of red bathtub water circling the drain
came to mind. All the while he kept repeating to himself,

I'm a man, I'll do things
that men do ... I'm a man,
I'll do things that men do
... I'm a man

The warm weight of his grandmother's rosary
gently pressed on his chest, and it was enough of a
distraction to keep him from drifting deeper into the crisis
mode of bloody bathwater and ash-ridden salt that he was
quickly becoming accustomed to. He discretely pressed his
palm onto his chest, pretending his breakfast was giving

him heartburn but still feeling the crucifix through his shirt, as he walked down the aisle toward the mural of Pastel Jesus wading in the water. The eyes of God were still looking up toward heaven, never breaking their gaze like yesterday, still waiting for the spirit to come down and anoint him. Michael looked up to the plaster ceiling spotted with water stains that looked like dried rose petals, expecting the numbness to trickle down his spine like it did yesterday. But it never came. All he could feel was the warm metal and beads on his skin.

The third pew on the right was the usual row for Manny and his family. But once the three of them had made their way through the rows of gossip, a few familiar faces from Manny's crew were already sitting there. Michael remembered seeing them at the end of the day yesterday. They sat aloof and sunken into the pew, ever watchful of how many of these well-dressed Americans walked by, and gave a pressed lip smile and a nod, but said nothing to them.

"Quiubo muchachos! Como están?"[63] Manny called out to them.

"Bien, Don Manuel, Gracias a Dios,"[64] they each said, and in almost near unison.

Michael and his mother squeezed by them to take their seats as Manny shook their hands and walked by, plopping himself in between his family and his workers, completing the Brown stripe in the Baptist Sea of Caucasia.

"Buenos dias, muchachos … como te llamas?"[65]

---

[63] "What's up, boys, how you doin'?"

[64] "Doing well, Mr. Manel, thank God."

[65] "Good morning, boys … what's your name?"

asked Magdalena as she reached across her husband, bypassing him to introduce herself.

"Buenos dias, Señora. Me llamo Jaime."[66]

"Mucho gusto, Jaime … y tu usted? Como se llama?"[67]

"Me llamo Raul, Señora."[68]

"Jaime y Raul … gusto en conocerlos."[69]

Manny, on the other hand, still was not going to be upstaged by his wife, so he stretched his right arm behind his wife on the wooden pew back like the other men in church. It was subtle enough, and it was his turn to remind Magdalena that although she may wear whatever she wanted, she was still his obedient and submissive wife.

Just when the tension had started to simmer between them, a familiar woman in a floral-printed blouse and a flowing olive-green skirt came up behind Magdalena. She knelt down in the row behind them and, in full perky cheerfulness, gently tapped Magdalena on the shoulder.

"Why, hi there, Magdalaayna …"

"Ahora que chingados quiere esta vieja?[70]" she quietly grumbled to Michael, rolling her eyes.

"How are you today?" the woman beamed.

"Hola, Rebecca, estoy muy bien, Gracias a Dios. Como estas tu?"[71] she replied as she turned around.

"Well, I'm doin' just fine. I've been tryin' to beat

---

[66] "Good morning, Mam. My name is Jaime."
[67] "Pleasure, Jaime … and you. What's your name?"
[68] "My name is Raul, Mam."
[69] "Jaime and Raul … pleasure to meet you two."
[70] "Now what the hell does this broad want?"
[71] "Hi, Rebecca, I am doing very well, thank God. How are you?"

this awful heat, you know. I think it's just getting hotter and hotter every year," she said, trying to fan herself and show off her freshly done manicure of stubby apple red fingernails.

"Pues, asi es el verano. Un feo calurrón!"[72]

"Well, I just wanted to stop by to ask you somethin'…"

"Que se le ofrece?"[73]

"Well you see, George has been on my case that he's cravin' tacos for a few weeks now, but he's just so dag-gome tired of those taco kits I get at the store."

"Ah si, son pesimos,"[74] Magdalena said wryly.

"He just won't let it go 'bout makin' some real authentic tacos, so I told myself, 'Good grief, Becky, why donchya just go and ask Magdalaayna? She's gotta know a thing or two 'bout makin' authentic tacos,' right?"

"Ah, si … jou wan to learn tacos autenticos?"

"Oh … yes … yes I would"

"Pues mira, el ingrediente mas importante para los tacos es un especia que se llama Chiltepín. Agarra como seis o siete bolitas de chiltepín, y los muele pero bien, bien finitas. Luego se las pone a la carne molida cuando ya se cocine. Y asi los tacos salen pero bien ricos," she said with a bit of subtle pleasure in her voice.

Rebecca's limited high school Spanish had finally reached its limit. She eventually just shook her head and said, "I didn't get a thing you said, sweetheart."

Magdalena turned around to Michael, who was trying to hold the giggles in. "Mijito, puedes traducir?"

---

[72] "Well, that's summer. An ugly heat!"
[73] "What can I help you with?"
[74] "Yes, they are appalling."

"Mom …"

"Hijo … anda …" she said to him with one raised eyebrow, and he begrudgingly obliged.

"My mother says that the most important ingredient is chiltepin. You need to get about six or seven little balls of chiltepín, and you have to grind them up really finely and mix it in the meat when it's done cooking, and your tacos will come out really good."

"Oh I don't think I've heard of that spice … what's it called? Chi . .chil … petin?"

"No no no, CHIL-TE-PÍN, chiltepín. Es muy facil!" Magdalena said loudly and slowly to overannunciate.

"OK, I think I got it."

"Es muy … good," Magdalena interjected.

"And is that some kinda spice?" Rebecca asked.

"Si, es muy espicey! Mmmm gooood!"

"Perfect, thank you so much, Magdalena, you're the best!" Rebecca beamed. "I'll see if I can find some of that chil … chile …"

"Chiltepín …"

"Yes, I'll see if I can find it at the store."

"No se precupe, Rebequita. Yo les triago unos. I brrring … jou … some!" Magdalena insisted.

"You'll bring me some?"

"Oh si, tengo muchos en las casa."

"Aww, Magdalena, you are such a sweetheart!" Rebecca replied as she got up, and she reached out to hug Magdalena. Magdalena hesitantly and uncomfortably held Rebecca by getting as close as she could without touching her.

"Thanks so much for translatin', darlin'," she said

to Michael.

"Oh, you're welcome."

"And by the way, you guys left the yard lookin' so good yesterday!"

"Thanks?" he said to her while she got up.

As she went about trying to find her husband, the effervescent and chipper demeanor evaporated instantaneously, like a splash of water in a hot pan, when she saw the two men sitting in the row with Michael and Magdalena. She clearly was not expecting to see the other gardeners from yesterday sitting in her church, and certainly not prepared enough to have anything to say, let alone in Spanish. Not knowing whether to extend her hand to Jaime and Raul, Rebecca did as any other woman in the church in her position would do. She looked at the two unknown Mexicans in front of her and gave the ubiquitous uncomfortable and hard-pressed lip smile, cocking her head to the side before turning around.

Magdalena whipped around to watch Rebecca briskly walk away before muttering under her breath, "Ya se fue la cabrona?"[75]

"Mom!" Michael said with quite a bit of embarrassment.

"Vez mijito?! Como te he dicho … no mas lo de ellos les importa."[76]

"So, what's wrong with that?"

"Pues que no se puede preguntar por mi o por mis cosas … ni podia saludar a estos muchachos."[77]

---

[75] "Did the bitch leave?"
[76] "You see, son?! Just like I told you … only their stuff is important."
[77] "Well can't she even ask about me or my things … she couldn't even say hello to these boys."

"Come on, Mom, she's don't even know them."

"Hay, no seas tonto mijito. Es un falta de respeto."[78]

"I'm not, it's just … I don't know … maybe she just wanted to know how to cook like you."

"Mijito, escuchame muy bien. Estos gabachos siempre estan enfocados en una cosa. Lo de ellos. Lo demas, les vale un pito de payaso."[79]

"You really think that way?"

"Veras! La proxima vez que ellos necesitan algo, alli estarán como el mejor amigo del mundo. Con el 'howarejou, good neyborr.' Pero cuando uno necesita algo, se largan a la chingada. Esta vieja me lo acaba de comprobár."[80]

Both Jaime and Raul overheard Magdalena talking to her son, and both started to chuckle quietly.

"Magda! Keep it down, people can hear you," snapped Manny.

"Hay como si todo estos Gringos entiendierán Español, Manuel! A ver si no te conviertes en un Gringo para que me dejes decir lo que me de la fregada gana!"[81]

Manny began to boil with frustration, but there

---

[78] "Oh son, don't be such a dummy. It's a lack of respect."
[79] "Son, listen to me and listen good. These Americans are always going to be focused on one thing. Their things. The rest, they could give a rat's ass."
[80] "Watch! The next time they need something, they are like the best friend in the world. With a 'how are you, good neighbor' But when you need something, they get the fuck out of Dodge. This broad just proved it."
[81] "Oh please like all these Gringos understand Spanish, Manny! Let's see if you turn into a Gringos that you can let me say whatever the hell I want!"

was little that he could do right then and there. The service was about start, and the pianist had already taken her seat at the old upright piano. Her golden cotton-candy hair rose over the open blue hymnal like the dawning of the morning sun as she began playing the first hymn of the morning. The cacophony of conversations around the church began dying down as people gathered in their pews and as gaggles of wives dispersed to roost with their respective husbands.

The worship pastor walked up from his front row pew and stood proudly behind the pulpit, ready to lead his small outfit battalion of faithful Christian believers into worship of the Pastel Jesus. Michael had generally regarded him as somewhat of an odd man, who at times was overtly open with his bothersome personality. Someone whose very blood seemed to pass through his veins with a lethargic and procrastinating effort. He was a rather heavyset fellow, his blond hair curly like a pig's tail. Unlike the other men in church, he was well into his forties and single, which often raised Michael's suspicions that Pastor Roberts was giving more appointments to others.

"Good morning!" he boomed from the pulpit.

"Good morning," said the congregation in obedient unison.

"How good is it to be in house of the Lord today?"

"Amen, brother!" someone in the back shouted.

"Amen, indeed!" the worship leader shouted back.

"Please continue standin' as we turn in our hymnals to hymn 251 as we sing." With a quick nod to the pianist, he lifted his hand to queue the downbeat to the untrained congregation. He took a deep breath, puffing up like a proud street pigeon, and began to sing.

> "I was sinking
> deep in sin,
> far from the
> peaceful shore,
> very deeply
> stained within
> sinking to rise no
> more, but the
> master of the sea
> heard my
> despairing cry,
> from the waters
> lifted me now safe
> am I."

Michael watched the worship pastor waving his hand like the master conductor of a world-class orchestra, but in reality he was chaotically herding the off-pitch voices into some semblance of a choir. But it mattered little to the ruddy and bright worship pastor. The man reveled in the Sunday morning songs and was brimming with overt joyfulness and exuberance. Even the joy of song at times made him forget that he was in front of his fellow believers. Often, Michael would catch him subtly straightening his wrists, just before his melodic voice seemed to overpower the howling of his fellow believer.

In a moment of selfish observance Michael looked down the row of Brown faces where he sat. The row of his people and his kind. His mother had the blue hymnal open to the song, but she stood in what can only be typified as her graceful contrarian nature, refraining from singing in protest of her husband's wishes. Manny, on the other hand, was deeply buried in the hymnal as he sheepishly sang along, horrifically out of tune. What made his singing worse was that he muddled and overenunciated his words trying to suppress his accent. It was one of the rare times when Michael ever saw him submissive to anyone or anything, like the wives of his fellow church men. Jaime and Raul paradoxically found themselves in the midst of a crowd but on the outside of a language, and oblivious, they had their hymnals open and mouths shut. Manny, standing next to them, did nothing to show them which page was the right song.

On the outside of the Brown strip was Manny's coveted life. The women with their immovable hair, tilting their closed eyes upward and imagining the satisfied Lord to whom they were singing. The men stood like solid stone, with steadfast gazes, like watchmen over the tiny congregation. All that Pastel Jesus stood for—family; order; and, above all else, straightness of one man and one woman in holy matrimony—was manifested there around them. At times, Michael loathed the things that Manny loved with as much contempt as he had for Manny himself, but even Michael wondered what life would be like if all three of them simply surrendered and became like the other people at church. If all the problems that they suffered through would simply vanish into Christian bliss; if only they themselves vanished into an American Gringo oblivion. If it were so, Manny may not be so hell-bent on striving for the picture-perfect example of a Christian family, because he would already have it, and maybe the weekly violence would be less or even nonexistent. Magdalena may not be so embittered toward her husband for wanting to make her into the perfect stay-at-home wife, who shared cobbler recipes with the other church women, and maybe her defensive machisma would be obsolete.

Michael may not be consumed with the crushing anxiety of second-guessing every step and wondering if every hand gesture was masculine enough for other people to accept him. In the end, maybe their Mexican lives were nothing more than ten thousand pieces of hostility and bitterness that reverberated and jostled against each other like half-lit coals in the fire.

He could feel the convergence of all three lives, drawing closer and tighter into the demands of Manny's singularity for practical and inescapable moral reasons. Manny wanted that life, and if Michael wanted Manny to have that life, then maybe he would find the life he wanted. A life free from queer nightmares. But even the prospect of Manny becoming the perfect Christian husband and father was on a completely different plane of existence for Michael. It still made no sense to him that salvation from this vortex of dysfunction was through the very sun-darkened hands that caused it in the first place. An impossibility that can happen only when the clouds part and God descends from heaven to make Earth spin backward. The far more detrimental possibility of an act of God never coming to fruition was that this may just be the random cruelty of the universe. Scarier, because then there was no hope for change, there was no hope that things could get better. It would just be him, the boy, and the girl in the salt desert of his mind forever.

"On the chorus one last time," the worship pastor shouted from the pulpit.

Michael snapped back to reality and looked down at the hymnal, fighting the temptation to think about the fantasies, which was trying to overwhelm him.

Burn - Flames - Searing - Ashes - Death - Numb

He opened his mouth and tried to sing the chorus along with everybody else.

> "Love lifted me,
> Love lifted me,
> when nothing else
> could help,
> Love lifted me"

6

The music had stopped, and the off-key singing finished like a car crashing into a wall. And there was the pastor, standing up, ready to preach. Proud and robust, Pastor Roberts walked up from the first pew carrying his Bible, wearing a new dark gray suit. He strolled with hubris and pious reverie as if entering into the very courts of heaven itself to have an audience with the almighty. His pinkish bald head glistened from with pre-sermon sweat as he sat his Bible down with an authoritative thud on the pulpit, sounding like a dead creature thrown on a butcher block for carving.

"Let us pray."

His pudgy, freckled fingers grabbed tightly at the pulpit as he steadied himself as if the whole of God's truth were slowly funneling down from above and sitting heavily on his shoulders. After breathing deeply, he whistled out through his slightly congested nostrils.

"Dear heav'nly Father, we're ask for your blessin' 'pon us today as we gather to hear your word and truth. We invite your Holy Spirit to enter into this place, that it may convict the hearts of the men that you have led to this church. We know that the times that we're livin' in are full o' wickedness, full o' sin, and the world around us is cryin' out for salvation. Lord, your redeemin' power and love saves us from death and teaches us the way to walk in godliness, and that's what we seek from you this day and every day. Guide us into righteousness, as we ask you to continue to change us into the image of your son, Jesus Christ. We ask these things in his holy and most precious name. Amen."

> "Amen Amen
> Amen   Amen   Amen
> Amen Amen Amen
> Amen   Amen
> Amen   Amen"

"Please be seated."

As Michael and his family sat back in their seats, Michael took a quick look around him, observing all the well-to-do men in the pews. They eagerly grabbed their Bibles and randomly opened them, then set them on the bookstands of their crossed legs. Their wives inched closer, cuddling to read their husband's holy book, as the words of the opening prayer and the hymns reverberated in their heads.

Pastor Roberts removed his glasses and then pulled out a handkerchief to clean the greasy fingerprints clouding his view while he spoke.

"Now, isn't this just a fine day to be in the house o' the Lord?"

> "Amen Amen
> Amen

Amen
Amen"

"Amen indeed, brothers 'n sisters. Are y'all ready to hear what the word o' God has for you today?"

"Amen, Pastor Roberts!"

"Hallelujah, Church, Ha-lle-lu-jah in-deed! If you'd turn in your Bibles to the Book of Romans this mornin', we'll be discussing Paul's message to the Roman Church."

People began flipping through the translucently thin Bible pages, all trimmed with shimmering gold leaf. The sound was like dried leaves tossed by an autumn breeze, and the rustiling filled the little church before quickly dying down again. Michael grabbed his tattered Bible and began to flip through it too. However, there was no shimmering cascade of gilded pages. The waking hours spent combing through scripture after scripture had rubbed off the warm gold and left the raw ascetic pages of a holy book exposed. Artful scribbles of blue and black ballpoint pen tagged the pages as if ancient cuneiform graffiti. Secret messages that only he could understand.

He glanced over at Manny as he laid his opened Bible on his folded leg, trying to mimic his brethren, while Magdalena pulled her shawl tighter around her, making sure that the tassels didn't touch her husband. Jaime and Raúl sat Bible-less, looking at each other with quixotic comprehension. There was no genuflecting, and there were no signs of the cross; there was only a man reading the Bible to them. A well-dressed man who looked more like he was trying to sell them car insurance than talking about

God.

"Now we'll begin with Chapter 1 verse 18,"
Pastor Roberts said, then let them the room
become still.

"For the wrath o' God is revealed from heav'n
against all ungodliness and unrighteousness of men,
who suppress the truth in unrighteousness,
because that which may be
known of God is manifest in them,
for God hath shewed it unto them.
For the invisible things of him from the creation
of the world are clearly seen,
bein' understood by the things that are made,
even His eternal power and Godhead,
so that they are without excuse."

Pastor Roberts often imagined himself like Jesus
preaching to his followers on the Mount. All of them were
expectantly waiting to hear the divinely inspired sermon
and the subsequent marching orders for how they will win
the souls of those born into sin. Although South Phoenix
was not a complete heart of darkness, in the eyes of the
believers there were plenty of people just a shade above
absolute paganism. To them, not being "saved" meant that
even if someone knew of Jesus, or may have even tried to
live a good life according to what they were told about
him, it wasn't the right Jesus. "Your Jesus isn't the true
Jesus" is what Michael and his mother were told time and
time again in the early days. Pastor Roberts, for better or
worse, was one of those turn-or-burn types of pastors. His
mission was to bring true light to the people lost in what he
saw as the artificial and corrupt light of Catholicism. His

prayers were for the Mexicans to shed their hold on the false Jesus of the priest and embrace the Pastel Jesus standing behind him in the baptistry. Of course, Magdalena was defiantly obstinate that she was right about her faith and was more than apt to adhere to the furthest ends of the belief spectrum out of pure spite. Besides, why wouldn't she? She was Mexican.

"Folks, let's just be honest, we're livin' in tryin' times."

"Amen!"

"We can see it all around. Why, Brother Jim right here was tellin' me just the other day 'bout all the ungodly things he saw on television the other day. Women who feel it's just all right to have an abortion 'cause they're just goin' from man to man to man."

"Lord have mercy!"

"Or what 'bout the nonstop flow of pornography pumped into your homes in the name of entertainment? Children's programs tellin' them that it's OK to be a fornicating homosexual? Tell me, church, is that somethin' we should just stand idly by and let happen?!"

"No, sir!"

"Right now, there are people in our nation's capital who are tryin' to make it so that sin is normalized in the name of bein' tolerant. And for what? At the cost of religious freedom? It's a travesty and an outrage that should drive God's people to seek him on our hands and knees in prayer!"

"Amen
　　Amen, brother!
　Amen"

"However, dear brothers and sisters, we know …
and boy, do we know it … that the Lord Almighty, creator
of heav'n and earth, he sees it all!"

"Amen!"

"He sees the wickedness that we're in, and he sees
all those ungodly people who fight against him, knowin'
that they're in direct disobedience to his word."

"Hallelujah!"

"The Bible says the wrath o' God is reveal'd from
heav'n. We ain't got any excuses to say that we don't
know what's right and what's wrong. Even the man who
isn't a Christian, who's an unbeliever, even he doesn't
have an excuse for the all evil things he does."

"Amen
　Amen
　Amen
　　Amen
Amen
　Amen"

"But what God's been doin' now for us as his
chosen people is exactly what he had done for the children

of Israel. Be assured, brothers and sisters, that just like the pillar o' fire that led the Israelites through the wilderness to the Land of Canaan, God is providin' a way for us through this wilderness of sin."

"Praise God, Hallelujah!"

"Now you can take comfort in that, my fellow Christian! You can take comfort that just like when God's glory dwelt in the Tabernacle, so too will the light of his truth shine forth from this church. You can rest in the promises of God that will never fail ya, just like he fulfilled his prophecy of returning the People of Israel to their homelands."

"Amen, praise Jesus!"

"You see, brothers and sisters, God does and will provide his cloak of protection to you, his chosen people. Protection for the people who love him and walk in his light and seek his righteousness. But just like the children of Israel, God can and does remove his protection. Oh yes. God can take his protection away if his people stray from him."

For the first time that whole morning, a somber silence fell across the congregation as Pastor Roberts continued.

"Lemme be honest with you, church! The judgment is gonna come. I believe that it's gonna come upon this nation if it hasn't already. Ain't gonna be no priest in some fancy church who's gonna save you. Mmm, no sir! Only the true word of God can save you from that. If God doesn't pour out his wrath and judgment upon this country for the vile wickedness that is spreading from sea to shining sea, then God sure does owe Sodom and Gomorrah an apology. Amen?!" he shouted.

"Amen!"

"But we shouldn't be surprised, brothers and sisters, that this is happenin' to this once great Christian nation, because the Lord prophesized about this in this passage. Look back at verse 24.

'Therefore, God also gave 'em up to uncleanness
in the lust o' their hearts,
to dishonor their bodies among themselves,
who exchanged the truth o' God for the lie,
and worshipped and served the creature
rather than the Creator, who is blessed forever, Amen.'

Lemme be clear on this, church. We simply cannot allow sin to come into our lives and think that it won't harm the soul. Once sin has a foothold in your life, you'll see the destruction that happens with it, each and every day that you refuse to give that sin over to Jesus. We can see this, as Paul writes,

'For this reason, God gave 'em up to vile passions.
For their women exchanged the natural use
for what's against nature.
Likewise, also the men, leavin'
the natural use of the woman,
burned in their lust for one another,
men with men committing what's shameful,
and receivin' in themselves the

penalty of their error which is due.'

Now, folks, there are some people who might think that what I'm 'bout to say is considered hate speech. And there are some people who say I should be in jail for speakin' out against a so-called lifestyle. But folks, last time I checked, God and not the president was still on the throne."

> "Amen
> Amen
> Amen"

"And I'd rather obey God than man when it comes to homosexuality. Amen?"

> "Amen!
> Amen!
> Amen!
> Amen!
> Amen!"

"And the honest truth, brothers and sisters, is that this whole thang 'bout being gay and gay men forcin' all o' us to see their sin up front and personal, that's just a symptom of a greater cancer. Just like the scripture says: when sin enters in and people don't lay it down before the feet of Jesus, God is just gonna give 'em right on over to their transgressions, just like that. Trust me on this, folks, I see this every day, where men like this are just addicted to these perverse desires. They can't look at another man and not think 'bout doin' somethin' sinful to them. They'll try so much as rapin' some poor boy off the street. And you wanna know why? Because they've forsaken what it means to be a man. And like I said earlier, they can't say that they didn't know that layin' with another man was a sin, 'cause the Bible says they're without excuse … . Look at the next verse.

'… knowing the righteous judgment of God,
that those who practice such things are deserving of death,
not only do the same but
also approve of those who practice them.'"

The small church seemed to empty itself of the booming voice of Pastor Roberts and the jeering responses of the faithful, all while the words *deserving of death* echoed in the vacuum of personal silence that enveloped Michael. The open sore of his fear was touched again and the terror of being outted radiated through his limbs to his fingertips, like ten thousand frozen needles poking at him. Michael glanced over at Manny and Magdalena, and he wondered if the gateway for sin to enter was in fact his family.

When he looked at his stoic and proud mother next to him, he saw the natural way she had carried herself these past few years—a formidable and strong woman who seemed to be more the head of the household than Manny. An unflappable feminine character who was not ready to conform to the expectations that were laid upon her. But even then, Michael wondered whether God judged her in the same manner that Pastor Roberts was judging him: that a person of uncompromising fortitude was an unfit follower of God. Was she one of these so-called women who exchanged their use for what is against nature?

"What's he mean by natural, anyway?" Michael said to himself.

He saw all the other wives sitting in church as ardently adherent to the church's concept of the ideal Christian woman—submissive, modest, meek, to be seen and rarely heard. None of those qualities he could see in Magdalena, and definitely not after marrying Manny. She was a fiery and passionate woman of utmost tact and bite. A woman who commanded and deserved the respect that she earned and had proven herself (at least to her young son) to be the father to her boy that her late husband could not. But even with the virtuous image of a female father in his mind, Michael still considered the validity of Pastor Roberts's remedy for his same-sex attractions to be true.

Michael had never felt treachery on the scale of Judas Iscariot like this before when it came to his upbringing. He would often think back to his childhood and the few years between his father's death and Manny, and he could remember the times when it was just the two of them trying to make ends meet. She never failed to provide all that she could, even down to the simple sopitas[82] of browned elbow macaroni, tomato, onion, and green chile that she would make for him. The times that she would scold him to do his homework on time, or those quiet Sundays listening to rancheras of José Alfredo Jiménez and Juan Gabriel. All this as she tried to fill the gap of a father and raise her son to be the image of a man whom she knew. A man deeply rooted in the ways of Mexico. A man like her father and brothers, who sought out formidable and strong women like her. His stomach tied in knots at the thought that in the simple act of being a

---

[82] Soups.

parent and just loving him, and rearing him in the identity of his heritage, it would have left him damaged in the eyes of Pastel Jesus.

Still, if all these things that Pastor Roberts was saying to him were true, that the favor of God would turn on America because of a willful drifting away from "God's intended natural way of things," then by that same virtue, wouldn't God's wrath fall upon his mother for not submitting to Manny, and upon him and his mother for their drifting away? For Michael, it came down to the one thing that he felt the universe was pressing on him: their selves were wrought with unimaginable corruption.

As Michael watched Manny bury himself deep in the pages of his Bible, he began to think about what Pastor Roberts said to him yesterday. God sent Manny to help him not to sin anymore. It seemed improbable that a man who rarely acted fatherly toward him was to be the heavenly sent father whom he needed in order to escape the hellish consequences of queer sin. And even as his mother was beautifully and admirably defiant to Manny and his way of thinking, Michael couldn't help but wonder whether maybe Manny was trying to save her from judgment as well, that her submission to acting like all the other White women of the church was his way of rescue. All of these uncertainties cut at Michael's confidence like a thousand daggers severing every little bit of himself that had precedence in the world. But even through all the questioning, he was still sure that his simmering loathing toward Manny was justified. He thought, *Most people would hate him too if they knew what happened any night when he wasn't home by six ...*

Whack! A loud smack of the pulpit startled Michael as Pastor Roberts slammed his hand down and his voice thundered.

> " '… For we know that the wages of sin
>   is Death, and all have fallen
>   short of the glory of God.'

Isn't that right, church?"

> "Amen
>   Amen
>   Amen
>   Amen"

Michael sat at attention and faced Pastor Roberts, who was now as red as a tomato with veins throbbing with indignant blood. The glint of bluish fluorescent light shined on the pastor's face as beads of sweat budded on his forehead. He was now hunched over the pulpit trying to hold himself up as the spiritual weight of heaven sank further onto his mortal and fragile back.

"However, brothers and sisters … we gotta give praise to God, the almighty … It was him that made a way for us. You know why? … It's 'cause he loves us. What does your Bible say? It says that

> 'God demonstrates His own love towards us,
>   in that while we were still sinners,
>   Christ died for is. Much more then,
>   having now been justified by the blood,
>   we shall be saved from wrath through Him.'

"Brothers and sisters, if God so loved the world, if he gave his only begotten son while we were sinners, then those that would reject him, those that would reject his son, those that would reject his salvation, why, they're just rejectin' his love!"

"Amen, Brother Roberts!"

"Amen indeed, brother … Amen indeed. 'Cause God don't have any other choice but to allow his wrath to be poured out on this wicked generation. Even those that would say that they love God, those that say that they follow his teachin's, those that say that they obey his commandments … if their lives don't show it, what does that mean?"

Pastor Roberts took a grand pause to let his words sink into the minds of his congregants.

"It's just like it says in First John, Chapter 1:

'If we say that we walk in the light,
but do not practice truth,
we are liars and the truth is not in us.'

So when someone from the World comes up to you and says to you that they believe in God, and are in a quote unquote gay relationship what do you know 'bout them? … You know that the truth ain't in them and you know that they don't love God!"

"Amen!
Amen!
Amen!
Amen!"

"When someone from the World comes up to you and says they believe in God and that it's OK to have an abortion, what do you know 'bout 'em? … You know that the truth ain't in 'em and, what? … That they don't love God neither!"

"Amen, brother Roberts!
Amen
Amen
Amen"

"When someone from the World comes up to you and says they believe in God and then goes on over to the bar and has beer after beer … you know by the grace and righteousness of God Almighty that the truth ain't in them and they sure don't love God!"

"Amen
Amen
Hallelujah
Amen"

"And just like the writer of the Book of Hebrews says in Chapter 2 verse 1:

'Therefore we must give the more earnest heed
to the things we have heard lest we drift away.'

And as we take this more earnest heed, it's our responsibility as the chosen people, as the elect that God has saved, to go out and preach the word of righteousness and truth."

"Amen!
Amen!
Amen!
Amen!"

"It's our responsibility to fulfill the great commission that Jesus himself told his disciples in the Gospel of Matthew!"

"Amen!
That's right, brother Roberts!
Amen!
Amen!"

"It's our responsibility to be the vessels of the holy spirit that God can use to convict the hearts of the World so that they can be drawn to him."

"Amen!
Amen!
Amen!
Amen!"

"And so they can be drawn into a lovin' and savin' relationship with his son, Jesus Christ!"

"Amen, brother!
Hallelujah!
Praise the Lord!"

One lowly voice in the pew erupted to join in on the frenzy of the people. "Amen!" shouted Manny as he glared with a side eye at his stepson. However, Michael could care less about another petty mid-sermon jab from him, and just like weeks before, he leaned back out of Manny's view. Hidden by the Morena silhouette of Magdalena and her black lace shawl, he slumped deeper into the pew. But it wasn't the glare from Manny, it was the words and the implications of what Pastor Roberts was saying that hit him like a third-round uppercut.

The haunting thoughts of his fantasies in the warm salt desert flooded his brain with a ravenous carnal euphoria, a gravity of covetousness, and a weight of morality that waged a silent war over his soul to tear him into little mortal pieces. He believed in God—at least, he wanted to. But the existence of the fantasies seemed to disqualify him at every turn for saying that he could ever truly believe in him. The thought even crossed his mind that he may be believing in the wrong God. He wondered if he had missed a minor detail, some forgotten catechism, or maybe he had misunderstood a word from a sermon that somehow led him to pray to a slightly adulterated version of God. He even thought that perhaps God, the correct God of the Pastel Jesus, was divinely whispering in Pastor Roberts's ear in that very moment, speaking through him to reach Michael with the truth, that the reason he was still afflicted with fantasies of men and women was that his faith was stuck in the belief of this strange, counterfeit, and impotent God, the one he assumed to be the Mexican Catholic God of his youth that Manny was fervently trying to eradicate from the house, Magdalena, and him.

As Michael looked down at the ragged pages of his Bible, opened to the Book of Romans, Pastor Roberts's voice faded softly while the oncoming buzzing in his head crescendoed again, into the now ubiquitous anthem of his desires and conscience. Trying to dissuade his mind from the eventual ashen remains of his psyche, Michael looked up at the crude mural in the baptistry, the correct blue-eyed God.

Burn – Flames – Searing – Ashes – Death – Numb

"Forgive me, Father, I have sinned!" he whispered to himself.

The rosary and crucifix felt warm and heavy against his skin again as if all the guilt and remorse for wearing this heretical relic to church had burned through his thin white T-shirt. Michael wanted to rid himself of it, to rip it off and shove it back in the shoebox along with everything else, just so he could make all these thoughts evaporate away.

> "They started comin' back
> when I put this on.
> That's gotta be it."

In a penitent panic, Michael tried to remember the course of events after leaving his appointment last night to when he came home in the evening. He meticulously combed through every detail as he felt the saving grace of God slip from his hands once again.

> "That's what God's been
> tryin' to tell me. That's why it
> keeps happenin' God's tryin' to
> get my attention!"

"As we come to a close," Pastor Roberts said with a shaky, emotional voice, "there are some here today who don't know what their eternal future holds for 'em. There are some o' you here this mornin' who if you were to get into a car accident when you leave this church, you wouldn't know if you were goin' to heaven or not. There are some o' you sittin' here who still have not put your faith in Jesus Christ. Now I ain't talkin' about some kinda weird ritual mumbo-jumbo with some man in a funny-lookin' robe sayin' your sins are forgiven and you get to go to heav'n. No sir-eee, I'm talkin' about a real true relationship with God. There are some o' you here who say that you know where you're goin' 'cause a long time ago someone sprinkled some lil' bit of water on you as a baby. Well, brothers and sisters, I cannot deny what the word of my God says, and it says that if you wanna be saved and see the reward laid up in heav'n for you, then you gotta confess with your lips that Jesus is Lord and that he is Lord over your entire life."

"God is talkin' to me!
He's talkin about the rosary!
God's gotta be talking to
Pastor Roberts 'bout me!"

"Right now I want everyone here to bow their heads and close their eyes while I lead us in prayer …"

Michael's beaten-up heart lit up for a moment because there was hope. Hope that even though he caused God to turn away from him on account of his treachery, there was still hope that he found the error of his ways. There was a means to fix it. There was another chance at redemption.

"Heav'nly Father, we know that you see the hearts of everyone here, and only you know the pleas and prayers of their hearts. Lord, as we've heard in your word today that you've made these things evident, and that you've made a way for ev'ry sinner to come into your righteousness by the blood of your son, Jesus, we ask that you come upon those here today who have not 'ccepted your son and you speak to their hearts …"

"Show me a sign, God.

Show me you're listenin'."

Pastor Roberts stood with a humble, grandiose pause, letting the words of his fervent prayer weigh on his congregation. "Now, with every head bowed and with every eye closed, let the Holy Spirit into your heart. This is your time to speak to the Lord. If in the depths o' your heart, you wanna 'ccept Jesus Christ as your personal savior, why don't you just raise ya hand. No one else can see you, just God. Just raise ya hand so that I may pray for you."

Michael's heart thudded loudly in his ears as he discreetly raised his hand. He tried not to make an overt motion that Manny or Magdalena could sense, even with their eyes closed. But he made it obvious enough so he could be seen squarely and plainly from the pulpit. Pastor Roberts was prowling around like a hungry tiger waiting for the zookeeper to throw in a near expiring porkchop in his pen, pacing behind his massive pulpit, waiting and watching for his God to hunt and strike a sinner's heart so he could claim their soul in the name of his Pastel Jesus.

"Don't let this chance pass you by. Jesus is here waiting for you," said Pastor Roberts.

Michael raised his hand a few inches higher, thinking that perhaps Pastor Roberts didn't see him. He even cracked open an eye just to make sure he was seen. He wanted Pastor Roberts to know that he was sorry and that he was repenting. He was ready to let the real Jesus in his heart this time. But his contrition was unnoticed. As he cracked his eye open even wider, he could see Pastor Roberts standing dead center in front of the pulpit, looking down the empty aisle of the church.

"Anyone? Come on, now, don't leave here without knowin' where you're gonna spend eternity!" pleaded Pastor Roberts. Michael wanted to start frantically waving his hand to get his attention, like a grade school student, contorting in urgency for knowing the answer that the teacher wants to hear. But he held steady, bottling up the exuberance inside, afraid that he may be asked afterward about the terrible sin for which he was so eager to beg forgiveness.

"I see those hands! God bless you!" shouted Pastor Roberts, pointing down the middle of the aisle as a quiet stream of whispers followed.

"Amen!
Hallelujah!
Praise Jesus!"

Michael opened both eyes, trying to see who had beaten him out in finding favor with God and Pastel Jesus.

"Now, with every head bowed and every eye still closed, I'm gonna ask Peggy to come up here and play us one more song, and as she does, I'm gonna ask those folks who raised their hands to make their way down here to the front so I can lead you in the Sinner's Prayer. Please, come …" Pastor Roberts gingerly said to the congregation as the worship pastor walked up behind the pulpit and the pianist took her seat. She turned to the back of the big blue hymnal book, and she began to play softly while the worship pastor led the congregation.

"Just as I am without one plea,
but that thy blood was shed for me,
and thou that bids't me come to thee

oh lamb of God I come, I come."

Each voice in the church began to sing like a warm candle glowing in a dim room. Soft and luminous, flickering independent of one another but together in the same incandescent tones of the hymn. Husbands and wives held each other, close as turtledoves, nestled in each other's wings as if a gentle drizzle of spring rain had begun falling. This was what they came for, to witness the miracle of salvation.

Michael was still trying to determine who exactly had raised their hand. He saw a few women walk down the aisle past Pastor Roberts and kneel on the steps next to the pulpit. Their cotton candy heads bowed into their folded hands that were clutching wads of tear-soaked tissues. Their calf-length skirts draped their legs and the floor around them, as if they were innocent peasant farm girls putting out a bountiful harvest before their lord and master.

"It can't be them. That's Rebecca!"

"Come on up, brothers, God is callin' you. It's OK!" Pastor Roberts shouted over the chorus of voices filling the church. "Jesus is callin' and waitin' right here for you!"

With the eyes of his followers still closed, Pastor Roberts finally turned to look toward Michael. Coyishly and in surprised disbelief, Michael mouthed the words "Me?" asking if God was indeed calling him to repent again. But no quicker did Pastor Roberts wave his hands to come forward that Manny urged and ushered Jaime and Raúl from their pew down the center aisle. From there, Pastor Roberts's transfixed gaze watched them as they made their way toward him, leaving Michael behind.

"Praise Jesus … Praise Jesus," Pastor Roberts said as he lifted his open hands up toward the ceiling.

"Hallelujah!"

People unable to hold their excitement finally opened their eyes and began applauding the two men as well, smiling and finally welcoming the dark-skinned strangers who had sat quietly in their midst since the beginning of the service.

For Michael it was treachery, pure and simple. His epiphany seemed to be so profound and real up until that moment that he was ready to ask for God's forgiveness in front of everyone. A great blank space of faith was set on him, and he didn't know what to do with so much emptiness. He couldn't help but remember the day when he and his mother walked down that same aisle. Walking to a supposed better life, a life that was past the death of his father, a life with the stability of a father figure. A chance for hope in a new church, and new god, and to some extent a new culture. But that hope that he had held on to was decimated just like the ashen boy in the salt desert, and he felt like a fool thinking that Pastel Jesus was genuinely seeking him and his soul. If before he felt lost in the mists of an adulterated God of the rosary, now he felt abandoned by the God of this little Protestant church, a church that he had been faithful to as child. He felt as if this God was interested not in him anymore but in the aggregation of more bodies to the whole. People were still clapping for Jaime and Raúl as they walked up to Pastor Robert. Clapping all the way up until the worship pastor finished the last run of the chorus.

> "… Oh Lamb of God I
> come, I come."

The piano rang its last notes as it faded into silence while Peggy stayed seated at the piano bench, and the worship pastor stepped back from the pulpit.

"Praise God, brothers and sisters … Praise God for convictin' the hearts of these two young men. Amen!"

> "AMEN!
> AMEN
> AMEN
> AMEN!"

"Now I wanna lead you boys in what's known as the Sinner's Prayer. A prayer to ask Jesus to come into your hearts and wash away all your sins. Are you two boys ready to do that and be welcomed into the family of God?" Pastor Roberts asked them while they glanced at each other.

They were dumbfounded as to what he was asking them to do, until one of them finally turned toward the pastor and said, "Pues … Lo que usted diga, señor."[83]

A look of modest surprise overtook Pastor Roberts. "No English?" he asked loudly, overenunciating every syllable. Both workers shook their head as they continued to look at this man standing in front of them. "Well folks, my apologies! Looks like we're gonna need a translator up in here."

Pastor Roberts gestured for Manny to come down to the front. Manny clumsily rushed up like a hyperactive

---

[83] "Well, whatever you say, sir."

Yorkshire terrier that was getting his treat after performing an obedience school parlor trick.

"Just wanna make sure the congregation has a chance to hear this wonderful and beautiful work that God's about to do. Let's bow our heads."

The room fell silent as each person bowed their heads and closed their eyes. Michael, on the other hand, was now resolute to see Manny's chicanery firsthand.

"Dear God, I know I'm a sinner, and I ask for your forgiveness. I believe Jesus Christ is your son. I believe that he died for my sin and that you raised him to life. I wanna accept him as my savior and follow him as Lord, from this day forward. I pray this in the name of Jesus, Amen."

As soon as Pastor Roberts finished the Sinner's Prayer, Manny began to translate, with Jaime and Raúl mumbling behind his words.

"Senor, yo se que soy pecador y pido tu perdon."

> *"Senor, yo se que soy pecador y pido tu perdon."*
> *"Senor, yo se que soy pecador y pido tu perdon."*

"Yo creo que Jesucristo es Tu Hijo."

> *"Yo creo que Jesucristo es Tu Hijo."*
> *"Yo creo que Jesucristo es Tu Hijo."*

"Yo creo que el murió por mis pecados"

> *"Yo creo que el murió por mis pecados"*

"Yo creo que el murió por mis pecados"

"y que tu lo resucitate a la vida."

"y que tu lo resucitate a la vida."
"y que tu lo resucitate a la vida."

"Yo quiero confiar en El como mi Salvador"

*"Yo quiero confiar en El como mi
Salvador"*
*"Yo quiero confiar en El como mi
Salvador"*

"y seguirlo como mi Señor."

"y seguirlo como mi Señor."
"y seguirlo como mi Señor."

"Te pido en el nombre de Jesus, Amen."

"Te pido en el nombre de Jesus, Amen."
"Te pido en el nombre de Jesus, Amen."

As the last mumbled words from Jaime and Raúl fell onto the old blue carpet, Pastor Roberts enthusiastically shouted, "Amen! All glory to God for the great things he hath done!"

The church erupted in applause as Pastor Roberts directed Jaime and Raúl to turn around and face the cheering congregation. Their uncomfortableness was on their faces in crooked smiles. Manny could barely contain himself as he clapped and stepped to the side to catch the spill-off glory from Pastel Jesus. But in the pew with the remaining Brown faces, Michael flexed his white knuckles while he gripped the back of the pew in front of him, trying to crush it into splinters.

"Increiblé, no?"[84] his mother quietly asked as she half-heartedly clapped, watching the scene unfold.

The people continued to applaud and say "Amen" and "Hallelujah" with exuberant enthusiasm, which was making Michael sick to his stomach.

"El los chantajeo, mijito. Asi como lo hizo con nosotros,[85]" his mother said with an unnerved resignation. "Cuando el ve que hay neccesidad, el toma ventaja."[86]

"It ain't right!" Michael protested. "Did God really do anythin'?" Michael fumed as he tried to talk low enough so only Magdalena could hear him.

Just then Pastor Roberts shouted over the applause, "Brothers and sisters, the service has ended. Go out into the world proclaimin' the Gospel o' Jesus Christ and praise him for the work he's done here today!" An upbeat hymn came from the piano as the clapping and cheering slowly died out and people swarmed the new converts, like a school of hungry nurse sharks swimming around a dying sea creature.

"Vez, ahora pueden saludar a los muchachos,"[87] she said.

"Why?!" asked Michael.

"Me imagino que piensan que ahora son como

---

[84] "Incredible, isn't it?"
[85] "He blackmailed them, son. Just like he did it with us."
[86] "He's just like that, whenever he sees a need he takes advantage."
[87] "See, now they can say hello to them."

ellos. Esta gente es tan predecible, no?"[88]

"It feel wrong, really wrong!"

"Vamonos, mijito. Aunque me veo muy santita, tambien puedo hacer muy cabrona,"[89] she said sternly as she gave her son and ally a reassuring smile.

She hurried Michael along out of the pew as she stepped out into the center aisle of the church. She pulled the black shawl tighter around her body, letting the lacy fabric cascade around her.

Her black shapely eyebrows arched above her honey-brown eyes, and her jet-black hair caught the dull light above like a halo. Jaime and Raúl were now standing off to the side, huddled and trying to avoid the people while Pastor Roberts and Manny relished in the conversion miracle.

"Hay, muchachos, que bueno que vinierón."[90]

"Pues si, señora, pero …"[91]

"Pero que? No me digas que mi marido les anda haciendo la vida pesada?"[92]

"Pues no señora, no era eso … Es que … pues … mire, no me lo tome mal, pero yo no queria venir.[93]"

"Y porque veniste?!"[94]

"Pues mira, señora, el patron … puesss … nos

---

[88] "I imagine it's because they're not dark-skinned Catholics anymore. These people are so predictable, aren't they?"
[89] "Let's go, son. Although I pass as a saint, I can also be a real bitch too."
[90] "Hey there, boys, so good of you to come."
[91] "Well of course, mam, but …"
[92] "But what? Don't tell me my husband is making life difficult for you?"
[93] "Well, mam, it's not that … It's just … well … don't take this the wrong way, but I didn't want to come."
[94] "Why did you come?!"

exigio, que teniamos que venir … que era parte de sus reglas para trabajar con el,"[95] answered Raúl.

"Hmmm … claro,"[96] she said, scoffing at that.

Out of the corner of his eye, Pastor Roberts noticed the small group forming around his new trophies.

"Isn't God great?! Praise Jesus for blessin' us today!" the pastor blurted out as he made his way back into the conversation, putting one hand on Jaime's shoulder and one on Raúl's.

"Si, gracias as Dios,"[97] she wryly responded.

"Yes, thank God indeed! How're you, sister Magdaleyna?"

"Muy bien, gracias por preguntar."[98]

"Dear Lord, where are my manners?! I never got the names of these two fine young men who decided to give their lives to Christ today," Pastor Roberts said as he extended his hand. "Uhm … yaaamo?! Co-mo yaaamo?!" he asked loudly.

"Soy Jaime."[99]

"Y yo soy Raúl."[100]

"Hi-may and … what is it again … ra … ra … uuuul?" Pastor Roberts asked.

"Si es Ra … ul, Raúl."

"Ra-a-wwl … humpf … Raaawl! Boy, that one

---

[95] "Well look, mam, the boss … weeeelll … kinda made us, he said that we had to come to his church … he said it was part of having to work with him."
[96] "Hmmm. Of course."
[97] "Yes, thanks be to God."
[98] "I'm well, thank you for asking."
[99] "My name is Jaime."
[100] "And I'm Raúl."

sure's a doozy from my White tongue! Aint it?" Pastor Roberts laughed as he gave hardy pats on his new converts' shoulders. "Anyway, uhm … Magdalena, I hear your boy is gonna be goin' to ASU this fall?"

"Si, mi Miguelito va empezar su carera este verano con el favor de Dios."

Unsure of what she just said, Pastor Roberts looked at Michael for a translation.

"She said, 'Yes, Michael is going to start in the fall, God willing.'"

"Ah, yes, yes, yes, God willin' … God willin' indeed, sister Magdalena."

"But he's gonna be workin with me this summer," blurted out Manny, "see if he really wants to go to school."

"Well, brother Manny, I really hope all that workin' with your boy is gonna get him ready to face all that school's gonna throw at him. I mean, that place is a den of sin if I've ever seen one. Isn't that right, son?" he said to Michael, smiling while inconspicuously winking at him.

"Cuales tentacíones?" she asked.

"She wants to know what you mean by that," Michael interpreted.

"Well, I uhm … I mean ASU is one of the biggest party schools around! Lotta kids doin' god knows what over there. I still wish you would've considered maybe goin' to a Bible college, son. Just to get away from all that …"

"Y porque?" retorted Magdalena.

"She asked why?" said Michael.

"Well, it'll help give you that strong Christian worldview, son. A view that you're gonna need to keep you straight in life, son. You definitely wouldn't have to worry about gettin' involved with any of them drunk and loose women over there," he said to Michael, giving him a reassuring and jovial pat on the shoulder.

"That'll be the day," Manny snidely remarked under his breath.

"But I gotta say, there's a lotta pretty girls on that campus, though! You just might find yourself a sweet little darlin' there." He laughed. "But just make sure she's a good Bible-believin' and God-fearin' woman, son."

"Hay pastor, no me diga que tiene celos de que mi hijo pueda conseguir una esposa antes que usted?"

Michael and Manny stood wide-eyed, and even Jaime and Raúl cracked smiles trying to hold in the laughter.

"What'd she say?" asked Pastor Roberts.

Initially Michael hesitated to respond, but Magdalena looked at her son with a raised eyebrow.

"Well, she asked if you were jealous that I'd be able to find a wife before you."

"Ha! Oh no, sister Magdalena, nothin' like that! I'm just like Jesus, married to the church and the only thing that's gotta hold on me is the word o' God."

"No me diga! Fijese que mi mama tenia un dicho para los hombres, que jale mas un par de tetas que un par de gueyes, será cierto?"[101] she sweetly and spiteful replied.

"Magda!" interjected Manny as he turned bright red. "She uhm … she says that's good that a man of faith is so dedicated to the church, isn't that right, honey?" Manny said apologetically as he glared at his wife.

---

[101] "Don't tell me! You know, my mom had a saying about men, that a pair of tits has more pull than a pair of donkeys, is that true?"

Michael, Jaime, and Raúl were trying their hardest not to laugh while a confused Pastor Roberts nervously smiled along.

"Uhm, Pastor Roberts, didn't you need, uh … to talk to me about the uhm … deacon board or somethin' like that … ?" Manny frantically asked.

"Oh heavens, I forgot 'bout that! Thank you so much for remindin' me!" he exclaimed as he looked around. "Why don't we go talk over there since this is more of a uh … private matter?" Before the pastor left, he shook the hands of those around him, starting with his adversary. "It sure was nice seein' you again, Magdalena."

"Igualmente,"[102] she said with a tight grin.

"Michael, we'll see you next Saturday?"

"Yes, sir," Michael responded.

"And once again Hi-may and Raaawl, welcome to the family of God," Pastor Roberts said loudly to the two men, giving each a tight hug and hearty pat on the back.

"Gracias," they responded as each one reciprocated with a quick one-handed hug.

"Hijo de su chingada madre,"[103] mumbled Magdalena as soon as Pastor Roberts and her husband were out of earshot. "Oigan, de verdad quieren estar aqui?"[104] she asked.

"Fijese que no, señora. Se me hizo muy raro todo esto,"[105] said Jaime.

"Entonces, me imagino que no quieren ser

---

[102] "Likewise."

[103] "Son of a bitch."

[104] "Listen up, boys, truthfully do you wanna be here?"

[105] "Honestly, mam. All of this was really strange to me."

miembros de la iglesia tampoco?"[106] she asked.

"Pues, no sabia lo que estaba pasando. Pensé que nos iban a dar comunión Doña Magdalena,"[107] said Raúl.

"No'hombre, no te van a dar nada,"[108] said Magdalena.

"Y porque nos hicieron creer que si?"[109] asked Jaime.

"Asi son, Jaimito. Asi son!"[110]

"No, no, no no, yo no dejo mi religion, para nada …"[111]

"Imaginate que diría tu mamá si supiera que dejaste lo que ella te enseñó! Imaginaté! Que pena!"[112]

"No, yo no dejo mi fe, no señora!"[113]

"Pues, yo diría que no volvieran,"[114] she said to them.

"Pero el patron … ?"[115] asked Raúl.

"Que tiene que ver mi marido con este asunto?"[116]

"Hay perdon Doña Magdalena, es que no quiero problemas con el."[117]

---

[106] "Then, I imagine that you guys don't want to be church members either?"

[107] "Well, I didn't know what was going on. I thought they were going to give us communion, Mrs. Magdalena."

[108] "No way, they ain't gonna give you anything."

[109] "So why did they make us believe they were?"

[110] "It's who they are, little Jaime. It's who they are."

[111] "No, no, no, no, I'm not giving up my religion, for nothin'!"

[112] "I mean just imagine what your mother might say if she found out that you left what she taught you! Imagine that! What a pity?"

[113] "No, I ain't leavin' my faith, no mam!"

[114] "I wouldn't either, I say that you don't come back."

[115] "But the boss … ?"

[116] "And what does my husband have to do with this?"

[117] "Excuse us, Mrs. Magdalena, we didn't want any trouble."

"Y que pedo puede tener con el?"[118]

"Es que su esposo nos exigió venir, si no, nos bota del trabajo. Y usted sabe que necesitamos la chamba, señora."[119]

"No te preocupes de mi esposo, el te necesita mas de lo que tu lo necesitas a el. Ademas, si el les pregunta, digan que yo les dijé que se regresarán a su parroquia."[120]

"Pero señora su esposo le puede …"[121]

"A mi me vale un pito de payaso lo que diga mi esposo. Ahorita, la que manda soy yo, y si tu patronsito tiene una problema, que venga a decirmelo a la cara."[122]

"Ouy, Señora!"[123]

"Fijate, ademas de ser bonita, tambien soy cabrona. Que te parece?"[124] she said with a confident smile.

Jaime and Raúl laughed as they stood uneasy in the middle of the church that was slowly emptying of people.

"Anda vayan a sus casa, y no se procupe del patroncito. Yo tambien tengo mis trucos con mi

---

[118] "And what problem would you have with him?"
[119] "It's just that your husband demanded that we come or we lose out jobs. And you know how much we need the work."
[120] "Don't you worry about my husband. He needs you just as much as you need him. Besides, if he asks you, tell him I told you to go back to the parish."
[121] "But, mam, your husband can do to you …"
[122] "I don't give a rat's ass what my husband says. Right now, the one that gives orders is me. If your little boss has a problem, he can come and tell me to my face."
[123] Whoa, mam!"
[124] "Am I right? Besides being beautiful, I can be a real bitch. What do you think?"

marido,"[125] she said proudly to them.

"Si Doña Magdalena, Gracias," Jaime said to Magdalena as he gave her a proper hug.

"Orale … Oye, Miguelito … nos vemos mañana?"[126] Raúl said to Michael, giving him a firm pat on the back before shaking his hand.

"Yeah, most definitely!"

"Que tengan buen dia!"[127] said Jaime.

The two men turned and walked out the front door into the bright sunlight. Each was lost in brilliant whiteness, never to return to the little church.

"What are you gonna tell Manny?" Michael asked Magdalena.

"No se. Una pendejada me magino."[128]

"Did you really mean all that, Mom?"

"Claro que si, mijito … Donde hay hambre hay necessidad. Ahorita el Manuel tiene hambre de vivir como un Gringo, y nosotros temenos hambre de vivir."[129]

"I don't think he'll put up with it for too long …"

"Pues que se aguanta … igual como yo lo aguanto."[130]

Mother and son found themselves alone again in a sea of White people. Everyone else was getting ready to go home to Sunday dinners, but they were waiting. Waiting

---

[125] "Go on and go home, and don't worry about your boss. I've got my little tricks with my husband."
[126] "Right on … Hey, Michael … we'll see you tomorrow?"
[127] "Have a good day!"
[128] "I dunno. Some stupid lie I imagine."
[129] "Of course I do, son … Where there's hunger there's necessity. Right now Manny's hungry to live like a White man, and me and you are hungry to live."
[130] "Well let him put up with it … the same way I put up with him."

for Manny, as one by one the faithful left them behind. They watched everyone go into the great white bright light in the doorway.

"You really think he played us back then, Mom?"

"O si, mijito. Ve lo que hizo con esos muchachos, y me acuerdo de todo. Mas claro no canta el gallo."[131]

"Do you think it's bad that you have to be like that with him?"

"Mijto, los perros no nacen, los hacen … a cuartazos,"[132] she said, holding back tears.

"I know, Mom, I know," Michael said with an ever-tightening tension in his stomach. "Hey, did you really just convince Jaime and Raúl to leave the church?"

"Te digo, quizás soy mejor pastor que ese tal Robertito."[133] She laughed as she squeezed her son's hand. As the last of the faithful women walked out the church and into the bright afternoon light, Magdalena and Michael were finally alone in the church with the open door beckoning them.

"Lástima que no tuvé los huevos años atras …"[134]

---

[131] "Oh yes, my son. Look what he did to those boys, and I remember everything. Can't get any clearer than that."

[132] "Son, bitches aren't born, they're made … by hitting them."

[133] "I told you, maybe I'm a better pastor than this little Robert guy."

[134] "It's just a shame that I didn't have the balls you do it years back …"

7

The summer was dragging on. The dry May winds had moistened into sultry air from the oncoming monsoon season. It wouldn't be long before the impeccable blue sky would become violently alive with thunderstorms that would forcefully roll through the valley. They would bring with them the gift of rain for the parched earth to drink, as well as the infamous dark clouds that swallowed up whole mountains and blotted the sun.

Manny and his crew were working overtime to try to keep even the hardiest of desert plants alive in the searing heat. The premature autumn colors hellishly burned themselves onto the tender leaves of trees and bushes. Everything seemed to wither, everything except the bougainvilleas; they loved the hellish heat and relished in the explosion of fuchsia and purple blooms. Like huge bunches of wine grapes, the brightly colored blossoms weighed down the boughs, ready for a stormy July harvest. Magdalena's wild bougainvillea had grown as well. She was now able to stretch out her branches of lush foliage in all directions as she tightly wrapped herself around the post of the dusty front porch, always leaving a carpet of pink petals on the ground for Michael when he left to go work with Manny.

His five a.m. drives from South Phoenix across the dried-up river to Gringolandia had become his summer routine now that school was out. The real day-to-day work with Manny had started to feel like a strange and unhappy déjà vu. Like other boys from that part of town the opportunities to get ahead were rare and on all the guys he worked with, he saw the same tired eyes reflecting an old story. Eyes that spoke of silent stories, of souls worn in by the work. But even though the tired working men were austere, he earned their prized respect, and he savored it like an expensive piece of chocolate, hiding it away and nibbling on it whenever he needed reassurance that he could be manly enough. At least manly enough around Mexican men.

Still, the echoing mantra of Pastor Roberts was in his ear over and over again—"Masculine begets Masculine"—and it clung to him like a haunting nightmare. And those men were not the right kind of men that he needed. But no man from church ever came alongside him to sweat and work with him. None ever talked to him or joshed him like one of the guys. In his own eyes he was man enough to be a hard-working Mexican but he couldn't even begin to reach the status of a straight Gringo of the church.

Michael was reminded of this every night when he closed his eyes and he would find himself enveloped in the velvety smooth dream where his fantasies lived: the white salt desert of his inner self, where he told Pastor Roberts that the boy remained entombed in a sarcophagus of ash beneath the shadow of the old twisted tree. And since that day when he saw Pastor Roberts lie to win a soul for Pastel

Jesus, Michael began to lie too. If Pastor Roberts could lie to save Jaime and Raul, then he too could lie to save the boy from the daily murder of the flame. He could not understand why he had to carry out such an elaborate lie to shield the boy in his dream from further harm. The more times he told Pastor Roberts that the boy was dead, the more he noticed Pastor Roberts trying less and less to make him murder an already supposed dead thing. Even with the assumption that the boy was dead, Michael still hated and yet loved him. Michael could sense his irresistible compassion touching him like a fresh wound whenever the girl in the fantasy came to the aid of the boy, removing the old ash from his first immolation as she healed him back to life.

****

Even though the scorching summer put high demands on Manny and his crew, Manny did have his moments of clemency. Manny granted them a reprieve by allowing them one extra day off during the week. Tuesdays happened to be Michael's day off, which he enthusiastically spent boxing with Coach Padilla. Michael left the house on a late summer Tuesday, as the midmorning sun was beating down on him hard. As he headed down the street to Round One on Central Avenue, the blasts of hot, bone-dry air blew past him on the busy shadeless street, burning his eyes as he squinted to see. The smell of molten asphalt and half-burnt motor exhaust filled his nostrils and covered any leftover scent of fresh-cut grass that he may have had in his nose from the day before. He could feel his golden tan skin baking into a darker and richer tone that matched his darkened hands.

The gym was mostly empty except for a few guys training on speed bags, which he could see through the cloudy glass of the storefront windows. The brick walls were rough and held up aging, exposed wood trusses. It was a place that did not lie about itself, nor could it if it tried. It was a humble and utilitarian temple for making men and boxers out of boys. The old aluminum and glass front door was propped open with a rock , and he could feel the damp air from the swamp coolers flooding out like a gust of stormy August wind. Michael stood in the doorway with a wide stance, his arms out to his side to let the cool air pass over him. His basketball shorts and T-shirt gently flapped in the outgoing breeze as he felt the soothing relief from the searing heat of the street.

"Better not be wastin' all my cold air standin' there like a pendejito!"[135] a deep voice called out from the back of the gym.

Michael looked through the darkness, squinting to see who it was.

"Well, I was lookin' for my coach and all I see is some fat gordo[136] runnin' his mouth!" Michael said with playful smile.

"Boy, if you're gonna train, then get yo' Brown ass in here!" said Coach Padilla.

Michael stepped inside, squinting harder to see in the dimly lit gym until his eyes adjusted. When the room came into focus, there in front of him was Coach Padilla picking up empty water bottles from the floor. He was a tall and massive man, built like an old refrigerator from the seventies. Broad and boxy, steadfast and calmly intense,

---

[135] Little dumbass.
[136] Fatty.

but at times temperamentally noisy when he needed to be. He was much darker than Michael, like melted piloncillo with a messy mop of curly salt-and-pepper hair and a thin, well-trimmed goatee. He gave a quick up nod to Michael as he smiled and walked over to him.

"Como te gusta chingar la paciencia, no?"[137] he said to Michael as he sat down on a bench.

"I'm just tryin' to keep you on your toes," Michael responded as he threw his gym bag down next to the coach and sat next to him. Michael hunched over and rested his elbows on his knees as he reached down and started to dig through his bag for his straps.

"Damn, boy!

"What?"

"You're gettin' dark! Pretty soon you're gonna be more prietito[138] than me!"

"It's all the work I've been doin' with Manny."

"Mira nada mas, guess you really are a Mexican, huh?!"

"What's that supposed to mean?!"

"It means you're bustin' your ass like your old man."

"He ain't my old man!" Michael responded in annoyance.

"Hay no seas tan serio hombre![139] I'm just playin with you, foo!" Coach Padilla said. He gave Michael a playful shove. "You're still tryin to get back at him, aren't you?"

"Wouldn't you?"

---

[137] "You really like to fuck with my patience, don't you?"
[138] Dark-skinned.
[139] "Hey, man, don't be so serious!"

"Yeah, but …"

"But what?"

"I dunno, for me gettin' back at someone usually means I'm throwin' some chingazos, asi … pa! Pa! You know what I'm sayin'?"

"Yeah, I know."

"Entonces?"[140]

"I've gotten close to it. Just watch, one of these days I'm gonna hit him, and I probably won't stop, you know. I'll just snap."

"What are you afraid of?"

"I ain't afraid of nothin'."

"No?! Then how come you havn't done it?"

"I dunno … I … I just haven't yet."

"I mean the shit he puts you and your mom through … hijole!"

"Yeah, I know …"

"You won't do it."

"You don't think I can?"

"No, I think you can, but you got too much to lose if you do."

"I guess …"

"Pero, you gotta a lot of corajitos[141] in that head of yours."

Michael clenched the hand he was wrapping, feeling the strap tighten in his fist the more he tried to flex out of it.

"Eh, there's a lot more than just that, a lot more," Michael said, as the growing sound of cicadas tried to creep into his hearing.

---

140 "Well then?"

141 Little fits of anger.

"What? You tryin' to prove you're the bigger man 'cause of that?"

"Cut it off

Cut it off"

"Ain't I?" Michael asked gruffly as he stared at his own shoes.

They both sat awkwardly in silence as the playfulness that he entered with, evaporated into the damp air of the gym. Michael wanted to tell him. He wanted to invite Coach to listen to everything that had plagued him. He wanted Coach to know how good it felt just to hear that he was within striking range of the prize, being called "Man enough." The enticing drug that called to him so many times, even though it wasn't from the right kind of place or the right kind of man, felt real nonetheless. It felt good. But at the same time, his bitter cynicism reached over from his psyche to whisper in his ear, to remind him that it was still only a question that coach asked, and not the answer.

> *"Maricon*
>
> > *Maricon*
>
> > *Maricon*
>
> > > *Maricon"*[142]

Spiritually severed him from the world, and the saddest part was that no one else knew just how far away he really was. Only he could understand the chasm between him and Coach Padilla. The words "I like that guy over there just as much as I like that girl over here" wanted to burst from his lips and break free from his guarded tongue. To simply say that openly and loudly would be the most liberating sentence he could utter. But he stopped himself like every time before, just like he stopped himself from ever hitting Manny. It wasn't proper. Straight men don't say they like guys, because they don't, and good Christian men don't hit their fathers, even if they are jerks. He had to practice the rites of Pastor Roberts to please Pastel Jesus, even in this temple of Mexican Machismo.

> > > *"Putito!*[143]
>
> > > *Jotito!*
>
> > > *Maricon!"*

"I really don't know why your mom puts up with his shit," said Coach Padilla.

"Huh? What were you sayin'?"

"No me oyes o que?"[144]

---

[142] Faggot.

[143] Little faggot.

[144] "Are you listening to me or what?"

"Yeah but … whatever …"

"I said, I don't know why your mom puts up with his bullshit. Your mom can do better! She deserves better."

"Yeah. I ask myself that all the time. But she's got her reasons."

"Marianna keeps sayin' that if you guys need to, she'll put a room out for you guys."

"I know. Coach ..."

"I mean it. You guys don't have to be out on the street."

"May be needin' it soon enough, Coach, you know … when I take her with me."

"Hay muchacho,[145] you're a good man for wantin' to look out for your mom like that. You've got a lot more huevos than that cabrón."[146]

> *"You can't trust him.*
> *He called you a boy first."*

"Yeah?"

"Most definitely."

> *"You're still a joto."*

"I'm glad someone sees it."

"What?! You're gonna tell me you don't feel like a man?"

> *"FAGGOT!"*

---

[145] Oh kiddo.
[146] Asshole.

"Sometimes … I don't. You know, you try and do everythin' right, but there's always somethin' or someone tellin' you that you ain't good enough. Even Pastor Roberts tells me that."

"You ain't a man, you fag."

"What kinda shit is that?! Sabes que, ese cabrón se puede ir mucho a la chingada![147] What the fuck does he know about being a man? Es mas puto que la chingada."[148]

"Don't say that."

"It's true. Un hombre tiene que tener huevos."[149]

"You think so?"

"You'll never be like that."

"Hell yeah, I do. Gringos like that little pastorcito[150] of yours think that lookin' like a man is what makes him a man. Chalé, hombre! Bein' a man is about how much shit you take and still stand up to keep on goin'. Asi como yo, un verdadero macho Mexicano."[151]

"Pinche Maricon!"[152]

Michael clicked his lips in scoff. "Eh!"

"Hey! I'm serious! I'll bet you when the shit hits

---

[147] "That asshole can go fuck himself!"
[148] "He is such a fucking fag."
[149] "A man has gotta have balls."
[150] Condescending form of "little pastor."
[151] "Just like a true macho Mexican man."
[152] "Fucking faggot!"

the fan, someone like that little pastor vato,[153] he'll be the first one to bail on you. Shit, even Manny, as much of an asshole as he is, still knows that. He wouldn't be tryin' so damn hard if he didn't."

"Hmm … you're right on that, Coach!" Michael laughed.

"No, Miguelito, don't you get sucked in to that bullshit. You got a lot goin' for you. If they don't like the way you are, pues que se vayan mucho a la chingada!"[154]

"I guess," Michael mumbled as he tightened the straps around his wrists.

"Orale pues,[155] you gonna get to workin out now or what?!"

"Yeah …"

"Pues andalé!"

As they got up to hit the speed bags, two figures came out of the hot white sun through the front door. One figure walked in with the slow strut of a calculating pit bull. His head was shaved smooth, and the faint shadow of his scalp was a sinuous line on his forehead, like the border of wet beach sand that's just been washed over by a great wave. The front of his white wifebeater plunged down like the parabola of a suspension bridge cable, and the faint black Old English lettering on his pecs were halfway hidden behind the hem. His baggy khaki Dickies hardly creased when he walked, and the sharply starched fold of the legs kept its edge like a brand-new knife.

The other figure was younger and about the same age as Michael, with a face of fear and unease about the

---

[153] Dude.
[154] "They can go fuck themselves!"
[155] "All right then."

world he'd just stepped into. He kept his hands in his pockets, trying to make himself as small as possible in the hopes that no one would notice him, or possibly he was trying to disappear into thin air. His hair was curly, like sheep's wool and black like the omen from some dreadful fortune. However, when he did muster up the courage to look up at the world around him, Michael managed to meet his gaze with his own. There was something intriguing about this timid boy. Something about the palpable sadness that he wore and the innocence of self. And it pulled Michael in like a whirlpool he couldn't escape.

Burn - Flames - Searing - Ashes - Death - Numb

It was open admiration, an indulgence that caught him off guard and made Michael feel as if he were struck with a forbidden beauty for the first time in his life. And he wanted more of it. He wanted time to freeze, for everyone around him to stop moving just so he could be a voyeur, enjoy something he wanted without shame or judgment. He had an urge to reach out and let his fingertip graze the skin of the boy's arm. To even embrace him and, by some metaphysical osmosis, absorb the fear that walked in with him and pass on to him his own shaky sense of comfort. But the more Michael wanted him, the more the cicadas in his head buzzed with fervency. He could not tell whether the flushing heat he felt was just his nerves or the inferno of his psyche bleeding out into reality. By now the buzzing cicadas had gotten so loud, he swore that underneath the monotonic symphony he could hear a boy screaming, buried in the noise.

"Orale, Coach, que onda?"[156]

"Que quires, Javi? You know I don't want you here."[157]

"Hey, can't a vato just stop by, ese?"

"I bounced your ass outta here for a reason."

"Relax, homie, I ain't here to start shit …"

"Then whatcha want, Javi?"

"Mira, carnal … I need a favor."

"Ha! You need a favor? I ain't got time for your shit."

"It's not for me, ese!"

"The answer is no, cabrón!"

"It's my cousin over there, ese …"

"I don't wanna hear it."

"C'mon, Coach … you know me!"

"Yeah, that's the problem."

"Hey, why you bein' like that, holmes!"

"'Cause, last time I helped you out …"

"I'm not askin' you to help me out."

"Hijo de tu chingada madre … como chingas!"[158]

"Hey, he got his ass jumped a couple days ago … OK?!"

"What did he do?"

"Pues, nothin', fool!"

"Bullshit, no one gets jumped unless they did somethin'."

"He didn't do anythin', I swear to God!"

"Yeah, whatever …"

"I'm serious, mira …"

---

[156] "What's up, Coach, what's happenin'?"
[157] "What do you want, Javi?"
[158] "Son of a bitch, you're fuckin' annoying!"

Javi pulled Coach Padilla off to the side, out of earshot from the two boys standing by the punching bags. Michael looked around the room awkwardly, trying to bounce his eyes to different objects, just like Pastor Roberts had taught him to. Anything he could do to avoid being pulled in to the seductive feelings and covetousness. Or even worse, being caught looking at the boy.

"Hey, I got feria, holmes … don't be like that!" said Javi with an elevate voice.

"Esta bien, esta bien … Miguelito!" shouted Coach Padilla.

"Yeah, Coach?"

"Hey, you're gonna be training with this little vato over here for today. I've got some extra straps and gloves in the office," he instructed Michael. "What's your name, shorty?"

"Diego," mumbled the boy as he tried to look up, fearful that the first thing that was going to happen to him was getting punched in the face.

"Diegito, huh? How old are ya?"

"I'm … a … I'm eighteen."

"Orale,"[159] Coach said. "Miguelito is 'bout the same age. He'll be a good matchup for you. You guys run some drills, then get goin' on bag work."

The boy nodded, but his feet still seemed to be weighted, as if he found it nearly impossible to lift them.

"Andale primo!"[160] shouted Javi.

Diego turned like a bashful child unwilling to meet new people. He whispered a plea to Javi as quietly as he could.

---

[159] "All right."
[160] "Go for it, little cousin!"

"Primo, c'mon, go learn to fight!"

"Javi, does he wanna train or not?" asked Coach Padilla.

"Hey, give me a minute, OK?!" shouted Javi, who then went back to whispering to Diego.

"C'mon, man, let's get to it!" said Michael, trying to coax his new training partner.

"Hey, mind your own fuckin' business!"

"I was just askin' …"

"Fuckin' joto …"

"What you call me?!" Michael shouted back at Javi.

"You heard me, puto!"[161]

In a split second, Michael felt the phantom flood of blood-tinted bathwater crashing around him, wetting his ankles. For everyone else the gym mats were bone dry, but he was already downing in a universe of seductive hatred.

> *I'm not a fag.*
> *Burn …*
> *I'm not a fag.*
> *Flames …*
> *I'm not a fag.*
> *Searing …*
> *I'm not a fag.*
> *Ashes …*
> *I'm not a fag.*
> *Death …*
> *I'm not a fag.*
> *Numb*
> *I'm not a fag …*

---

[161] Faggot.

"Call me a puto again and see what happens. I ain't scared-a you!" Michael said as he stepped up to Javi, getting up in his face before shoving him away.

"I'll beat the fuckin' shit outta you, fuckin' joto, if you don't get out my way," Javi retorted as he shoved Michael back. Both were in fighting stance, with fists up ready to go to blows, right before Coach Padilla stepped in between them.

"Knock it off! Quitos!"[162] Coach Padilla shouted.

"You're gonna hide behind him, pinche maricon!"[163] shouted Javi as he tried to get around Coach Padilla.

I'M NOT A FAG!

"Ya basta, Javi!"[164] commanded Coach Padilla.

"Who you callin' a maricón? I'll kick your ass right now!" Michael shouted as Coach Padilla hooked his massive arm around Michael, holding him back as if Michael were an angry Rottweiler on a leash.

"That's enough! Javi, get the fuck outta here! I'm tired of your goddamn shit!" Coach Padilla commanded.

"Fine, I'll go. You just tell that pinche mamón[165] he better watch his back!"

"I swear to God, I'll hurt you!" responded Michael.

GOTTA BE A MAN! I'M NOT A FAG!

---

[162] "Calm down!"
[163] "You fucking fag!"
[164] "That's enough, Javi!"
[165] "Fucking cocksucker."

"Yeah? I'll fuckin' jump his ass, fool!" Javi shouted back.

"Ya! Vete, cabrón!"[166] Coach Padilla shouted.

By this time Michael had devolved into a rabid, animalistic beast of a human, yelling in grunts and growls, which just made Coach Padilla squeeze him tighter.

"Is that what you sound like when you're gettin' fucked in the ass, you fuckin' joto!" Javi taunted.

"GET THE FUCK OUT, JAVI!", roared Coach Padilla as his voice echoed through the rafters of the old building. Javi continued to relish in the moment as he strut slowly and proudly back out of the front door, back into the sweltering heat, all the while devilishly smiling at Michael who was still being held back.

I'M NOT A FAG!

"Miguelito, ya! Hombre … ya … ya …"[167] Coach said forcefully as Michael continued to wriggle in Coach's grip.

GOTTA BE A MAN, NOT A FAG!

"Miguelito ya calmate!"[168] he shouted louder, trying to make Michael snap out of it.

"MIGUELITO! YA! CALAMATE, CABRÓN!"[169] he screamed, managing to grab Michael's face and squeeze his cheeks so as to bring Michael's eyes level to his.

---

[166] "Enough man! Get outta here!"
[167] "Mikey, enough!"
[168] :Mikey, enough! Calm down!"
[169] "Mikey, Calm down, dumbass!"

The vivid wrath that had erupted earlier receded into the dark recess of Michael's soul as Coach Padilla's voice and dominating laserlike gaze broke through the cacophony in his head. Michael seemed almost incoherent, but his grunts had slowed to gulping pants as he looked around his feet frantically to check whether the bloody bathwater had disappeared.

"Ya hombre, ya … ya,"[170] Coach Padilla kept repeating, while Diego stood frozen.

Finally, Michael said, "I'm OK, Coach. I'm fine."

"Hijole,[171] I'd hate to be in the ring with you!" Coach Padilla said. "All right, all you shortys get back to it! There ain't nothin' to see here."

The onlookers turned away from the scene, leaving Coach Padilla and Michael in the middle of the mat and Diego standing nervously in a corner.

"Oye, en serio … estas bien?" Coach Padilla asked in a discreet whisper.

"Yeah … I'm … I'm OK."

"Man, you scared the shit out of me!"

"Yeah, I … I uhm … I dunno. I just heard 'joto' and …"

"Ya, ya, ya … it's over, it's over. Don't let that pendejo get to you."

"Did I hit him?"

"Nah, that pichón[172] walked his ass outta here before you could land a punch."

"Uhm … OK."

---

[170] "Enough, man … enough."
[171] "Oh man"
[172] Squab.

"Hey, go chill my office for a bit. Para que te calmes un poco."

"Nah, I'll … I'll be fine … seriously!"

"You sure?"

"Yeah … yeah I'm ready, I wanna get started."

"Orale … go get Diego and show him around."

"Where is he?"

"Lil' vato's in the corner. Looks like he's about to piss himself."

"OK, I … I can do this."

"Deveras?"[173]

"Yeah?"

"Start 'm off easy with some warm-ups."

"I can do that."

"I'm gonna get straps and gloves for him."

"OK …"

"You sure you're OK?"

"Yeah, I'm fine …"

As the coach walked back to his office, Michael led Diego to the front of the gym near the windows to start with the jump rope. The blinding fury of his outburst still hung around the room like the smell of old sweat, stubbornly clingng to the walls. But the residual adrenaline that was still pumping in his veins did help him talk to Diego without sounding like some tongue-tied voyeur.

"You … wanna get started?" Michael asked.

"Uhm … yeah … I guess"

Diego was awkwardly silent as he looked around at the posters Coach Padilla had hung on the walls. Old-school boxers posing with their championship belts, like saints of masculinity watching over the young initiates

---

[173] "Seriously?"

while they practiced their craft. Under the poster of
Muhammad Ali and Sonny Liston, Michael grabbed jump
ropes that were hanging on a hook while he tried to make
small talk.

"Hey, sorry 'bout actin like that."

"Don't worry 'bout it."

"You sure it ain't no thing?"

"Yeah, it's no problem."

"Your cousin … he's a …"

"You can say it. He's kind of a jerk."

"Is he always like that?"

"Nah, he's just protective …"

"Of you?"

"You could say that …"

"He said you got jumped?"

"Yeah."

"What for?"

"N … Nothin' …"

"Nothin?!"

"Yeah, nothin'."

"Nobody gets jumped for nothin'. What happened?
What'd you do?"

"Uhm … some cholos … they uhm … uhm?"

Diego's arms began to tremble as he clenched his
fists so tight that his knuckles turned white. Even in the
damp air of the gym, his teeth chattered with chilling angst
as wave after wave of a vivid memory kept crashing onto
him. His brown eyes looked straight through the floor as
they turned into perfectly glazed spheres, as if his soul had
quickly retreated from the windows of his skull to hide in a
deeper part of himself.

Is he OK?
I will not see other men
as objects of lust.

Michael thought of the girl in the salt desert and how she tended to his secret fantasy that was left in ashes. From that image, a simple human urge kindled in the bleakness of the subsiding rage. Like a gentle flower sprouting in the dry dirt, Michael wanted to reach out with genuine kindness, to tell him in what few words he could think of that it was OK, even if Michael himself didn't know what OK was. He reached out his hand and rested it on Diego's shoulder, just like the men at church would do to pray or bless someone.

Don't touch him.

But instead of the warm humanity of kindness, he felt the trembling in his own hand, and in the rush of the tumultuous desert he plunged into the place where the flames and ashes had consumed the boy.

This will make you fall.

The infinite numbness and fear seemed to flow from Diego, like osmotic sin. It was a kindred compassion that Michael intimately knew but couldn't let back in.

Burn - Flames - Searing - Ashes - Death - Numb

There could be no compassion for Diego, not like this, anyway. The boy was infected with Michael's lust, and he felt it. And as much as Michael wanted to give in, a fear sat in him like a heavy stone. For the preservation of his own soul, Michael had to go back to being at arm's length.

"Here, gonna start with jump rope for 'bout ten minutes," Michael responded coldly as he pulled his hand away.

He handed Diego a jump rope. As Michael started to jump rope, he hoped that the soft rat-a-tat-tat of the rope tapping the floor would tap out Diego's shuttered breathing. He hoped that if they could just start doing something, anything, Diego would forget what was bothering him and Michael could stop being callous.

8

The damp afternoon breeze signaled the approaching monsoon, and while the craggy mass of South Mountain obscured the view of the open desert, the clouds bloomed high over the peaks like desert flowers swallowing the rich turquoise sky. The bougainvilleas shed their lush purple and pink paper flowers like confetti. They were celebrating the end of the oppressive heat and bracing for the violent storms that would usher in autumn. August was only a few days away, and for Michael the shady tree-lined streets of campus life would be a welcome change from the dusty and blighted sidewalks of Central Avenue. School was a place where he hoped that he and Magdalena could just slip away—from the authoritarianism of Manny, the lies of Pastor Roberts, and the people of Pastel Jesus. He hoped that it would be a place and a future where the dreamscape of the salt desert could finally blur into a sublime wallpaper of memory like all the hundreds of other dreams he would have in his lifetime.

Michael had finished an afternoon training session at the Round One gym when the storm loomed overhead. He was pleased that after only a few weeks, Diego had started to open up and gain confidence. Michael and Coach Padilla were able to get him to throw a few basic combos while staying light on his toes. Michael secretly enjoyed the company, though there were times he would let his eyes drift to Diego's body, admiring him for a brief and indulgent second before the painful sounds of the cicadas chastised him back into submission. "Pleasure/Pain" is what he eventually started calling it—the pain he would have to make himself feel for the pleasure he wasn't supposed to have. The pain of watching the boy in the desert die, the noise of the cicadas, and the back-and-forth catechisms all served to tell him that what he was doing was right.

As Michael walked home, the sun beat down on him through the wispy tips of the thunderheads that were reaching out to grab the golden orb and hide it from Earth. It would start raining soon, and from the looks of the billowing underbelly of dark clouds, this was going to be an impressive storm. When he finally turned the corner, he could see Pastor Roberts's Cadillac parked in the driveway of his house. Before he could get any closer, Pastor Roberts waddled out alone, passing under his mother's bougainvillea. A few thorny boughs bobbed in the breeze and caught the pastor with a few scratches. He got into his car and headed toward Central Avenue. He waved at his young acolyte behind the rolled-up windows, jovially smiling as he drove by. Michael was confused to say the least as he waved back at the shiny car rolling past him.

When he got to the house, he could see that the front door was left wide open and in the darkened cave, he could hear arguing in the kitchen. For a brief second, Michael's stomach churned with the acidic memories of fights and brawls from the past, and at the same time he was oddly comforted by the familiarity of it, a tenacious old friend that comes back to stir up peaceful waters. He knew what to do and why he had to do it. No one had to teach him how to numb himself to the fights; it was all a part of surviving Manny. He quietly slipped into the house, trying to not be noticed, and crouched in the shadows of the hallway. He was out of sight but within earshot of Manny and Magdalena. He did it to bear witness so later he could judge once again who was ultimately right and who was guilty.

"… Everythin' I've done for you, and you can't do this for me?" yelled Manny.

"Ya te dije que no! No quiero!"[174] shouted Magdalena.

"Why you have to be so difficult, huh?"

"Porque asi soy! Para aguantar tantas pedejadas de ese pinche pastorcito!"[175]

"You don't understand. You know what this means to me?!"

"Yo no te'intiendo? Hay, Manuel, no seas tan pendejo …"[176]

"Hey, treat me with respect. I'm the man of the house and …"

"Y yo soy la mujer que merece tu respeto!"[177]

"Why are you actin' like this, huh? Why?!"

"Porque?! Porque estoy cansada, cansada de batallar cada dia, de no perderme en esta pinche secta! No

---

[174] "I already told you! I don't want to!"

[175] "Because that's the way I am! To put up with all the stupidities of that fucking two-bit pastor!"

[176] "I don't understand you? Please, Manuel, don't be so stupid …"

[177] "And I'm the woman that deserves your respect!"

quiero perderme en el mundo de ellos, entiendelo, Manuel! No soy como ellos!"[178]

"Hey, I'm not the one stuck in the past. You left everythin' behind … this is your new life, 'member? I'm just tryin' to be 'merican, Magda!"

"No me andes con eso, Manuel. Tu sabes muy bien que nunca me ha gustado que esa bola de hipocritas crean que soy una pinche chencha o una ilegal que apenitas cruzó."[179]

"Well, if you would stop actin' like a wetback …"

"Ya, Manuel! Por dios! Parale con tus chingaderas!"[180]

"I ain't gonna stop … and you know why? 'Cause you don't know what it feels like to get just a lil' bit of respect from 'em. You don't know what it's like for those gringos to treat you like you're one of 'em, 'stead of the guy that's there to clean up after 'em? Huh, do you?"

"Hay, Manuel, como chingas con los pinche gringos … No te cansas de la misma chingadera?"[181]

"Yes! I'm tired of bein' looked at like a piece of shit, Magda! I'm tired of people thinkin' I'm just a good-for-nothin' Mexican! You gonna tell me I'm a bad person for wantin' what George has?"

---

[178] "Why?! Because I'm tired, tired of havin' to fight everyday so I don't get lost in the fuckin' cult! I don't want to get lost in their world, can't you understand that, Manuel! I'm not like them!"

[179] "Don't give me none of that, Manuel. You know very well that I've never liked that bunch of hypocrites that think that I'm some fuckin' housekeeper or some illegal that just crossed over."

[180] "Oh my God, Manuel, enough! Stop it with your fuckin' bullshit!"

[181] "Geez, Manuel, you just don't stop bitchin' about those fuckin' gringos … Don't you get tired of the same bitches, or what?"

"Pues vete! Vete con tus pinche gringos, porque yo no me voy a rebajar quien soy para nadie! Me entiendes? NA-DIE!"[182]

"You know somethin'?!"

"Ya ni la chingues …"[183]

"I'm tired of listenin' to you. I'm getting outta here. You don't understand a damn thing of what I want!"

"Andale vete … pinche cobardé!"[184]

Manny stormed out of the house like he always did, punching the wall, but never hard enough to go through, not yet at least. Just enough to make the wooden studs rattle a bit. The signal for war had been given, and tonight Manny would enlist his monster, his most trusted ally, to make sure he did in fact have the last word. It was just a matter of going off and fetching him and negotiating what kind of punishment Magdalena should receive for her insubordination and disrespect to him. And by the sound of squealing tires piercing the air, the deal making for Manny's monster would be a swift affair. When he finally sprung up from his hiding place, Michael went into the kitchen to find his mother fuming at the kitchen table.

"… Puta madre!"[185] muttered Magdalena.

"Hey …"

"Hay, mijito, no te escuché!"[186]

"What did he get mad 'bout this time?"

---

[182] "Well leave! Go with your fuckin' gringos, because I don't lower myself for no one! You hear me? NO ONE!"

[183] "Enough with the bitchin' already …"

[184] "Fine, leave … fucking coward!"

[185] "… God damnit!"

[186] "Hey, son, I didn't hear you!"

"Ya no se mijito, ya no se."[187]

"What happened? I saw Pastor Roberts leave and …"

"Pendejadas, mijito, puras pendejadas!"[188]

"Over what?"

"Pues … pa'que decir?"[189]

"C'mon, you can tell me …"

"No … no, quiero que te metas con esto."[190]

"I'm gonna find out either way, Mom …"

"Pues … mira … vino el pastorcito a decirnos que a manuel lo iban hacer diacono … pero …"[191] Magdalena responded with apprenhension.

"But what?"

"Pero alguien les dijo que no soy una mujer adequada …"[192]

"What?! Who said that?"

"No, nos dijo, no mas que no me porto como una mujer Cristiana …"[193]

"They just realized that now?" Michael grimaced as he tried to make a joke.

"No seas grocero …"[194]

"Sorry."

"Pues eso fue lo que nos dijo el pendejo!"[195]

---

[187] "You know I don't know anymore son, I don't know."
[188] "Stupidities, son, plain ol' stupidities!"
[189] "Well … what can I say?"
[190] "No … no, I don't want you to get involved in this."
[191] "Well … look … he came to tell us that Manuel was going to be a deacon … but …"
[192] "But someone told him that I wasn't an adequate woman …"
[193] "No, he didn't tell us anything, just that I don't behave like Christian woman …"
[194] "Don't be smart with me …"
[195] "Well that's what the idiot told us!"

"Really?"

"En mi cara me dijo que soy una mala influencia … fíjate nomás!"[196]

"To who? It's not like you talk to anybody at church … just Rebecca."

"No se, mijito … es que me da tanto corajé … y fíjate que lo peor es que el Manuel no me respalda, para nada!"[197]

"Well, he's too busy with church and work. He ain't got time for us … I mean, other than to yell at us."

"Pues el Manuel tuvo los huevos a decir al pastor que todavia tengo mi rosario, mis santos de mis papás …"[198]

"Oooh, I bet that went over well."

"El baboso me dijo que tengo que entregarle todo, o quemarlos …"[199]

"What's that gotta do with anythin'?"

"Siempre la misma cantaleta de esta pinche secta."[200]

"That whole fight was because of that? You're kiddin' me?!"

"Te digo, fue mi culpa mijito … mi maldita culpa!"[201] scoffed Magdalena.

---

[196] "He told me to my face that I'm a bad influence … can you believe it!"

[197] "I don't know, son … it's just that it makes me so angry … and notice that the worst part of it is that Manuel doesn't back me up for anything!"

[198] "Apparently Manuel had the balls to tell the pastor that I still have my rosary, and my saints from my parents …"

[199] "That drooling idiot told me I have to give them to him, or burn them …"

[200] "The same old song from this damn cult."

[201] "I told you, son, it's my fault … it's my damn fault!"

"No it's not, Mom. It's not!"

"No, mijito, asi es … porque soy mujer … la mujer siempre carga la mierda de otros …"[202]

"Yeah, but they don't know him like we do."

"Que pena que no sepan … que pena …"[203]

They stared out the open door as the slowly darkening sky stole more and more daylight from them. The big bougainvillea of the front porch reached her heavy flower laden branches out towards the empty street. Almost as if she wanted to hold Manny back from going out and making another deal with the monster.

"Is it gonna be one of those nights?"

"Creo que si, mijito, creo que si."[204]

"How much time you think we got?"

"Estaba bien enrabiado el cabrón … Quizas sies, siete whiskies."[205]

"It's only 'bout four hours."

"Anda! Ve bañate y alista tu maleta. Te voy hacer algo de comer. No hay nada mas que podemos hacer … nomás esperar."[206]

Michael had forgotten at what point Manny's fights stopped being personal cataclysm and instead became grand inconveniences to plan for. After a time, viciousness and cruelty had an odd way of hardening someone up. At least for them both, the predictability of

---

[202] "I don't know, son, it just is … because I'm a woman … the woman is always carrying the shit of others …"
[203] "It's a shame they don't know … what a shame …"
[204] "I think so, son."
[205] "That asshole was pretty enraged … Perhaps six, seven whiskies."
[206] "Go on! Take a shower and get your bag ready. I'll make you something to eat. There's nothing else we can do … but wait."

violence made them feel as if they could conquer anything like this. This was not an impossibility to survive, but because they survived so many times it became mundane, like taking out the trash. Only this trash was rabid mountain lion. There was no reward for surviving Manny, only a promise to do it again when times shifted and when circumstances wobbled in a way to make the perfect world he was trying to build topple like a house of cards

Michael headed down the dark hallway to his room with gym bag in tow, knowing the drill by heart. He took from the smelly bag his extra set of workout clothes to make more room. He went through his drawers, pulling out socks, underwear, and T-shirts, methodically laying them out on his bed. He pulled out the shoebox and opened the lid to do a quick inventory. The pictures and other keepsakes were still there, squirreled away from Manny's hands. He closed the lid, undid one of the shoelaces of the cradle, and tied it around the box to keep the lid closed before packing it in his gym bag with the rest of his clothes. Once everything was neatly set, he zipped the bag closed and hid it with his backpack in his closet.

Magdalena soon came in, carrying her own bag filled with clothes and photo albums that she too had been hiding from Manny. Like a well-rehearsed play, she handed over her bag and the purse to her son, knowing that in the middle of the next act their drama would eventually be played out here in his room. He took them and hid them alongside his gym bag and backpack, then slid the closet door shut. They looked at each other with halfhearted resolve in the face of an impending battle and the predictability of being a refugee away from their home.

Magdalena said nothing to her son, communicating everything she had to say to him in a hug. She couldn't express that everything was going to be OK, because despite all her boldness she couldn't believe that any of this was OK. She squeezed Michael tight, offering through her embrace to be by his side no matter what was about to happen. With as much dignity as she could muster, she turned around and headed back to the kitchen to make Manny a quick dinner.

Finally alone in his room, Michael could hear the cicadas buzzing softly in his ear as he stared down the open door where the monster would soon be lurking. There wasn't anything right about tonight. It was nothing like the others. So many injustices had gone unanswered, left as open wounds that festered and bled at the slightest provocation. In the quiet he thought about every one of Manny's transgressions against him and Magdalena. He thought about the way Pastor Roberts asked him to kill an innocent boy who haunted his dreams. He thought about the way Jaime and Raul had been tricked into converting. And he thought about Javi and his abrasive behavior toward Diego. All these moments needed something. They lacked resolution and, in Michael's eyes, they warranted a hero. There needed to be someone to right the wrongs. And possibly, through the will to commit righteousness in the name of justice, these might just be the catalysts for him to do manly things. He could be that man whom he needed to be and grow into his straightness. Wasn't that what all the repetitious catechisms inferred?

> *I'll fight against anythin' that*
> *says that I'm not a man.*

The amber eyes of the whiskey monster would be home soon, and his time for prepping would soon be over.

He stripped off his damp workout clothes as the sun was swallowed up behind the darkened clouds in the sky and the last orange glow leaked through the old mini blinds in his room like daggers of gold. While standing there naked and alone in his room, he closed his eyes and pinched the crucifix of the rosary hanging around his neck between his thumb and forefinger, and he prayed:

> *God, please let me be strong for this ...*
> *let this happen so I can be straight ...*
> *let me prove that I can be a man ...*

At the kitchen table, the smell of slightly charred flour tortillas and beans did little to entice their appetites, but they forced down what they could, chewing in obstinate silence. The clouds overhead billowed higher and farther north as the wind began to pick up speed and the southern horizon grew increasingly dark, heralding the oncoming dust that would soon crest the top of South Mountain and rush down the slopes to the neighborhood below. Michael washed their dishes and put them away while Magdalena prepared a single plate of food that she set out on the table, ready for whenever Manny and the monster decided to come home that night. Waiting for war meant that it never started on time, and the crushing anticipation gnawed at their nerves like some desert scavenger finding a less-than-fresh carcass. Magdalena took a seat at the table with a glass of water in her hand, taking sips from it out of a compulsion.

"A ver que pasa, hijo. A ver que pasa,"[207] she said.

It would easily be another hour before the rumble

---

[207] "We'll see what happens, son. We'll see what happens."

of Manny's beat-up truck would come klunking down the street, and by then the plate of food Magdalena had set out on the table would be cold and the beans would be crusty like dried mud. The rumble of thunder shook the roof harder than Manny's fist, and the boom permeated skin like a ghost trying to tickle their hearts. But eventually their heads perked up when the dull yellow headlights pierced the hazy desert dusk and the living room window as Manny crookedly rolled up onto the driveway. The truck lights flooded the house, casting horizontal shadows on the walls from the mini blinds as the long branches of Magdalena's bougainvillea danced in the wind, fluttering in silhouette. The engine puttered for a few minutes as Manny clumsily struggled to put on the parking brake before the muffler shuttered still.

"No te metas, me intiendes?"[208] Magdalena asked Michael as she squeezed his hand.

> *I'll fight against anythin' that*
> *says that I'm not a man.*

"I know … I'll keep my mouth shut."

The door to the truck creaked open as Manny incoherently mumbled as he got out. He slammed the door and stumbled to the front of the house, at times shuffling his feet to make sure they were still on the gritty sidewalk.

"… telllll me I ain't ennnough … she donnn't knnnow …"

He came up to the front door, opened it, and held himself with one hand at the doorjamb while letting the other hand dangle at his side. Manny's eyes were already

---

[208] "Don't get involved, you understand me?"

bloodshot and squinty with dirt. Every now and then, Michael could see the fleeting amber glimmer of a half-drunken whiskey in his eyes. The monster came home tonight, and it leaned in the doorway with an air of grandiosity. The monster had come to do what it does best. To whisper in Manny's ear, telling him just what to do and how to do it. Letting him know that not only was it permissible to get what he wanted, but he must get what he deserved. Besides, he was the man of the house.

The air behind him turned muddy like the cloudy water of July flash flood, and the streetlamps on the other side of the road faded into faint specks of light in the howling winds. Manny took a step into the house, making sure that his footing was solid before he heaved himself awkwardly toward his next step, allowing blowing dirt to come inside. He walked toward them, stepping crookedly but managing to remain upright and smug, until he leaned up against the open doorway of the kitchen. A contemptuous smile grew on his face as he looked at Magdalena and Michael sitting at the kitchen table, not ready to give him a dignified peek at their eyes.

"Well … i-fffff it ain't … m-mmy lovin'… family."

The whiskey monster pulled and pushed Manny's heavy drunk legs toward the table while his spine seemed to be rippling with every tug.

"Te hice cena,"[209] Magdalena said coldly as she slid the plate of food toward him.

"Pffff," Manny scoffed as he looked down at the plate. "You-ssee … that boy?! Mmmm, Looksss-like sheee's good for somethin', huh?"

---

[209] "I made you dinner."

The smell of Manny's whiskey-soaked throat hit Michael's nose with a forceful punch while fine powdery grains of dirt stuck on his tongue and crunched in between his molars. Michael tried to close his eyes to escape the present, but the memories of every night just like this one came bombarding from the past in millisecond replays. Echoes of Manny's angry voice reverberated through the soft tissues of Michael's head, and the disillusioned cries of Magdalena lingered against his eardrums.

I need to fight!

He could not let another night go by without trying to make it stop. Even Magdalena's command for him to stoically stand down hurt Michael. For him, there was a bottle of manliness deep down inside that needed to be poured out to protect the innocent, or else it would explode as a red-hot supernova of uncontrollable rage. He wanted to feel Manny's face crunch on his knuckles, just once. He wanted him to feel pain, real physical pain by his own hand. He wanted Manny to feel scared of the violence that was due to him. He wanted to be drunk with the most primal sense of man. He needed this so he could keep on living. He needed to prove himself. And he needed to know that he was stronger than any faggot that he might be confused with.

"Vas a comer?"[210] she tersely asked her husband.

Manny's head kept wobbling on his relaxed neck as he pointed with disappointment at the cold plate in front of him.

"You … you want-mmme … da eat dis? Disss …

---

[210] "Are you going to eat?"

beaner sshit?”

"Si no lo queires ..."[211] she said as she reached for the plate.

"Noooo!" he shouted as he pushed her hand away.

Manny stared down at the plate of cold crusty beans and began to weep. His lips blubbered in spastic and gasping angst while his eyes squeezed out the tears that streaked the powdery dust into haunting darts of mud, tears that fell to moisten the dried-out food on his plate.

"Why … Why are you-ssso mean to-me?" he cried as the years of pathological inadequacies coalesced into one simmering eruption. "HUH?! … WHY?!"

Both Magdalena and Michael continued to sit in steadfast silence while the outburst unfolded.

"WHY, GODDAMNIT!?" he screamed, smacking the table with his dirty hands. The fork rattled while Michael and Magdalena held themselves down instead of jumping up. The whiskey monster was now making itself fully known to them. Previously, it pulled Manny around like cheap marionette. Now it was being birthed from the mouth of Manny into an amber-colored snake.

"I justed … wanteded some'in better for me's!" he cried. "And you! You took-it … away from me's, like you alwyasssdo … jus' … 'cause you couldn't be like'emm!"

Magdalena pressed her lips tight so as not to let more of her instigating sarcasm fall into the fire of rage. Even though she wanted to speak, she had every memory flooding back, and the invisible bruises of the past whispered caution to her whenever Manny felt drunkenly sorry for himself.

"You know … I'm … I'm tired of bein' the-fuckin

------

[211] "Well if you don't want it …"

dirty … wetback! 'nd, 'nd I gotta chance to not be that! I gotta chance to feel-like sssome big shot gringo, to feel-like a somebody. Donnn-I got a goddamn right to want dat? Don't I?! … ANSWER ME!"

"Miguel vete a tu cuarto,"[212] Magdalena calmly and discreetly commanded her son.

"NO! GODDAMNIT! Sit your-ass down. You-ain't doin ss-shit to help," Manny said, pointing at Michael.

"No le halbes asi a mi hijo!"[213]

"Howareya gonna let her treat me likes this, huh?! Arenchu my son?! I-been a father da-you, but you-dd-don't give a fuck-bout me's, after all I done-frr you!"

"Ya basta, Manuel! Miguel no tiene nada que a ver con esto!"[214]

"No! Fuck that! It'sss both-f you. You-think I like drinkin? You mmmake-me drink! I drink cause you make mmmeee feel lika ssshit!" he yelled, trying to stand up as he held on to the kitchen table.

"Ya deja a mi hijo, cabrón!"[215]

"GOD DAMNIT W'MAN, WE'RE IN FUCKIN' U-U-UNITED ESTATES, SPEAK ENGLISH YOU-WETBACK MM-BITCH!"

"Don't you talk to her like that!" shouted Michael as he immediately shot up and shoved Manny backward.

"Miguel, no te metas! Por Dios, ponte quieto!"[216] Magdalena shouted as she stood up, ready to get in

---

[212] "Miguel, go to your room."
[213] "Do not talk to my son like that!"
[214] "That's enough, Manuel! Miguel has nothing to do with this!"
[215] "Leave my son alone, you asshole!"
[216] "Miguel, don't get involved! For the love of God, calm down!"

between them.

"Oh-you fuckin lil-shit!" growled Manny as he lunged at Michael, grasping and twisting his shirt, trying to hold him. Michael grabbed Manny's clinched hands hard as he grunted and struggled against the whiskey monster, working to break Manny's grip on him. Magdalena tried to pull Manny off, but the loose mass of his arms shoved her away and onto the floor. Michael was unaware that in the scuffle, something had slipped into Manny's view, one of the few secrets Michael had tried to keep to himself. In the incandescent kitchen light was a quick shimmer of crystalline beads that appeared just above Manny's hand, and despite his dizzy focus, Manny recognized what it was.

"What th-fuck is-this?!"

"Get off me, Manny!"

Manny grabbed the rosary tightly in his fist as if trying to pulverize the beads against the crucifix.

"I tol-you I don-wan dis-shit in my goddamn-house!" Manny screamed as he ripped the rosary from Michael's neck. Glass beads shot in all directions with shimmers of multicolored light before the darkness swallowed them up, as if they were fast-burning shooting stars. Instantly, the cicada buzz in his head grew to a piercing volume that made his ears ache and drowned out the noise of the fight.

Suddenly, there in the middle of the kitchen, Michael saw the gnarly dried-up tree in front of him. Droplets of bright red blood were blossoming and falling like ripened fruit, staining the pure white salt where he was standing. But when Michael looked around for the fantasies, all he could find was Manny at the foot of the tree, rolling and holding his face while lying on the linoleum floor. Michael was confused as to where he was, looking to see if his own feet were on salt or on the kitchen floor. The ground at his feet quickly flooded with warm bath water as the red blossoms of the tree dripped around him, swirling in the current around his ankles as Michael tried to find an escape from this all-too-real immersion in his mind. Just as quickly as the tree had appeared, the cicada's song began to die down and Michael could hear the faint voice of a woman shouting behind him. His right hand began to ache sharply from his knuckles and wrist. Suddenly the voice of the woman in his half dream became crystal clear.

"MIGUEL!!!"

When Michael turned around, he was back in the kitchen of Manny's house. Dazed and disoriented, he wondered why a slow-moving Magdalena was pulling his aching arm, begging him to run. He looked down in front of him to see Manny writhing on the floor, but the gnarly old tree was gone. No salt, no crimson bath water. All that was at his feet were the scattered bits of beads and silver chain from his grandmother's rosary.

"Vamonos mijito, por Dios![217]" Magdalena yelled out as she pulled her near catatonic son away. Time finally caught up to Michael and lashed him to realize what he had done. He only had seconds to react before the whiskey monster and Manny clawed their way to their feet in order to get back at him.

Men protect ... I've gotta protect.

Michael turned around and grabbed his mother's hand as they ran out of the kitchen and through the dusty

---

[217] "For God's sake, son, let's get outta here!"

living room. They could only think of one thing—get to Michael's room, where they could lock themselves away from the whiskey monster.

As soon as they were in his room, Michael slammed the door shut, grabbed the old wooden chair at his desk, and used it to barricade the door.

"Maldito perro!"[218] Magdalena cried out as she ran her fingers through her long, loose black hair and then gripped it tightly. "Porque haces esto maldito?! Porque?! Porque?! PORQUUUUEEEE?!?!?!?!"[219] she continued yelling while she pulled her hair, the dark locks undulating in waves from her hands. She tried to rip out her hair, screaming, "Ya no puedo, mijo! Ya no puedo!"[220]

Michael. who had been pushing against the closed door and bracing for the attack, looked back and saw his mother finally breaking down under the pressure. Through all the hard nights, he had never seen his mother beaten down like this. For Magdalena, each stinging tug reminded her of the depressing reality that she was in and had been trapped in for years. But for Michael, the fact that tonight was also his doing was stuck in his mind. His punch is what brought the fury and fire of hell on them, and yet he wanted it still. According to all the catechisms that he was taught, someone had to pay the price of violence so that he could live. Eventually everyone's luxury came at the cost of someone else's oppression. It was odd that it was not the Pastel Jesus doing the sacrificing tonight.

But despite this thirst for the fight, Michael fell to his mom's side with a clash of instinctual mercy as she too

---

[218] "Damn dog"

[219] "God damnit, why do you do this?! Why?! Why?! WHHHHYYYY?!?!?!?!"

[220] "I can't anymore, son! I can't anymore!"

collapsed in the flowering spread of her long skirt. He slid his hands over her arms, locking them down, trying desperately to hold her tight so she would stop pulling her sweaty tangled hair. He calmly and gently rocked her back and forth like she used to do to him, whispering, "You're OK, Mom, it's OK." It was in moments like these during the fight nights that he felt truly alone, where he would come to the precipice of his world and stare at the immense gulf between him and everyone else in his life. And now more than ever, he wondered where all the people from the church were when he needed help.

Peace would not come so easily, and Michael could hear Manny, clumsily getting himself off the kitchen floor, screaming in a deep roar, "Hijo-de-la shingada!"[221] The drunken steps of Manny made clumsy thuds on the floor as he stumbled down the dark hallway with the fury of a stunned bull. He managed to reach Michael's bedroom.

Bang, Bang, Bang …

"Op'n … th-door, Michael!"

"Op'n … th-door ddammnit!"

---

[221] "Son of a bitch!"

Magdalena had stopped weeping as they sat huddled on the floor. Each held their breath and tried their best not to make any noise in the vain hope that Manny would think they had somehow vanished into thin air.

"Op'n … the goddamn-door … Now, you lil-shit!"

Bang …   Bang …   Bang …

"Why you two do-thisss to-me huh?! Aft-everythin' I-do fo-you, this-th'fuckin' thanksss-I get?!" he demanded loudly.

Thud …

Thud …

Thud …

Manny's shoulder hit the door like heavy meat landing on a butcher's slab. The whiskey monster was determined to get in, even if meant using Manny as a battering ram.

"Op'n … th-door Michael this'ss-my house!"
"Leave us alone!" yelled Michael.

Thud …

Thud …

"Op'n th-door, god damnit!" Manny screamed, as the rickety chair Michael had propped up against the door began creaking and loosening every time it took a hit.

Manny's thuds were still heavy, but his rhythm was slowing as he took more and more time to breathe through his whiskey-choked lungs. But even though Manny was locked out of the room, the whiskey monster's venom of hate still seeped in around the door. The seed of revulsion was starting to grow in Michael more with each pound of Manny's body, so much so that Michael's grip on Magdalena's sweaty arms began to tremble and tighten as if he were ready to unleash every fight night he had ever lived through back onto Manny. Every blow by blow and every punch by punch. Magdalena had sat in her son's arms long enough, her tears caught in the folds of her long skirt. As a mother she could not let her son defile himself anymore and fall into the trap of violence that Manny was already lost to.

"Que quieres, Manuel?"[222] she called out as she got up and faced the door.

"Magda!"

It was clear by now that the exhaustion from ramming the door had gotten to Manny. He slumped against the door, trying to hold his limp body up by the doorjamb. His sweaty, dusty face pressed dark smears on the dented white door, and he breathed heavily as he made his plea.

"Magda, jusss-op'n the'goddamn door," he proposed. "Please, Magda, you-owe it'me!"

---

[222] "What do you want ,Manuel?"

"No te debo nada. Me escuchas? Eh? Ahora tu dime … que chingados quieres?"[223]

"Magda, com'on."

Michael got up and was ready to charge the door, open it wide to start raining down blows on the half-incapacitated man, but Magdalena stopped him.

"Vete a la chingada!"[224] she yelled out.

"Whatcha say to'me?"

"Te dije que te vayas mucho a la chingada! Tu y tu puta madre!"[225]

"You'bitch!" he yelled as he kicked the door with his dusty workboot. "This-ss my'house. You-nd'dat lil-shit jus'live here!" Manny mustered up what little whiskey strength remained to kick and punch the seemingly impenetrable door in an unrelenting barrage.

"Ya vete cabron!"[226] she yelled. "Estoy cansada de tus pinche borracheras!"[227] She stepped closer to the door, clenching her fists, tasting the same infectious whiskey monster venom as her son.

"Fine! You wanme-to leave, I'-leave. But when-I come back you'nd the lil-shit better'be outta my'house!" he yelled before stumbling back down the hallway. "Goddamn w'man …"

---

[223] "I don't owe you anything. You listenin' to me? Huh? Now you tell me …what the hell you want?"
[224] "Go fuck yourself!"
[225] "I said go fuck yourself! You and that two-timing whore of a mother of yours!"
[226] "Leave now!"
[227] "I'm tired of your fucking drinking benders!"

Thud

Bang

Thud

"After e'rthing I do for 'em …"

Thud … thud

Bang

Scrape

"Won't e'vn lemme be who I'wanna be."

Thud.

"And dis shit … ?"

Thrash
Thrash
Thrash

The roar of Manny's truck echoed loudly through the house but faded quickly in an eerie post-monsoon silence. It was over for tonight. Magdalena had saved her son from being tainted and lured into the violence of her husband. Michael listened as his opportunity to become straight, his challenge to prove his manliness, walked away from him into the night.

9

The dented door to Michael's bedroom slowly cracked open as a sliver of warm light cut through the darkness. The stench of body odor and raw whiskey breath saturated the air as if Manny's own spirit were still watching them. Michael's silhouette passed over the light as he peeked out into the blackness, trying to see if any lingering demons were still lurking. It had been an hour since Manny left.

"I think he's gone."

"Hay que ya irnos, hijo. No nos podemos quedar aqui,"[228] said Magdalena as she wiped the dripping snot and the salty tears.

"C'mon, get your stuff and let's get outta here," Michael said.

Michael slid open the closet door and grabbed their bags. He handed Magdalena her purse and bag, and he slung on his backpack, ready to lead her to their hideout. Before they left, he scanned the room one last time to make sure he had not forgotten anything. There was one thing,

---

[228] "Let's just leave now, son. We can't stay here."

one small nagging relic that called out to him to not be left behind. There on the nightstand was his torn-up Bible, unassuming with its dull gold-leaf edges. He went to grab and shove it into his backpack like he had always done, but when his fingers touched the worn-out leather cover, it gave him pause.

Where was the help?

It was an absurd hopefulness that he wanted to cling to, that someday in some miraculous way the teachings of Pastel Jesus would bring relief. His feeling rested on the naive notion that the anticipated recompense would be that sweet, sweet rest he read about every time he passed under the Bible verse above the entrance to the church. So what happened? Was God disappointed in him because he didn't seize the opportunity to cure himself? Or worse, did he commit the same sins that Magdalena had been committing, putting the God of her past, the God of her family's rosary, and memory of all that was Mexican before Pastel Jesus?

"Mijito … ?"

He could not help but stare down at the Bible and feel sadness. Sadness that something he did had caused this.

"Mijito, ya vamonos,"[229] said Magdalena.

He looked back at his mother, who was at the door with bag in hand, ready to venture out into the night. He left the Bible on the nightstand, unsure if doing so would bring more retribution upon them for abandoning it. He prayed that Pastel Jesus would give him a little leeway in

---

[229] "Son, let's just go."

his obligations to him, just enough so he could figure out whether what he did was truly that bad.

Michael opened the door to allow the glow of his bedroom to flood the abysmal black void. The luminous rays caught the microscopic desert dust particles still floating, swirling through gentle eddies and vortices of space. As they walked down the hallway, Michael could taste the earthiness in the air just as a solitary bougainvillea flower petal floated along the dingy carpet. As they cautiously made their way to the living room, the odd and dramatic angles of light coming from the floor elevated and enlarged the shadows into abstract phantoms on the walls. Then they rounded the corner into the living room, they could see the hiding place from where obtuse shadow demons were loosed.

The wide-open front door welcomed the dirt to float in gently and blanket the furniture in a layer of talcum-like brown powder, accompanied by soft, paper-thin bougainvillea flowers. The ferocious winds had died to a gentle post-monsoon breeze that blew across the aluminum mini blinds, rattling them in a metallic flutter. Clouds billowed from the floor with each of their steps in an already turbid atmosphere, like astronauts walking on an inhospitable moonscape. Chards of broken thrift store knickknacks littered the floor as shattered artifacts to the tenuous peace. The table lamp lay in pieces, and the shade was mangled like abstract origami, which cast fantastically angular shapes on the bare white walls.

As they stepped carefully through all the brokenness, the magnitude of the mess was of little surprise to them. This had become a familiar calling card of the whiskey monster inside Manny's house. However, when they walked out the front door, they witnessed the extension of violence that the whiskey monster had brought to Magdalena's beloved bougainvillea. Delicate petals floated past them in groups of vibrant pink as they fell away from the mutilated trunk, like final breaths from a loved one In the halogen orange glow of the streetlamp, the torn and fibrous ends of the heavy, flowery boughs lay in savage disarray around the porch and yard. Verdant leaves had been ripped up by the whiskey monster and were now erratic green smears on the concrete, trampled by Manny's boots. Among the many stains on the porch floor, Manny's blood and chlorophyl mingled in splatters, marking the final moments when all that Manny wanted to do was destroy something that Magdalena loved.

For Magdalena, this was far more than the culmination of petty arguments over her skirt length and makeup. She had struck Manny with unrelenting attacks at the one thing he wanted most in life—the respect and affirmation of White men. She had come to recognize that because of her humiliating emasculation, the restraints keeping the putrid and boiling resentment inside him were now broken. And given all that she had experienced, and all that she had endured in her marriage, Magdalena still wanted to inflict more. She wanted the same thing as her son, her unconditional victory over Manny. His complete subjugation and the eventual liberation from the forces of American misogyny. More so because she knew that Manny had cunningly made her dependent on him for everything. She had no job, because the church says that a woman's place is in the home. She had no money, because the church says that the man is head of the household and finances. She had nothing to her name other than the clothes in her bag, because the church says that a man should love and care for his wife as Christ did for the church. She could leave now for a few days to let the hangover pass and for the whiskey monster to retreat into its bottle. With each passing second, she wanted to run farther and farther, but it would only be a matter of time before hunger would lead her back to the necessity of marriage.

"Come on, let's go. There ain't nothin' for us here," Michael said pulling her arm.

Magdalena could feel every mangled flower and every shredded branch cry out from the barren dirt of Manny's front yard. They cried out for mercy and remembrance. Manny had taken everything from her, and she was once again wandering the night looking for refuge. In these times of unprecedent violence, she could not simply stand idly by and let this happen. She needed her dignity, even if it was only fragments of herself. Otherwise, she would just disappear, like everything else.

"Sabes que, ya basta con estas chingaderas!"[230]

She went back into the house and searched the kitchen cabinets for a towel, slamming doors and rustling through drawers. When she found one, she ran it under the faucet until it was dripping wet. When she turned around, the rainbow sparkle of crystalline beads on the floor caught her eye. She pulled out a clean plastic sandwich bag from another drawer and went over and picked up as many beads as she could find, crawling under the table to search for the crucifix and pieces of chain. She took the sopping wet towel and the sandwich bag outside with her, dripping on the floor and making a trail of muddy splatters in the living room. When she returned outside, she handed Michael the pieces of her mother's rosary and her purse.

---

[230] "You know what, son, enough with this fucking bullshit!"

"Detenme esto!"[231]" She knelt down among the remains of her bougainvillea, "Hijo de su chingada madre! A ver si no te pago con la misma moneda y te doy chingazo, tus huevos cabrón!"[232]"

She carefully pulled out the most salvageable branch she could find, a sturdy branch on which the leaves had not yet wilted and flowers were still blossoming like Aaron's staff. She laid the branch in the towel and wrapped it as if she were swaddling a baby, letting it drink deeply so as not to wither away. Regaining what dignity she could, Magdalena wiped the final tears from her eyes, stood up, and slung her purse over her shoulder.

"Nos vamos hijo. Me canse de ver las pendjedads de tu padrastro,"[233] she commanded as she and Michael left the house, with the door wide open.

The rolling hum of overheated tires on semimolten asphalt beckoned them as they neared the main drag of Central Avenue. The oncoming headlights rushed closer to them, only to taunt an instantaneous flash as cars zoomed past the impersonal and barren sidewalk. The monsoon storm was traveling well northward toward the high country, and ricochets of lighting arced in the fluffy indigo lantern of the thunderhead. The bluish strobes could be seen beyond the silhouette of the downtown towers as office lights shimmered in the distortive heat of the city. In the orange of the streetlamps, Michael's and Magdalena's shadows grew and shrank as they hurried along, hoping to

---

[231] "Hold this for me!"
[232] "That fucking son of a bitch! We'll see if I don't repay you and punch you in the balls, you asshole!"
[233] "Let's go. son. I'm tired of looking at the stupidities of your stepfather."

avoid an even more inebriated Manny who could easily chase them right back behind the locked bedroom door. Luckily, even if Manny tried to hunt them, the trail of dripping water from Magdalena's bougainvillea branch had slowed to sporadic drops on the sidewalk that quickly evaporated.

It was close to nine p.m. when they approached the Round One Boxing gym with milk-colored puddles of fluorescent light illuminating the gritty sidewalk. Coach Padilla stepped out onto the street, kicking the large rock that propped open the door so he could lock up for the night. The two phantom shadows startled him as they approached, searching for their posada as had become their custom.

"A chingado,[234] you scared the shit outta me!"

"Hey, Coach," said Michael.

"Are you guys all right? Did Manny start shit again?"

"Yeah …"

"Did he hurt you?!"

"No … no, not this time."

"Bueno … que bueno …" he said, letting the plans for retaliation recede.

"But it got kinda bad, though … Can we stay here again?"

"Hay, Miguelito, why do you even ask? Claro que si!"

"Thanks, Coach."

"Butchya know you guys don't gotta sleep here, right?"

"I know, Coach, but it's only for couple of nights."

---

[234] "Oh shit."

"Y que?"

"We don't have a car and don't wantchu to be drivin' us back and forth."

"You know it ain't no problem. You can stay with me and Marianna."

"Hay Felipe, muchas gracias pero no queremos molestarte,"[235] answered Magdalena.

"Señora, no me molesta."[236]

"Vamos estar bien aqui, en serio."[237]

"Deveras pueden quedarse con nosotros, no hay problema."[238]

"Solo va hacer un par de dias Felipe …"[239]

"Está bien señora, está bien," he finally relinquished. "Oye, que tienes en la mano?"[240]

"Hay, una ramita de mi bugambilia. Me puedes prestar un vasito de agua?"[241]

"Si, si claro. Pasale, pasale."[242]

Without any more hesitation, Coach Padilla ushered mother and son into the empty boxing gym. The lingering smell of cleaner and bleach wafted in the damp cool air and welcomed them to their inn for the night. The Mexican and American flags hanging in the rafters lay still, and the posters of boxers watched over them like sweaty macho saints.

---

[235] "Oh Felipe, thank you but we don't want to be a bother."
[236] "Mam, It's no bother."
[237] "We'll be fine here, seriously."
[238] "You sure, you can stay with us, there is no problem."
[239] "It's only going to be for a couple of days, Felipe …"
[240] "Whatcha got in your hand?"
[241] "Oh, just little branch from my bougainvillea. Do you have a little glass of water that you can lend me?"
[242] "Yeah, yeah sure. Come on in, come on in."

"Mire, señora, tengo unos vasos aqui …"[243] said Coach Padilla as he started rummaging through closets and drawers looking for some empty cups.

While Coach and Magdalena were occupied, Michael headed into Coach's office. He dropped his bag and backpack onto the concrete floor as he looked around at the pictures and memorabilia that Coach had collected over the years—a few championship belts in picture frames, a pair of worn-out boxing gloves dangling on a hook, and many pictures in a patchwork mosaic on the walls. One grainy photo caught Michael's attention. Coach Padilla was in the ring as a young heavyweight fighter, shirtless and sweaty, throwing a last-minute uppercut just before the bell rang. Michael felt an envious admiration for Coach Padilla whenever he looked at this photo. He hoped that one day he could achieve that level of manliness and roughness that was demanded of him. He played back the events of the evening, but the seductive memory of actually striking Manny was fading quickly, soon to be lost under the gains of salt and buried under the gnarly old tree. The only true record of it was the sore and tight tendons in his right hand as they pulled across his knuckles when he made a fist. The chance to prove his manliness was gone.

"Oye! Was this one pretty bad or what?" Coach Padilla shouted out to Michael as he walked into the office.

"Yeah, it got pretty bad, Coach."

"Hijole, your mom looks pretty upset."

"It was worse than last time."

"Pues si, you can just see it on her face."

---

[243] "You know, mam, I've got some cups around here somewhere …"

"See what?"

"La tristeza …"[244] Coach Padilla shook his head in disbelief. "Your mom is a good woman. She doesn't deserve that."

"No, she doesn't … where is she?"

"Oh, she went to the bathroom. I found her a water bottle someone left behind for her little ramita. By the way, what's up with that?"

"That's all Manny's doin' …"

"Huh?"

"I haven't seen him blow up like that. We usually just lock ourselves in my room when he gets mad and let him blow off some steam in the living room and then he leaves. But this one … this one was big!"

"Que hizo el cabrón?"[245]

"He came after us, then he tried to break into my room. When he couldn't get in, he went outside and tore up my mom's plant."

"Oh shit!? Are you serious? Did he hurt you guys?"

"Nah, but I punched him …"

"Deveras?!"[246] Coach Padilla exclaimed.

"Yeah, bare knuckles. My hand still hurts."

"Orale, chingón!"[247] he said, happily trying to play box with Michael.

"Hey, hey, hey, watch it … I ain't proud of it."

"Como que no?!"[248]

"I don't even 'member hittin' him, just blanked

---

244 "The sadness …"
245 "What'd that asshole do?"
246 "Really?!"
247 "Right on, you badass!"
248 "Why not?!"

out, and next thing I know he was on the floor."

"A la verga!"[249]

Michael let out a small chuckle before he stared off again.

"It's gettin' bad, Coach, real bad … And I'm scared he's gonna get worse."

"You shouldn't be havin' to take shit from anyone like that!"

"I know, but what can you do?"

"Man, if I could I'd go over there right now and have it out with Manny. I tell you what, there wouldn't be just one chingazo between me and him, you know what I mean?"

"I know you would, 'cause I want it too."

"It's a lotta bullshit you two have to put up with, but you guys aren't alone. You and your mom can live with us. It don't have to be like this."

"I know, I know! I keep thinkin' about when I leave for ASU and takin' my mom with me. Get her outta the house and just leave all this behind. We've had enough practice leavin'. For once, just once, I want it to be the last time."

"And how come you don't?"

Michael couldn't look at his face, fearing that his eyes were traitors to his secret. So instead he stared blankly through the photo of Coach Padilla on the wall, past the cheering spectators into the infinite blackness between the faces. There was some primitive survival instinct that made going with Coach and his wife the most logical decision of his life. He could even smell the roses of peace if he would just say yes. However, he could not break the binding

---

[249] "Oh fuck!" (Literally – to the dick!)

chains that held him to Manny. As long as he was haunted by the dream and the boy, he still needed Manny in the end. Either as the father he needed, or as the object of insidious prejudice that could kill the effeminate. Even now the prophetic words of Pastor Roberts were ringing in his brain:

> *Older gay men prey on young*
> *boys looking for father figures.*

"I got my reasons, Coach. Still have some things to figure out."

"What kinda things, other than him bein' an asshole."

"Dad things …" Michael said rather coyishly.

"Really?! You got daddy issues with a man that ain't even your real dad?"

"Yeah … it's hard to explain … but I do. I don't wanna leave without figurin' them out, at least for me to be OK with not knowing I tried."

"Hay, Miguelito, ain't no one in this world that don't have daddy issues."

"E'rybody?"

"Claro que si! You see that guy in my corner right there?" Coach pointed to the photo Michael was staring at. "That's my old man, 'El Bronco.' Man, did we used to get into it!"

"Really?"

"O si, tanto que me jodiaba.[250] Always wanted me to fight like him, after me to press and press my opponent till he got tired. Never understood that's not my style. I like

---

[250] "Oh yeah, he used to try my fuckin' patience."

to take my time, you know. Wait for them to make a mistake. God, we used to get in so many fights about that shit."

"Geez!"

"I shit you not, we just couldn't be around each other in the end, so I had to go off and do my own thing, you know?"

"I guess …"

"Hay hombre, no me andes con eso![251] You gotta make your own life, just like everyone else."

"Yeah, I know. There's just a lotta stuff goin' on in my head, you know?"

"What kinda stuff?"

The possibility of divulging his secret to Coach put him on edge, so he tried to find another scapegoat for his trepidation.

"What if leavin' is the wrong thing to do? Like the way I wanna."

"What you mean?"

"What if God punishes me for makin' my mom leave? What if God's been punishin' us because we have been leavin'?"

Coach Padilla began awkwardly and strangely looking up at the ceiling and exposed rafters above their heads.

"What?"

"Nothin'."

"Whatchu lookin at?" Michael asked.

"Just waitin'."

"Waitin for what?"

"You punched Manny?"

---

[251] "Come on, man, don't be playin' me like that!"

"Yeah …"

"Just waitin for lightin' to hit you," he said.

"Shut up!"

"No, I'm serious! Manny's gotta be La Gran Caca for you to be scared of him like that!"

"I ain't scared of him. I'm just tryin' to do the right thing."

"Chalé!"[252]

Just as they were talking, Magdalena graced the threshold of the doorway with a full water bottle in hand and her refreshed bougainvillea branch peacefully reclined in the water.

"Mijito, tienes mi maleta?"[253]

"Yeah, it's in here, Mom."

As she walked into the office, Coach Padilla tried one last time.

"Señora, esta segura de que se quieren quedar aqui? No hay problema si se quedan con nosotros."[254]

"Si, Felipe, yo y Miguel vamos estar bien aqui. En serio, no somos Desamparados, nomás andamos vagando por ahorita. A ver que pasa en la mañana."[255]

"Esta bien, pero si por cualquier razón quieren irse a la casa no mas me dicé."[256]

"Gracias, Felipe," she said, setting the plastic water bottle and branch on Manny's old green desk.

---

[252] "Fuck that!"

[253] "Son, you got my bag?"

[254] "Mam, are you sure you want to stay here? It's not a problem if you stay with us."

[255] "Yes, Felipe, me and Michael are going to be fine here. We're not destitute, just being vagabonds for now. We'll see what happens in the morning."

[256] "All right, but if for any reason you want to go to the house, just lemme know."

"Mira, te tengo unas cobijitas, sabanas, almouadas, y un catre escondiditas aqui para ustedes,"[257] he said to her as he opened a small broom closet in his office.

"Hay, Felipe, haces de mas."[258]

"No se preocupe, señora, de tanto que vienen compre todo esto para ustedes."[259]

"Hay, gracias, Felipe. Deveras."

"Mira, para que no anden preocupados, mañana viene mi mujer con desayuno para ustedes."[260]

"Thanks, Coach."

"You like chorizo and egg burritos?"

"I do."

Coach gave Michael a pat on the back as he shook Magdalena's hand.

"Se les ofrece halgo mas …"[261]

"Si, yo se, Felipe, yo se,"[262] she said as she cracked a smile.

"Voy a cerrar la puerta. Buenas noches."[263]

"Buenas noches, Felipe."

"Night, Coach."

Coach Padilla's long shadow slipped farther away from them as he dragged it to the front door. With a loud click, the lights in the gym shut off, and the rolling clunk of the deadbolt locked them inside their little haven. All

---

[257] "Look, I have some blankets, bedsheets, pillows, and a cot that I've been hiding away for you guys."

[258] "Oh, Felipe, you do more than you have to."

[259] "Don't worry, mam, for as many times as you guys come, I bought them for you guys to have here."

[260] "Look, so that you guys don't have to worry, tomorrow my wife will come with breakfast for you."

[261] "If you need anything …"

[262] "Yes, I know, Felipe. I know."

[263] "I'll go lock the door. Good night."

that was left was the bare bulb lights of Coach's office, which created long, deep, and sharp shadows on their faces, especially around Magdalena's puffy eyes. Michael sat down next to her as he had done countless times when he was a little boy, silent and wide-eyed even now at age 18. They felt the warmth of their bodies in such a narrow space, together in harmonious mourning.

"Ay mijito, como quisiera que tuvieras otra vida. Una vida sin estas pendejadas de ese cabrón."[264]

Michael gingerly slipped his sweaty tanned hand into hers, and she tried to wipe the salt crust left behind from the tears on her face.

"I know. There's a lotta things I wish were different too. A lotta things."

"Yo nunca queria que tu vida fuera esto. Vale madre vivir asi!"[265]

"It's not your fault. None of it is."

"Yo se mijito. Pero ni modo, mereces mejor!"[266]

He felt his stomach cringe tightly when his mom said that. He and Magadalena knew they both deserved more than this and that life could not be the long valley of tears that the church and Pastor Roberts made it out to be. This wall was equally as impossible to scale every time they ran into it. They knew that respite and sanctuary were just on the other side if only they could get there. Faith kept telling him that one day things would change if he just believed in Pastel Jesus. One day Manny would change. One day the desire for men would go away. One day he

---

[264] "Son, you don't know how much I wish that you had a different life. A life without this bullshit from that asshole."
[265] "I never wanted your life to be this. It's bullshit to live like this."
[266] "I know, son. But nonetheless you deserve better!"

wouldn't have to hide himself or the family relics. But reason patiently and gracefully impressed upon him the reality and likelihood that change would not come to him through benevolence like it did for the believing White people at church. Change would happen only if either he or Magdalena did something to birth that change.

As he continued to ponder this, Michael pulled his hand from her clammy palm and reached around to hug Magdalena, pulling her closer. She laid her head on his chest so the soft and gentle rhythmic thuds of his heart would give her hope that her sorrow could be assuaged. Even though Pastor Roberts was explicit that Michael maintain a distance from his mother so he could shed his queer and effeminate ways, the feeling of another human cleaving to him like a wounded bird finding refuge made him feel like the man was supposed to be. It was an extraordinarily intoxicating sense of self, an almost narcotic euphoria, and he did not want it to end. He was baffled that he didn't get this feeling from a firm handshake or the practice of catechisms or the psychological murder of fantasies. He couldn't tell whether God had bestowed masculinity on him. It was strange, because he hadn't earned this sense. It was as if the sense of self was always there, buried beneath the obligation to ideas and covenants not his own.

"Mom?"

"Si mijito?"

"How do you put up with so much?"

"Es que uno aprende muy pronto como aguantar …"[267]

---

[267] "It's because one learns really quick how to put up with a lot …"

"You ever afraid this will make you bitter like Manny?"

"Quizas … porque los perros no nacen, los hacen a cuartazos."[268]

"What happens if you turn into a dog like them?"

"Quizas tendre los huevos para confronter la vida, mijito."[269]

That night Michael began a metamorphosis, in that he could no longer see Manny, Pastor Roberts, George, or any of the other men as possessing the same fortitude as the Mexican woman sitting next to him. How was it that the cure for his affliction was supposed to have come by following the footsteps of the men before him but now evidently had arrived by the way of a woman?

Before Magdalena had a chance to drift off to sleep, Michael quietly got up and went to the closet to pull a bedsheet. Then he knelt down next to his bag, rummaging through the underwear, socks, and T-shirts to find the old shoebox of family treasures still tied up with the shoestring. He reverently untied the knots and lifted the lid like Moses opening the Ark of the Covenant, taking account of all the family relics.

Behind the desk on a shelf under the picture, Coach Padilla kept a little tape-deck radio.

"Mom, is it too quiet in here?"

"Si mijito."

Michael went over and turned it on, tuning it past the KPRY station until the static cleared up near the end of the dial. The speaker let forth the soft weeping melody of

---

[268] "Perhaps … because dogs aren't born, they're made by hitting them."

[269] "Perhaps I'd have the balls to confront life, son."

mariachi violins that came floating into the office like a spirit.

"Hay mijito! Subele!"[270] Magdalena said as her thirsty soul drank in the bitter tequila-flavored words of the song, giving meaning to all her sorrow.

She closed her eyes and was instantly transported back home. The cold, crisp blue sky and the mountains were around her while songs like this played on the old radio in their home. She could see her family and her husband when he was alive, and the time before America, Manny, and the Church. It was a stunningly beautiful and tragic sentiment that her own words could not express, yet she felt vividly in every fiber of her skin. There was a happiness to be felt in the sadness and longing for the nostalgia instead of the hollow hope she lived in now.

When Michael sat back down on the couch, he unfolded the light-blue bedsheet and draped it around them, pulling her close to him once again in the dim light of the office.

"Here, been keepin' this safe for you," he said as he lowered the plastic sandwich bag of loose rosary beads into her hand.

"Que bonito, no? Aunque esté quebrado."[271] She smiled, feeling the familiarity of her past as she pulled out a chain of unbroken beads from the bag.

There, locked up in the dim office of the boxing gym, they surrounded themselves with the things denied to them for so long. With Magdalena resting on him holding the pieces of her mother's rosary, Michael drifted in and out of consciousness. His heavy lids transported him back

---

[270] "Son! Turn it up!"

[271] "It's pretty, isn't it? Even though it's broken."

to the salt desert and the gnarly old tree. There, he found his male and female fantasies sitting under the twisted shadows of the branches and the warm sun, and for the first time in a long time he didn't want to disturb them. He wanted to leave them alone as they peacefully gathered in their favorite place like two wild deer, innocent and quiet. As the infinite indigo-blue horizon encircled him, no stinging song of the cicadas could be heard, with only the soft breeze whistling past his ears, kindly whispering,

"Padre nuestro que estas en los cielos, sanctificado sea tu nombre ..."[272]

---

[272] "Our Father who art in heaven, hallowed be your name ..."

10

The morning light cut through the sand-etched glass of the Round One gym, making the copper-colored skin of all the young men glow like new ingots from the smelter. Bobbing heads capped by charcoal-smudged hair moved about while they kept light on their toes. The praxis of this aggressive ballet was taking place on the stage of the boxing ring, under the gently waving Mexican and American flags. Standing around the heavy bags near the storefront windows, Michael tried to shake off last night's events while working with Diego.

Smack-Smack–Smack-Smack.
Smack-Smack–Smack-Smack.
Smack-Smack–Smack-Smack.

"Hold up, hold up, hold up man," Michael said to Diego.

"What?! What I'do? What's wrong?"

"You ain't getting your full reach, man."

"Am I too close, or what?"

"Yeah. Here, put your arm out like your gonna

234

throw a jab."

"Like this?"

"Yeah, that's 'bout how far away you should be. Try it like that."

"Like this?" asked Diego as he threw a hard jab at the bag.

"Yeah, just like that."

After a few more combos, Diego dropped his hands to shake them out. "Ain't you gonna do some bag work?"

"Nah, man, I'm takin' it easy today. Kinda hurt my hand yesterday."

"You serious?"

"Yeah, it's nothin. Just a lil' accident, that's all."

"You sure?"

"Yeah, it ain't no thing."

Diego's ropey arms flexed, showing off his bourgeoning strength as he resumed with punch after punch. All the while, Michael caught himself in one those familiar moments of covetousness, breathing heavily while biting his lip. He knew he should not have allowed himself to watch Diego for so long, but he just wanted a few more moments to feel the warm thrill of carnal human desire before the reactive and well-entrenched catechisms pulled his attention to much more bland subjects. Once in his life, he wanted to experience something other than the pain or consternation of not being human enough, even if that feeling was deemed "sinful."

> *I'd thought it would have gone away by now.*
> *Something should've changed.*

Although he was afraid to bring the thought

forward, there was an ominous possibility that he had never considered until now, since doing so was a severe taboo.

Is all this a lie?

Michael was scared to question the God he was raised to know, let alone the methods of redemption and sanctification that were guaranteed to work for him if he just had one more ounce of faith. He was sure that last night he sensed a primordial oneness of being male. Somewhere between punching Manny and hearing Magdalena pray, he was certain that an inalienable part of being human awoke in him that was as much a part of him as his hands and feet. But he worried that what he had been searching for had evaporated when Diego walked in, and he was stuck with his desires again. He would close his eyes to replay the fresh memory on the backs of his eyelids, of his mother seeking consolation and with the powerful euphoric feeling of being a hero to someone hurt even while he himself was swirling in the same summer sandstorm of whiskey, violence, and delicate flower petals. The purely instinctual electricity running through every fiber of his nerves to comfort and shelter Magdalena from all the cruelties in the world surely must have catapulted him into the ranks of manhood, where his sexualization of men would be satiated.

Yet there was no parting of the heavens later that night, and no dove of the Holy Spirit cascading down to anoint him in permanent and irrevocable straightness. He felt as if the promised miracle was denied to him as soon as the golden Arizona sun peeked over the eastern mountains and illuminated Diego when he walked in that morning.

While he tried to hold on to that intoxicating rush of that feeling for as long as he could, the image of Magdalena leaning on him quickly disintegrated into a shimmering mirage on the great salt desert of his dreamscape. And just as quickly, his two fantasies were there to greet and haunt him again, standing silent, stoic, and barefooted in the salt grains, shaded by the sparse shadow of the dead gnarly tree. Peacefully they watched in anticipation of Michael drawing near to either of them, but deep down Michael wanted to kill one of them.

He wanted to resort to flames like he had been taught, to rid himself of this plague. The boy who insidiously stripped him of his maleness again and again and caused him to fall deep in the trap of fantasizing about malice. But how he? Michael was them, and they were Michael. But Michael still could not bring himself to murder the boy more than he already had. It was one thing to imagine the boy wrapped in the shroud of amber flames, but it was another to try to cut that part of him out altogether. The more Michael thought of it, the more the cicadas buzzed in his ears.

Gotta think of somethin' else,
gotta think of somethin' else ...

He opened his eyes and looked up at the open roof and its old wood trusses as a quick inert object to focus on while the stinging buzz slowly waned. Like a desperate chain smoker taking a long drag from a cigarette, Michael breathed in deep his neutral relief as he came back to earth.

"You OK? You kinda spaced out there," said Diego.

"Yeah, I'll be fine …"

They continued training for a while, until the front door to the gym opened and out of the early morning heat strutted in a fine young girl with long black hair, tight jeans, and simple T-shirt. Her tanned bouncing curves immediately cut through the thick testosterone ambiance, making heads turn.

"Quiuvole chulita!"[273] called out one of the guys who was sparring in the ring.

"Chinga tu madre, baboso!"[274] she said, rolling her eyes and crisply flipping him off.

"Ohhhhh shit, she called you out, bro!" another guy taunted with a laugh, causing the guy who catcalled to retreat into the background noise.

The determined and unwavering young woman made a beeline for Michael and Diego, who by now were standing next to the swinging bag wondering what all the commotion was about.

"Diego! Vamonos ya!"[275] she said with a snap of her fingers.

"Why? What for?"

"We need to go baboso! Andalé!"

"Patti, I'm in the middle of …"

"No andes chingando cabrón![276] Mom needs to go to the store."

"Why doesn't she just go? You don't need me!"

"We need someone to babysit Juanito, pendejo!"

"And why can't you?"

"'Cause I'm drivin'! Andale, go get your stuff! We're goin righ'now!"

---

[273] "What's up cutie!"
[274] "Go fuck your mother, dumbass!"
[275] "Come on! Let's go!"
[276] "Don't be fuckin' around with me, asshole!"

Diego scoffed by smacking his lips "ehhhh."

"Siguele, cabron, a ver que pasa!"[277]

Diego begrudgingly pulled off his gloves and started gathering his things while still mumbling displeasure.

Michael was immediately struck by this morena beauty who had abruptly commandeered his lust away from her brother. Sure, he still liked the tight physique of Diego, but there was something about an angry Mexican woman that made her more interesting than any of the other women he knew. Michael even wondered whether his earlier thoughts did end up falling on the soft ears of Pastel Jesus and whether this could possibly be a divine response, another miraculous chance for him to redeem himself. He had already let the feeling of being a man slip away into the salt desert, and if he was too much of a coward to kill the desire for men, then he would have to choose the one over the other. He would have to make a move now.

"Hi! I'm, uhm ..." Michael stammered.

"Yeah?!"

"I'm Michael," he awkwardly blurted out, extending his hand to shake hers but forgetting that he was still wearing his boxing gloves.

"Soy Patti." She smirked as he bashfully pulled his hand back. "So, you're the one teaching little Diegito to fight, huh?"

"I am."

"OK, do I pay you now or ....?"

"What?! Pay? Nah nah ... I'm, I'm just one the guys that ... works out here."

---

[277] "Keep it up, asshole, see what'll happen!"

"So, you ain't the coach?"

"Nah, Coach Padilla is that big guy over there …"

"So whattayou do here?"

"Oh, I just uhm … I train, yup, that's what I do … I practice, maybe help Coach with some sparring … you know, the usual."

"Hmmmm …" She huffed at him while giving a wry little smile.

"What?"

"Nothin'."

"Nah seriously, what?"

"I hope your fightin' is better than your game ..." She smiled.

"Game?! What game?"

"Wow, OK … I'm gonna go now." She laughed before turning her attention back to her brother. "Andale mocoso! We have to go! Mom's waiting in the car!"

"Hay voy, hay voy!" whined Diego. "Thanks for workin' with me, Miguel. See you tomorrow?"

"Yeah, sure thing!" Michael muttered.

"Andale, chamaco mugroso,"[278] scolded Patti as she pressed her lips together, making sure her laugh didn't escape.

And with that, she quickly ushered Diego out of the gym and into the searing Arizona sun. Michael stood alone in the white daylight coming in from the window. Patti's waves of commotion were quickly swallowed up by the gym's testosterone. But that giggle pulled at him like a hook caught in the gills of a fish.

---

[278] "Come on, you snot-nosed little brat."

******

It was a couple of days later and the heat was beating down outside as the swamp coolers squealed nonstop to fight off the Arizona summer. They had not heard anything from Manny, and Manny knew better than to come to the gym. It was just best to wait about a week for his temper to cool down. By that time, he would usually get hungry and realize that without Magdalena, he would starve. It was a sharp contrast to how Magdalena was passing her day, completely secluded from mostly everyone. She constantly questioned whether this was a right place for her and Michael and considered how easy it would be to disappear with her son and start all over again. The damnation of this seemingly endless cycle of abuse was only in its second year now, and even her brilliant resilience and fortitude was wearing out.

Michael was finding it difficult to concentrate on anything else. His hand was still throbbing, and the more he trained, the more he felt the dull ache radiate up his arm. He couldn't take much more training. So he strolled back to Coach's office, looking forward taking to a hot shower and putting on clean clothes. When Michael got to the door of the office, he found that it was left open slightly enough for him to hear two women talking inside. Earlier that morning, Marianna had brought them burritos for breakfast again, which left the lingering and satisfying bold aroma of chile and pork in the air. Hungry for more than just food, Magdalena took the opportunity to comadrear with someone she trusted. A streak of mischievous intrigue came over Michael, and he decided to eavesdrop on the conversation. So he crouched out of sight of any of the guys in the gym, leaning against the doorjamb.

"Hay, Magda, no te cansas de tanto pleito con tu marido, o que?"[279] Marianna asked Magdalena

"Pues claro que me canso Marianita, como no?"[280]

"Pues es lo que te estaba diciendo, esto es de mas comadre! Como pueden aguantar tanto? Necesitan un cambio!"[281]

"Es que no hay remedio, Marianita, entiendelo no hay salida. No hay nada que pueda hacer, nomás tengo que aguantar el peoresnada de mi esposo."[282]

"Claro que te entinedo comadre pero no seas tan bruta. A mi, como mujer … a mi me da mucho coraje como los tratan. A ti no te da coraje como el Manny se trata a tu hijo?"[283]

"Como no! Me quema hasta el corazon."[284]
"Entonces?"[285]

"Estoy atrapada! No tengo dinero, ni chamba, ni madre, para salvarnos. No tengo na-da."[286]

"Por Dios, comadre. Sabes muy bien que se

---

[279] "Oh, Magdalena, don't you get tired of all these fights with your husband, or what?"
[280] "Well of course I get tired of this Marianita, how could I not?"
[281] "Well it is like I was saying, it's too much comadre! How can you guys put up with so much? You guys need a change!"
[282] "It's because there is no other way, Marianita, understand there is no way out. There is nothing that I can do, other than put up with this good-for-nothing husband."
[283] "Of course I understand you, comadre please don't be so blunt. It's just for me, as a woman … I just get really angry with how he treats you guys. Don't you get angry with how Manny treats your son?"
[284] "How could I not! It even scorches my heart."
[285] "Well then?"
[286] "I'm trapped! I don't have any money, I don't a job, I don't have shit to save us from this. I've nothing."

pueden quedar con nosotros. Hasta que puedas encontrar chambita por haí!"[287]

"Gracias, Marianita. Pero no es questíon de dinero. Es que … es que hay … algunas … cosas que me tienan atada con Manuel."[288]

"Como que?"[289]

"Es … no no no mejor no digo."[290]

"Dime, comadre, por fa?"[291]

"Es que … algo me dice que el Manuel esta tratando de quitarme a mi hijo."[292]

"Que, que?"[293]

"Te estoy diciendo la verdad, esta jugando chueco con Miguel."[294]

"Pero como, comadre? Ni es el padre del pobre muchacho, como te lo va quitar?"[295]

"No se, no se, pero siento algo muy profundo en mi ser de que las cosas no estan bien. Hace mucho que

---

[287] "My God, comadre! You know very well that you can stay with us. Even until you can find a job somewhere!"
[288] "Thank you, Marianita. It's not a question of money. It's that … it's that there's … something … that still has me tied to Manuel.
[289] "Like what?"
[290] "It's … no, no no it's better not to say anything."
[291] "Tell me, comadre, please?"
[292] "It's that … something tells me that Manuel is trying to take away my son."
[293] "Wait, what?"
[294] "I'm telling you the truth, he's doing something crooked with Miguel."
[295] "But how, comadre? He's not even the poor kid's dad, how's he going to take him away?"

Miguel ha cambiado."[296]

"Cambiado como que, en contra de ti?"[297]

"No tanto en mi contra, olvidate de eso. Desde que empezo a ir con el … cara mil chingazos del pastor, Miguel ha cambiado. Muchismo! Como muy alejado de mi."[298]

"Pero como comadre. Tu y tu hijo son como uña y mugre."[299]

"Te lo juro, Marianita. Me he fijado, como quiere decirme algo pero … algo lo detiene."[300]

"Y nunca has hablo con el de esto."[301]

"No … nunca, de los nuncas ha podido hablar de eso. Porque cada vez que trato de pregunatarle, me sale con una mentira."[302]

"A lo mejor no es nada, tu sabes como son los hombres. Si no hay cerveza y comida, no se fíjan en nada."[303]

---

[296] "I dunno, I dunno, but I feel something really profoundly in me that things are not right. It's been a long time since Miguel had changed."

[297] "Changed like how, that he's against you?"

[298] "Not so much against me, forget about that. Ever since he started going to see the pastor with a face like someone punched him one thousand times, Miguel had changed. Like he is really distant from me."

[299] "But how, comadre. You two are like two peas in a pod." (Literal translation: you two are close like fingernails and the dirt under the fingernails.)

[300] "I swear to you, Marianita. I've just noticed, like he wants to tell me something … but something holds him back."

[301] "And you've never just talked about it with him?"

[302] "No …never, never have I been able to talk to him about it. Because every time I try to ask him, he ends up lying to me."

[303] "Maybe it's nothing, you know how men are. If there is no beer and food, they ain't gonna notice anything."

"Ojala, Marianita, ojala … pero fijate que hay otra cosa, otra cosita que me he fijado en el."[304]

"Dime."[305]

"Hace poca que empezo a dicerle 'papa' al Manuel."[306]

"Ahh jodido!"[307]

"Exacatamente! Que babosadas son esas?!"[308]

"Pensé que el Miguel lo odiaba?"[309]

"Yo tambien, pero ahora sale con esto! Que chingados!?"[310]

"Hay, comadre, eso es muy canijo! Como le puede coresponderle asi, como papá. Con tanto daño que les ha hecho a ustedes?!"[311]

"No se, pero yo digo hay algo que tiene que ver con ese pastorsito, el desgraciado!"[312]

"Hay ni lo mencionas a ese tipo enfrente de Felipe, no puede ver lo ni en pintura al cabrón!"[313]

"Felipe no lo quiere?"[314]

---

[304] "Hopefully Marianita, hopefully … but there's something else, one other thing that I've noticed."

[305] "Tell me."

[306] "It hasn't been that long that I heard him calling Manuel 'Dad.'"

[307] "Oh fuck!"

[308] "Exactly! What kinda bullshit is that?!"

[309] "I thought Miguel hated him?"

[310] "I did too, but then he comes out with this! What the fuck!?"

[311] "Oh, comadre, that is really fucked up! How can he just give him that place of being his father. With all the harm that he's done to you guys?!"

[312] "I don't know, but I say it has something to do with that little bastard of a pastor!"

[313] "Oh, don't even mention his name in front of Felipe, he can't even stand the sight of that asshole!"

[314] "Felipe doesn't like him?"

"O no, comadre. Se pone muy rabioso con el."[315]

"A poco?"[316]

"Veras, una vez vino aqui al ginmasio para hablar con Felipé. Y empezo con que la iglesia catolica no es Cristiana, que todo lo que dice la iglesia es mentira, que nos tenemos que convertir a su iglesia, y esto y el otro. Te imaginas comadre? Diciendo eso a un boxeador corajudo como mi esposo? Olvidate!"[317]

"A dio! Tuvo suerte el condenado que no le metio sus buenos chingazos."[318]

"Pues con esa cara, a la mejor alguien ya le habría dado sus mil chingazos,"[319] said Mariania as the two women cackled. "Entonces crees que ese cabrón tiene que ver algo con el Miguel?"[320]

"Si, definitivamente si. Hace mucho que engatuzo a Manuel con esas chingaderas que tiene que hacer como gringo pa'que lo acceptan en la iglesia. Y creo que esta tratando de hacer lo mismo con mi hijo."[321]

---

[315] "Oh no, camadre. He's gets enraged with him!"

[316] "You're kidding me?"

[317] "Lemme tell you, one time he came here to the gym to talk to Felipe. And he started with that the Catholic church isn't really Christian, that everything the church says is a lie, that all have to convert to his church, and this and that. Can you imagine, comadre? Saying that to my husband, a boxer with a short temper? Forget it!"

[318] "Holy shit! The jerk was lucky that he didn't get punched."

[319] "With a face like that, someone probably already did!"

[320] "So you think that asshole has got something to do with Miguel?"

[321] "Yes, definitely yes! For a while he brainwashed Manny with that bullshit that he has to be like a gringo to be accepted in the church. And I think he's trying to do the same thing with my son."

"Por eso no quieres dejar a tu marido?"[322]

"Desgraciadamente … tengo miedo que si dejo a Manuel, los dos pueden poner mi hijo en mi contra. Ya hizo un desmadre con el Manuel y ahora estoy pagando los consequencias."[323]

"A poco, comadre?"[324]

"Si! Fijate que el pastor le dijo al Manuel que la razon por cual no puede ser diacano, fui por mi!"[325]

"Te culpó a ti, comadre? De que? Como?!"[326]

"De ser una mujer muy puta!"[327]

"A chingado! Te dijo eso, comadre? Ese hijo de su chingada madre!"[328]

"Fijate! Nomás porque me pongo maquillaje y no ando como las nagüdas de la Iglesia soy la puta mas puta! La pinche reina de las putas!"[329] said Magdalena trying to be angry but still crackling a smile.

"Hay comadre, que feo!"[330]

"Pero cuidado! Puede decir que soy muy puta,

---

[322] "And that's why you don't wanna leave your husband?"
[323] "Unfortunately … I'm afraid that if I leave Manuel, that guy can pit my son against me. He already did that bullshit with Manny and now I'm paying the consequences."
[324] "Really, comadre?"
[325] "Yeah! Let me tell you that the pastor told Manuel that the reason he couldn't be a deacon was me!"
[326] "He blamed you, comadre?! Of what? How?!"
[327] "For being a whore of a woman!"
[328] "Oh fuck! He told you that, comadre? That son of a bitch!"
[329] "I'm tellin' you! Just because I don't wear makeup and I'm not like those long-skirted women in the church, I'm the most whorish whore. The fucking queen of the whores!"
[330] "Oh comadre, that's awful!"

pero le aseguro que soy mas cabrona que puta."[331]

"A chingado!"[332]

"Un dia lo va ver."[333]

"Oiga, porque ese tipo será tan entrometido? Que busca que es tan importante?"[334]

"Pues asi son, Marianita. Como no respetan la privacidad, no respetan quien soy, y todos se metén en los asuntos de otros. Es una barbaridad!"[335]

"Oye, comadre, y porque te metiste en esa iglesia?"[336]

Magdalena took stock of her severed bougainvillea perking up in the water bottle on the desk before she could give a proper answer.

"Porque me casé por necesidad."[337]

While crouching next to the door, Michael could remember the slow transformation of Manny in hindsight. The benevolent image of a savior reaching out his hand of mercy to them to save them both from abject poverty, only to grip them tightly in obligation according to the teachings of Pastor Roberts. He knew all too well what it felt like to be trapped in the pit of necessity that conveniently has ways to escape that are just out of reach.

"Oye comadre, crees que algun dia el Manuel

---

[331] "But he better be careful! He can say that I may say I'm the biggest whore, but I can assure you that I'm way more of a bitch than a whore."

[332] "Oh fuck!"

[333] "One day he'll see it."

[334] "Hey, why is that guy so nosy? What's so important to him?"

[335] "Well that's how they are, Marianita. Like they don't respect privacy, they don't respect who you are, and everybody gets into everyone else's business. It's barbaric!"

[336] "Oh, comadre, why did you get involved in that church?"

[337] "Because I married out of necessity."

cambiará?"[338]

Magdalena remorsefully searched her soul to find her passionate boldness to say no, but she remembered the saving that she and Michael needed years ago.

"No se, Marianita … ojala."[339]

There were no open windows in Michael's skull to let all the silent screaming out. The immutable truth of his stepfather was something that he just could not deny or accept. He wanted God to simply change him into a man who was kinder, gentler, and loving, but he also knew the near impossibility of doing so. Anything short of a miracle from God himself could never undo the horrid and volatile personality that blossomed in cheap whiskey. Michael was so lost in the ruminating riptide of "what if" that he was completely unaware of the presence that was making its way through the gym. Its saccharine arrival was marked only by the scent of talcum powder wafting past his nose and masking the pungent stench of sweat, body, and rubberized floors.

"Well, hey there, darlin', how's it goin'?" she asked.

Michael turned around to see Rebecca standing behind him, wearing a high-cut floral print blouse and a string of pearls around her honey milk–colored neck.

"I'm doin' a'ight … what … whatchya doin' here?" he asked.

"Well, honey, loooooong story, but Pastor Roberts gave George a call this mornin', askin' for some godly advice. And I guess after they talked some, God just told them that if they wanted to get down to the bottom of their

---

[338] "Hey comadre, do you think one day Manuel will change?"
[339] "I don't know, Marianita … hopefully."

lil' problem, then they're just gonna needed some womanly help. You know, a mission o' mercy," she responded in a chipper voice.

"A mission of mercy?"

"Well, I know that just sounds like a trifle thang, but I was told that your mom and daddy had bit of a spat the other night."

"You mean stepfather."

"Oh yes, I'm so sorry, your stepdaddy. Lord help me with my manners." She laughed.

"Why didn't Pastor Roberts come?"

"Oh, you know, this'll be a whole lotta girl talk, nothin' any of 'em really wanna deal with. Come to think of it, he really didn't give George a reason why he couldn't come. I guess he's just busy callin' people on the prayer chain for your mom and daddy."

"So e'rbody knows?"

"Just about."

"Oh boy …" Michael sighed. "Hold on. I think she's in here with her friend. Lemme check."

Michael slid into the barely open door, closing it enough to hide the surprise guest.

"Uhm … Mom … Rebecca is here."

Magdalena turned back to Mariana. "Que te acabo de decir, eh?"[340]

She crossed her legs and sat up on the old couch while patting down the few stray hairs on her head. She fed on the ire of this woman intruding on her sanctuary as she extended her neck by lifting her chin upward, reminiscent of a coiled rattlesnake dripping with sharp and sarcastic venom from its fangs.

---

[340] "What did I just tell you, huh?"

"Que pase la vieja mijito."[341]

Michael snuck back out of the office to retrieve Rebecca, who by that time had grown increasingly unnerved at the shouts and kissing noises from the men in the gym. She nervously gripped the strap of her fine leather purse as she began to sweat from the damp air.

"Come in. My mom's inside," Michael said.

Rebecca scurried into the small office, away from the catcalls and into the lair of women. Coach Padilla had stopped his lesson in the ring to check out the unknown guest to his gym. He looked over at Michael, nodded his head, and gestured with his eyes to ask if Michael knew this person. Michael nodded back, assuring Coach that the stranger was here to see them.

"Well, hi there, Magdalena, how are you?"

Magdalena looked at Mariana with sense of contempt but engagement as she sized up her target.

"Estoy bien, gracias a Dios. Conoces a mi amiga, Mariana?"[342] Magdalena gestured at Mariana.

"Oh, I don't think we've met, but it sure is to nice meet you, Mary Ann. I'm Rebecca," she said as she extended her hand to shake.

"It's Mariana," said Mariana.

"Oh, dear Lord, what did I say?"

"You said Mary Ann. It's Mariana."

"Oh, I'm so sorry, Maryanna? Did I get that right?"

"It's close enough. Nice to meet you, Rebecca. How do you know Magdalena?"

---

[341] "Let the broad come in, son."
[342] "I'm doing fine, thank God. Have you met my friend Mariana?"

"Oh, well, we're sisters in Christ at the lil' church just down the street right over there."

"You're from the church?"

"Oh absolutely, part of one big happy Jesus-lovin' family." Rebecca laughed.

Mariana tried not to be overtly obvious in confirming all that Magdalena had said earlier, so she just politely smiled at this strange happy woman.

"Have a seat," Mariana said to Rebecca as she got up and pulled a chair for her from the corner.

"Oh, thank you, Maryana."

Sensing the cat-and-mouse game that Magdalena was about to play, Michael tried to slip out of the office.

"Mom, I'm just gonna wait outside till ..."

"No mijo, quedate. Quiero un testigo."[343]

Not wanting to be disobedient in front of Mariana, he resigned himself to leaning up against the doorjamb as a fly on the wall. Rebecca cheerfully took her seat as the interrogation was about to begin. Magdalena stared down at her prey, from the cotton candy hair and white pearls to her flat taupe shoes. While she remained composed and quiet, her brown eyes could not help but silently say, "Con tanto dinero, y asi llegaste en esas garras!"[344]

"Well, Magdalena, I just came by to see how you and Michael are doin' and all. Pastor Roberts was worried sick 'bout you two."

"O si?"

"Oh absolutely, honey. I was tellin' your son that Manny called the pastor this mornin' in an absolute tizzy sayin' that you and Michael had up and left, and well I just

---

[343] "No, son, you stay. I want a witness."

[344] "With so much money and you show up in these rags!"

felt so gosh darn horrible when I heard that. So I dropped to my knees and started prayin', 'Please, Lord Jesus, please! Help to heal the hurt in this couple's marriage. In the name a' Jesus, don't let the enemy destroy what God has brought together.'" Rebecca lifted her hand in the air and closed her eyes.

Mariana looked at Magdalena as she quietly mouthed the words "Que, que?!"

Magdalena just shook her head and rolled her eyes and mouthed the word "Nada," then said, "Si es horrible cuando alguien quiere destruir lo tuyo, no?"

Rebecca's limited high school Spanish had brought her just into the start of the conversation before failing fantastically. She was desperate to know what was said, so she turned to Mariana and whispered, "I don't understand what she's sayin'."

"She said that it's really horrible when someone wants to destroy what's yours, don't you think?"

"OH YES! IT'S MALO, MUY MALO," Rebecca said slowly and loudly.

"Perdoname, Rebequita, pero porque viniestes? Aunque agradezco la visita, se me hace que viniestes con un proposito. Si quieres hablar con migo hay que a hablar mujer a mujer, no? Entonce dime ... a que vino chencha?" asked Magdalena.

"She said, 'Excuse me, Rebecca, but why did you come? Although I appreciate the visit, somethin' tells me that you came here with a motive. If you want to talk to me, let's talk women to women, right? So ... tell me, what did you come here for?'" repeated Mariana.

"Oh ... well, yeah ... uhm ... are you ... sure you want Michael in here for this? I was kinda hopin' this was gonna be more of girl talk."

"Mi hijo se queda."

"She said, 'Her son stays.'"

"Oh … well, OK," said Rebecca as she tried smiling despite Magdalena's blunt demeanor.

"Dime, porque no vino Manuel?"

"'Tell me, why didn't Manny come?'" responded Mariana.

"Uhm … well, ya see, it's not, uhm … well, when Pastor Roberts called George and they talked, you know how the deacons do, they felt that it'd be more appropriate if one of the deacon's wives come and talk to ya."

"Entonces ganaste el premio de visitarmé."

"'So you won the prize to come visit me.'"

"Guilty as charged." Rebecca giggled.

"Y mandarón un diacano con el Manuel?"

"'And did they send a deacon to Manny?'"

"I … I … think George had said somethin' 'bout the whole deacon board gettin' together to talk to Manny. You know how the boys are, gotta have their man time too."

"Hmm, mandarón un chingatal de gente con el Manuel, y a mi una mujercita. Que bonito!"

"'So they sent a bunch of people to Manuel, and they sent only one woman to me? That's nice.'"

Magdalena's honey-brown eyes stalked her prey, and Rebecca could feel the flush of nervous heat radiate through her body as it became trapped in her high-cut blouse.

"Y el Manuel no les dijo que sucedio?" asked Magdalena.

"'And Manny didn't say what happened?'"

"Well, all I know he was pretty upset 'bout not gettin' on the board and all …"

"Y eso fue todo?"

"'And that was it?'"

"Uhm … well … I, uh …"

"Si tienes que decirme algo Rebequita hay que decirlo."

"She said, 'If you got something to say, then say it.'"

"Well, I … gosh darn it … I didn't want to say this in front of Michael, but there was some talk that Michael assaulted Manny last night."

"Asalto!?" asked Magdalena. "Y no dijo porque Miguel le dio un buen chingazo?"

"'And he didn't say why Michael punched him?'"

Rebecca's hesitation to answer grew with each question as she tried to reformulate the message that was relayed to her. Michael was still leaning up against the doorjamb and saw his mother's surprised eyes dart over to him as the accusation hit him like a sucker punch.

"Well, again, I just heard this from George, who heard from Pastor Roberts, who heard it from Manny himself, but he told me that you guys had gotten into a fight and that Manny left, came back, and that's when Michael hit him."

"Y el no dijo adonde se fue?"

"'And he didn't say where he went?'"

Rebecca could feel the cold look of the two women around her, but in her mind she had to be the honorable Christian Soldier and stand in the face of uncomfortableness if it meant bringing the light of God into the situation. She knew no other way.

"No, sweetie, they didn't tell me anythin' 'bout that."

"Y no confesó nada de sus boracheras?

"'He didn't confess anythin' 'bout the times he's been drunk?'"

"What?! … No! … Manny drunk? … Are you kiddin', Magdalena? I just … No … I, I, I can't believe that … Manny would never drink, I mean he's such a good godly man!"

Magdalena turned to her trusted comadre, who herself couldn't offer much in the way of consolation. The lie was deep, and only served to embolden Magdalena and twist the knife of truth further with Rebecca. She didn't want to just be right, she wanted to make Rebecca feel the nausea of deception. She wanted her to feel pain.

From his corner, Michael replayed the event in his mind. He knew very well what he saw the other night—whiskey vapors of malice caressing the scattered brilliance of glass rosary beads thrown across the kitchen. He kept quiet about knowing that, but he too could feel the rage. And as it grew, he could swear the buzzing cicadas were nesting now in the rafters of the little office. He closed his eyes to force the sound back down and out of his head, but he must have shoved it so far down that he swore that he could feel the sensation of warm blood-tinted water surrounding his feet.

"Pues tu dime Rebequita, cual es la verdad? Que mi hijo le metio un chingazo a su padrastro porque le dio la fregada gana? O el borracho de Manuel lo provocó? A ver, dime!"

"She wants you to tell what's true. That her son punched his stepfather just because he felt like it? Or that Manny got drunk and he did it."

"Oh, Magdalena, I know how you feel! Honestly, honey, I do, but I've just never seen Manny like that! I just know him as the man who wants to please the Lord and provide for his family. I mean, he's a believer, and with faith in Jesus there ain't no room in his life for gettin' drunk."

"Fijate no mas, mi hijo asaltando un santo, y su puta madre abandondo su matrimonio."

"She said, 'Isn't it funny, my son—'"

"No le vas a intepretar eso!" Magdalena interjected.

"What, what'd she say?!" Rebecca asked.

"Entonces que queiren? Te mandarón a convencerme que me regresé con mi esposo?"

"She said, 'So what do they want? Did they send you to convince me to go back with my husband?'"

"Magdalena, I don't want you to think I'm here to be the bad guy. I just want what God wants for you. To be in a happy marriage that honors God, even through this rough patch."

"Mira Rebequita, nadie sabe las razones de uno. Yo no creo que mi hijo cometio una falta, y no creo que hice mal en irme."

"She said, 'Nobody knows anybody's motives.' She doesn't believe her son committed a crime, and she doesn't believe she did anythin' wrong in leavin'."

"Oh Lord Jesus, help me …" Rebecca sighed. "I know this is hard, Magdalena. It's hard when it's your son that we're talkin about, but even Pastor Roberts said that all this boxin' and fightin' is probably makin' Michael a lil' too aggressive."

It was a depressingly poignant remark, even if it came second- or thirdhand. Michael looked at his hands tightly bound in straps and wondered if his stubbornness to stay involved in the sport despite the Pastor Roberts's objections had really caused the jeopardy he found himself in. Coach Padilla may have been looking for lightning to strike the other night, but divine punishment arrived in a soft-spoken southern accent from a messenger wearing pearls.

"Pues asi deben de hacer los hombres, no? Con huevos para defender sus seres queridos! Y tambien las mujeres deben de tener ovarios mas grandes para ser mas cabronas."

"'Well, that's how men should be, right? To have the balls to defend their loved ones! And women should have even bigger ovaries to be more of a bitch.'"

"Oh, honey, no, no, no, I didn't mean it that way! It's just that we gotta have some bit of civility. We can't be goin' 'round solvin' all our problems by hittin' people. You know it's just like Jesus tellin' us to turn the other cheek. Someone has to keep the peace."

"Y si hay abuso? Entonces que? Debo de voltear la cara y perdonarlo?"

"'What if there's abuse? Then what? Do I turn the cheek and forgive him?'"

"Well, yeah, we're supposed to, sweetie. We're Christian, and we oughtta forgive just like we've been forgiven. Now, I don't know if there's any abuse, Magdalena, but ya just keep sayin' things about Manny that just don't seem like him. It may have been a bad fight, but this is just the one time, right?"

"No! No es la primera, ni la segunada, y ni la tercera vez."

"'No! It ain't the first, or the second, or the third time.'"

"Oh! I, uh … I didn't … know that …"

Mariana and Michael stood waiting as spectators in an arena as Rebecca, the meek gladiator, faced the lioness that was ready to pounce.

"Te dije, hay que hablar con la verdad, Rebequita. La neta neta. Por qué te mandarón, eh? Por qué viniestes? Darme sermones es una perdida de tiempo. Vinistes con proposito, ahora dime!"

"She said, 'I told you, you gotta be speakin' the truth with me. The real, real reason. Why did you come, huh? 'Cause coming here to give me sermons is a waste of time. You came with a motive, now tell me!'"

Rebecca's heart pounded underneath her blouse and her jugular veins pulsated under her high collar as sweat began to bead on her spine. She had known Magdalena as the bold and unconforming woman at Sunday service, but she had never experienced her blunt, confrontational approach to life firsthand. Rebecca mustered enough courage to part her dry lips and give an answer.

"I … oh my gosh … OK … I'll tell you what happened. When Pastor Roberts called my husband and he told George about Michael punchin' your husband, they we're talkin' about pressin' charges against Michael. Assualt charges."

"Cargos! A mi hijo?!"

"Please, Magdalena! It's why I asked them to let me come down and talk to you first. I told them that if it's God's will, y'all would go back home. Then they wouldn't need to file them charges!"

Magdalena, the fierce lioness, was trembling furiously at the thought of charges. Mariana and Michael could feel the air escape their lungs, leaving a vacuum.

"Entonces, me estan chantageando. Que hijos de la chingada!"

"'So they're blackmailin' me. What sons of

bitches!'"

"Dear Lord, Magdalena, I don't wanna make this about that, please! I just didn't wanna see your son have to go through that. He's too good of a kid to be put through that, and you're a good Christian woman to just throw it all away!"

"Pero es mejor que temenos que suffrir el abuso del Manuel, o que?"

"'So it's better we put up with Manny's abuse, or what?'"

"No! No, it's not better, Magdalena, but God doesn't want families to be split up! He don't want you to leave your husband just as much as he don't want Michael to go to jail."

"Y quien eres tu para decir lo que quiere dios, y menos lo que yo quiero?"

"'Who are you to tell me what God wants, or even of what I want?'"

"Oh my God, Magdalena! Where's this all comin' from?! I'm … I'm just tryin' to help you! I don't want you to be angry with me, and I don't want anythin' to happen to your son, for God's sake! We just have to believe that God is gonna see us through these hard times, and he will. I just know he will," pleaded Rebecca through tears.

"Claro! Para ti será facil creer en eso, no? Será facil tener esa fe en que todo va salir bien, que todos van a tener esa familia perfecta, y toda esas chingaderas! Pero yo, no soy como tu. Yo he tenido que vivir sabiendo que estoy sola en este pais. Solomante tengo a mi hijo y un poco de paisanos que me respaldan. No hay ayuda de ti, ni de la iglesia. La imagen de la familia perfecta que nunca fue. Yo no necesito a nadie me diga quien soy o quien debo de ser! Soy la misma que emigró hace uno años, nomás que estoy mas amargada por aguantar a todos!"

Mariana, trying to lean further back in her chair, calmly rendered her interpretation.

"She said, 'Of course! For you it's easy to believe? It's easy to believe that everythin' is going to be all right, that everybody is goin' to have the perfect family, and all that bullshit.' But she said that she's not like you! She's had to live knowin' that she's alone in this country and that she only has her son and few others who have her back. There is no help, not from you and not even from the church. That picture-perfect family never happened. She doesn't need anyone to tell her who she is or who she should be. She's the same woman who immigrated, just more bitter for having to put up with everyone."

A sullen Rebecca sat in the small uncomfortable chair, fragile and weeping. She could not bring herself to look directly into Magdalena's fiery eyes, as she had never encountered acidic remarks from someone she sincerely thought of as a fellow sister in Christ.

"Dime un cosa, si tu estuvieras en mi lugar, regresarias?" Magdalena asked in a stern yet quieter tone.

"She wants to know, if you were in her place, would you go back?"

Trying to hold back the tears, Rebecca managed to squeak out, "Yes … Magdalena, I would go back. I … I just can't believe that God wouldn't do what he said he'll do. I can't live in a world where my faith don't count for nothin'." Tears continued to run down Rebecca's makeup-free face.

"Alli esta! Tienes mas miedo de que muera tu dios, a que yo y mi hijo suframos el abuso."

"She said that you are more afraid that your God

dies than if she and her son suffer abuse."

An oppressive and deafening silence filled the tiny office, so thick that not even the smacking of punching bags could be heard. The only sound came from the short weeping gasps from Rebecca as she tried to hold steadfast.

Magdalena was stewing. She looked over to Michael leaning against the doorjamb, and her maternal instinct could not conceive of freedom without her son tasting it as well.

"Pues, no hay otra opción. Tengo que regresar … por mi hijo."

"She says that there are no other options. She's gotta go back, for her son."

Rebecca finally found the courage to look up at the subdued lioness in front of her. She was the victorious gladiator, but winning did not bring the joy she had hoped for. She had fallen into a strange new world where the black-and-white moral code by which she operated failed to capture the vibrant, dynamic color in front of her. It was terrifying that no simple Bible verse or quip from a sermon could provide the salve for the deep wounds in Magdalena's heart and Rebecca's faith. In all her years of trying to rescue the unbelieving and unrepentant, Rebecca had finally come to the limits of her beliefs, realizing that to praise God meant condemning her sister in Christ.

"Diles que yo y mi hijo regresaramos manana."

"She said to tell them that she and her son will go back tomorrow."

Rebecca's blue watery eyes opened wide as she nodded, affirming that she would relay the message. Her shaking hands wiped away tears as she rose to her feet and started to head out.

"Oye, Rebequita!" Magdalena called out before

she reached the door.

"Por lo menos, hablaste con la verdad. Agradezco que pensaras en mi hijo. Gracias, en serio muchas gracias."

Rebecca turned her weeping gaze one last time to Mariana.

"She said, 'At least you spoke the truth.' She appreciates that you were thinking about her son. She said, 'Thank you, thank you very much.'"

Rebecca turned to open the office door, where Michael had been standing immobile, trying to fight off the noises in his head. She reached out for his wrapped-up hands and squeezed tightly, trying to osmotically pass her genuine empathy to him. She managed to squeeze out a smile before making her exit back into the sounds of the gym.

Smack-Smack—Smack-Smack.

11

"Ya sure you guys don't wanna stay?" asked Coach Padilla.

"I'm sure, Coach … things went sideways you know, and … we gotta go," responded Michael.

"Door's always open if you need it."

"I know."

"Señora, no es demasiado tarde si quieren quedarse,"[345] said Coach Padilla.

"Gracias, Felipe, lo agradezco muchismo, pero nos tenenos que ir,"[346] said Magdalena, with her full purse slung around her shoulder and the water bottle with her severed branch in her hand.

"Pues … esta bien señora, esta bien. No estoy de acuerdo de que se vayan pero lo intiendo. Quieren que los lleve a su casa?"[347]

---

[345] "Mam, it's not too late if you guys want to stay."
[346] "Thank you, Felipe, I really appreciate it, but we have to go."
[347] "Well … it's OK, Mam, it's OK. I don't want you guys to leave but I understand. Do you want me to drive you guys to your house."

"No, no, no, mejor caminamos. No esta lejos y no quiero que el Manuel te vea y se arme un escandalo."[348]

"Hay señora. Tenga mucho cuidado con el, pero por lo menos el ya sabe que su hijo la puede defender."[349]

Coach Padilla's kind words were like a fleeting ghost, bright and shimmering but quickly gone the moment Michael wanted to hold on to them.

"Claro que si … hijo, estas listo?"[350] she called out to Michael.

"Thanks, Coach!" Michael shouted back as he waved goodbye.

The hazy, golden sunlight had already started to bake the sidewalk and cast long shadows as it peeked over the buildings in the east. The neighborhood was starkly silent as Coach stood outside the gym watching them walk away, hoping that even as they made their way back home, the two would spontaneously about-face and return to the safety that he and his wife offered.

As for Michael and Magdalena, there was a familiar despair associated with the very first step back to their house. Whereas only a few days ago the same gritty and worn-out concrete was their path to peace, now it had morphed back into the loop of irredeemable conformity, bringing them back to the sleeping whiskey monster. They walked heavy with their burdens, Magdalena's ankle-length skirt flapping in the breeze.

"Mom?"

---

[348] "No, no, no, it's better if we walk. It's not far and I don't want Manuel to see you and cause a scene."
[349] "Oh, Mam. Just be careful with him, at least he knows that your son can defend you."
[350] "Well, of course … son, you ready?"

"Si, hijo?[351]"

"You still believe in God?"

"Hay mijito! Porque me preguntas eso?"[352]

"I dunno … just …"

"A ver hijo, dime, que etas pensando."[353]

"When you were talkin' to Rebecca, It kinda seemed like you didn't …"

"Hay mijito."[354]

"Well, do you?"

"Claro que si mijito, como no!"[355]

"Then why'd you act like you didn't care about God?"

"Es algo muy profundo hijo, mucho mas de lo que tu vez."[356]

"Yeah?"

"No es que no creo en Dios, es que no creo en el Dios de ella."[357]

"Isn't it all the same?"

"Nos dicen que si, pero no es mijito … no es."[358]

"But there shouldn't be a difference, right?"

"No … pero hay. Siempre ha habido."[359]

"Pastor Roberts says God is God no matter what."

"O si? Y porque tengo que rezar a Dios en

---

[351] "Yes, son?"

[352] "Oh my son! Why do you ask me that?"

[353] "Come on, tell me what's on your mind."

[354] "Oh son."

[355] "Of course I do, son. How can I not!"

[356] "It's something very profound, much more than what you see."

[357] "It's not that I don't believe in God, it's that I don't believe in her God."

[358] "They tell us that … but it's not."

[359] "No … but there is. There always has been."

ingles?"[360]

"I … I dunno … why?"

"Eso es el punto … Para ellos, no somos de ellos si no somos como ellos."[361]

"Isn't God supposed to love us no matter what?"

"Yo se que mi tatito Dios me quiere, te quire a ti … pero no creo que el Dios de ellos nos quiere igual."[362]

"Mom?"

"Si mijito."

"Am I turnin' into them … am I lookin' like the men at church?"

A mischievous smirk came across her face while juggling the bag slung over her shoulder. She managed to free her hand to make a tight fist. She then pointed to the tanned fleshy folds of her hand and her curled-up index finger.

"Mira! Sabes donde te pareces a ellos. Aqui! En las arrugas de tu fundillo. Mira! Igualitos!"[363]

"Ma, I'm serious!"

"Yo tambien, mijito!"[364]

"Am I turnin' into a man like them? Like George or Pastor Roberts?"

"Te dije, en las arrugas de los fundillos somos todos iguales."[365]

---

[360] "Oh yeah? Then why do I have to pray to God in English?"
[361] "That's the thing. son … For them, we aren't them unless we are them."
[362] "I know my God loves me, he loves you … but I don't believe their God wants us, the same as them."
[363] "You know where you're starting to look like them? In the wrinkles of your butthole! Look! Exactly the same!"
[364] "I am too, son!"
[365] "I told you, in the wrinkles of our buttholes we are all the same."

"Ma! Am I?"

"No! Como vas aparecerte! No eres nada como esos hombres."[366]

"Shouldn't I? Isn't it a sin to not be?"

"Eres mas hombre que ellos, eso te lo digo."[367]

"I don't feel like it. Shouldn't they say that I am?"

"Quires hacer como ellos?"[368]

"I …"

"Hijo, dime …"[369]

"I've wanted to."

"Para que. Están tratando de hacer lo mismo contigo?"[370]

"No …"

"Entonces, que negocios tienes de querer ser como ellos?"[371]

"'Cause, maybe all this bad stuff that happens to us is 'cause we're not like them. Maybe if were like them, then we wouldn't be walkin' back home like this!"

"Hijo, entiende lo que te voy a decir. Nunca vamos a ser sufficiente para ellos, y menos al Dios de ellos. Nunca de los nuncas!"[372]

"Then why are we going back?"

"Porque … porque no hay otra salida. No hay

---

[366] "No! How are you going to be like them! You're nothing like them."

[367] "You're more of a man than they are, I can tell you that."

[368] "You wanna be like them?"

[369] "Son, tell me …"

[370] "For what? Are they trying to do the same thing that you are?"

[371] "Well then, what business do you have trying to be like them?"

[372] "Son, listen to what I'm about to tell you. We will never be enough for them, and even less for their God. Never!"

remedio, hijo."[373]

The heavy air weighed on Michael more and more as they walked. Sweat and apprehension trickled down like little shackles, chains that seemed to reach from Manny's house to as far as they could run.

"Ven, dame un abrazo," Magdalena said as she pulled him closer. "Mira, siempre voy estar contigo. Me oistes? Siempre, siempre, siempre. Algun dia mijito, vamos a salir de esto."

"Yeah?"

"Si, algun dia vamos estar libre. Pero ahora tenemos que aguantar, y eso es algo que los cabrones de la iglesia no saben hacer. Aguantar lo peor para tener lo mejor."[374]

"Sometimes I wish we could leave now, not have to put up with this anymore."

"Yo tambien hijo, yo tambien. Pero vamos a solucionar esto. No se como, pero tu y yo no podemos seguir viviendo asi. Yo no quiero vivir con chantajes, ni andar pidiendo limosnas. Ojala un dia encontremos como huir de aqui."[375]

---

[373] "Because … because there is no way out. There is no other solution, son."

[374] "Come here and give me a hug. Look, I'm always going to be with you. You hear me? Always. Together we are going to get out of this. One day, son. One day we'll be free, where no one will tell us we are less than anyone. But for now we are going to have to tolerate, and that's something those assholes at the church don't know how to do. Tolerate the worst to have the best.

[375] "Me too, son, me too. But we are going to solve this. I don't know how, but you and I can't keep living like this. I don't want to be living with blackmail, and asking for alms. Hopefully one day we can find some way to get away from here."

Dread and anticipation sunk in when they turned the corner and stared down the converging parallel sidewalks of their street. Along the cracked and deteriorated asphalt, they could see Pastor Roberts's car, freshly washed and waxed after last week's storm, parked in front of the house. The blinding white glare from the polished paint eclipsed Manny's dull and rusted truck that was sitting quietly and reverently in the driveway. It was a peculiarity for Manny to take the day off and had been happening more frequently since Manny had figured out the secret recipe for the "come back to the house" sauce that he cooked up after their fights.

"Quieres apostar?"[376]

"About what?"

"De los regalos que nos tiene alli?"[377]

"I've lost track of what he's bought me."

"Pendejadas, mijo, puras pendejadas."[378]

When they walked closer, they could see the newly exposed part of the house where Magdalena's big, wild bougainvillea tree once stood. Parts of the eaves that were once shaded by the healthy green leaves were darkened, and the outer edges that were exposed to the southern sun were bleached and coated with the fine white chalkiness of old paint. From where they were standing, they could see the tan monotone moonscape of the desert dirt highlighted by the few remaining fuchsia flowers that littered the front yard. Some had dried in the clutches of the blighted brown weeds that survived the fierce monsoon winds a few days before, whereas others had shattered after being scorched

---

[376] "You want to place a bet?"

[377] "On what gifts he'll heave for us?"

[378] "They're bullshit, son, just pure bullshit."

by the sun and were strewn like confetti from a birthday party.

As they approached, Michael and Magdalena could see that even the chain link fence had amassed clumps of flowers in its metal nets. The ghost of the mighty tree seemed to have huddled herself in the rustling petals, seeking refuge in the farthest corner from Manny. The dust-covered flowers triggered Michael to smell the half-drunken whiskey vapors mixing with the scent of dirt wafting through the air. Magdalena, on the other hand, could hear the slurred insults and sporadic rhythm of Manny's fists on the wooden bedroom door reverberating between her eardrums. Memories their bodies kept like badges of honor, ways that the events could be made real for the mother and son when everyone else denied them.

"Ingrato!"[379] said Magdalena as she looked closer at the front door, where her majestic bougainvillea tree was once planted. Fresh dark potting soil carpeted the dry pebble-laden dirt and hot ornamental bars of a new trellis surrounded a young, frail, and scrawny shrub of sparse leaves and pink flowers. Her tender stems branching out from the spindly trunk were pulled outward and meticulously pinned to the crossbars of this new cage. Her entire form was crafted and sculpted by her bound-up stems.

"Con esto me quires callar, carbón,"[380] she muttered, loud enough for Michael to hear.

Magdalena wanted to cry again, but she knew what would be required of her when she walked in the front door, and she could not falter if she wanted peace, even if

---

[379] "Ungrateful bastard!"
[380] "With this you want to shut me up, you asshole."

that peace was short-lived. She sat the water bottle with her salvaged branch on the hood of Manny's truck while she tried to fix the few stray hairs that were flying in the hot breeze. Even though the front door was closed, they could hear the rich southern accent of Pastor Roberts waxing eloquently on some virtue of Christianity to Manny.

"Ahora vamos a ver que pacto hizo con el diablo,"[381] she said. "Estas listo?"

"I've got too much practice doin' this?"

"Yo se hijo, volvimos a la chingaderas. A ver que quire este lambion! En el nombre del Padre, el Hijo, y el Espiritu Santo."[382]

Magdalena took one last deep breath before she turned the brass doorknob and slowly pushed it open, allowing the morning sun to flood into the dark, plain white, and unadorned living room. The two chattering men fell silent as they beheld the wayward woman and her son who had returned home.

Michael could feel the instantaneous gravitational pull back into the orbit around Manny while he peered into the black infinite abyss of his home and saw nothing in the void. No remnants of pink flowers, whiskey bottles, or regrets could be found in the vast emptiness of that living room. Just the chaotic accretion of broken promises and cynical hopes swirling around the master of this small little universe.

"Magda!" exclaimed Manny as he and Pastor Roberts rose to their feet. "Thank God you're home!" he blubbered while oozing saccharine joy.

---

[381] "Let's see what pact he made with the devil now."
[382] "I know, son, we came back to this fucking shit. Let's see what this brownnoser wants." ("Lambion" denotes the licking of a repentant dog.)

Manny was dressed in his typical old Sunday suit. He slowly walked over to embrace his wife, who was still trying to keep her cold distance. Knowing the stakes of his game, she allowed him to invade her space and wrap his arms around her, encircling her tightly to express that she should never leave him again. And just like that, he subtly settled her back into his same old life.

She slowly acquiesced to his advance, and every exhalation allowed the affectionate serpent to tighten his hold on her.

"I'm so happy you're home," he said with a quivering voice.

"Well, hallelujah and praise God almighty for this!" exclaimed a beaming and overtly joyous Pastor Roberts.

"God, I missed you, Magda. You don't know how much I missed you!" he quietly sobbed onto her shoulder.

Magdalena could do little else than slowly close her eyes and say nothing while trying to imagine some faraway place to escape the bombardment of sentiment. Deep, vivid memories of her childhood in Mexico, of walking the plaza and eating duros from a street vendor flooded her imagination, much like her son's thoughts for him. A time before Manny, America, and the church where she didn't feel the crushing external pressures. It was with these memories that the profound despair of a life lost welled up in her to the point that she wanted to weep. But she held back the tears like a closely guarded secret. She did not want Manny or the Pastor to assume that her tears were of remorse for leaving, or even an act of contrition. She just let Manny's arms squeeze her childhood from her, leaving her heart just a little more callused.

"I gotcha new bougainvillea. You see it outside?"

Manny asked her.

"Si la vi … Gracias,"[383] she responded diplomatically.

"I don't know what I'd do without you, Magda," he awkwardly blurted out. "I didn't know where you were. I was so scared to lose you."

"Amen, brother, Amen!" interjected Pastor Roberts.

"Please, Magda, don't ever leave me like that again!"

Michael, who was still standing in the front door, watched the scene unfold as if it were a melodrama—as if his mother, Manny, and even Pastor Roberts assumed scripted roles in a soap opera that debuted years ago but had been cursed to never-ending weekday matinees whenever the happily-ever-after ending failed to come to a lasting fruition. From Michael's vantage point, both Manny and Pastor Roberts gave bold and impassioned performances meant to enthrall even the most uninterested audiences.

Magdalena, however, lacked the same motivation to act her part, bemusing the whole scene with indifference but still trying to hide her melancholy sentiment from watchful eyes. Even the living room setting had been well staged. The broken lamp that cast eerie shadows with its crumpled shade had been replaced with a dated and mismatched lamp salvaged from the thrift store. The carpet was vacuumed clean of its glittering luster of ten thousand shattered glass stars and ceramic shards. But despite Manny's efforts, he could not get rid of the extrafine desert dust that with each of their steps still faintly wafted upward

---

[383] "I saw it … thank you."

in dancing and undulating swirls in the morning sunbeams. The swirls were the presence of Michael's cosmic God breathing in the lowly, unnoticed parts of the house, still watching him as he had in every Saturday appointment. The only action left to do in this scene was to forgive.

"Mijito, no quieres dejar tu maleta a tu recamara?"[384] Magdalena asked her son.

Michael's tongue was stuck to the roof of his mouth, cemented with dry saliva that was far more binding than any word he could have squeak out. He nodded, looked down, and silently excused himself into the shadowy hallway.

In the dark corridor, the past events were on the walls like cave paintings. Only the witnesses of their creation could read the hidden meanings of the smears of sweat on the white paint. When Michael went to open his bedroom door, the soft dents in the thin wood veneer boomed with the sound of the whiskey monster as he traced each one with his fingers,

> *Op'n ... the goddamn-door ...*
> *Now, you lil-shit!*

The ghosts of violence, the vestiges of normalized horror, glorified themselves with each and every passage through the vernacular temple of memory. The schism of forgiveness and the urge to flee collided and feverishly tugged at his conscience while he stood in the doorway. The notion that Manny would never change and the damnation to this nomadic homelife made it difficult to breathe in the warm dark hallway. He looked up at the

---

[384] "Son, you don't wanna take your bag into your bedroom?"

glittering popcorn ceiling.

Where's the rest you promised?

Just then, Magdalena came quietly walking down the hallway. "Hijo, esconde esto,"[385] she said, pulling the broken rosary from her pocket. Seeing the delicate sparkles, he quickly stuffed it into his pocket.

"Un dia mijito, un dia vamos a salir de esto."[386]

"I know, Mom."

"Anda! El lambion quiere darte algo."[387]

"What is it?"

"No se … hazte el pendejo mijo, y a ver que pasa."[388]

Reluctantly Michael walked out, and Magdalena followed him to Manny and Pastor Roberts in the living room. Manny was waiting in the center of the room, and Pastor Roberts had plopped himself back on the couch, hunched over and resting his arms on his knees.

"Hey, Michael …"

"Yeah?"

"Hey, I … I wantchyou to know I missed you and your mom these past few days."

"You did?"

"Yeah, it made me realize just what you guys mean to me."

"Really?!"

"Come on now, son, your daddy's been all beat up

---

[385] "Son, hide this."

[386] "One day, son, one day we'll get out of this."

[387] "Go on! The brownnoser wants to give you something."

[388] "I don't know … just play stupid, son, and see what he wants."

over this. Least you can do is hear him out," said Pastor Roberts.

"Like I said, you and your mom mean a lot to me and I want things to be better with us."

"Better how?"

"Well, I want you to start to trustin' me like … you know … a dad."

"You want me to trust you? I'm gonna be outta of the house to college in a few weeks. Seems a lil' late."

"It's never too late to start," he said while handing Michael a simple brown paper package.

"What is it?" asked Michael.

"Well, open it, son, and let's find out!" Pastor Roberts blurted out.

Michael turned the package over and began to gently undo the clear tape, all in the name of keeping the peace. He let the brown packing paper fall to the ground, revealing a burgundy patent leather-bound Bible.

"It's … a Bible," said Michael.

"Yeah, I saw your old one was pretty beat-up."

"You went into my room?"

"Not gonna lie, it was a hard night. I went in there and seein' an empty bed, I just started cryin' my eyes out. It really hurt me that you guys weren't home."

"It hurt you?" Michael respectfully retorted.

"Oh, come on now, son, er'body hurts when things like this happ'n. Ain't no shame in Manny tellin' y'all. Ain't that right, Magdalena?" chided Pastor Roberts.

"Si," said Magdalena through tight lips.

"Son, whatever happens, we gotta forgive when someone is askin' for it. If we don't forgive, then just what exactly did Jesus die for?" asked Pastor Roberts.

And with that, Pastor Roberts fated Michael's

gravitational orbit back around Manny's darkness. Now there was no escaping the accelerating speed of Michael's sense of self revolving in the chaotic trajectory of Manny's life, glowing and giving light through his own personal decay so that the blackness of this home could appear to be illuminated. Michael didn't know how long it would be before he and Magdalena would be pulled into the singularity of Manny's negating existence, fusing themselves to him, Pastor Roberts, the church, and Pastel Jesus. At that point, it did not seem that even the physical distance of a college dorm would be far enough to escape the rippling forces of this dynamic.

"Thanks," Michael sheepishly mumbled.

"Son, why don't you and I go outside for a bit and let your momma and your daddy have a lil' time to talk." Pastor Roberts pushed his large body up from the couch and waddled out the front door.

"Come on, Magda, we'll talk in the kitchen," Manny said as he gingerly took her by the hand and began leading her into the dark recess of the kitchen.

"Son, you comin out or what?" shouted Pastor Roberts from the front porch.

As Michael stepped out, the grinding of sand grains under his shoes echoed the Sisyphean steps from the night of their escape. Magdalena's severed little branch was still sitting outside in the water bottle, waiting for someone to bring her in.

"Come on, son, I ain't got all day!" Pastor Roberts called out.

Michael went to Manny's beat-up truck, where Pastor Roberts was standing, and picked up his mom's bottle. There was a certain happiness to Pastor Roberts's face as he surveyed the dirt around him. Poverty of spirit had been vanquished and a renewed hope for Christian harmony and bliss had come into the home. His work as the shepherd of his flock had borne fruit. And there was only one stain, one malady left to redeem.

"All right, son, let's have a look at that new Bible of yours!"

Michael placed the Bible into his pudgy hands as the gold-leaf edges of the pages shone in the warm glow of sunlight. The front cover cracked as Pastor Roberts opened the new Bible, the virgin patent leather spread open to release the faint aroma of plastic. The pastor's thick and meaty fingers felt up the new pages, and he read from the inside cover.

"Hmmm, well, how 'bout that."

"What?"

"Looks like your daddy already dedicated this Bible to ya!"

Michael took the open Bible from his hands. "This Bible is dedicated to my son Michael, from your father Manny," he read out loud.

"Amen!"

"Hmmm."

"Well, there you go, son. If you ever had doubts that your daddy loves you …"

"Stepdad … he's my stepdad."

"Ohhh, come on now, he sure has been tryin'."

"Tryin' what?"

"To be the father figure you need, son!"

"Didn't seem like it the other night!"

"Son, er'yone makes mistakes."

"Yeah, but not like that!"

"Hey hey hey, don't be mouthin' off like that, boy! You know just as well as I do that if we can be forgiven, then we gotta forgive too."

"But I can't."

"Can't or won't?"

"Won't."

"Boy, don't be goin' against God."

"You're tellin' me that God's makin' me forgive someone I don't want to?"

"If you don't believe me, you open up that Bible and get to usin' it. Look it up! Go on! Look up Matthew chapter 6 verse 15, and you tell me what God says 'bout forgivin' others."

Reluctantly, Michael took the Bible, cracked the binding himself, and began thumbing through the tissue-thin pages until he arrived at the verse.

"Go ahead and read it out loud, son," demanded Pastor Roberts.

"But if ye forgive not men their trespasses, neither will your Father forgive your trespasses …"

"There you go, boy. Can't say it any clearer than that!"

"Why do I gotta do it? I ain't needin forgiveness for anythin'."

"No?"

"No!"

"What 'bout hittin' him the other night?"

"Yeah, but …"

"Son! What you did was assault, plain and simple! It ain't right what you did. What's the Bible say? 'Thou shall honor thy mother and father' … or you need to look that one up too?!"

"But he deserved it!"

"Now, see, this is why I don't want you goin' to that boxin' gym!"

"Why! 'Cause I'll fight back?!"

"'Cause you're pickin' up all'em worldly habits from those hoodlums, gangbangers, and whatnot! I know you Mexicans like to solve things that way, but in the United States we don't do that!"

"I ain't pickin' up nothin'!"

"Son, tell me the truth. You wanna fix your problem?"

"What problem?"

"You heard me, son. That little problem you have with wantin' men!"

"What about it?"

"You want me to go right in there and tell your momma all 'bout what you been wantin' to do with boys? Huh?! You want me to tell her how you been wantin' to act like a faggot? You want me to do that?"

"No! I just ..."

"You want me to tell her 'bout all'em dreams you've been havin' about that one boy?"

"NO, I wanna ..."

"Or 'bout how Manny found out 'bout you? I'm sure he'll go right ahead and back me up in front of your momma!"

"NO, I ... I ..." Michael stammered, trying to hold back the tears.

"Stop cryin', son! Cryin' is for girls and faggots. You got that?!" Pastor Roberts demanded as he continued, "You best be gettin' in gear 'cause God is givin' you opportunity after opportunity to fix 'erthing and all you're doin' is just wastin' 'em! You know how lucky you are that you got someone that's willin' to step in and be that man to show you the way out? Manny's your God-givin' salvation, so you don't end up like one 'em queers. But you and your momma are just too hardheaded to see when God's trying to save you two. Y'all don't know when a good thing is starin' you right in the face."

"I ain't hardheaded!"

"No? Then prove it! That lil' twig is your momma's?"

"Yeah"

"Then throw it away."

"What?"

"You heard me, boy. Throw that water out and toss that twig in the trash. Start showin' me that you know how to be a man and put a woman in her place."

"I can't, this is …"

"Son, if you don't put your foot down, then your momma's gonna be runnin' out er'ytime there's a lil' ol' fight. And if you don't take a stand against your momma, you aint provin' to yourself that you got what it takes to be a man. She's gotta learn to accept when God's tryin' to get her attention, 'stead of bein' her own woman."

Michael tightly gripped the bottle, which was now warm from the late morning sun. The tender leaves of Magdalena's branch fluttered gently in the wind just like the old bougainvillea tree used to. Even a few days after the big tree was ripped down, the confetti of dried pink flower petals still littered the dirt by the driveway and Michael's feet. Even though she was slowly being buried like an ancient artifact beneath the sand, her ghost was still there with him, reminding him that she hadn't left.

"Son? I ain't got all day."

Michael stood frozen, and the sound of cicadas stung his eardrums as he fought against the erupting sentiment. He wanted the earth to swallow him whole, to be buried under the pebbles and sand and to vanish forever into the ground with all the pink flowers.

"Look, son, I know it's hard, but you can't forget what Jesus did and what he does is 'cause he loves you. Just like the church loves you, and I love you! We all just want you to live in the grace that Jesus' given you."

Michael couldn't bring himself to look up at Pastor Roberts, who had already placed his hand on his shoulder, which felt like cold lead pulling him down.

"If you don't do it, son, God'll let all 'em lustful feelings come after you. You want that?"

The wetness of Michael's subtle tears rained down like a spring drizzle at his feet. The dirt drank up his watery fears, an indifferent salve for him that was impotent in the face of betrayal to Magdalena.

"Fine, have it your way, son. God'll get your attention, just you see. We'll see when you come for your last appointment."

As Pastor Roberts strolled down the driveway, he began to hum and sing to himself while the hellish Phoenix winds carried the melody away.

> "Just as I am without one plea
> But that thy blood was shed for me
> And that Thou bid'st me come to thee
> Oh, lamb of God I come, I come …"

The soft rumble of a clean engine crescendoed as Pastor Roberts's car came to life and then rolled past Michael, who still leaned against Manny's truck. Michael could recall most of what Pastor Roberts scolded him over right up until the threat of divulging his secret and accusations of addiction. From then on, the rest of the conversation disintegrated into a jumble of a thousand barely recognizable pieces, and the only words he could remember was the verse.

> *"But if ye forgive not men their trespasses, neither will your Father forgive your trespasses."*

It was a jarring proposition to impose the interdependence of faith and salvation on the nexus of his command to forgive. A necessity for a necessity that would result in mutual assured benefit. But the running account of wandering nights, finding places of refuge to sleep, and the insecure and constant feeling of having a bag of clothes ready at hand seemed to be a hefty debt that Manny owed in exchange for the corrupt thoughts that manifested in the salt desert of Michael's dream.

By now, the great ball of light was rising higher in the sky, and he could feel the sweat beads on his brow and back as the hunk of rusted metal that he was leaning against baked. It was the inevitable return that was waiting for him at the threshold. The hopes of breaking free this time were finally dashed and lay scattered like the remains of the many dusty pink flowers. In reluctant resignation, he turned around to head back inside.

Once he came back into the house, Michael saw that the scene had managed to change from the overt and melodramatic contrition to the routine and mundane trappings of Manny's life. He quickly glanced into the kitchen, and he saw that Manny sat at the table having said all he had needed to say, reverently and quietly waiting for food while Magdalena tied an apron around her waist to start cooking, but not without first turning the radio on ...

"You're listening to KPRY,
broadcasting the truth of God
across the state of Arizona …"

Neither Manny nor Magdalena noticed him sneak back into the house while they finished the last few rehearsed actions of their soap opera rerun. Michael stealthily made his way back down the dark hallway and into his bedroom to quickly drop the new gift on his bed before going into the bathroom. He quietly turned the faucet on and then filled his water bottle before he snuck back into his bedroom and searched for a place to hide his mom's prized plant. He couldn't hide it under the bed or in the box spring cradle without water spilling, so the best he could do in the meantime was place it on the floor next to his dresser, obscured from the view of Manny in the doorway.

"Hijo?" Magdalena called out.

"Oh! Geez, you scared me"

"Perdon hijo, pero no quieres algo de comer."[389]

"Nah, I'm not really that hungry."

"Ni yo tampoco, pero hay que complacer al hombre … por mientras," she said, rolling her eyes. "Oye hijo, no has visto mi ramita por ahi."[390]

"Yeah, I found it and hid it in here."

"A que bueno, a ver si la panto esta semana."[391]

"Ok, you might wanna let it get a 'lil stronger, it took a beatin' outside."

---

[389] "Did you want something to eat?"
[390] "Me neither, but gotta make the man happy. Hey, son, you haven't seen my little branch around here, have you?"
[391] "Oh good, we'll see if I plant it next week."

"Esta bien. Ahorita se va el Manuel a trabajar."[392]

"OK …"

"A ver si nos hacemos unas quesadillas y escuhar musica como el otro dia."[393]

"Sure, we can do that," he said, displaying a warm smile. "Mom?"

"Si, hijo?"

"You miss Mexico?"

Despite all her machisma, the question softened Magdalena as all the memories of her childhood, her family, her music, and every copper-speckled summer sunset in the Sonoran sky sparkled in the liquid jewels of her tears.

"Sabes que, hijo … llevo una gota de Mexico en mi, ojala que pueda beber por una vida con tan poquito."[394]

The air was still and quiet as she left to attend to her contrite husband. The house was back just as it was, but Michael and Magdalena were one notch lower. Nothing could erase the injustices that he and Magdalena had endured those few short days. A growing litany of transgressions that for everyone in the sphere of Manny and Pastor Roberts seemed to easily justify. It was becoming increasingly clear that his mother may be right. Maybe for the people at church, their God lived in a state of constant existential threat unless sin could be purged from them. To him, it seemed that her unwillingness to conform to being a White, ladylike Christian woman and

---

[392] "That's fine, Manny will leave to work in a bit"

[393] "All right. Manuel is going to head off to work in a little bit. We can make some quesadillas and listen to music like the other day."

[394] "You know what, son … I take a drop of Mexico with me, hopefully I can drink for a lifetime on so little."

his incessant failure at correcting his sexual deviancy were the iniquity, the kryptonic threat to Pastel Jesus's very being. It was a frightening power that he did not want, the ability to undo God with his own desires. So, when faced with the perplexities of life, he did what he had been taught to do. He opened his new Bible to the verse Pastor Roberts pointed out earlier, except this time he started to read a few verses earlier:

> *And when thou prayest,*
> *thou shalt not be as the hypocrites are:*
> *for they love to pray standing*
> *in the synagogues and in*
> *the corners of the streets,*
> *that they may be seen by men.*

12

That afternoon, the last Saturday before the start of the ASU fall semester, was to be 117 degrees. Autumn in Arizona typically meant a resurrection of scorched greenery that rose out of the brown and crispy remains. The monsoons had brought little reprieve in the way of rain, but they had managed to delicately cake the city with the powdery dust on the streets and homes, at least until Manny brought in his army of leaf blowers to kick it up off the north side of town.

Even though Manny's regular customers were a good drive away, all that dirt seemed to find its way to Manny's front yard. Drifts of sand rippled across the barren yard as if forming a miniature Sahara. The only thing keeping the growing dunes down were the hands of Magdalena as she tended to her new bougainvillea. She managed to save face by nurturing the one that Manny planted, even going so far as cutting the twine bindings that tied her to the trellis. At the very least Magdalena could give her freedom while she waited for her little branch to get stronger and sprout some roots. It was expected that, as with most of his gifts, Manny would lose interest in why he bought them in the first place. There was no need for him to pay attention anymore, now that Magdalena had walked back into the house and right back into his marriage.

And in the same way, the fleeting promise of a surrogate father to Michael had blown over like a sandstorm rolling over the mountains. It was of little concern to Michael, since Manny's ambivalence usually meant that he and his mother were left alone in the tenuous but somewhat livable peace. Michael felt lucky that the ambivalence also brought with it liberation from early Saturday morning workdays. So, with his newly found free time, he decided to foster the one last relationship he had hoped to have before he would venture out and into the world of sin that Pastor Roberts cautioned him about.

****

"Jab – Uppercut – Hook … again … Jab – Uppercut – Hook … good, again … Jab – Uppercut – Hook," commanded Michael.

"Man! How many of these we gonna do?" asked Diego.

"Just one more set. Then I gotta go."

"Alrighty …"

"Jab – Uppercut – Hook … again … Jab – Uppercut – Hook …"

The Saturday rhythm of the gym had settled in after the early morning hours when Michael arrived. He wanted to make sure that he was there as long as possible to see Diego before he left. It was almost noon, and Manny would be coming by to pick him for his final appointment, the last time he would have to see Pastor Roberts.

"All right, man, that's good enough for today."

"Thanks, Miguel."

"No problem. You gonna be keepin' this up when

I'm gone?"

"I hope so …"

"Has it been helpin'?"

"Yeah … I mean, as much as it can."

"Good."

"I can't believe this is your last day, man!"

"Yeah, I know! Summer just flew by!"

"I'm gonna miss you whenever I come here."

"I know, me too."

Michael fidgeted awkwardly as he tried to fish out a way to ask Diego.

"Oye, Miguelito!" called out a booming voice from behind him.

"Yeah, Coach?"

"Hey, can you take out the trash from the office and bathrooms? I left it right there. I got a lesson right now."

"Sure!"

"Thanks, Miguelito! What's up, Diego, how ya been?"

"Doin' all right, Coach," said Diego.

"All right, all right, boys!" said Coach Padilla cheerfully.

Michael was unable to speak for a bit as he still searched for a way to ask Diego. He could feel the tingling in his stomach as he looked at Diego covertly, admiring him still.

"Well … I better go get my stuff. Patti will be here to pick me up."

"Well, hey … uhm … that's what I wanted to, uhm … kinda ask you?"

"What's that?"

"Would it be … OK … if you gave me her number?"

"You want her number?"

"Unless you think it'll be weird, then I'll …"

"Nah, that's fine … I mean … I didn't know you liked her."

"Well … yeah, I kinda do … and I wanna get to know her and all, so …"

"Yeah, I'll give you her number … it's 480-21 …"

"Whoa, whoa, hold up, man, I need somethin' to write it down."

"Uhm … sure, I kinda need to get my gloves off anyways."

"Cool, cool."

Michael bolted for the trash bags that were sitting outside Coach's office. Any excuse to get him out of the painfully obtuse conversation of asking, for the very first time in his life, for a girl's phone number.

He went outside to the back alley where the dumpsters were under a scraggly and twisted ironwood tree, growing out of the patchy pavement. He tossed the bags overhead into the speckled sunlight falling around the dull green leaves above, and then he leaned against the hot metal of the dumpster.

"God, I made a fool outta myself!" he whispered as he let his head fall back against the steel in a booming thud. He was so lost in his inner thoughts that he didn't notice Diego standing in the doorway, quietly watching him rewind and mouth the words he wanted to say.

"Hey," Diego gently called out.

"Heeeey … man," Michael said, startled. "Did you get your sister's number?"

"Yeah, I did, but I wanna ask you somethin' first."

"What's that?"

"You really like her?"

"Do I like her? Come on, man, I wouldn't be askin' if I didn't like her."

"You sure?"

"Look, I know 'cause you're her brother you wanna …"

"Well, yeah, she's my sister, so I gotta know."

"Other than me just being straight up witchyou, how else are you gonna know?"

"Like this …"

Diego lunged forward and clenched a handful of Michael's shirt, pulling Michael into his waiting kiss. When their lips touched, Michael felt the electric elation coursing up and down his body as passion bloomed from a neglected bud deep in the recesses of his self. Michael could feel the universe slowing down as the two locked in, and Michael, in a momentary lapse of restraint, slowly allowed himself to kiss Diego back. The softness of Diego's lips pulled him deeper as he found it almost impossible to breathe, and his heartbeat echoed in his veins. In one instant, the longing gazes and minor lapses that entire summer crashed into a thousand little pieces as he felt the illumination of his desire finally realized in the flesh. It was the boy in the salt desert. He finally had his way.

But as soon as Diego pulled away, air and consequence rushed back into Michael like a riptide. In one breath, the serpent of regret sunk its fangs into him to deaden the novel euphoria with its venom of fear and guilt. The quickening of this reaction made Michael's lungs quiver at the grave sin he had just committed.

> *I am a man ... Dirty little faggot*
> *I am made in the image of God ... hyprocrites ...*
> *... You-nd dat lil-shit jus-live here ...*
> *Cryin' is for girls and faggots!*
> *Op'n the-door you lil' shit! ...*
> *but that they blood was shed for me ...*
> *I will not see other men ... burned in their lust ...*
> *I am a man*

Dizzy with judgment, Michael could feel the walls of the alley spinning around him as the temple of two emotionally wrought years of honed conformity came crashing down in a fantastic ecstasy of destruction. The mere shock of his first kiss made him feel as if the fires of hell were already licking the soles of his feet. He looked down to see the imagined bathwater rushing at his feet again, blushed with his own judgment, that only ran redder and redder the more he stared at his shoes. Faintly in the distance, the low rumble of Manny's truck could be heard idling in the parking lot of the gym.

"I ... I ... gotta go," Michael said, stumbling and pushing past Diego, who was expectantly waiting for the reward to his gamble. But with every clumsy and heavy-footed step away from him, Diego could feel the collapse of his chest into the growing cavity of loss. Whether he had misread the looks he would catch from Michael, or whether his own infatuations had blinded him, Diego watched the boy whom he thought he could love turn his back on him and walk away.

"What's wrong with you?" asked Manny as Michael climbed into the truck.

"Nothin'," said Michael as he started to shiver inside the sweltering cab.

"Whatever …"

As Manny let off the brake and rolled out of the parking lot, Michael looked back through the hazy and dusty glass of the truck window. Diego stood in the parking lot waiting and hoping that his object of affection would come back instead of escaping from his life forever. Even though he was strapped into the seat, Michael's legs urged him to jump out of the moving truck and make a mad dash back to kiss Diego. But between the dirty glass and the moral chains of Pastel Jesus, he could not.

I've gotta kill him, the boy.

As Manny pulled into the empty church parking lot, the crew of dark-skinned men were already getting to work, blowing around dust and trash. The humming drone of gasoline leaf blowers penetrated the cab before Manny could kill the engine. Without saying a word, Michael slipped out and slammed shut the door of the truck.

"Hey, don't be slammin' my door! … Michael! … Michael! … Este chamaco!" shouted Manny.

But Michael headed straight for the front doors, determined to seek out his immediate cure. Under the shadow of the white steeple and a cloud of brown dust from Manny's crew, the ubiquitous words above the entrance met him once again.

"Come unto me, all ye that labour and are heavy laden and I will give you rest"

He wanted the words to be real. They needed to be real. He wanted to be free from this, once and for all. Michael could see through the words to the brief dark flashes of the future if this continued.

Diego, how could you?

"Well, mornin', son!" Pastor Roberts said cheerfully as he came waddling out through the double doors.

"We need to start now!" Michael said pointedly as he slid past the pastor's damp, sweaty belly and into the dark shadows of the church. He headed down the middle aisle like so many times before, aggravated by the urgency for redemption. However, the soothing reminders of peace and affection from the divine were scrambled in the buzzing cauldron of thoughts that kept boiling over within him as he passed through every sunbeam that cut through the darkness. The familiar swirling nebulous dust was gentle, each bit illuminated in golden sunlight like a terrestrial star before being swallowed by the blackness.

Michael stopped in the aisle, looking at the empty pews around him. Now, not even the ghosts of his memory prayed for him. He was forsaken to this universe of solitude, where only the hints of Cosmic God lived in the dark. Slowly, a frightening premonition crept in—that those who had prayed for his salvation as a child were now going to abandon him one by one.

"Son, you're actin' as crazy as a sprayed cockroach!" Pastor Roberts billowed as he stood guard over the slightly open front door.

Michael thought he could hide the tears streaming down his face, but even in the dim light, Pastor Roberts could see the shimmer of rivulets on his soft brown cheeks.

"Somethin' bad happened."

"Somethin' bad? Well, what kinda 'bad' thing are we talkin' 'bout, son?" Pastor Roberts asked sternly.

"I ... I ..."

"Boy, spit it out!" Pastor Roberts commanded as he waddled his way down the middle aisle.

"I kissed someone!"

"Oh, Lord in heav'n!"

"I didn't mean to! It just happened!" Michael sobbed.

"Son, I …" He stopped midsentence as his nostrils puffed out. "Lord, help me with this boy!"

He stopped waddling for a moment as he closed his eyes.

"Son, I'm only gonna ask you once, so you better be truthful with me, 'cause God don't like no liars, you hear me?"

Michael nodded.

"Did you go out and kiss a man?"

Pastor Roberts was barely visible through the kaleidoscope of tears. Truth was pulling at the very corners of Michael's face . He said nothing, and nodded again.

"Son, I just … how could you?! Huh?! After all God's done for you, how can you turn your back on him like that?"

Michael was silent and started shivering like a cowering dog being scolded for soiling the living room carpet.

"Whatcha gotta say for yo'self, boy? Huh?"

Michael tried to speak, but he felt his tongue retreat to guard his words.

"Boy, you better answer me! Don't be actin' like them queers, you hear me?! It's 'bout time you start actin' like a man. Now answer me!"

"I … I … want … want it … to stop."

"Son, you've been sayin' that for two long years and now you come in here and tell me that you're only a few steps away from fornicatin' with a man?"

"I just wanna stop it!"

"How am I supposed to believe you wanna change when you're out there doin' all that sinnin'?!"

Unable to speak, Michael lowered his eyes before Pastor Roberts as he watched the watery contortions of the blue carpet change with every teardrop falling to the floor.

"I … I dunno! Heav'n help me!" Pastor Roberts prayed out.

"I really don't wanna be like this."

"C'mon now, son, don't be givin' me no lip service, ya hear?"

"I wanna change!"

"You wanna change that bad?"

"Yeah!"

"You're gonna have to convince me, son!"

"Don't you believe me?"

"Nope! 'Cause right now I can't even believe you're a believer what with all this backslidin'!"

"I wanna to change!!" Michael said a little more forcefully.

"You think just by whinin' and cryin like a lil' girl that you've shown me that you wanna change?"

"I WANT to change!" he said louder and with more command.

"Son, you gotta be beggin' a lot louder than that. God hears only the voices of righteous men."

"I WANT TO CHANGE!" he screamed.

"What do wanna change, boy?!"

"I wanna stop sinnin'!"

"What sin, boy? God can't forgive you unless you ask for it."

"My sin of … my sin … my …"

"Say it out loud, son!"

"My sin of thinkin' 'bout guys."

"Boy, donchya be lyin' to God in front of me! This is now more than just thinkin' 'bout men! Go on! Confess to God whatcha really are!"

"I'm a sinner!"

"No, son! Confess to God what kind of sinner you are!"

Michael looked at him with watery eyes, terrified to say it. The word—that name he had tried to fight against all these years. The word that embodied everything he was afraid of.

"C'mon, son! Say it."

"I'm … I'm gay," Michael confessed.

"That's right, boy, you're a faggot! A dirty, vile faggot! Say it again!"

"I'm … I'm a faggot," he said hesitantly.

"And again, son, you cry out to God in heaven! Let him hear your cry!"

"I'm a faggot!"

"YES, LORD! Hear the cry of a repentant sinner, in the name of your son, Jesus!"

"I'M A FAGGOT, GOD! I'M A FAGGOT, I'M A FAGGOT, I'M A FAGGOT!"

"Hallelujah, thank you, Jesus!" Pastor Roberts yelled out as he lifted his hands high in the air.

Michael stood in the abyss of the dim church clenching his hands into white knuckle fists, looking up at the dark wooden beams and pale white plaster hoping that God heard him.

"Son, you better be straight with me this time."

"I will …"

"You wanna be free from the burden of your filthy

sin?"

"I do! I dunno how else to say it!"

"All right, son, all right. God don't leave a soul out to fend for itself if it cries out for mercy."

"It's what I want."

"Trouble is, you've gotta a taste for lust now, boy."

"I know."

"You know what it's like, and you're gonna be wantin' it."

Michael just nodded.

"We gotta make sure you know that touchin' a man like that is a sin. I'm gonna teach it to you. I wanna make it so you feel how bad it is, and you'll never wanna do it again."

"I don't wanna feel like this again."

"Come on up, son. Come on up here behind the pulpit. We gotta lotta work to do."

Pastor Robert waddled and led Michael up to the rows of chairs for the choir. He pulled two of them out and placed them to face each other in front of Pastel Jesus.

"Sit down, son," commanded Pastor Roberts as he made his way to the back of the church.

Michael took his seat at the right hand of Pastel Jesus. The fluorescent bulbs above him flickered on, and the droning hum of their bluish-white glow banished the darkness, the natural light, and the nebulous dust in the air. Michael wiped the last few tears from his face as he looked up at Pastel Jesus's blue eyes. He seemed so serene, as all the other times before, but Michael wished that just once he would break his gaze from heaven to look at him.

"Son, I'm gonna be straight witchyou. We're gonna have to do some pretty heavy prayin', you got that?"

Pastor Roberts heaved and sweated as he walked back to Michael, wincing and flipping through the pristine golden pages of his Bible.

"Right here, this is where God'll have us start," Pastor Roberts said. "Here you go, son." His pudgy fingers handed Michael the Bible. "Read verse 13, son."

"And he was there in the wilderness forty days, tempted of Satan; and was with the wild beasts; and the angels ministered unto him," Michael recited.

"Praise Jesus!"

"You sayin' I gotta wait forty days?"

"No, I'm sayin' that you're in a wilderness. You're gonna be in a place away from your daddy and your momma. The devil is temptin' you right now. We're gonna pray for angels to come and minister to you. You get what I'm sayin'?"

Michael mumbled, "Yeah, I understand."

"Now you listen to me and you listen good! Jesus was tempted and resisted, so you gotta be able to resist the Devil too. You understand me? Everythin' you feel that's callin' you to lust after men, I want you to resist it. Ya hear me?"

"Yes, sir."

"We're gonna do the same thing we've done before, but you gotta swear to God Almighty that you resist every temptation that's gonna come at ya. You got that?"

"I'll try."

"I don't need you to try, son. You gotta step up and be a man of God, like I told ya. Just keep askin' God to deliver you from this evil, and he'll help you resist."

The old wooden chair creaked under the weight of Pastor Roberts as he sat down with his legs open wide and as close to Michael as possible. As he leaned forward and laid the open Bible on the floor between them, Michael could feel his knobby warm knee touch his just as the smell of coffee breath and thickened saliva wafted from Pastor Roberts's mouth. In a pious attempt to hide from the pungent smell, Michael buried his face in his hands and hunched over the open Bible. He believed wholeheartedly that this was his redemption and this was what would ultimately define him in his hopes to receive his divine rest. He heard the cavernous sigh from Pastor Roberts before he began to speak.

"Let us pray."

A lifeless silence swallowed Michael and the air around him. Despite the minor hums and drones of lights and work crews, everything seemed muffled and far away. Everything except for what was in the tiny huddle of prayer around him. The pounding pulse of his anxious heart beat on his eardrums, and the veins in his neck throbbed with the rush of blood, all while Pastor Roberts heaved hot blasts through his nostrils that brushed across Michael's short black hair.

> *God, I just wanna be right with you.*
> *I wanna be good.*

"Heav'nly Father, we come before you askin' for your miraculous and atonin' mercy to fall on this boy. Lord, you know the sin that has plagued him for so long. A foul and vile sin of the highest order that brings with it disease, death, and damnation from your holy and righteous judgment. Father, we know that the Enemy himself has come to lay claim to this boy. He has come to tempt him into a life of sin that you can save him from with the power of your precious merciful blood. We know that you have brought him here to this place, that you've been workin' in his heart to prepare the seed of your truth to be planted in the soil of his soul. And just as Jesus was led into the desert for forty days and tempted by the devil, we ask that you bring Michael into the desert of his mind to face the demon of sexual perversion and that you strengthen him to resist temptations, knowin' that you will bring about salvation to him."

Michael tried to slow his breathing as he whispered, "Please, God, let this be the last time."

"Son, before we keep goin', is there anythin' you want to say to God? Anythin' at all?"

Confused by the request, Michael lifted his head out of his hands and prayed what he thought God wanted to hear.

"God, I … I'm sorry for what I've done. I'm sorry for what I am. Please, I need help to be good. I just wanna be good."

"Son, aren't you gonna confess your sins to God?"

"I've already said it."

"It don't matter, you say it again. You can't be forgiven if you don't confess it."

"I'm … I'm …"

"Go on, son."

"I'm … I'm confused. I'm confused about what I want …"

"Son, you ain't confused. Say what you are."

"I'm …"

"Say it … you're a faggot, plain and simple."

"I'm a faggot …"

"Call sin what it is! Cry out to God and ask for forgiveness for bein' a faggot!"

"God … I'm a faggot."

"Amen, son, confess it again to the Lord!"

"I'm a faggot."

"Hallelujah! Confess to God and repent, son!"

"God, I'm a faggot, please forgive me for bein' a faggot!"

"Praise Jesus! Praise God Almighty!"

The acrid flavor of this new label numbed Michael's lips where Diego had kissed him. It was as if a piece of cold coal had been smeared across his mouth, leaving a charred residue that covered the intimacy and innocence of human pleasure he had experienced earlier that day.

"All right, son, just like last week I want you to let God take you back to the dream that you keep havin'. And I want you to focus on the last part. Can you do that?"

"I can do that."

"OK, son, just keep your eyes closed and tell me when you see."

The back of Michael's eyelids darkened as he released control of his mind and allowed himself to drift back into the tunnel of his imagination, until the dim light of the desert grew and eventually surrounded him in the blinding white flash of pure subconsciousness. He could see with absolute clarity the silhouette of the nearly monochrome purple mountains surrounding him, the white salt flats stretched out in all directions. He turned as he had before to see the long, imposing shadow of the old dead tree as it traced its sinuous form on the dry salt grains. Like before, his mind's eye would follow the shadow figure to meet his two familiar fantasies—the young male and female desires that he kept secret in the inner world. However, there was no hiding for one of them this time.

                      Are you in that place now, son?
Yeah, I am.
                           Whatcha see, son?
I see … I see the tree like before …
                            Is that boy there?
Michael hesitated to divulge his refugee.
                  Answer me, son, is that boy there?!
Yeah, he is.

                        Oh, heav'nly Father,
                 the Devil has come and rooted
              himself in the mind of this boy.
                We beg you that you dispatch
                    your angels to him.
                 Please minister to him.
              Son, is there anythin' else
             you can tell me about him?
Nothin' really.
He looks the same as before.
                 Look a little closer, son.
I told you he lo—

                 Just take a closer look, son.
               I know what I'm tellin' you.

     While immersed in the world of his imagination, Michael walked closer to the twisted tree, hearing the quiet breeze of the desert and the crunch of salt grains under his feet. Nearing the male fantasy, Michael looked closely at his face, which so many times before was pleasing but wasn't of anyone he recognized. What seemed like a bouquet of fluttering butterflies grew in his belly, and he could feel the magnetism he had felt when Diego's lips touched his, a sensual warmth and ecstasy inviting him to partake in human pleasure. It filled his body, budding and blossoming from his shortly repressed adolescent drive. The fresh memory of Diego's ambush kiss flashed in front of him like lightning in the desert under a clear blue sky. Anxious cicadas began their song as he looked around the valley of his subconscious, vigilant of the changes occurring in this protected inner world. The female fantasy sensed the change in her surroundings as well, and like a frightened doe she began to run toward the horizon for safety, disappearing into the liquid line between white salt and purple mountains. He turned once more to the boy, still standing by the dead tree, and staring back at Michael with honest and gentle brown eyes was Diego.

> Son! Can you tell me what
> God is showin' you?
> Who is that boy?

It's … uhm … it's the guy …

> Go on, son, you can do this.

It's the guy that kissed me.

> Father, have mercy on this boy.
> Lord Jesus, send down your
> grace from heav'n.

What's wrong?

> Jesus, we beg that you come
> and minister to his soul!

Why is he in my dream?

> Heavn'ly Father! In the name of Jesus,
> we demand that the Devil
> bow his knee to you!
> We ask in the most precious
> and holy name of Jesus that

the Devil release his hold on the boy!
In the name of Jesus,
creator of heaven and earth,
we command that
the Devil leave this boy,
that he be free from the bondage
of homosexuality,
that he be free to live
the way you intended!

The bouquet of butterflies in Michael's belly
flapped frantically, sensing the same dread and fear that
drove his young female fantasy to flee.

Son, listen to me.
In the name of Jesus,
do you turn from this sin?!

Y-y-yes.

Son, do you wanna walk in
the light of God's grace?!

Yes, I do.

Do you reject the abhorrent
lifestyle of a faggot?!

Yes.

Say it louder, son!

Yes!

Louder, son, so the Devil
knows you mean business!

YES!

Do profess your faith in Jesus?

Yes!

Is he your one and
only Lord and savior?!

Yes!

>   Do you wanna be washed in
>   the blood of Christ for all your sins?

Yes … yes, I do!

>   And son, do you still feel
>   like fornicatin' with that boy?

His lips fell suddenly silent as he squeezed his
eyes even tighter so as not to let any more of the reality
around him infiltrate the serenity of his secret place. But he
could not stay quiet, as his lungs shivered with every deep
breath, shaking and vibrating the air in his throat.

>   Son, I'm gonna ask you again …
>   you feel like fornicatin' with that boy?

Staring at the image of Diego in front of him,
Michael felt the tears of remorse cascade down to the
parched white earth at his feet.

>   Son, you better answ—

Yes, I still do.

>   Stand up right now, boy!
>   Come on, stand up,
>   and keep your eyes closed!

Pastor Roberts's heavy and frustrated breathing
was growing by the minute.

>   Son … listen to me, all right?
>   The Devil has got a real strong
>   foothold on you already,
>   but the God that you and I believe

in is stronger than the Devil. Am I right?
Yes, sir.

Say Amen, son,
like you believe in Jesus!
Amen!

If you want God to save you,
your gonna have to resist the temptation
to fall into all that fornication you feel.
You got that?
Yeah, I got it. I mean, Amen!

I want you to look that
boy straight in the eye
and I want to you to
repeat that sayin' I taught you.
You understand me?
Amen!

Whatever lustin' you might feel,
you stand strong and resist it.
Whatever you feel, resist it!
I'll be right here prayin' witchyou.
OK.

With his eyes still closed, Michael took in one last breath before falling back into the place halfway between reality and dreams. Once he was in the salt desert, he saw his object of desire next to the dead tree. He came up close to him and did as Pastor Roberts commanded, gazing deep into his rich chocolate brown eyes. All the regret of running away poured out of him like an artesian spring, and he felt the pull of Diego drawing him in. This time, there was no fistfull of his shirt to draw him close. It was Michael wanting it for himself, wanting to recapture the missed opportunity and to repay Diego for his bravery. But

before they could bring their lips together, Michael began
to weep, as echoes seeped from the purple mountains
around him, shaking the ground and sky.

I'm a man.
>   Jesus, son of God and savior of mankind.
I'm made in the image of God,
as he chose and destined me to be.
>   Command that this devil of
>   perversion leave the soul of this boy.

       The light-blue sky turned to a rich indigo as the
sound of screeching cicadas could be heard in the distance,
like an approaching plague billowing into massive clouds
from behind him. Suddenly, while deeply entranced by
Diego's eyes, Michael sensed what felt like a heavy snake
on his left shoulder. Afraid to look, he maintained his
focus on resisting temptation. But the heavy snake felt
distinctly like immense emptiness and deadness. At the
same time, the weight caused a new sensation that excited
him in a strange way, a way that only the recent kiss from
Diego had ever done. Without being able to break his
concentration and look for himself, Michael figured that
whatever was tempting him and commanding him to leave
must be making itself known in this way.

I'll serve God as the
man he calls me to be!"
>   Instill in him a right spirit that
>   you have destined for him, Lord!
I'll love my wife as
Jesus loves the church!
>   Give him power to resist the

temptations of that faggot's lies!

Michael could see the pained look in Diego's eyes as his words grew louder to keep up with the pastor's voluminous prayers. However, both voices were competing to overcome the noise of the approaching horde of cicadas as each forceful prayer from Pastor Roberts seemed to change the salt desert and make it more tumultuous. The phantom snake brushed along Michael's neck in a gentle yet numbing caress, moving slowly and sensuously down to the collar of his shirt. The arousal intensified. The Devil was trying harder to tempt him.

I'll seek to do things that other men do!
Send your mighty angels to minister
to him that he may withstand this lust!
I'll affirm that I'm a man to
myself and others!
Teach this boy to reject the urges
to act like a woman!

The cloudless sky was growing even darker as the edges of the distant mountains melted in the monochromatic indigo of the atmosphere. Soon the great dome of the sky would envelope them in the darkest, silkiest blue, absent the warm, soothing tones of a typical fiery orange sunset. The shouts from Pastor Roberts to resist temptation bounced off the disappearing mountains like bullets ricocheting off steel. The phantom snake had continued its deadening and arousing track as it slid from his neck and now slithered around his chest. Carnal sensuality radiated like a cooling warmth through his body while causing his stomach to turn in anxious knots. He

wanted to wake up and run out of the church to get away
from the feeling, but he fought the urge, adamant that this
time he would be cured.

I'll turn away from anything
that would say I'm not a man!

Bring the light and truth of what
it means to be a man of God to
this boy, Lord!

I'll not see other men as objects of lusts!

Destroy the lie of homosexuality
that is in this boy!

Michael could feel the great tectonic shifts beneath
his feet as the ground vibrated and rumbled, while the
mountains ruptured with each of his and the pastor's
boisterous shouts. His throat felt raw, as if he had gargled
with sharp pebbles and broken glass, but he was adamant
that each time he shouted, he would strengthen his
willpower to conquer the sin. He had still not broken his
gaze with Diego, who was also distressed by the
catastrophic destruction around him. Terror, like that of a
child dreaming their first nightmare, had glazed his brown
eyes, which seemed to scream in mute pleas that this was
far worse than the immolation from before. However, as
the light in the desert was slowly fading, the phantom
snake had slithered its way farther along, to Michael's
belly, propagating the dueling sensual exhilaration and
paralyzing him with fear. With every inch it traveled, it
made his skin cold, as if blackness were straying from its
path to swallow him up and erase him. This feeling was
like suffocation, making Michael gulp for air in shallow,
spasmodic breaths. Involuntary shivers made his body

twitch in an orgasm of fear. Then the heavy phantom snake slowed its trek, finding its destination as it began to softly caress his crotch. The serpent opened its jaws to swallow its captured prey, and it gripped him in pulsating and undulating motions. Sexualized venom was released instantaneously, a numbness that shot up from his loins into the rest of his body. Like a gut punch, he felt the wind get knocked out of him. Air fled his lungs without a struggle. The venom stopped the convulsions, but it wasn't relief. It was an anesthesia that made him aware of what was happening and that he would be unable to do anything to make it stop. Diego seemed to feel the exact same intrusion on his body, silently pleading with Michael to end it while he cried in the looming darkness.

I'll see my fellow men as examples
of manliness.

> Jesus, let this destroy his lust.
> Let this teach him to hate this sin.

I'm a man.

> Lord, let this be what drives
> him away from being a faggot!

In the deafeningly quiet and dim salt desert, the blackness had swallowed nearly the entirety of his imagination, and only the shadow of the tree and Diego remained in front of him. The snake continued to arouse and tantalize him as he found himself in a strange equilibrium of consciousness and sleep. As he screamed his last affirmation into the dark and palpable indigo, his final words evaporated into the infinite space around him while Pastor Roberts had quieted his praises to God in his usual post-sermon whisper. He assumed that the numbness that traveled through his body and tingled in his joints was the antidote he always prayed for—a divine power to restrain his lusts, causing him to feel repulsed if he were to ever look at another man. He thought that this was his awakening into heterosexual rebirth and the rest he had sought for so long. But his burgeoning curiosity finally broke his sensual paralysis to look down at the mysterious creature still touching him. He expected to see Diego's hand still touching and trying to seduce him.

The ground was not covered in usual twilight lit salt but rather covered in old commercial carpet stretched tightly, softly illuminated by the bluish florescent light. Resting on the ground were the pristine white pages of the open Bible, its glowing golden edges untouched in the ambient light. And hovering above the open Bible was the thick, pale-skinned serpent of Pastor Roberts's pudgy arm fondling Michael through his shorts.

The sour flavor of stomach acid splashed on the back of his tongue. His whole body shook, not in prudish eroticism but in instinctual rage that had to be dealt with immediately. He wanted to scream so someone from Manny's crew could come in and see what was happening, but he could hear only the sound of air passing through his throat. He watched as the pink, bald, sweaty head of Pastor Roberts lifted from it posture of prayer like a cobra raising its head to hypnotize its prey. With his eyes still shut and his one free hand raised in worship, he continued to whisper praise.

"Yes, Jesus, yes. Show your mercy to him, yes, Lord Jesus."

For the first time, Michael heard no inner sound to his rage. There were no cicadas buzzing in his head. There were no affirmations repeating in his ear. Just savage silence and caveman instinct. He then acted on it.

Michael felt crushing cartilage and flesh against his fingers as his indignation uncoiled on the unsuspecting pastor. The impact echoed in his own bones like the recoil of a pistol, as his arm drove his fist deep into the pastor's face in one of the best right hooks he had ever thrown. He watched the plump pervert roll his surprised eyes back into his head and collapse to his knees in front of Michael, falling ungraciously from his seat of mercy into the crosshairs of judgment. Blood from his lip and nose flowed in streams of crimson that splattered onto the pristine white pages of the Bible. All of this occurred before the visage of Pastel Jesus, still gazing and waiting for the spirit of God to fall like a dove from heaven.

"Why'd … you … ?" coughed Pastor Roberts.

In his savage aggression, Michael could only think about doing what he was told to do. The snake had tempted him, and he had to destroy the snake. So he kicked Pastor Roberts in the chest. The thud to his torso faded quickly as Pastor Roberts writhed on the floor, gasping for air.

"Stop!"

Michael kicked him again in his stomach as Pastor Roberts screamed out.

"I just … wanna … help you!"

He had never seen Pastor Roberts truly cry. He had never seen a man reduced to a blubbering and beaten mess in front of him. The pastor lay on the ground as Michael continued to kick him over and over again. His breathing was shallow as bubbles of blood popped like fresh berries around his mouth, and he choked out his plea to Michael.

"I wanna … help … I wanna … help …"

Michael's rage may have subsided a bit, but the anesthetic blackness of the snake felt as if it were now seeping out of Pastor Roberts and coming to claim him. Guilt, remorse, and indignation hit Michael in waves the longer Pastor Roberts lay on the ground motionless. So Michael ran.

He charged straight for the front door of the church, his legs accelerating him as he left Pastor Roberts behind. Michael pushed the heavy wooden door wide open into a cloud of earth-colored dust and the daylight.

In a full sprint, Michael ran past Manny and his crew, toward Central Avenue. Luckily, traffic was stopped at a red light. He weaved his way around the rumbling cars, dodging exhaust clouds and the ever-present pungent smell of semi-liquid asphalt. Even through the cacophony of car sounds, he swore he could hear a distinct familiar voice calling out to him.

"Michael! Michael!"

He ignored the calls, afraid that Manny was chasing. He was ready to tackle Manny and beat him the same way he had beat Pastor Roberts. He darted behind a repair shop with a hand-painted sign and into a dusty barren alleyway in the back. His legs ached with acid as he tried to put more distance between him and the church, trying with all his might to push the whole planet away from him. Puffs of dust shot out from the soles of his feet, and he felt the burning rays of the midday sun scorching his body. Sweat soaked his clothes, making them heavy, and his legs chaffed as the sound of an approaching truck seemed to stalk him from behind.

"Michael!"

He tried to run even faster down the back alley, until he found a small hiding place next to a building and a dumpster and under the shade of a Palo Verde tree. He slipped into the narrow space that reeked of rotted garbage and fetid grease, hoping that Manny would pass him by. Even though the adrenaline was starting to wear off, his heart was still pounding hard to where he could feel it in his throat as he tried to catch his breath. He hunched over and slowly collapsed to his knees, dry heaving from breathing in the stench of decaying trash. His skin began to tingle from what he thought were ten thousand malevolent insects as they swarmed him, and icy cold sweats made him shiver in the unrelenting Arizona summer heat.

He could hear the faint gravelly footsteps through the street noise in the otherwise quiet alley. In the pit of his stomach, raw and anxious acid churned as the freshly minted memory of his latest appointment began to replay in microsecond-long movies in his head. Over and over the scenes played out, and his body remembered the very real sensations. The same sexually numbing venom as before radiated from the phantom fingers of Pastor Roberts seductively rubbing him. Michael tried digging his fingernails into the skin of his forearms, trying to claw off the flesh that could not stop remembering. Tiny red droplets erupted from the deep scratches, like the agonizing blossoms from the dead tree in his dream. The sting from salty sweat helped to distract him from feeling the invisible hand on him in every unrelenting recollection. The footstep grew closer.

Michael squeezed his eyes tighter and hit his head hard, whispering and trying to console himself. "Go away, just go away, just go away."

Suddenly he felt the snake's jaws clamp down on his arm. He was not going to let this happen again. He flailed frantically in the small hiding space, trying to hit and claw whoever had found him and was trying to touch him again.

LEAVE ME ALONE …
DON'T FUCKIN' TOUCH ME!

> Michael!

NO, LET ME GO,
I SAID LET ME GO!

> Michael!!

STOP TOUCHIN' ME!!!
NO!!! STOP!!!

> Miguelito, it's me!!!

The booming voice was warm and familiar to Michael, as hands gripped his face and smooshed his cheeks. Michael realized that he hadn't opened his eyes the entire time, as if he were trapped in some never-wake nightmare. When he finally did open them, Coach Padilla was staring him down.

"Hey, it's OK, it's OK, it's OK!"

"Don't let him find me, Coach!" Michael cried. "Don't let him find me!"

"Ya, ya, ya calmate … calmate."

"He's gonna come after me, he's gonna come after me!"

"Estas bien, did someone do somethin' to you? What happened?"

Without any noise in his head to tell him otherwise, Michael lunged toward Coach Padilla and buried himself in his chest. He didn't care anymore if crying in the arms of another man made him feel like a faggot.

"Hey, hey, it's OK, Miguelito … It's OK, que te paso?"

"He touched me."

"Que, que?"

"Coach … he touched me!"

"Who touched you?! Manny?!"

Michael sheepishly shook his head, trying to vomit the truth.

"The pastor …"

"What?! Where?! Where'd he touch you?!"

"He … he touched my dick, Coach. HE TOUCHED MY DICK!!!!" Michael sobbed as he muffled his screams in Coach's chest.

Both sat in the muck of the ally, among the trash and dirt. Both men shook in each other's arms.

"You're OK, Miguelito, you're OK now … No one's gonna hurt you …"

"I just wanted it to go away … I just wanted it to go away …" Michael whispered.

13

The dingy linoleum in Coach's office warped and twisted whenever Michael looked down through the bottom of the empty shot glass, a little universe that he could escape to and glimpse at through this tiny circular window, like a spyglass. Unfortunately, on this side of the shot glass, regret was as real as the serpent's touch from Pastor Roberts.

Michael sat on the couch where he had spent countless nights sleeping. He could not shake the throbbing numbness in his hand. The scorching afternoon had stretched on for hours, and the waning yellow-white sunlight of the day had turned to a citrus orange flame that was being swallowed the dusk. He was far away from the inquisitive eyes of the young men swinging at the heavy bags outside. He was a little calmer now, though his chest and throat still burned a little as the dizziness from his first-ever taste of tequila had started to wear off. The glass was bone dry, with the faint smell of aged alcohol lingering only on Michael's breath. Michael imagined that every sad ranchera that Magdalena listened to carried with it the same secret and intoxicating agave smell of bitter memories.

"You know, I said I'd never drink 'cause of Manny," muttered Michael.

"You worried you're gonna end up like him?" asked Coach Padilla.

"Lil' bit."

"I wouldn't worry ..."

"Why not?"

"A lil' drink every once in a while ain't gonna make you like that. That shit takes years."

"I guess so," said Michael, staring again into the squiggly world at the bottom of the glass. "How many have you had?"

"Mmmm, only four so far ..."

"I think I'd be out for the count with that many."

"I figure that if after ten shots I still wanna go over to the church and beat the shit outta him, then I've thought it through ... Marianna can call a lawyer."

"You still wanna beat him up, even after four?"

Coach Padilla brazenly tipped his glass to his lips, and the golden tequila slid into his mouth in one gulp.

"Ahhhhh ... yup, still do ... Guess I need more." He picked up the bottle of warm tequila and poured himself another shot. "By the way, don't tell your mom I gave you booze. She'd kill me"

"There's a lot I don't tell her."

"Yeah?"

"Yeah ..."

"Why not?"

"It's my thing, you know? Ain't no one else's."

"You ever gonna tell her about all this?"

"No ... I just wanna forget it ever happened. Just

crawl into some dark hole and hide."

"I don't think you can, Miguelito, that shit … it stays with you forever."

Coach Padilla spoke while he stared off into the collection of the photographs on the walls. A massive collage of 4 x 6" trophies and enumerated masculine achievements over his lifetime. He silently beckoned to them like saints in a shrine dedicated to machismo, praying for wisdom to the gods he knew.

"You know, Miguelito … I … psss," he scoffed by smacking his lips, "… no se … no se!"[395]

"What?"

"You know … I've seen a lot a shit growin' up here. A lotta shit that I can't forget. And just the way I heard you screamin', it uhm … hijole … the way you sounded ahorita[396] just brought up some ..."

The tranquilizing effects of his single shot of tequila had all but evaporated by now, and as Michael closed his eyes, the vivid smells and sensations of his hiding place behind the dumpster began to intensify. Coach Padilla plopped himself on the couch, and Michael could feel his warm presence as if he were an incubus. The closeness of even a familiar man kindled within him an icy-cold distance.

"Oye, que te pasa, estas bien?"[397] asked Coach Padilla as he softly put his hand on Michael's shoulder. The feeling reminded Michael of the serpent's touch, tracing its path down his torso and to its eventual destination. The numbing venom radiated outward again,

---

[395] "… I don't know … I don't know!"
[396] Just now.
[397] "Hey, what's goin' on, are you OK?"

and his body began to tremble with cold shivers and helpless, spastic whimpering.

"Oye, oye, oye … it's okay, it's okay," Coach said softly.

"I … I … I feel him touchin' me again, Coach … I want it to go away, go away, GO AWAY!" Michael sobbed as he tried curling up in a ball, smacking his head.

"Oye, Miguel, open your eyes. Come on, mira me.[398] It's okay, it's okay … I'm not gonna hurt you, I'm not gonna hurt you."

Like a soul freed from an exorcised spirit, Michael collapsed into Coach's chest once again seeking comfort and refuge in the place that for two years he was told was forbidden.

"He was supposed to fix me, Coach … he was supposed to make it better."

Coach Padilla pulled Michael from his chest and tried to prop him up to speak to him.

"Listen to me, Miguelito, don't believe that shit! Me oiste?[399] You're better than that. If anyone needs fixin', it's that son of a bitch!"

"I know, Coach, but how am I gonna go on if I can't even be a man, huh? All this that I've been doin' and it don't work. I can't even stop cryin'!"

"You don't feel like you're a man?"

"I just hear everythin' in my head tellin' me that I'm not."

"Because he touched you?"

"Kinda …"

"Then what?"

---

[398] "Look at me."
[399] "You hear me?"

Michael cracked an uncomfortable crooked smile as he wiped his face of tears and snot before he could answer.

"Am I a fag, Coach?"

"Does it matter?"

"For me it does."

"You wanna be?"

"Sometimes I think I do, then sometimes no …"

"Hmmm …"

"You ever deal with somethin' like this, Coach?"

"You mean me? Know someone … that's …"

"Yeah."

"No, I don't … you just don't talk 'bout it where I grew up."

"Then who do I talk to … I've got no one."

"I don't know, Miguelito … sometimes you just have to make your own way."

It would be another hour before the sunset in the western Arizona sky and the little bit of orangey daylight burnt out to cooler shades of red and purple that glowed in the one window to the office. Michael lay back feeling a tenuous if not novel sense of relief. He tried to fall asleep, but even though his eyelids were weighted with booze, his fear of what was next propped his eyelids open like theaters curtains during a show.

The respite was cut short when the office phone rang. Coach got up, still relaxed from his last shot of tequila when he answered, "Round One Boxing, Felipe speaking … Señora! … Si, el esta aqui conmigo … que pas …"[400]

Michael, recognizing the faint sound of

---

[400] "Yes, mam … he's here with me … what happ …"

Magdalena's voice on the receiver, perked up immediately.

"Miguelito, it's your mom …"

Michael got up from the couch and took the receiver from Coach Padilla.

"Mom?"

"Hay mijito, donde andabas, por dios?"[401]

"Mom, what's wrong!?"

"Estas bien?!"[402]

"Yeah, I'm OK. I've been here with Coach …"

"Ay hijo, hubo un gran pedo aqui con Manuel."[403]

"Already? How bad?"

"Pues, anduvo aqui, gritandome de ti, que golpeaste al pastor."[404]

"Are you OK? Did he hurt you?"

"Si estoy bien pero … no se hijo … esta bien bravo esta vez."[405]

"Did he tell you anythin' else?"

"No, nomás eso hijo … pero es cierto?"[406]

"What's that?"

"Es cierto que golpeaste al pastor?"[407]

"I'll, uhm … I'll tell you when I get home, it's better that way. Is he still there?"

"Se acaba de ir … pero te anda buzcando mijito. Le dije que a la mejor andas con un aimgo tuyo para que no se vaya alla con Felipe. Estaba bien enrabaiado, el

---

[401] "Oh my god, son, where have you been?"

[402] "Are you all right?!"

[403] "Oh, son, there was a big fight here with Manuel."

[404] "Well, he was here, yelling at me about you, that you had hit the pastor."

[405] "Yeah I'm fine but … I don't know, son … he was pretty wild this time."

[406] "No, nothing else, son … but is it true?"

[407] "Is it true that you hit the pastor?"

cabron!"[408]

Michael turned to Coach Padilla, who was emptying his last shot of tequila into his mouth as he overheard bits of the conversation.

"Manny is out lookin' for me."

"Did he do something to your mom?"

"No … not yet."

"Go get your mom. You guys are gonna stay with us, for good. You hear me? No more of this back-and-forth shit."

"You sure?"

"Manny ain't gonna let up if you guys are there, and I don't wanna leave you guys here anymore."

"You serious?"

"Yeah, I'm fuckin' serious. Enough is enough."

"OK, I'll go get her."

"You want me to go with you?"

"Nah, if he sees you, it'll get real bad."

"Esta bien, but go get her right now. Don't leave her alone with that cabrón!"

Michael turned his attention back to the phone.

"Mom, go pack your bag. I'm comin' to get you."

"Esta bien hijo, yo te espero."[409]

"Get your stuff and go lock yourself in my room. We're goin' with Coach and Mariana tonight."

"Ten cuidado hijo."[410]

"I will …"

---

[408] "He just left … but he's out lookin' for you. I told him that more than likely you're with one of your friends so he wouldn't go over there with Felipe. That asshole was pretty pissed off!"
[409] "OK, son, I'll wait for you."
[410] "Be careful, son."

"Hijo … te quiero."[411]

"Me too, Mom," Michael said as he hung up the phone.

"You didn't wanna tell her why you punched him?" asked Coach Padilla.

"I dunno if she's ready for that right now."

"Tarde o temprano,[412] you gotta tell her."

"I know, just not tonight."

"Estas bien? You seem really calm."

"Usually there is so much noise in my head when I'm like this. Like I'm tryin' to tune in to ten thousand radio stations. But it's quiet now. There ain't no more noise, it's just empty."

Michael sat the empty shot glass on Coach's desk before slipping out the back door and into the sweltering summer night. The orange halogen streetlights of Central Ave hummed as he jogged his way back to the house. The growing and shrinking shadows of his body reminded him of what he experienced only a few weeks ago, when he and Magdalena fled in the middle of the night. He was well aware of Manny's possible retribution, which may have already begun—his telltale campaign motivated by pride and intent on vengeance. The memories, both distant and recent, clashed into one another like a massive freeway pileup as he ran into the night. And with every broken lamp and dent in the door, each memory asked of him, "Why?"

Even as Michael rounded the corner, he tried to reconcile how he came to this exact moment. If it were not for that one kiss, that glorious and yet damning kiss, would

---

[411] "Son … I love you."
[412] Sooner or later.

he have been able to wait it out, to leave unscathed? Even though the confusing sensations of violation, sex, and shame from the pastor's touch had plagued him all afternoon, he could not help but still hold Diego and his own lust in contempt for this disaster. The words of Coach Padilla had done little to assuage this particular guilt that was leveraged to him, as Michael saw himself as judge, prosecutor, and defendant in the courtroom of his own soul, tried in infinite jeopardy. And yet, even if he and Magdalena could escape tonight, if this could be their last flight from harm, he questioned whether he would ever find true and lasting peace from himself. It seemed to him that this was just the beginning of a fugitive life from the abuse at home, the unattainable morality of his faith, and the stark yet true nature of his being.

The house's barren front yard was still as he came up the street. Catching his breath, he could see the miniature wind-sculpted sand dunes that rippled like an ocean of dry water, lapping at the dark edges of the house. The unforgiving desert had done its best to leave the ground at Manny's house ripe with neglect, ready to sprout its late-season crop of animosity. Walking up to the front door and past the chain link fence, Michael saw that Manny's truck was missing from the driveway but the remnants of his violence were already evident. The new and well-groomed bougainvillea that had replaced Magdalena's wild and lush predecessor lay destroyed on the sandy ground. Her young, tender stems were splayed in tightly wound fibrous spirals, all from the ferocious lacerations that her young body could barely withstand. Her perfectly trimmed leaves were trampled under the workboots of the pitiless gardener. She had spilled her green blood on the concrete to join the stains of Manny's shoeprints in old chlorophyl. She had not lived long enough to blossom her delicate paper flowers in the pageantry of desert survival like the rest of her kind. There would be no carpet of fuchsia confetti on the dirt this year, no color to cover the monotone blight of the house. There would not even be a piece to salvage for rebirth in a new home. Tonight was different. Tonight wasn't about destroying something Magdalena loved. Tonight was about breaking the things that even Manny wanted.

Michael walked into the house to see that the weeks-old thrift store table lamps had been flung across the room, tethered to the wall by the noose of the electrical cord. The one bare bulb that survived projected an eerie white light through the crushed lampshade that scintillated irregular shapes on the walls like an amorphous phantom emerging from the wreck. Shards of picture frame glass crunched under his shoes as he moved through the quiet house. The glass fragments knitted their way deeper into the frayed loops of the dirty carpet with each step, joining the other glittering specks of fractured light in the terrestrial galaxy of shattered memories. The few photographs of him and his mom lay on the floor, trampled like the leaves of the bougainvillea outside. Michael picked up the photos and shook off the broken glass, planning to stow them in his shoebox of treasures. He continued making his way past the wreckage of the living room, hoping to find his mother safe in his hiding place.

"Mom, it's me."

The clunking of the wooden chair echoed in the shadowy hallway as a dagger of incandescent light pierced Michael's face through the darkness.

"Mijito!?"

"You OK?" he asked while shutting the door.

"Hay, mijo … tu sabes. Las mismas chingaderas."[413]

"What happened? What'd he tell you?"

"Pues vino en la tarde pero bien, bien enrabiado. Que acaba de venir del hospital …"[414]

"The hospital?"

"Si … y estaba gritandome que golpeaste al pastor. Que le iba hablar a la policía y …"[415]

"Is that all he said?"

"Pues si, de allí empezó el pedo hijo."[416]

"Oh God …"

"Aventó las cosas, me gritó que nosotros no lo dejamos ser buen Cristiano. Y ya despues que hizo su desmadre, se largo … a buscarte me imagino."[417]

"You think he's at the bar again?"

"No se la verdad."[418]

"I hope not …"

"Pero sabes que, mijito? Ya estoy harta de esta mierda."[419]

"I know, Mom … I know …"

"Que no tiene alma ese hombre?"[420]

"No … no, he doesn't."

---

[413] "Oh, son … you know. The same shit."

[414] "Well he came in the afternoon, but he was really pissed off. Said that he just came from the hospital …"

[415] "Yes … and he was yellin' at me that you had hit the pastor. That he was gonna call the police and …"

[416] "Well yeah, the whole fight started from there."

[417] "He threw things, he yelled at me that we don't let him be a good Christian. And after he made that whole mess, he left … to go look for you I figured."

[418] "I don't know to tell you the truth."

[419] "But you know what, son? I've had enough of this shit."

[420] "Doesn't that man have a soul?"

"Como estoy cansada de cargar las fallas de el."[421]

"I know, Mom …"

"Y no quiero que se te cargen mas problemas a ti hijo, pero mi alma …"[422]

"Mom …"

"Mi alma ya no resisté. No puedo mas … ya no puedo!"[423] she cried.

"It's OK, Mom, it's OK."

Michael wrapped his arms around her, trying by osmosis to absorb her sorrow. Her tears rained down like the estranged July monsoons, soaking his T-shirt. Her maternal tenderness engendered that old, familiar intoxicating sense in him, a primal call to be the hero. It was a warm and empowering sensation that seemed to fill the dark void within him. But as he looked over her shoulder to the Bibles on his nightstand, the omnipresent dread stared right back at him. He knew that as soon as she let go, the numbing venom of guilt would seep back in, stealing whatever light had started to glow. And the thought of Diego, for that matter, only served to magnify the numbness to excruciating heights.

"You got your stuff ready?"

"Si alli esta mi maleta …"[424]

"Did you pack enough clothes, though?"

"Pues, no mas por unos dias como siempre."[425]

"You're gonna need more than that."

---

[421] "You don't know how tired I am of having to carry his failures."

[422] "And I don't want you to have to carry more problems, son, but my soul …"

[423] "My soul can't resist anymore. I can't anymore … I can't!"

[424] "Yeah, my bag is right there …"

[425] "Well, only for a few days like always."

"Como?"

"Don't think we're comin' back this time …"

"Que, que?"[426]

"I don't think we can stay after this one. I know I can't."

"Hay, hijo, pero como? Como vamos a vivir? Estas seguro?"[427]

"You wanna be pickin' up the broken pieces of our lives again and again?"

"Pues no …"

"Good, 'cause they're never gonna come back together, Mom, not as long as we're still here."

"Pero de que vamos a vivir? A donde …"[428]

"We always talk about leavin', and I'm tired of talkin' 'bout it but never doin' it."

"Si pero …"

"I want somethin' better for the both of us. Somethin' more than whiskey fights."

"Si hijo … yo se … pero tengo miedo. Entiendeme, tengo mucho miedo de que nos va obligar."[429]

"What else can we do? Let's just go … let's go far away where he can't find us no more. Somewhere where we can listen to music, out in the open. Somewhere where you can wear what you want and no one is gonna tell you to not wear makeup."

The years of countless fights rushed past her in a seemingly effortless recollection, like the ebb and flow of waves on a beach. Manny's stinging judgmental cut

---

[426] "Wait, what?"

[427] "Oh, son, but how? How are we gonna live? Are you sure?"

[428] "But how are we going to live? Where … "

[429] "Well yes, son … I know that … But I'm scared. I'm scared that he is just gonna make us come back again."

through from the past, coloring her memories in a fantastical version of truth like the mural of Jesus in the church. She could stay and stand against the pressures of conventionality around her, but with Michael ready to walk out the door, she had to ask herself if it was even worth staying and fighting.

"Esta bien, esta bien, hijo … nos vamos."[430]

"Let's go."

Michael began pulling clothes from drawers and his closet, tossing them on the bed trying to make sure he took as much as he could with him. Magdalena helped by quickly folding shirts and jeans into tight little bundles and packing them in his gym bag. He knelt down beside his bed and reached into the shoestring cradle inside the box spring to pull out the box of family artifacts. He managed to stuff these last few items into his gym bag, safely tucked away until they reached Coach Padilla's house.

"Es todo, hijo?[431]" asked Magdalena as she slung her bag and purse over her shoulder.

"I think so."

As he scanned his room one last time, he noticed there on his nightstand he had left his old and new Bibles. His old one was dog-eared and beaten up, whereas the new one still had a fresh plastic-infused leather smell.

Mijito …

He reached down and thumbed through the pages of the older Bible, revisiting the neurotic and frantic scribblings in the blank white spaces of almost every single

---

[430] "All right, all right, son … we'll leave."
[431] "Is that everything, son?"

page. Hopeful postulates and notes next to any verse that might give him absolution from the plague within. Absolution that never came.

Mijito! ...

He knew that if he could just close his eyes, he could hear the familiar rustling of delicate Bible pages and his own voice reciting scripture out loud, only to be interrupted by the sound of thick drops of blood splattering on tissue-thin pages and his fists making contact with Pastor Roberts. Deep down he still wanted to believe, but he just didn't how he would believe—whether it was wise to trust the hymns and preaching of a different church with a different Pastel Jesus or necessary to rely on the sterling silver saints and crystalline rosary beads of his family to find God.

"Mijito, ya ..." Magdalena called out to him.

"OK ... OK ... I'm ready!"

Michael turned back and left the pristine Bible on the nightstand as an offering on the altar of justice. A blind hope for freedom from a law that never sought to liberate him but enslave him. But even more so, an act of bravery to trust the divine grace that his fellow congregation extoled but never dared to rely on.

Michael stuff the old Bible in his gym bag and then slung it across his shoulder, the treasures of his shoebox rattling inside, ready to make the journey to their new place. He grabbed Magdalena's clammy hand as he led her back out into the aftermath of Manny's rage in the living room.

"Is there anythin' else you wanna get before we go?" Michael asked as they emerged from the dark hallway.

"Where the fuck you think you're goin'?" growled a low and rough voice.

Manny's imposing figure was already in the hallway covered by a half silhouette, the long, obtuse shadows of his body and face wrapped around him, consuming him in spotty and sober darkness. Michael braced himself for the typical whiff of whiskey breath, but nothing passed by him. The whiskey monster would not meet them tonight, Manny's wrath would be acting alone.

"You thought you could just come in my house and take my wife just like? Huh!?"

"My mom isn't yours to keep, Manny!"

"No andes con esas pendejadas,[432] she ain't goin nowhere … me entiendes?!"[433]

"She's goin with me, and there ain't nothin' you can do 'bout it!"

"Bullshit there ain't nothin I can do 'bout it. Did you forget I'm the man of this house, huh?"

"So what?!"

"Yo soy el que manda aqui![434] Who gave you the life you have now?! Who gave you the clothes on your back and the roof over your head?!"

"So what?! I'm supposed to owe you somethin'?"

"Yeah, a little goddamn respect for this house, and for me!"

"You know what, I don't need this."

"I told you I didn't want your cochinada[435] in my house. I told you to get it fixed, but you couldn't even do

---

[432] "Don't be givin' me any of that stupid bullshit."
[433] "You understand me?!"
[434] "I'm the one who gives orders around here!"
[435] Dirtiness.

that, could you?!"

"Help?! You call that help?"

"You're damn right I do!"

"Do you even know what he did to me today, huh?! Do you?!""

"Claro que si! He told me when they were tryin' to keep him alive at the goddamn hospital!"

"Yeah!? And did he say that he molested me too, huh?! Did he tell you that?!"

"You're so full of it, you know that?"

"Did he tell you that he touched me?! Did he tell you that he felt me up right there at church?!"

"Que dijiste?![436]" exclaimed an infuriated Magdalena.

"If that's what it takes to fix you …"

"Don't gimme none of that!"

"Or are you just too much of a lil' bitch?!"

"What'd you say to me?"

"You think when people find out 'bout you that they're gonna treat like a real man out there?"

"I'm so sick and tired of people tellin' me I ain't man enough 'cause of that!"

"Que le hiceste a mi hijo, Manuel?! Alguien por dios, digame lo que esta pasando!!!"[437]

"You think the world is gonna be nice to you because of that, boy?! Look around you, you think people are gonna give a shit when they see your Brown ass too?"

"At least I'm not tryin' to suck up to no Gringo like you!"

---

[436] "What did you say?!"

[437] "What did you do to my son, Manuel?! For the love of God, someone please tell me what going on!!!"

"You'd would know all about that, wouldn't you, fuckin' joto!"

"Don't you call me that!" screamed Michael.

"You haven't told your mom that you're a goddamn joto? A maricón?[438] A puto?!"[439]

"Stop it!"

"Andalé, tell her! Tell her how much you wanna be a little Mexican bitch. Go on, tell her!"

"Que chingados estas diciendo, Manuel?!"[440]

"Mom, don't listen to him", Michael shouted as he started to guard Magdalena behind him.

"I told you, I don't want no maricónadas[441] in my house!"

"Cut it out, Manny, I swear to God I'll hurt you!"

"What are you gonna do, huh?"

"Basta! Manuel no le hables asi a mi hijo!"[442] Magdalena shouted back.

"I'LL TALK TO HIM HOW EVER THE FUCK I WANT TO!!"

"Ve chinga a tu puta madre!"[443] Magdalena yelled.

With the reflexes of a mountain lion, Manny swung his fist past Michael's head and landed a right hook on Magdalena's unsuspecting face. She let out a loud yelp as the blunt force knocked her down, and she crumpled into a ball there in the hallway behind her son.

"Don't you fuckin' hit her, you piece of shit!"

---

[438] Effeminate faggot.

[439] Promiscuous faggot.

[440] "What the fuck are you saying, Manuel?!"

[441] Pejorative—behaviors and traits of an effeminate faggot.

[442] "That's enough! Don't be saying that to my son, Manuel!"

[443] "Go fuck your whore of a mother!"

screamed Michael as he tried to push Manny away but got entangled in Manny's arms. Manny latched on to a fistful of Michael's shirt and swung his whole body around, slamming him up against the white wall, pinning him and holding him up off the floor with a clenched hand around his throat. Michael tried to pry away Manny's sun-darkened fingers while the veins in his head started to swell. Michael's voiceless gagging gurgled what little air he could get past Manny's grip, and his fearful eyes peered deeply into the beady black pupils of the sober devil.

Manny got close to his stepson's ear and in perfect calmness and composure he whispered, "I'd rather you be dead than have a faggot stepson."

His words sent a haunting chill down Michael's spine as he distinctly felt the rage-filled fingers crushing his neck. But just as much, the sensation of another man touching him on the same scarred erogenous skin as Pastor Roberts enraged Michael, and he burst into a blind fury of savage instinct, where all he wanted to do was one thing and one thing only: destroy the devil in front of him. Michael quickly kicked up Manny's shin as hard as he could, raising his foot between Manny's legs and crushing his crotch. Manny immediately released the grip on Michael's throat.

Manny dropped to the floor, coughing and gagging as Michael, gasping for air, scrambled over and with immediate impunity started kicking Manny in the stomach. He could feel the angry air escape Manny with every contact from his foot, and was not satisfied by just seeing Manny's body fold over and collapse. Then, between one of his cathartic kicks, Manny managed to catch Michael's leg and wrestle him down to the floor.

Manny climbed on top of Michael, pressing his

weight down as he straddled Michael's chest. The shards of glass that were embedded in the carpet cut Michael's back, smearing his copper skin with blossoming blood. Manny wrapped his hands around Michael's neck again, and Michael worked to push him off and wriggle free. Michael could see the eerie white light above him, like an ominous aura on the ceiling, between the blows that Manny rained down while screaming, "I don't want … SMACK … no fuckin' … SMACK … jotos … SMACK … livin' here!"

Michael could taste the warm metallic blood from his lip seeping onto his tongue while the fury and adrenaline that were raging within him numbed his face. He tried to pull Manny's vicelike grip off his throat as the room went dark. He feared that he might have already succumbed to the choke, but then he felt Manny's weight lift up and off his chest. Slightly dazed and concussed, Michael rose up to see Magdalena, her face bleeding, wrapping the lamp cord around Manny's neck as he thrashed around the room like a fish flopping around on dry land.

"Corre, hijo! Corre!"[444] she screamed.

In a daze, Michael looked around the dark living room to find his gym bag on the floor.

"Come on, Mom, let's go! Let's get outta here!" he yelled as he grabbed his bag.

"Corre, hijo, yo te sigó!"[445]

Without a second thought, Michael bolted out the front door into the Arizona night. As he ran down the driveway, he could hear the faint crashing of bodies in the

---

[444] "Run son! Run!"
[445] "Run, son! I'll follow you!"

house as Manny and Magdalena screamed and wrestled for control. Michael ran so fast and far that he quickly heard only the tat-tat-tat-tat of his shoes on the gritty sidewalk, the pounding of his pulse in his head, and the echoing beat of the shoebox of family treasures rattling in his bag. They were going to be free. It finally happened. They were going to be free.

Romp-thwat-romp-thwat-romp-thwat-romp-thwat

14

The bright headlights and honking horns of cars speeding down Central Avenue had little effect on Michael as he darted off the sidewalk and ran straight through oncoming traffic. He dodged roaring metal beasts while weaving in and out of the stampede that he found himself in. The softened asphalt squished under his tennis shoes, sticking to him and slowing him down. The squealing tires around him melted into the last screams he heard from Magdalena, which were still filling his ears. Despite his disregard for traffic, surly drivers sat and watched him dash by like some sort of horrific phantom from a slasher movie. The lacerations on his face and lips dripped warm blood that glistened like black ink under the orange streetlamps. As he ran, the splotchy crimson stains from his back made him look like someone who just escaped a scourging.

When he got to the other side of Central Ave, he bolted past the few shops still open at that hour. Their bluish florescent light spilled out onto the sidewalk like puddles of old milk. His instincts were screaming at him to hide, hide the way he had that afternoon. He needed to find somewhere to huddle in a ball and shield himself from reality, a reality that was as pervasive as the cuts and bruises on his body. If it meant running farther and farther away from the fluorescent lights, and deeper into the illusionary shallow tides of blood-tinged bathwater, he would find safety wherever it was.

> *God, don't let her get hit by a car,*
> *don't let her get hit by a car!*

He was sure that Magdalena would be following the same erratic path that he laid for her. Navigating the same pools of milky light so they could be free together. Fear kept him from looking back, a fear that Manny might be there behind her, giving chase, trying to recapture the family he needed. Michael couldn't let that happen. Not this time, and not ever again. He had to keep moving forward, leading the way for her.

Michael had run so far by now that he came to the intersection of Broadway and Central. He went straight into the crosswalk, again dodging the cars and trucks that raced toward him in the ever-darkening roadway. By now, the sweat had started to seep into his open wounds, and the salts stung deep like hot knives. The acid building up in legs made his muscles cramp and ache, while the hot desert air had dried out his lungs to the point that he swore he could taste the metallic flavor of fresh blood in the back of his throat. The last car horn blared to a crescendo before the car sped off behind him, and he stumbled up onto the curb, now fully immersed in the city's darkness and far enough away from Manny's house and the puddles of milk-colored light. Finally, he was alone.

He dropped his gym bag on the ground and hunched over to catch his breath. The racing tha-thump-tha-thump-tha-thump of his heart pulsating in his neck began to slow with the subsiding adrenaline. When he turned around, he saw the intermittent strobes of distant red, yellow, and green traffic signals and the pale-yellow headlights of cars sailing by. His short yet quick escape was illuminated right in front of him like some life-size porcelain Christmas village. It was familiar and yet it felt inhumanely distant from where he stood, as if he had stepped out into another world and the turmoil he lived in was left behind him, seething like a rabid dog. He could see the street and sidewalk toward Manny's house, and he saw the Round One Boxing gym. The lights were still on, waiting for him and Magdalena to walk right in. Just above the shops and businesses on the street, the random checkerboard patterns of office lights in the glass towers jutted up from downtown, crowned by slow, pulsating red jewels at their tops. It was a view he rarely had the chance to see, the diorama of his poor blighted city in the foreground and the wealth of the American dream in the distance. These two worlds pushed and pulled like the gravity of two dueling bodies, shaping and shifting his life and purpose in blunt yet often asymmetrically elegant ways.

But what he did not see was Manny. He watched intently to see whether he could find a dark figure running on the same sidewalks and in front of the headlights looking for him or chasing after a figure ahead of him. Michael felt a small bit of relief that the city was serene, almost calmly ambivalent to the violence he just ran from. But that relief was quickly swallowed by the worry that Magdalena was just as absent.

Michael stood in the shadows, waiting and watching the distant street. He expected that at any minute her figure would be coming down the sidewalk looking for him, and at least it would let him know that his prayers were answered. Michael didn't know exactly where he was, just that he had stumbled upon an unlit lot of South Phoenix like so many others. When he turned around to see what was behind him, the velvet darkness seemed to roll away from him and the lights of houses on the other side looked like distant stars peeking over the horizon. But looming over him was the shadowy outline of a steeple, crisply cutting the city lights behind it and swallowing them whole.

The church that he had grown up in stood in unfamiliar contrast to the rest of the city, like a stranger lurking behind him. The only thing that Michael recognized was the telltale padlock and chain coiled and looped around the handles of the wooden double doors. The stoop was bathed in the sickening yellow glow of a bug light, and only with the help of the occasional headlights could he even see the faint lettering of the hand-painted sign above the door.

Despite the fervent urgency to find his mother, Michael was captivated by a hypnotic morbid curiosity in seeing the place that only a few hours ago unleashed the very fury of hell upon him. He closed his eyes momentarily to try to erase the imposing shadow from his retinas, but being so close to the church transmitted the unforgettable sounds of hymns and Pastor Roberts.

... very deeply stained within ...

... But the wages of sin is death! ...

Sinking to rise no more ...

... Don't you know what's good for you!

I am a man made in the image of God ...

... But the master of the sea heard my despairing cry ...

... I don't want no maricónadas in my house!

...Corre hijo, yo te sigo!

"Mom, where are you?" he whispered to the night as he opened his eyes once again to the imposing shadow in front of him.

The open cuts and busted lip felt as if they had crusted over. His cotton T-shirt with stains of crimson stuck to the wounds on his back like gauze, pulling open the drying scabs with the slightest movement. His stomach rolled, wringing out the acid and pushing the sour taste to the back of his tongue with every minute that passed without Magdalena showing up.

"C'mon, Mom, please ... you said you'd follow me!"

The empty lot where he stood seemed to be growing abnormally invisible to the life of the streets around him with every passing minute. Traffic rolled past

the church in apathetic irreverence, avoiding the darkness
that enveloped him out of what he thought was the fear of
being pulled in and becoming trapped by barrio.
Occasionally a passing car would kick up tiny bits of street
dust into the air and blow it and the rising asphalt vapor
toward Michael, blessing him with the scent of earth and
petroleum. Nebulous dust moved in memorizing swirls.
Subtle glittering silica floated in front of him, like ocean
waves lapping long an invisible vertical coast. It breathed
with him, expanding its spatial lungs to live briefly before
exhaling and dispersing into the night over and over again.
Uninhibited by the bounds of brick and mortar of the
church, the presence of the divine—the Cosmic God—was
now made manifest and not in the flesh.

"Where's my mom?! How come she's not
comin'?!" he asked the dust.

The dust said nothing in response and floated by
him, quiet and unassuming. Michael's restlessness grew
with this mute ambivalence while he was desperately
fighting back the tears welling up. His watery eyes made
all the lights of the city around him scatter into brilliant
bursting stars and tangled halos of filaments like glowing
spiderwebs. He was determined to stand watch through the
sparkling shattered light until his mother showed up. She
had to show up. She must show up.

Off in the distance the faint wailing of sirens
echoed through the streets and back alleys as Michael
turned to see the flashing blue and red lights rapidly
exploding like never-ending fireworks. At first, he didn't
think much of it, since sirens in the barrio were common
enough. But the pitch was getting closer and louder, and
although he could not see the actual police cars through his
teary eyes, he could see the flashing red and blue lights

making their way up Central Ave.

As the lights closed the gap, passing the Round One Boxing gym and turning onto Manny's street, Michael felt a sharp coldness sting him in the chest, a heavy and alien sensation that pushed out against the heat of the desert. Breath escaped him in silent screams and crackling hisses from his throat. He had run with the dread that tragedy would visit him again, and now it appeared and punched him in the gut as he collapsed to his knees on the sidewalk, huddling down to shield himself from the force of the universe's cruelty. His crusty wounds cracked open like parched earth as tears and blood flowed out of him again, and at his first chance to gasp in air, he heaved erratically, his face in the dirt. His hoarse wail rose up from the shadows like the cry of the first human to experience loss, confronting the tremendous invisible pain. But the lights, the street, and the city still didn't care about his pain. His cries fell on the deaf ears of the world around him and the church behind him, carrying on without a skip in the beat as the traffic signals turned from red to green.

She's needs to be with me!

We were gonna listen to her music.

This wasn't supposed to be like this!

He cried out, pressing his teary cheek on the bare, gritty sidewalk, sprawling, clawing the ground with his fingertips.

"I should've stayed, Mom! I should've stayed!"

His weeping became more intense every time he cycled through everything that happened today, believing that he was finally paying for all his sins. His conscience tore at him like the shards of glass in the carpet—that his never being able to change had led to this somber night. Nothing had been good enough, and nothing would ever be good enough. And it was the injustice of Magdalena having to pay for his sins that ignited the simmering rage toward the one person who stood between him and God.

"FUCK YOU!" he growled into the night, scrambling to his feet and charging toward the front doors of the church.

"Fuck you, you piece of shit!" he screamed as he reached the doors, ramming his shoulder into them and rebounding off the wood.

"I did everythin' you asked me to!" he screamed as he kicked the doors.

"I'm a man, you asshole … I ain't the lil' pussy you made me out to be!" he shouted as he banged on the doors with his fists.

"Let me in, damnit! I'm good enough! Let me in! Let me the fuck in!" he screamed as the cathartic rage expended itself through his lips and fists, slowly evaporating into the night. But no matter how hard his fists hit the wood, or how many times he screamed at the locks, the doors held tight. Bound by the clanging steel of the chain that would never give him entrance to see Pastel Jesus again. He had gone as far as he could into the dark heart of his religion, and now his religion had no need for him.

"Bring her back, God! Bring her back!" he wept as his tired body leaned against the wooden doors.

He clawed himself upright to peer inside the tiny windows in the door, cupping his hands around his face to see better into the dimly lit church. The headlights of the passing cars and buses cast their dancing light through the narrow cloudy windows, briefly illuminating the rows of pews and the pulpit as their long shadows stretched and glided across the bare plaster walls. He could see the faint figures of all the people he knew, singing hymns happily and without worry. He could see the back of his own head sitting in the pew with his mom glowing in a radiant innocence that he longed for. With each passing headlight he could see this new dream created out of the darkness, this other world that he wished he could be in—the heaven of Pastel Jesus, where there was no pain and no sorrow, where every tear that he had shed in his life would finally be wiped away and where the rest that he sought with faithful tenacity would finally be his. There, they would be inside the church forever listening and worshiping among the White people who never talked to her, but at least they were there together.

"God please, lemme in. She's right there.

She's waitin' there for me, she's waitin' so that we can go home.

Please lemme go in and get her! Just lemme go in, God.

I did everythin' I'm supposed to! I was good … I was good!

Please God, lemme back in to make it right!

I promise I'll be better this time!"

He slid down the wooden doors to the bare concrete stoop, sinking beneath the sickening yellow light and away from the rapturous sight inside.

"Please God, don't take her away 'cause of me, please, God … Please."

Of the many black holes that Michael carried with him, this was by far the most destructive. Manny had swallowed time, Pastor Roberts had swallowed trust, but the collapse and implosion of this light in Michael swallowed up hope. Before, he could look out over the dry river to the towers downtown and say to himself,

I know things are bad now,
 but one day it be different.

One day I'll get that
dream on the other side …

... One day the drinkin' will stop ...

> *... One day I will be what the*
> *church wants me to be ...*

> > *... One day I'll grow out*
> > *of these feelings for Diego*

> > > *... One day ...*

Lost under the stars and lights of the city, he gazed out at the traffic, indiscriminately passing by him, unaware of the abandoned tragedy at the church's doorstep. He felt the heaviness of his limp body unable to get back up on his feet. Even if he could, he didn't want to amidst the delirium of loss and the one principle that he had wrestled with his entire life weighing on his heart: Sin, in all its forms, destroys. His sin had come for his mother, and the more damning revelation was that his punishment did not take place yet in the fires of hell but existed now in the scorched earth of the empty desert lot where he slumped.

Exhaustion was starting to seep into his head as he drifted in and out of consciousness. He tried to hold to that one vision, the single moment of hope where he and his mother were sitting quietly in the pew, before it vanished into the black cloud of his memory. Crumpled on the stoop, he tried cuddling the flat and obtuse door like a hurt child would, trying to transcend physicality to enter the locked church where his memory of her was kept. His tired voice even began mumbling the words of a hymn, trying to force his brain to remember the image before it began to fade from his eyelids.

"Just as
I am without
one plea,
but that
thy blood
was shed
for me
and that thou
b-bid'st
me come
to thee
O Lamb
Of God I come,
I come

Time seemingly passed without him as he lay there, when a shadowy figure made its appearance from the city, slowly inching its way toward him from the street corner. The glow of the sailing headlights cloaked this figure in an aura of dust that glowed and shimmered like a dimly lit sun after a summer sandstorm. The apparition might have been mistaken for a homeless person searching for shelter. Even more telling was that the figure stumbled like a drunk, dragging a booze-lame foot behind with each step. The night embraced the figure with shadows like a lace prayer shawl as it neared Michael, who was strewn like a raggedy marionette.

As the figure came closer, the orange glow of a streetlight cascaded upon the nest of matted hair and illuminated the rich black filaments like golden harp strings bound together by clumps of scabbed blood in a chaotic tapestry that only violence can weave. The same black ink stains of cooled crimson blood crusted the profile of the figure's face, and jagged scabs consumed the soft swelling skin in tectonically torn trails of red. Had Michael looked up from his despondency, he would have seen in the figure's silhouette the golden orbs of stud earrings, but instead the feeble voice cracked and scratched from bruised vocal cords to call out to him.

"Mijito …"

Like Lazarus hearing his master's voice, Michael was stunned out of his catatonic misery and wrestled himself away from the curse of memories trapped in the church. As he stumbled out of the bug light's nauseating yellow rays, he quickly touched the apparition to see that it was real, that the shadow that called him out was made of flesh and bone. The moans of still-fresh cuts and bruises bled into the night from his embrace as he wept for the miracle that had just walked into his life.

"Mom!" he exclaimed, feeling her warmth through his bare arms as he held her tight. "I'm sorry I didn't wait for you, Mom. I'm sorry, I'm so sorry!"

"Ya hijito, ya, ya, ya … todo esta bien … ya se acabó."[446]

"I shouldn'tve left you there, I should've stayed with you!"

"Ya hijo, ya,"[447] she said softly.

As Michael blubbered in spastic sobs, his tears moistened the already-dried blood on his face, creating new crimson rivers as each little tinged drop plopped on

---

[446] "There, there, son … everything is OK … It's all over."
[447] "It's OK, son, it's OK."

Magdalena's shoulders. Michael could still smell someone else's anger in her hair. Manny's sweat and dirt had followed her here and hovered like a watchman over them.

For a brief moment, Michael wanted to be selfish. It was an addictive and intoxicating sensation of purest joy that burst forth from him. She was alive, and she was consoling him. Perhaps Pastel Jesus had heard him banging outside of the locked doors, and even though Michael was angry with his pastor, mercy might have been extended to him. Magdalena also sensed something that Michael had locked away for years, gushing out like a monsoon rain.

"Mira mijito, te quiero pedir una cosa, y solamente una cosa …"[448]

"What's that?"

"Eres Mexicano?"[449]

"Yeah."

"Y yo? Soy Mexicana?"[450]

"Well … yeah …"

"Entonces porque insistes en hablarme en ingles?"[451]

"I … I … dunno?"

"Ya deja esas chingaderas de la iglesia,"[452] she said, looking at the looming steeple.

"Así amá?"[453] He sniffled and smiled.

"Ahorra si!"[454]

---

[448] "Look, son, I want to ask you one thing, and only one thing."
[449] "Are you a Mexican?"
[450] "And me? Am I Mexican?"
[451] "Then why do you insist on talking to me in English?"
[452] "Now, leave all that bullshit of the church."
[453] "Like this, Mom?"
[454] "There we go!"

"Esta bien, amá, esta bien."[455]

"Hay hijo, que chinga, no?"[456]

"Esta fue uno de los peores."[457]

"Se nos ve en la cara, no?"[458]

"Hasta los huesos."[459]

"Veras como estoy cansado … nos sentamos?"[460]

"Pero en donde?"[461]

"Pues no veo a nadie aqui, ayudame, hijo."[462]

Magdalena knelt down on the dusty sidewalk, leaning on her son for support as the slightest movement pulled and twisted her bruises and cracked open the cuts on her body.

"Buenos chingazos me metío el baboso,"[463] she said with clenched teeth. "Maldigo la panocha que lo hechó al mundo."[464]

"Hay ma!"[465]

"Que, hijo?"[466]

"Todavia le vas a hechar?"[467]

"Pues si hijo. Si no reniegas, todo ese coraje se queda en el alma."[468]

---

[455] "All right, Mom, all right."
[456] "Oh son, this is a lot of shit, right?"
[457] "This was one of the worst."
[458] "You can see it in our faces, right?"
[459] "Down to the bones."
[460] "Can't tell you how tired I am … let's sit down."
[461] "But where?"
[462] "Well, I don't see anyone here, help me, son."
[463] "Geez, what beating that asshole gave me."
[464] "I curse the pussy that brought him into this world."
[465] "Mom!"
[466] "What, son?"
[467] "You're still going to curse him?"
[468] "Well of course, son. If you don't curse, all that anger stays in your soul."

Michael rolled his eyes as she sat down.

"Andalé, sientate aqui conmigo, hijo. Me imagino que estas bien cansado tambien. Tirate aqui un ratito.[469]"

Aching from his own cuts, Michael managed to unceremoniously plop himself down next to his mother. There was a rigid and childish clumsiness in him, turning over to lay his sweaty head in her waiting lap as he had done the night his father died. The night when they first felt what it was like to be alone in the world. Resting on her legs, he watched the whole world of the barrio turn on its side as his eyes aligned themselves with the flat horizon of the sidewalk. The cars passing by in the street looked as if they shot upward to the heaven above his head, and the glass towers of downtown gave up their reach toward the sky. Instead, their square pixels dappled like the reflection of a square moon on a corporate glass ocean.

"Estas segura que no quires sentarte allá en la entrada, amá?"[470]

"Que no tienes vergüenza? No tenemos nada que a ver con esa iglesia, mijito. Ya no."[471]

"Ah dio?!"[472]

"No, no, no no, hijo, es la verdad. No voy a darles el gusto de sentarme allí. Hay que mantener la dignidad."[473]

Taken aback at her rebuttal, Michael cocked his

---

[469] "Come on, sit here with me, son. I can imagine that you are pretty tired too. Just lie here for a bit."

[470] "You sure you don't wanna sit there at the front door, Mom?"

[471] "Don't you have any shame? We've got nothin' to do with that church anymore. No more."

[472] "Oh really?!"

[473] "No, no, no, no, son, it's the truth. I'm not gonna give them the pleasure of sittin' there at the front door. We've gotta maintain a little bit of dignity."

head up from Magdalena's lap to look at the sideways black steeple behind her. Even though he had just seen his and Magdalena's past ghosts through the windows of the front door, blackness flooded the backs of his eyelids whenever he tried to remember them in the pews, and in one short breath those phantom memories were gone. He wanted to get up and peer inside the church one more time, to see what kind of other ghosts might be illuminated with the passing headlights of cars, but he was also fearful that he would revive them only to see them vanish like the others or even worse. The memories of Pastor Roberts would never go away.

"Amá?"

"Si hijo?" she asked, trying to dust off the flakes of dry blood from his chin.

"Que nos paso?"[474]

"Como?"[475]

"Como llegamos aqui, sin casa. Sin iglesia. Sin nada."[476]

"No se."[477]

"Ama, como que no sabes?"[478]

"Pues, si se que las chingaderas de Manuel …"[479]

"No ama, no de eso. Quiero saber porque Dios nos hizo esto?"[480]

Magdalena sat for a long time as she stared off into

---

[474] "What happened to us?"

[475] "What do you mean?"

[476] "How did we get here without a home. Without a church. Without anything."

[477] "I dunno."

[478] "Mom, how is it that you don't know?"

[479] "Well, I know that Manny's bullshit is …"

[480] "No, Mom, not about that. Why did God do this to us?"

the same night sky.

"Pues, no tengo respuesta, hijo … yo nunca he sabido porque la vida nos chingo asi … solamente se que tenia que seguir."[481]

He lay back and let his eyes open wide to the sphere of the sky that appeared to turn above them like a great celestial clock, slowly spinning stars around them as they sat on the ground with the electric lights of the world flickering on and off. The outline of mountains shimmered with silvery light from the rising crescent moon that effortlessly slid across the silky cloak of an indigo night. It was as elegant as it was surreal to sit under the sky and watch Earth move, and to see the creation that he was taught to believe in, working with an unspoken order to itself. He found it funny that in all the times he would sit in church, he would wonder and question what heaven would be. What would that place of sereness look like? The place where there were no more tears and no more pain. The place where all the wrongs of the world would be made right. Whenever he looked up from the pews to try to see it, he saw only the dingy white plaster ceiling. Even with the chaotic flickering of the milk-colored lights from the shops, the orange sprays of the streetlights on the roadway, and the strobing traffic signals around him, it felt otherworldly to lay in that empty spot with his mother. It was as if they were on the dark side of the moon and the glowing bodies of orbiting chaos rotated around them like the theater for God to show himself without anything to get in the way. But to Michael, it was too easy. It was too easy to see God in such ordinary things and by such sin-filled

---

[481] "Well, I don't have an answer, son … I don't know why life fucked us over like this … all I know is I have to keep going."

people.

"Quiero volver, ama."[482]

"A la casa de Manuel?!"[483]

"Hay no! Quiero volver a mi niñes …"[484]

"Porque?"

"Eran buenos tiempos, ama."[485]

"Si eran, mijito."[486]

"Prefiero esos tiempos que estos."[487]

"Como no, hijo …"[488]

"Podemos volver? A Mexico?"[489]

"Podemos … pero no va hacer igual."[490]

"Porque?"[491]

"Es que somos diferentes. Hemos vivido mucho …"[492]

"Entones adonde vamos?"[493]

"Donde nos den posada, mijito."[494]

Michael's heart didn't want to sit still with all these unanswered questions fluttering around him like moths swarming the useless bug light. Lying there in her lap, he looked up at the night sky again, silently asking the sparse and twinkling specks of blue lights above. He

---

[482] "I wanna go back, Mom"
[483] "To Manny's house?!"
[484] "Oh no! I want to go back to my childhood …"
[485] "Those were good times, Mom."
[486] "Yes they were, son."
[487] "I prefer those times over these."
[488] "How could you not, son …"
[489] "Can we go back? To Mexico?"
[490] "We could … but it won't be the same."
[491] "Why?"
[492] "It's because we're different. We have lived a lot …"
[493] "Then where do we go?"
[494] "With whoever lets us in, son."

wanted the answers to come from the sky, from the very face of God. Why did this happen to him and his mom? Why could he not remember the way the blood splattered on the Bible, or the way Magdalena looked sitting in the Sunday pew? Was this the cure?

The sky would remain silent as he lay there. It never gave up its answers. He felt far more naked in his thinking and reasoning of the world than he ever had before. He even yearned to go back into the dreamland of his mind, where his fantasies lived around the gnarly old tree; at least he knew that, even though he feared it. He missed the vivid sensation of the salt crunching under his feet and the explosion of colors in the sky as the orb of the sun dipped behind the mountains. He wanted to feel the tranquility of the salt when the last flame of orange sunlight burnt out among the darkening violet and blue hues of the sky. Once more, he wanted to feel sunlight in the warm salt on his bare feet after dusk. He even wanted to see the blossoming buds of blood on the gnarly old tree by silvery moonlight. But this, too, vanished like the memories from before. In a flash of opulent brilliance, they evaporated like the sparks from a firework.

For now, he would have to make his own tranquility in the empty lot, being thrown headfirst as a nomad in the desert of milky light. The pungent smell of slowly cooling asphalt and half-burnt gasoline wafted from the street toward them, reminding him of the mundaneness of their impromptu sacred place. Pristineness and Whiteness had escaped him, and he was left with dirt on a hot night. There was nowhere to run now. He had come to the reducing reality that the sanctuary of his mind was gone and in its place was a bottomless grave of memories. Its headstone was the church steeple with the now ominous inscription, "Come ye all who are burdened and heavy laden, and I will give you rest." Neither he nor Magdalena could fix it.

"Y ahora?"[495] asked Michael.

"Creo que tenemos que empezar de nuevo …"[496]

"Nos vamos con el Coach?"[497]

Magdalena pulled her bruised-up son tight to her chest, as he snaked his arms around her. For Michael it was a strangely new and yet intimately familiar feeling. A feeling that he knew was right, and he would have known only in the moment that he found it. Perhaps this was the rest that he searched for for so long in the gaze of Pastel Jesus and, oddly enough, found in the arms of his Mexican mother. Maybe it was something even more than that. A beginning, instead of waiting for a dreadful end. It was understood that in their liberty, they were now sinners, heretics, and heathens—dissidents of the lowest order and cursed to wander the blighted land beyond the perfections and Whiteness that Manny had wanted so badly for himself. But maybe life outside that unachievable Eden was better. Perhaps the Cosmic God whom they could see in the stars at night would forgive them the wrongs they had done instead of the trespasses for the people they could never be.

"Pues, creo que el Coach nos esta esperando,[498]" said Michael.

"Si hijo, vamonos. Tienes tu maleta?"[499]

"Aahhh … no … se … créo que lo dejé alli en la

---

[495] "And now?"

[496] "I think we've gotta start from scratch …"

[497] "Shall we go with Coach?"

[498] "Well, I think Coach is waiting for us."

[499] "Yes, son. Let's go. Do you have your bag?"

entrada. Esperame, voy por ella."[500]

Michael stood back up, his stiff muscles aching and the tightness of the scabs itching under his shirt. The barrio was a little wobbly as it reoriented itself to how he had found it, back into the order of living in it.

"Oye, amá, a ver si el coach nos deja escuchar una musiquita cuando llegemós a su casa. Unas rancheritas para mi amá, que no?"[501]

---

[500] "Aahhh ... I ... don't ... know. I think I left it at the front door. Wait for me, and I'll go get it."
[501] "Hey, Mom, let's see if Coach will let us listen to a little music when we get to his house. Play some rancheras for my mom, right?"

"Amá?!"[502]

"Amá?! No me oyes?"[503]

"Amá!"

---

[502] "Mom?!"
[503] "Mom?! Are listening to me?"

The sidewalk was empty when Michael turned around, finding it still and quiet, like the whisper to a beloved. Under the indigo mantle of the sky, clothed with summer stars and anchored by the rising crescent moon, one of them found freedom that night, the other found rest.

ABOUT THE AUTHOR

At the age of 20, Lalo León was placed into conversion therapy through his local church and remained an ardent adherent to the practice for 10 years. It was not until a series of compounding crisis, that he stopped the therapy and began to deconstruct the falsehoods that he had been led to believe. "Las Bugambilias – A bilingual queer novel" is a cathartic culmination of his time in conversion therapy and retroactively explores not only the damaging effects of conversion therapy, but also the Americentric views of maleness that lie at the heart of the practice. Lalo is a proud Mexican-American, born and raised in Southern New Mexico. He holds an engineering degree from New Mexico State University, and master's degree from Arizona State University.

9 798991 382403